"She likes being snuggled," Corinne whispered.

"I see that." Gabe was whispering, too. "I think you're both enjoying this."

"Immensely." She smiled. "The years are flying by with my kids. I miss this."

Her sweet regret painted another picture for him.

Corinne.

A baby.

A child to raise together.

The thought held an appealing mix of hope for the future. And then panic. His palms went damp, and he backed off from the image instantly.

"Do you want me to take her?" Part of him wanted her to say no while another part longed to protect.

She nodded and handed him Jessie. He leaned back, almost loving the feel of her on his chest, scared about how easy it would be to fall into a trap he couldn't afford—the trap of love.

He'd been there before and had nothing to show for it, but somehow holding Jessie made it feel almost possible…and that might be

Multipublished bestselling author **Ruth Logan Herne** loves God, her country, her family, dogs, chocolate and coffee! Married to a very patient man, she lives in an old farmhouse in Upstate New York and thinks possums should leave the cat food alone and snakes should always live outside. There are no exceptions to either rule! Visit Ruth at ruthloganherne.com.

Award-winning author **Mindy Obenhaus** lives on a ranch in Texas with her husband, two sassy pups, and countless cattle and deer. She's passionate about touching readers with biblical truths in an entertaining, and sometimes adventurous, manner. When she's not writing, you'll usually find her in the kitchen, spending time with family or roaming the ranch. She'd love to connect with you via her website, mindyobenhaus.com.

Her Holiday Lawman

USA TODAY Bestselling Author

Ruth Logan Herne

&

Mindy Obenhaus

2 Uplifting Stories

The Lawman's Yuletide Baby and *The Deputy's Holiday Family*

LOVE INSPIRED®
INSPIRATIONAL ROMANCE

Recycling programs for this product may not exist in your area.

ISBN-13: 978-1-335-42994-0

Her Holiday Lawman

For questions and comments about the quality of this book, please contact us at CustomerService@Harlequin.com.

Love Inspired
22 Adelaide St. West, 41st Floor
Toronto, Ontario M5H 4E3, Canada
www.LoveInspired.com

Printed in U.S.A.

CONTENTS

THE LAWMAN'S YULETIDE BABY

USA TODAY Bestselling Author

Ruth Logan Herne

This book marks my twentieth book with Love Inspired, and I am blessed to be part of their outstanding group of authors. I am offering huge thanks, not only for this particular story, but for all those that have come before and are yet to come, to Melissa Endlich, my editor, guide and mentor, the person who took a chance on me in 2009 and launched a beautiful career with a phone message I still have on my voice mail—a voice mail I have never deleted because it marked a bend in the road I longed for all my life. So, to Melissa I say thank you. *Thank you so much.* And may God bless you.

The Lord is close to the brokenhearted
and saves those who are crushed in spirit.
—*Psalms* 34:18

Chapter One

This couldn't be happening.

Corinne Gallagher watched as the Realtor tacked a Sold sign on the year-round lakefront home less than a hundred feet from hers.

It wasn't the sign that made her heart take notice.

It was the man shaking the Realtor's hand.

New York State Trooper Gabe Cutler stood facing the real estate salesperson as if he'd just clinched the deal of a lifetime.

She swallowed hard as his gaze shifted from the Realtor to her.

Her heart ground to a painful stop.

So did her breath.

He stared at her, then her house, then her again.

She stood rooted to the ground, unable or maybe just unwilling to move.

Her twelve-year-old daughter had no such qualms. "Coach!" Theresa, known to the world as "Tee" Gallagher, streaked across the yard beneath a canopy of late October color. The blend of breeze and tinted leaves signaled another change of seasons.

Corinne was determined to ignore the passage of time. It's what she did best.

Day by day, year by year, she looked forward, making sure her children were grounded, faithful, safe and kind. She purposely didn't look right or left. It was a job she did well because Corinne Gallagher did everything well.

"Coach, are you moving into the Penskis' house for real? Callan won't believe it!" Tee leaped at him, hugging the man who'd been coaching her brother for the last three years. Three very long years for Corinne to pretend she wasn't attracted to the decorated state trooper. Three years of watching him counsel and teach youngsters the rules of the game...and the rules of life. Three years of maintaining a distance because she would never willingly put herself in the position to bury another man in uniform.

He couldn't be moving in next door.

He lived nearly fifteen miles away, toward the south end of Canandaigua Lake, surrounded by vineyards. She'd Googled him on purpose during a weak moment.

Look at you. Stalking the baseball coach.

She hadn't stalked him. Not really. She'd just been curious. And lonely. And possibly wondering about the man behind the uniform, behind the stubborn set of his jaw as they met weekly to firm up the plans before the upcoming holiday-themed Christkindl festival.

And here he was, one arm around Tee, gazing her way.

This couldn't be happening.

And yet...it was.

"Coach, is that you?" Fourteen-year-old Callan poked his head out from the sliding glass door leading to the deck. "Are you kidding me? You're moving in next door? That's awesome!" The high school freshman loped across the yard, all arms and legs, a boy in the thick of adolescence. He pumped Gabe's hand, excited, then shoved his hands into his pockets as if unsure what to do with them.

Tee had no such qualms. She kept her arm linked through Gabe's as if she'd just acquired a new BFF. "Can you believe it, Mom?" She screeched the words as Corinne moved their way. "Coach is here! He's moving in! Right next door!"

Tee lived in a world full of exclamation points. Nothing stagnated in Tee's world. Her roller-coaster personality kept life humming around her, a total contrast to her more sober older brother.

Callan took after Corinne, focused and cautious and steadfast.

Tee was total Gallagher, a feminine image of the father she'd never known. She was a spontaneous, fearless know-it-all, and there wasn't a day that went by when Corinne didn't thank God for these kids. They were a piece of Dave to keep close by her side, but that honor came with mega responsibility, a task she never took lightly.

"So." Gabe watched her approach.

Caramel-brown eyes, with hints of gold that brightened when he smiled. Medium brown hair, always cut short. Strong shoulders, a broad chest, made broader by his protective vest when he was in uniform.

But protective vests could only do so much. She'd found that out the hard way.

"We've just become neighbors." He didn't shift his gaze as she walked, and she didn't hurry her steps because she needed every single second to grab hold of the calm facade she'd need for this new bend in the road.

She nodded to the Realtor to gain a few extra seconds, then faced Gabe directly. "So it would seem. I had no idea you were looking for a house, Gabe."

He lifted one brow and paused, and when he did, her heart paused, too. "I didn't want to make a big deal out of it. I've always wanted to live in a quiet spot on the water. To throw my boat in now and again and drop a line. When this came on the market three weeks back, I knew it was perfect."

It wasn't perfect.

Having the strong, stoic trooper next door was the exact opposite of perfect.

Perfect was her safe, sound world, surrounded by Gallagher family and friends, a low-risk pool of normal.

Perfect was her administrative position at the hospital, where she'd graduated from the ups and downs of crisis pregnancy care to being a very capable paper pusher.

Ideal was having as much quiet control as she could get while not appearing to be one of those helicopter parents, hovering around everything their children did, thought or tried.

She'd tucked herself into this quiet corner of the lake, her grandparents' old house, determined to do things her way without appearing crazy neurotic.

Gabe Cutler's arrival just rocked a boat she'd kept calm for a long, long time.

Gabe Cutler had spent years purposely keeping himself on life's outer edges. He worked, he coached, he fished and he took good care of Tucker, his dog.

It was enough because he made it enough.

And now he'd managed to sign papers tucking him next door to Corinne Gallagher and her delightful kids, Callan and Tee.

How had this happened?

Corinne and the kids didn't live on the water. They lived in a simple split-level just off Route 20A. He'd dropped Callan off there a couple of times the year before.

And yet…

Here they were.

The kids looked delighted to see him, because they'd been buds for several years. He'd coached Callan, and laughed over Tee's antics.

Corinne looked surprised and maybe chagrined about the whole thing.

She helped with team stuff when she could. She organized fundraisers and structured team gatherings when they had out-of-town tournaments. She stayed friendly while keeping her distance, a neat trick she maneuvered well, which meant she was well practiced. Like him.

He smiled for a selfie with Callan, his star shortstop, then winced inside when Callan blasted the pic to the rest of the team with a wide, easy grin.

So much for keeping his private life private. A part of him wanted to sigh, because this was his fault for not checking the town's records before signing the purchase offer.

He wouldn't have chosen the house if he'd known Corinne and the kids lived next door. Gabe didn't just like his privacy. He craved it. He needed that downtime, where he could split wood or fish or do whatever he needed to do to get through the calendar year. And now—

Two bright-eyed kids, kids that he liked, grinned up at him as if this was a wonderful turn of events.

It wasn't anything of the kind.

"Is Tucker coming with you?"

The team loved his trusty mutt, a great dog. He'd rescued the tricolor collie mix from a shelter four years before, but it might have been the other way around. The goofy, loyal dog might have been the rescuer all along. "He is."

"Yes!" Tee fist-pumped the air. "Can I take him swimming? And for walks along the road? Because there is like no one living down here in the winter, Coach." She dramatized the words with perfect adolescent accentuation. "Well, a few people," she conceded. "But most of them go to Florida for the winter, so the road is crazy quiet now!"

And with all of those quiet, empty cottages dotting the shore, the only affordable house that had gone up for sale along the waterfront was right next to a busy, vibrant family. Was God laughing right now?

Although if this was some sort of master plan, Gabe failed to see the purpose. Or the humor, for that matter. "Tee Gallagher and a quiet road?" He hiked a brow that actually made Corinne smile. "Why does that seem hard to compute?"

"Even I can't make enough noise to liven up a whole road on my own," the girl told him. "But I do my best."

"That's for sure." Callan sent his text. He started to pocket his phone, but replies began flooding in, fast and furious. "My phone's blowing up, Coach." He laughed as he moved over to their honey-stained picnic table. "Gotta answer these."

"If I had a phone, I could share this news, too." Tee shifted her attention to Corinne.

"A conversation we've had way too often," Corinne told her. "You don't need a phone. When you're in high school, yes. I'll get you a phone and you can help pay for it. There's no need to do that now."

"Everyone in junior high has one. And I mean everyone."

A stat that didn't bode well in the school, Gabe knew. Some of those kids' phones were being used for things far beyond what a seventh grader should be considering, much less doing. He respected Corinne for taking a stand that clearly made her unpopular with her strong-willed daughter.

"Junior high kids have survived without phones for centuries. You'll be fine, Tee."

"Laura Ingalls didn't have a phone, so Tee Gallagher doesn't get one?" Tee hiked both brows, then rolled her eyes. "That's totally apples and oranges, Mom. Let's stay in the current century for comparison's sake." She shot Corinne a dimpled look, and Gabe couldn't hold back his smile.

The kid had sass.

She never gave up, she smiled a lot and she faced life fearlessly.

If Gracie had lived, he figured she'd be a lot like Tee Gallagher. But she didn't live. Neither did her mother. He had a host of regrets a mile long about that.

He'd messed up once.

He'd broken a good woman's heart and possibly her spirit, and the truth of that weighed heavily even nine years later.

He'd cost two lives that day. Three, if you counted his own by aftermath.

No, he couldn't afford to let this sweet family get under his skin. They treated him like he was a stand-up guy.

That's because they didn't know the truth. If they did, they'd think differently.

"Coach, I am just so crazy excited to have you here!" Tee hugged his arm again, and the shot of pain that jabbed his chest was quite real.

He realized that Gracie would have been Tee's age now. She would have had a mop of brown curls, and an unerring talent for winsome smiles, enough to grab his heart and hold it tight, all these years.

His chest constricted.

The real estate agent must have sensed the change in mood because she reached out a hand to Corinne. "You inherited this place from your parents, didn't you, Mrs. Gallagher?"

Corinne accepted the light handshake. "My grandmother, actually. Gram wanted to keep it in the family, and my late husband loved the water. He said you could learn more about a woman by watching the lake change than any self-help book on the market."

The Realtor laughed. "My husband would agree. Well, if you ever think about selling, give me a call." She handed Corinne a business card. "I know you haven't been back on the water for long, but we never have enough lakefront property to fill the demand. No pressure, of course."

Corinne stared at the card, and Gabe felt like a complete jerk. Was she really that bothered because he moved in next door? Or because he'd disagreed with her stance on the Christmas festival committee the week before? Would she really stay upset about that?

He didn't know her well enough to know, but he hoped not.

"Coach, when are you moving in?" Callan's excitement lightened the moment. "I can help if it's on the weekend."

"I closed the deal this morning, and I'm working this weekend, so next weekend is move-in time."

"Mom." Callan swung around. "I bet me and some of the guys—"

"And me!" Tee cut in.

Callan frowned at her, then continued, "I bet we could help Coach get everything moved. What do you think?"

The kid meant well, but he'd just corralled his mother, so Gabe stepped in. "Listen, Corinne, if you're working that weekend, it's no problem." He was offering her an out if she wanted to take it. "I know your schedule can get complicated."

"Not anymore." Tee caroled the words. "Mom isn't doing regular nursing anymore. She's got an office and she's one of the people who make sure everything gets done right."

"You've moved up?" She nodded, but looked more resigned than happy, as if moving up the ladder of success wasn't all it was cracked up to be. "That's a big change."

"Takes some getting used to," she told him, then directed her attention to Callan. "Cal, I think it would be great for you guys to help Coach move in. If he wants the help, that is."

What could he say and not sound like a total curmudgeon? "I'd love it."

"And then we can do hot dogs and stuff at our house if the weather stays nice," Tee exclaimed. "Right, Mom? You're here on the weekends now, and if the guys haul all Coach's stuff, we can make food for them, just like Grandma does whenever we do things. She always makes it so special to help."

"Your grandma has a way of putting a shine on life like no other woman I've ever known. Except possibly your Aunt Kimberly," Corinne conceded. "Tee, that sounds like a great idea. If it's all right with Coach."

"What kind of guy would refuse an offer of help and food?" He gave Tee a half hug, then dropped his arm.

"Sounds like a plan. And now." He turned back to the Realtor. "I've got to head home and get ready for work. I'm on the late shift today."

"Like at night?" Tee asked.

He nodded. "We switch things up. I don't do nights as much as I used to, but I told them I'd help out as needed from now through December." He didn't mention that he grabbed whatever hours he could late in the year. Working didn't just keep him busy during the deluge of holiday forums embraced by their sweet, small town. It kept him sane. "We've got a couple of guys who needed day shifts. And one who just had a baby, so he's out for a couple of weeks. I think they were in your unit, actually." He lifted his eyes to Corinne. "Jason and Shelly Montgomery. Shelly had some problems, and was in the hospital for the last four weeks, then the baby was in the NICU for a few weeks. But now everyone is home, no one is sleeping and life is good."

"I heard they were a very nice couple. I didn't know Jason was a trooper."

That surprised him, because the baseball parents seemed to open up to Corinne, and then he put two and two together. "Of course, the new job. Off the floor. So you wouldn't get to know people the same way. Well." He stepped back. "Gotta go. I'll see you guys at tomorrow night's game."

"Last game of fall ball," said Tee. "And then we blast right into the holidays. This will be our first Christmas on the water! Maybe we can decorate the dock and everything, like Grandpa used to do!"

Callan reached out and pumped Gabe's hand. "This is great, Coach! Really great! I can't believe it!"

It wasn't great. It was the opposite of great because

Gabe Cutler didn't do holidays. He didn't do family gatherings or twinkle lights, and if he could disengage himself from endless loops of sappy carols, he'd do it in a heartbeat. Holidays forced him to think about what he'd lost.

And now he'd be next door to twinkle lights–loving Tee and her intrinsic optimism.

Corinne was watching him. Her brows shifted together in concern. Because he'd slipped and let his dark side show?

Maybe.

But then she hid that emotion and began backpedaling to her place. "Kids, let's go so Coach can get to work. We've got homework and laundry waiting for us."

"And then can we take the boat out?" Tee gazed at the water with longing. "You said we could this weekend. You promised."

Corinne tapped her watch. "All depends on time, kid. Let's roll."

Callan strode back toward the house.

Tee slumped her shoulders. "I don't know why we live on a lake when we can't ever do anything on the lake."

"Yeah, yeah, yeah." Corinne reached to put an arm around Tee's shoulders.

The girl shrugged her off, chin down.

Corinne looked at Tee, then him, then lifted her hands. "Welcome to the neighborhood, Gabe, where moods change faster than the weather, and that's mighty fast around here."

She was right. Weather on the water could be unpredictable. That's one of the things he loved about it.

Would Gracie have loved the water like he did?

He'd never know. He'd never know her favorite color,

her favorite song, her favorite dolls because she was gone too soon.

He wanted to remind Corinne how precious life was. He wanted to encourage her to leave the stupid laundry and fire up that outboard. The changing seasons meant fewer trips on the water.

He kept quiet on purpose.

She knew the pros and cons, just like he did. She'd also loved and lost, and didn't need his advice. And after working together on the intertown baseball league, and then the festival committee, he was pretty sure she wouldn't take his advice, anyway.

She wasn't cool or judgmental or obnoxious, but she kept her guard in place.

Uptight people tended to annoy him because he'd grown up surrounded by them. His mother's family lived their lives tightly wound about everything from religion to politics to food choices.

And yet, with all they had, all the blessings abounding, they were never satisfied. Never content. His mother wasn't like that. Neither was Gabe.

He'd lost his contentment through his own fault. But it bothered him when folks didn't understand the blessings of a child. Any child. And how, if he had it to do all over again, he'd make whatever sacrifice needed to keep a kid safe and happy and content.

So you'd give Tee a phone? Even though you know better?

He wouldn't, he realized, as Tee stomped into her house. He'd do exactly what Corinne was doing, but he'd hate every single stinkin' minute of it.

But it would never be an issue because he'd had his chance once and blew it. And that was that.

And here he was, next door to a woman who kept a cool distance in what she did. Not exactly an ice queen, but not all that warm, either.

The sale was complete.

The deed had changed hands. He'd have to make the best of it. So would she.

Corinne resisted change. She wasn't a fighter, but she quietly blocked it in her own way.

Did she know how blessed she was to have those two kids? He couldn't look at Tee and not remember Gracie. And a fine kid like Callan, hardworking and devoted to playing ball. A young man, ready to explore so much of the world around him.

Not your business.

He knew that. And it wouldn't become his business, no matter how pretty those blue eyes were when she looked his way.

He'd made a promise when he laid his baby girl into the ground, a pledge he intended to keep. He'd been given the gold ring once and lost it by his lack of attention.

He'd laid flowers on her grave and promised God he'd never take that chance again, and he meant every word, but when Corinne Gallagher waved from her back deck, his fickle heart tried to pry itself open.

He slammed it shut.

He'd had it all once and ruined it. He had absolutely no right to wish for more than what he had now. A great job keeping people safe, a small boat and a house on the water.

A house that seemed pretty empty compared with the busy family living next door.

Chapter Two

Gabe had just finished packing dozens of boxes when his landline phone rang the following Saturday. He almost tripped getting through the confusing maze, but when he saw his mother's number in the display, he grabbed the call quickly. "Hey, Mom. What's up?"

"Gabe. Do you have a minute?"

Worry wrenched her voice. He was pretty sure she was crying, and he was nearly four hours away with a moving crew on the way, but if she needed him, he'd hop in the car and head toward Albany because Linda Cutler had gone the distance for him too many times to count. And with his mother's crazy, mixed-up, dysfunctional family, Gabe knew he'd been blessed to be on the normal end of the spectrum. "Of course I do. Take your time. I'm right here."

"I know. I just..." She breathed out a sigh. "Aunt Maureen just got off the phone with me, screaming about life's injustices, and how unfair things are. She's blaming the police and the world for everything that went wrong with Adrianna. I tried to calm her down, but it didn't work. She hung up on me, but not before she called me unkind names."

"I'm sure she's hurting, but that's no reason to take it out on you. I'm sorry, Mom. You know Aunt Maureen. It's always someone else's fault." His narrow-minded aunt had recently buried the daughter she'd disowned years before. Adrianna had gotten herself into a mess of trouble as a teen, then again as a young adult. She'd done time, and her parents made sure that everyone knew they wanted nothing to do with their wayward child.

She'd died in a convenience store robbery gone bad, a tragic end to a life filled with flawed choices.

"My sister is mean, Gabe. Just plain mean, and it's got nothing to do with her faith or her church, it's her. No wonder that poor girl went rogue. And now look what it's all come to."

She was right. His mom's younger sister had a sharp tongue and always held a grudge. She and his uncle had little regard for Christ's instruction on forgiveness. "Aunt Maureen is probably second-guessing her actions, Mom—maybe wishing she hadn't thrown Adrianna out of the house, or been so strict with her."

"Or she's blaming everyone but herself for her family problems."

That sounded more like it. "Do you want me to come down there? I can. I've got the next two days off." He didn't mention that he was supposed to be moving because she'd refuse his help if she thought she was inconveniencing him.

She'd blessed him from the day he was born, or at least as far back as he could remember. She'd been a single mom at a time when being a single mother wasn't overtly accepted, but she'd been great. And still was.

And through it all, her sister Maureen had held Linda's mistakes up like a banner, making sure everyone knew that Linda lived a life of bad choices.

But in the end, Gabe had turned out just fine and Maureen's two daughters had brought nothing but trouble on themselves. That had always infuriated his fire-and-brimstone aunt. "Why did you take her call?"

"Because she just lost her daughter."

Gabe would have done the same. "Do you want to come up here for a visit?"

"No, I just needed to vent. Maureen is just..." She paused, then drew a deep breath. "Well, you know. She needs to lay this at someone else's door, and that finger of blame will never fall back on her. Maybe if she'd shown those girls a little kindness, a little understanding—" She paused again. "No use rehashing all of that. And you're right, if she calls again, I'll let it go to voice mail. I'm working overtime this weekend, so that will gain me some distance."

His mother worked at a manufacturing facility outside Albany. "You sure you're okay?"

"Yes, I just needed someone to talk to. It's been a rough couple of months down here, and losing Adrianna like that has stirred some old pots."

"Aunt Maureen and Uncle Blake had choices, Mom. So did Adrianna."

"I know. And I knew I could only do so much when their mother was dead set against anyone helping those girls out, but it weighs on me, Gabe, knowing Adrianna longed for help and thought no one would provide it."

Guilt.

It was an emotion he knew well. Too well. "We pray, Mom. And we keep our eyes open for other ways to help people. Like you taught me all along." The noise of pickup trucks pulling into the driveway made him turn. "You sure you don't want me to head down there? I can be there by lunchtime."

"I'm sure. Just glad you don't mind talking with your mom now and again."

"Mind?" He laughed because throughout his times of trouble, Linda Cutler had been the calm voice of faith, hope and reason. "I love it, Mom. And I love you."

He pictured her smile in the softer note in her voice. "I love you, too. Bye, honey."

He hung up, knowing she'd be okay, but it wasn't easy to dodge angry family members, especially when proximity allowed them access.

That was another reason he'd moved four hours northwest when everything fell apart. Distance from his mother's family wasn't a choice, it had been a life-saving measure.

The first two trucks rolled to a stop, and half a dozen boys and men aimed for his door. He swung it wide in welcome.

He might not have family here, but between the troopers and the baseball team, his needs were covered.

By ten o'clock they were on their way to 2312 Lakeshore Drive with the first wave of belongings.

He thought it would take all day to move things.

He was wrong.

A single guy who worked long hours and coached three seasons of baseball didn't accumulate a lot of stuff.

They pulled the trucks into the lakefront driveway one at a time. Tee spotted them and raced across the narrow yards, hurdling the short privet hedge on the property line. "Can I help?"

He spotted Corinne's bemused expression next door. Hands up, she gestured to the tables and chairs she'd been setting out and then her daughter. "You help here," he told her. "I'll go help your mother move the tables."

"Oops." Looking a little guilty, Tee spun and waved. "Sorry, Mom!"

"I'll bet she is," Corinne noted as Gabe drew closer. "She'd much rather help the team than be stuck helping her mother."

"Pretty normal, I expect. But I can help her mother," Gabe added as he lifted one of the tables. "Tell me where you want them and I'll get them in order for you."

"You've got a whole house to arrange," she scolded. "I can handle this."

Gabe moved the first table closer to the lake as he replied, "I've got bedroom stuff, kitchen stuff and living room stuff, which means half the rooms of the house will sit empty. I bet they can figure it out, Corinne. And my buddy Mack is over there with his wife, and when Susie MacIntosh takes charge, we all smile and nod and follow orders."

"My kind of gal." Corinne started setting up folding chairs. "Should we start the fire now, if you guys don't have to make too many more trips back to your old place?"

"One more trip should do it, so that's probably a good idea." He settled the next table close to the first. "And if I'm setting these in the wrong spots, tell me. Don't wait until I'm gone, then change them."

"Well, it's a simple afternoon barbecue, so I'm pretty sure anywhere is good."

Her tone was easy, but it didn't take a real smart guy to sense something amiss. "Listen, Corinne. I didn't get a chance to talk to you after the committee meeting the other night." He was working as the safety liaison for the upcoming Christkindl festival, a huge annual event that netted tens of thousands of dollars for the Police Benevolence Fund. The fund helped widows and children of fallen officers. As a widow, Corinne had headed the committee for half a dozen years, but the current committee had voted in some major changes she didn't like. Changes he approved, which might make him persona non grata with his new neighbor.

"Because you were mobbed by triumphant town retailers and I had to get home to the kids."

That was true, but law enforcement was schooled in undercurrents, and the one on this deck rivaled an East Coast riptide. "I don't want you to think we were trying to undercut your position."

A momentary pause of her hands was her only outward reaction, which meant she was hiding her feelings, a move he recognized because he'd hidden his share. Watching her, he realized she was just as good as he was at disguising his true emotions. Maybe better. "When you, Lizzie and Maura took places on the committee, it meant we all needed to work together," she replied in a soft, even voice. "Although neither Kate nor I was invited to the impromptu meeting you guys had on Tuesday."

It hadn't been a meeting at all. He'd run into two other committee members at the Bayou Barbecue, and the two women had hijacked his quiet supper with committee talk.

"It wasn't a meeting. I was having supper at Josie's place. Lizzie and Maura came in and sat down, so we compared notes. Then I got a call on the south end of the lake, and Josie bagged my food for later. That's all it was, pure coincidence."

"You don't owe me explanations, Gabe."

He didn't...but he did. Corinne had invested years in this festival because she'd buried a first responder, and he didn't take that lightly. Nor should anyone else. "I do, because Lizzie made it sound like we held a prearranged meeting. It wasn't anything of the kind."

"And yet there's no reason it couldn't be, is there, Gabe?" She paused again, watching him from the far side of the deck, holding a floral porch pillow in her hands. She looked...cautiously beautiful, if there was such a thing, and there must be, because he was seeing it, right now.

No reason...

"Of course there's a reason. To go behind your back and usurp the time and effort you've put into this whole thing would be ludicrous. I can't imagine someone doing that, and if they did, they'd have to answer to me. That's not how things are done, Corinne. Not in police brotherhoods, anyway."

She watched him, still clutching the pillow, and when he was done with his little spiel, she still watched.

And then she smiled, ever so slightly, as she set the pillow down.

Her smile intrigued him.

He wasn't sure why, because she did absolutely nothing to try to intrigue him. In fact, she went out of her way to be carefully level and polite, like the model nurses you saw on TV.

As she looked down, her lips quirked up, as if he'd pleased her.

He wasn't looking to please anyone. He'd won the race once. He'd had it all until he lost it, way too quick and far too easy.

Yes, he was older. Smarter. But he was just as guilty now as he'd been when Gracie climbed into his SUV all those years ago. A stupid football party, parents, kids, pizza and beer…

He swallowed hard. "I just didn't want you thinking we were plotting behind your back. Or Kate's back." Corinne's mother-in-law had built a highly regarded event business in Grace Haven. She'd shared her expertise by helping with the festival for years.

"Kate's a smart woman. She saw the way things were trending from the beginning, and that's why she volunteered to work with Lizzie and Maura."

"To keep an eye on them?"

"That sounds far too sinister, even for a small town." She crossed the decking and moved more chairs into place. "More like she wants to keep her finger on the pulse of the area. When you run an event center, it's important to be on the inside informational loop. And I'm sure she wanted to keep me updated so I wouldn't get clotheslined by whatever changes came about. Kate knows I'm busy, and she takes an understandable special interest in the benevolence fund."

Of course she did. She'd buried a son, and her husband had been chief of police for over twenty years. The Gallaghers appreciated law enforcement like few families could. They'd lived it for over two generations. "She's protective of you."

"Sure she is." She drew up more chairs. "They love me, and they love these kids. That's pretty much how the family rolls. And they know being a single mom isn't easy. But we're doing okay."

After being raised in a single-parent house, he knew the truth of it, and it was never an easy gig to be top provider, rule maker and beloved parent to kids. "I'd say you're doing great, Corinne."

"Well. Thank you." She took the compliment lightly. Maybe too lightly. "It's too early to start the grill, but if you call me from the truck, I'll have it heated up when you guys get back."

"Sounds good." He touched a long-nosed lighter to the kindling in the fire pit, waiting for the first flickers of success. "If you ever need anything..." He waited until she looked up, and when she did, there it was again. A tiny spark of connection when his eyes met hers. "Call me, okay? I'm right over there, and I'm happy to help."

"That's a really nice offer." Sincerity deepened her tone, while her expression stayed matter-of-fact. "The Penskis were gone a lot, so I'd only seen them twice since we moved in last year. And when the weather turns, it's kind of desolate down here. Like Tee said, most folks use these as summer homes, so there aren't too many neighbors during the winter. It will be nice to have you nearby."

He puffed on the kindling until a curl of smoke burst into tiny licks of flame. "I saw that little park at the end of the road by the turnoff. It's got a small baseball field."

"A relic from times past, when neighborhoods got together to play ball. That's Welch Grove Park."

"It's quiet and I can practice ball with the kids there whenever they're available."

"I played ball on that field when I was a girl." She tapped the grill as if tapping home plate and took a batter's stance.

"You lived here?"

"Off and on, with my grandparents."

She didn't elaborate and it wasn't his business to delve, but why hadn't she been with her parents?

Not his business, so he kept to baseball. "They had softball there?"

"Hardball."

She'd surprised him again. "You played hardball?"

"Seven years. When I got to high school girls could only play softball, and that's a whole other game." She moved a chair that didn't need moving and shrugged. "I moved on to other things. That's why I loved seeing Amy make the team when Drew Slade came back to town. A girl with that kind of talent shouldn't be relegated to a minimal role in anything."

"If you're good enough, you play." It made sense to him, regardless of gender.

"That's something you and I can agree on." She didn't mention the festival controversy per se, but he understood the meaning behind the words.

"Gabe." Mack called his name from across the yards. "We need to know how you want some of the things set up."

"Coming." He tipped his ball cap slightly. "One more load to get, and that should do it on our end. I'll be happy to man the grill when we get back."

"I am delighted to accept the offer."

"Good."

He jogged back to his place.

He'd hurried over there to clear the air over Thursday's meeting. She'd lost an important battle, one that meant she'd be facing angry vendors at the upcoming holiday festival. The out-of-town vendors had paid a significant fee to contract their space on the grounds of the historic Gallagher farm at the edge of town. They weren't expecting to have local buses transporting their shoppers downtown every fifteen minutes. There would be backlash, mostly directed at Corinne because she headed the committee. It wasn't her fault, and he felt bad about that. He'd sided with the local businesses from a practical angle. Putting Corinne in the crosshairs hadn't been the intention, but it was a probable outcome.

Would she hold a grudge?

He hoped not, but her guarded nature didn't make her an easy read.

"Coach, I can't wait for you to see how many fish there are in the lake! Grandpa showed me so many hot spots, it's amazing! Do you like perch and bass?" Tee grabbed his hand in an excited grip as he crossed the yard.

He loved both. He nodded as the old weight redescended.

"Then maybe we can go fishing sometime together," Tee exclaimed. "I can ask Mom, I bet she won't mind, and I won't be noisy. I know not to be noisy on the boat, because Grandpa threatened to toss me overboard if I scared the fish. And I love eating fish, so why would I scare them?"

She talked at light speed, like Gracie had.

Her hands danced in the air, alive with excitement.

Her eyes so blue.

Gracie's had been a lighter shade of blue, tinged green, but with that same kind of sparkle and joy.

Gone.

His heart choked.

So did his voice, because he couldn't form a word around the massive lump clogging his throat.

He'd thought it would get better in time, and it had,

but when he was around Tee Gallagher and her crew of funny, adolescent girlfriends, all he could think of was how sweetly Gracie would have fit into their crowd. Laughing, dancing, climbing…

"Come with me." Susie MacIntosh thrust her arm through his and propelled him into the house. "Focus on the simple and the mundane."

Susie had known him all those years ago, years before they both moved upstate to Grace Haven.

"You've got to forgive yourself, Gabe. God doesn't want you to spend your life beating yourself up. He wants you whole and happy again."

Susie's opinion was similar to the reverend's talk last Sunday.

And maybe it would have worked out that way, if Elise had been okay. But she wasn't all right, ever again. Then she was gone, too.

"We make choices, Gabe. All of us. You, me, Mack. Elise."

He couldn't listen to this, because there was no way he could lay any of this on Elise. He'd left the door of the SUV slightly open. He must have. He was the last person in it. He'd pulled into his buddy's driveway and parked. Then he'd gotten Gracie out of her car seat and walked into the broad backyard of Jim Clayton, another state trooper.

He was the designated driver, so he grabbed some cold iced tea and talked NFL prospects, waiting for the four o'clock kickoff in Jim's man cave–style barn toward the back of the property.

And then came the scream.

Nine years later, he still heard the scream.

Elise's voice, screaming his name, screaming for

help, and Gracie Lynn, their beautiful little girl, lying so still in the grueling heat of the SUV.

Her death was ruled accidental, but he knew better. He was her father. She was his responsibility, and he'd failed her over football stats and arguments about team superiority. All while his baby girl lay perishing in the unyielding temperatures of an SUV parked beneath a brilliant September sun.

No, there were no second chances for stupid fathers.

God was big enough to forgive because he was God.

But Gabe was a mere man, and there was no way on this earth he could forgive himself. And that was that.

Chapter Three

The group of young movers crossed from Gabe's yard into hers when the final load had been brought and distributed, but Corinne's heart went into overdrive as the tall, square-shouldered policeman followed in their wake. Gabe Cutler, chatting with "Mack" MacIntosh, another local trooper.

"Mom, we're going to check out the cove, okay?" Callan and five of his teammates got to her first.

"No swimming," she reminded them. "It's too cold for that."

"No swimming. But we might throw Tee into the water, just because she's a pest."

Tee pretended innocence, but Corinne knew the truth. Tee was a hoot, but she could be a pain in the neck to her big brother, and no way did she want the twelve-year-old hanging out with fourteen-and fifteen-year-old boys. "I'm keeping Tee here to help me. You guys did all the heavy lifting. We're doing food."

"Mom." Tee folded her arms and scowled. "Girls don't have to stay home and cook while the brave hunter goes in search of food anymore. We can actually *do* things, just like they can. It's called the new millennium." She hooked her thumb toward the teenage ballplayers, heading for the cove up the beach. "I could have helped move things. And I should be able to go to the cove. I'm twelve."

"I know how old you are. I was present at your birth, remember?"

But Tee saw nothing amusing in her reply. "We've got food ready, and everything's done. Why can't I go?"

What could she say? That she wasn't sure the boys' conversations would be okay for Tee's ears? And that Callan deserved some time away from his nosy little sister?

The boys were good kids, but they were hormone-struck teens, and she wasn't ready to have to deal with Tee and crushes and heartbreaks. Why had the idea of kids spaced so close together appealed to her a dozen years ago?

Oh, that's right.

Because she didn't know any better.

Tee huffed into the house as Gabe, Susie and Mack climbed the short steps on one side while the boys raced across the short stretch of open beach. "They did a great job today."

"I'm so glad." She opened the grill, judged it ready and pointed out the grilling tools hanging from a head-high two-by-four. "Tools of the trade. And the meat is in the cooler. Where's Tucker?"

"I put him in the house. He'll need to get a feel for his boundaries, so for now he's napping on the floor. Or staring at us through the sliding glass doors, which seems to be more accurate at the moment."

They all turned. The black, brown and white dog peered at them through the glass, tongue lolling, hoping they'd notice.

"That's a tough face to ignore," noted Mack.

"And he knows it. But better safe than sorry." He moved toward the cooler. "I'll save him a hot dog. Tucker forgives anything if there's a hot dog involved."

"I wonder if there's a similar system that works on kids," Corinne mused. "It's definitely cheaper than a cell phone, which is our current argument of the day."

"Tee doesn't let things go, does she?"

"No. And I hate being the bad guy 24/7, but that's kind of how things shake down."

Understanding marked his gaze. "My mom said that, too. She raised me on her own, and she always said the hardest part was being the tough one, all the time. No respite. But it worked out in the end."

"That's my hope and prayer, right there. That they grow up to have full and happy lives. Like you did."

His face drew down slightly as he began laying the meat on the hot grill surface. She started to chat with Susie as the hamburgers, hot dogs and Italian sausage sent meat-scented smoke their way.

Corinne breathed deeply, loving the scents of a cookout on the lake. Susie turned a pale shade of gray-green and looked dreadful.

Pregnant.

Corinne had dealt with morning sickness both personally and on a professional level. She took Susie's hand and led her toward the house. "I'm going to show Susie around inside. You guys okay?"

"Just fine."

"Yup." Mack lifted a cold bottle of iced tea their way. "See you in a few."

She got Susie inside to the bathroom just in time,

then gave her a cool, damp washcloth to lay across her forehead. "Sit down and breathe easy, and it will pass."

"I'm so embarrassed." Susie's mouth scrunched up below the wet cloth. "Corinne, you don't even know me."

"No time like the present." Corinne laughed. "But I've seen this particular malady often enough because I'm a nurse in the crisis pregnancy unit. How far along are you?"

"Eighteen weeks. But we've kept it pretty quiet because pregnancy hasn't gone well with us."

"Susie, I'm sorry."

Susie shrugged beneath the cool cloth, but her chin quivered. "I'm with a new doctor and she's determined. And I've never been sick like this before."

"A well-set pregnancy makes its presence known."

"Is that true?" Susie sat up and whisked the damp cloth from her forehead. "Because the doctor said that, too."

"It is in my experience. And I'm putting you on my prayer list right now because this would be so exciting." She reached over and pressed Susie's hand lightly. "A new baby coming to visit the lake next spring." A baby…so sweet, so special, such an amazing blessing. And so very difficult for some. She saw that on her hospital unit. She'd dealt with the mercurial highs and lows of crisis pregnancy.

She'd wanted a house full of kids. She'd wanted to chase babies and toddlers and push strollers long after Tee was running and climbing and shrugging off any offers of help. Her dream had been thwarted by a felon's bullet, but she had two beautiful children, and that was something to be grateful for.

She spotted movement on the deck. "Susie, pretend you're looking at something."

"Which I am, of course." Susie picked up a book from the table as Mack came to the sliding screen door separating them from the broad wooden deck.

"How we doing in there?"

"We've finished the grand tour and Susie's checking out a book I recommended."

"Great." He smiled through the screen at his wife. "Gabe says we've got about five minutes until everything's done."

"I'll bring out the rest of the stuff. Susie, feel free to borrow that and tell me what you think."

"Thank you, Corinne."

"Tee?" Corinne called upstairs from the first floor. "Can you help me with food?" Long seconds of silence ensued before she heard Tee's footsteps on the floor above.

Shouts from up the beach indicated the boys' return. Corinne carried a hot potato salad out to the deck. Tee followed with a cold pasta salad, and dragged her feet every inch of the way, right up until the boys made it to the deck.

Then everything changed.

Tee raised her chin.

Her eyes sparkled.

Shoulders back, she was the epitome of charm once the deck was filled with five young baseball players.

Corinne wanted to smack a hand to her head, because if Tee was crushing on one of Callan's friends, the result could be gut-wrenching for brother and sister.

Callan loved Tee. He'd given her that name as a toddler. She was his "Tee-Tee," and the name stuck.

But they were stepping into uncharted waters now. And while Corinne didn't have to do too many weekend shifts anymore, the idea of teens with too much time on their hands was worrisome. Time alone and internet access, texting, unlimited phone use…

She wanted normal for these two, but how could she strike that balance, keep them safe and allow them to grow in current times?

"She's got a thing for Brandon."

Gabe's soft voice made her turn. "You think?" Brandon was the team's center fielder.

"Oh, yeah. She's being subtle around him and a little too loud with the other boys, as if trying to gain his attention. And he's oblivious."

Corinne glanced behind her and agreed. "Can I lock her away? At least until sophomore year of college?"

He laughed softly as he removed meat from the grill. "I think that's an excellent idea. And this road is out of the way enough that the boys won't be visiting down here, unless they're coming to see Callan."

"Which they do on a regular basis."

He exaggerated a wince. "That means team dynamics are about to change. We'll go from total dedication to the game to split attention because of *G-I-R-L-S*. There goes our guaranteed spot in the state playoffs."

She couldn't help it. She laughed. "We're not that bad, are we?"

"At that age?" He raised the tongs and indicated the boys and one lovestruck tween. "No contest."

He was right. There was nothing like the bittersweet moments of young romance to mess with a kid's head.

She dreaded it, not because she didn't want the kids to grow up. That was normal. But the older they got, the less she could fix for them, and affairs of the heart were not easily mended.

She sighed because she knew the truth in that. Broken romances were mended only by time, faith and experience. "No one asked my opinion on this particular timeline, but if asked, I'd have put it off another year. Or two."

"And yet, no one offers options," Mack said as he came up alongside them. "We deal with what comes our way, the good and the bad."

Gabe's jaw tightened. He stared down as he flipped the meat, then piled it all onto her large platter. "I'll put the meat on the ledge."

He didn't look at Mack. He didn't look at her. He crossed the open patio overlooking the water, set the tray down and walked to the water's edge.

Mack scrubbed a hand to his jaw, watching Gabe. Then he sighed, turned and called out to the guys. "Food's ready!"

"Great!"

"Awesome!"

"Thanks for doing this, Mrs. G.!"

The grown-ups waited while the boys filled their plates, and when they all gravitated toward the water—and their beloved coach—the adults had a quiet patio to themselves.

Gabe stayed by the water, talking with the boys. Should she go get him? Remind him that the food was getting cold? He'd been fine, working, cooking, talking, and then…not fine.

He started their way a few minutes later.

He didn't look at her. Didn't look at anyone, not really. If alone in a crowd had a face, it was Gabe Cutler's expression, right now.

"The burgers came out perfect, Gabe. Thank you for cooking them."

"Happy to help."

But he didn't look happy at all. He kept his gaze averted and his shoulders square as if a wall had sprung up between him and the rest of the world.

Just as well.

Once the busyness of his move settled down, she'd keep a comfortable distance because she wasn't a moonstruck adolescent.

She was a grown woman who'd already buried one lawman. Nothing in this world would make her take a chance on facing that a second time.

Chapter Four

Gabe faced a new normal through his spacious lakefront picture window later that afternoon. His shaded yard tapered down to a strip of sandy beach. The dock stood to the right of the property line. Corinne's was on the left of her line, offering a wide expanse of sweet, shallow water.

Tucker would love living here.

He'd given his trusty friend a tour of the yard on a leash, reminding him of boundaries. Tucker learned quickly, but Gabe wanted to make sure he understood the commands of a new place. Chasing a rabbit up the hill to the much-busier four-lane road could be deadly, so a little time spent now was well worth it until the dog felt acclimated.

Him or you?

The mental question had Gabe scratching the back of his head.

Corinne was right. The lake was quiet in the fall. Maybe too quiet. He liked quiet in theory, but there was a soothing monotony in the noise and traffic and activity of a busy country road.

There was no busy on Lakeshore Drive in November. That meant he better do something to create his own distractions. A dozen stuffed packing boxes on the second floor should do it.

He went upstairs. He and Mack and one of the team dads had set up the furniture. Susie had put sheets and blankets on the bed, and she'd freshened the pillowcases. She'd probably cringed while doing it, because Gabe didn't swap them out as often as he should, but she faced his grimy cases like a true friend.

That made him smile as he pulled another box open and began putting things in drawers.

A noise made him pause.

He looked outside, then down the hall and saw nothing.

Heard nothing.

He moved back to the room and resumed his task, one thing after another.

It came again. A noise. A small noise, like a tiny animal's cry.

He had the front windows open to the fresh fall air. He peered out. A bird, maybe?

But then Tucker barked down below. He barked again as Gabe came across the open hallway above, then the big dog paced back and forth by the door. "Have you got to go out again, fella?"

Tucker panted by the street-side door, paced, then panted again.

The noise came again, closer now.

Tucker bounded up, laying two big front paws against the hardwood door, and he barked, twice.

"Down."

The dog came down.

Gabe gave him a hand command to sit and be quiet. Tucker obeyed quickly but kept his canine attention locked on the door.

Gabe peeked outside from the side window, one hand on the weapon he carried in his back waistband.

Was someone casing the place? Skulking around?

Woven vines along the lattice blocked his view of the small covered porch. He kept his hand on the gun and quietly opened the door.

His heart stopped. And then he dropped his hands, leaving the weapon right where it was.

A baby.

Sound asleep. In a car seat. On his front step.

He stared for too many seconds, then dropped down as if someone had drawn a bead on him.

The baby sighed, thought to stick a hand into a tiny mouth, then thought better of it and dozed back off, utterly content.

His heart stopped.

A diaper bag lay next to the baby. And the baby's wrappings appeared clean and fresh, although the car seat carrier looked worn.

Snugged in pink…

A girl, then? Most likely.

He reached out a tentative hand, then realized he was being foolish. She wasn't going to explode if he touched her and she couldn't stay outside on the stoop. He lifted the carrier and brought her inside.

She frowned, wriggled, then dozed right back off.

A baby.

He scratched his head and never thought twice about what he did next. He crossed the room, swung open his door and hollered for Corinne. She popped out of her sliding glass door with reading glasses perched on her head and waved. "What's up? Do you need something?"

"Can you come over here? Nów?"

"Of course." She slipped into a pair of canvas shoes sitting on the deck and crossed the yards. "What's wrong?"

He pointed.

She followed the direction of his hand. Her mouth dropped open in a perfect circle. "It's a baby."

"Yup."

"Whose?"

He shook his head. "I have no idea."

"What?" Disbelief formed a W between her eyes. "That's impossible."

"It's quite possible, actually. I came down from upstairs and there she was, on the front porch stoop, sound asleep."

"No note?"

He crossed to the bag and rummaged around. "I didn't look. I was too surprised by the baby."

"A little girl." Corinne whispered the words and sounded absolutely joyful as she did. "Oh, Gabe, she is beautiful."

"Except no one in their right mind abandons a beautiful baby."

"A mother needing sanctuary for her child, maybe? You are a cop and you work in a sanctuary building."

"Except this is my home. Not the troop house." He pulled a zippered pocket of the bag open and found a thick envelope inside. It wasn't sealed and he yanked out a sheaf of papers quickly. The first sheet was a letter, to him, and it was signed by his late cousin, Adrianna.

Gabe,
If you're reading this, it's because I'm gone. My friend Nita and I had this all worked out, and I was going to bring Jess to you, but I'm not sure what will happen now. These guys, the guys I'm working with, well…they don't care. Not about themselves, not about their women, and they sure don't care about innocent babies.

I stayed sober a long time, Gabe, but I'm not straight now and I can't live with myself if something happens to her because I'm stupid and selfish. I tried to give her up to strangers, but I couldn't do it. I just couldn't.

You're the best person I know. My parents disowned me and they want nothing to do with Jessie. They called her a child of sin. My sister has her hands full. Her husband left when he lost his job, and that's a mess.

I have no one else, Gabe. I have you, and you always tried to see the good in me.

That good is gone, and I'm sorry about that. So sorry. But I was sober until after Jessie was born, so she won't have any problems from her foolish mother.

I wish I listened when I was younger, Gabe. You tried to help. So did your mom, but I couldn't be bothered.

We're going on a run tonight. I don't know how it will end, but Nita promised to bring Jessie to you.

I got these forms online. They give you custody and permission to adopt Jessie, and the free lawyer at the center told me I'd done all the right things. You would be good for her. And I think she would be good for you.

Sister Martha at the mission helped me get some things together that Jessie might need, enough to tide you over for a couple of days.

Please pray for me. This isn't how life was supposed to be, but I've got only myself to blame. And if you can't find it within yourself to raise her, will you find someone who is really nice to do it? I want her surrounded by goodness, and that's not going to happen if she stays with me or my family.

I love you.

Adrianna.

Attached to the two-page letter were official-looking legal documents signed by his cousin Adrianna and witnessed by two people. The stamp of a notary public from Schoharie County indicated that Adrianna had followed the directions of the legal website and the attorney.

"Oh, Gabe." Sympathy deepened Corinne's features. "She sounds like she's in a bad way."

"She's gone, Corinne." He scrubbed a hand to his face, then his neck as the baby slept. "I went to her memorial service two weeks ago, and there were only a handful of us there. Adrianna died while she and her crooked friends were robbing a Thruway exit convenience store. And my mother never said anything about a baby. I can't believe she wouldn't have told me during one of our phone calls."

"Did your mother live near her?" she asked.

"My family is in Saratoga County, on the upper side

of Albany. Adrianna got herself mixed up with a bunch of gang members after she dropped out of high school. A wild crowd, according to Mom. She's done time, twice. And now this."

The baby squirmed, stretched and blinked.

"Is there a bottle in there?"

Gabe searched the bag. "No. But there is a can of formula."

"Try the insulated pocket on the side."

He did and withdrew a cool bottle. "How'd you know that was there?"

"Between my two sisters-in-law, I am surrounded by babies. I think all diaper bags have insulated pockets now, but not when I was dragging things around for Tee and Callan."

"Right." He didn't remember that with Gracie's diaper bag, either.

"You might want to heat that quickly, because when she decides she's hungry, she's going to let us know in no uncertain terms."

He remembered that, too, but there was no way Corinne would know he had actual experience because he didn't talk about it. To anyone. Ever.

He hurried to the kitchen, set the bottle in a large coffee mug and filled it with really warm water as he hit Mack's number in his cell phone. He and Susie not only knew Gabe's background, they were familiar with the rough family dynamics. They'd give honest advice. Then he hit 9-1-1, reported what happened and brought the warmed bottle into the living room just as the darkened sky painted an end to their Indian summer day. The wind picked up.

He handed Corinne the bottle because the last thing

he was about to do was sit and feed a baby. "I've got to shut the door against that wind."

"I've got this." She lifted Jessie from the carrier as if she did it every day, then snugged her into the crook of her left arm once she settled into his big, broad recliner. She leaned back and stroked the baby's cheek with one slim finger.

The baby turned eagerly. When she found the soft tip of the bottle, she latched on as if it might be her last meal.

"Isn't it amazing, Gabe?"

"Finding an abandoned baby on your doorstep?" Talk about an understatement. "Yes."

"Well, that." She looked at the baby with a smile so sweet and warm that her cool and careful image dissolved before his eyes. "How instinctive we are for survival. God's plan, to nourish us and nurture us. She knows she needs food, she demands it unequivocally, and when she gets full, I bet she smiles up at me to say thank you."

He recalled that oft-played scenario. Gracie's smile. Her first tear. The way she gripped his finger in the hospital nursery…

He remembered every single moment, which was exactly why there was no way he could ever do it again.

Three cars pulled into his driveway minutes later. Mack and Susie climbed out of the unmarked car and hurried to the door.

Chief of Police Drew Slade and a uniformed officer followed from their respective vehicles.

"Gabe Cutler, what's going on?" Susie kicked off her shoes and crossed to Corinne's side as if magnetized by the sight of such a small baby. "Oh, have you ever seen anything more beautiful?" she whispered softly. "Mack, come see."

Mack raised a questioning brow toward Gabe, then followed Susie. "It's a baby, all right."

Susie jabbed him with her elbow. "It's an amazingly beautiful and wondrous gift from God," she scolded, only half teasing. "And someone left her here, Gabe?"

He waited until Drew was inside, then shared the details.

"I'm not sure of any other particulars," he said, "but it seems we have a situation on our hands."

"Not a situation." The baby fussed and didn't burp, so Corinne stood and circled the room. She rubbed the tiny girl's back and murmured soft and sweet encouragement. "She's a baby, not a situation. There is a big difference."

"A baby whose presence has caused a situation, then," he acknowledged. Now what on earth was he going to do about it?

"Then Jessie is your cousin, Gabe?" Susie eyed the baby from her spot in the middle of the room, and he'd have to be blind to miss the look of longing in her gaze. She and Mack had been trying for years to have a baby, with no success.

"Well, kind of. Her mother is, so I guess she is, too."

"She's your first cousin once removed," Corinne said softly. "If you have kids someday, she'd be their second cousin. Oh, there," she crooned when the baby let forth a burp far too big for such a tiny child. "Good girl, doesn't that feel so much better?"

The baby pulled her little head back and smiled a big, wide, toothless grin of agreement.

The entire room stood still.

"Oh, Gabe." Susie looked over at him, then Mack. "She is so perfect."

"And I expect she wants the rest of that bottle now," Corinne supposed. "Susie, do you want to feed her?"

"May I?" She exchanged one of those feminine looks with Corinne, the kind men recognize but can never quite comprehend.

"It would be rude of me not to offer," Corinne told her as she laid Adrianna's daughter into Susie's arms. "This way we both get our baby fix."

Susie sank onto the couch and began feeding the baby.

"Well, it is a tough situation." Drew didn't mess around with semantics. "Gabe, she may have left the baby with you but not with your consent, so we're still talking a possible case of child abandonment here. Except with Adrianna gone, the baby becomes a ward of the state, I believe."

"Leaving her with her cousin isn't the same as on a stranger's doorstep." Corinne didn't hesitate to jump in, but then Drew was her brother-in-law. "She had the presence of mind to draw up legal papers countersigned by witnesses and a notary. I think she did way more than most desperate mothers might do under the circumstances. She had a contingency plan when things went bad and had her friend implement the plan, but the mother's intent is clearly defined in these papers." She held up the legal forms Gabe had retrieved from the diaper bag.

"There's protocol, Corinne."

"Drew. Darling." She crossed the room and looped her arm through her brother-in-law's and Gabe knew the chief of police didn't stand a chance. "There is always protocol. And sometimes there are moments when protocol gets bested by common sense. Gabe's cousin did one of the smartest things she could have done for her baby girl. She left her with a man who'll see to her future as long as it takes."

"He'll what?" Gabe stared at her, dismayed. "You mean watch over whoever takes her, right?"

"Takes her?"

The disbelief in his neighbor's eyes should have shamed him, but this wasn't his fault. Adrianna should have known better. She knew his past. Corinne didn't. "She can't stay here, Corinne."

"She can't?"

Mack frowned when Susie tucked the baby closer to her chest. "What are you going to do with her, Gabe?"

Silence reigned.

Corinne stood less than ten feet away. Was she disappointed in him?

Well, join the club because he'd been disappointed in himself for years.

The uniformed officer cleared his throat and Drew withdrew his phone. "I can call Child Protective Services, Gabe. They'll find a foster home for her. They've always got emergency placement homes lined up."

Foster care.

It was a viable alternative. He could drop by and visit the baby, make sure everything was all right. It would give him time to think. Time to rationalize the irrationality of finding babies on doorsteps.

She cooed just then. She leaned back, away from the bottle, and when Gabe looked down, the soft coo of her voice tunneled him back twelve years.

Elise, nursing their baby girl, then Gracie pausing

her meal to smile up at him. At her dad. At the man who pledged to keep her safe and sound, all of her days.

He couldn't do this.

He crossed to the door, needing space, needing air, needing—

He barged through to the outside and hauled in a deep breath.

It wasn't enough air, not nearly enough.

A wind gust brought a flutter of last leaves down around him, gold and red and orange and yellow, spiraling to the ground.

People around town spouted how they loved fall; the parade of colors; the crisp, cold nights; the sun-swept hills of tree-changing splendor.

They were stupid.

The change of colors signified one thing: loss of life. The leaf got one shot at being glorious before being trampled.

Dark thoughts ran through his head. He'd failed before, miserably. How could Adrianna think him good enough to look after such a prize? Such a perfectly wonderful tiny soul?

"Gabe."

He turned.

Corinne stood in the doorway. She beckoned him in.

The cold wind picked up, tossing her hair over her shoulders, into her face.

She'd never understand.

Well, she won't if you don't give her a chance, his conscience reasoned. *She might surprise you because people who've loved and lost are pretty empathetic.*

He saw Drew beyond the window, his phone to his ear.

Susie was holding the baby as if wishing she could

change places with him. The young officer stood off to the side, quiet and still, uncertain.

But not as uncertain as Gabe at that moment. He pulled his keys out of his pocket and raised them up. "I'll be back."

"Gabe." She moved across the narrow porch, her arms clutched around her middle. "Come back, Gabe. Please. Drew's making arrangements."

Making arrangements.

Just like that, as if one word from him sealed the baby's fate. Adrianna had offered him a chance—

A chance he didn't dare take.

"Tell him to go ahead. I need time, Corinne. Just..." He settled into his car and backed it out, around Drew's cruiser. And then he drove north, away from the lake, and then west, away from people because the last thing Gabe Cutler wanted to do was fail another innocent child.

Gabe's driveway sat empty when he pulled back into the house two hours later.

Drew had sent him a text shortly after he left the lakeshore. Baby in good hands. Take your time figuring this out. We locked up the house.

They'd left. And they'd taken that sweet, innocent baby with them.

Good.

That was better for her. Better than being in his care.

Is it? his conscience wondered. *Is being with strangers better for Jess? Or better for you?*

He pulled into the drive, shut off the engine and hung his head, ashamed.

He'd run away in that baby's hour of need. What kind of person did that?

A surprised one?

He ignored the mental sensibility. Gabe wasn't about to let himself off that easy. Sure, he was surprised, but it wasn't surprise that sent him scurrying into the hills. It was panic, pure and simple.

The wind swept in from the west, an early glimpse of the coming winter. Leaves spiraled and tumbled in the surrounding darkness, adding touches of color to fading leaf clutter already on the ground.

He parked the car in the garage and climbed out on leaden legs.

Adrianna was gone, but tied up in a swirl of bad choices, she'd tried to do something right. Only it wasn't right. She said she trusted him with her child, but what she messed up—what she couldn't possibly understand—was that he didn't trust himself.

And that made all the difference.

Chapter Five

"Hey, what was going on over at Coach's house today?" Tee asked as she and Corinne cleared the table from dinner. Callan had gone upstairs to write a report due on Monday. "I saw a bunch of cars there, including Uncle Drew's, but then they were all gone by the time I was done with my Revolutionary War project profile. Did they have to move more stuff in?"

Corinne shaded the truth to give Gabe time to figure things out. "A case they'd been working on needed some fine-tuning."

"On a Saturday when he moves into a new house?"

"The law never rests."

"I guess." Tee rinsed the last bowls and tucked them into the dishwasher, then asked a question she hadn't asked in a long while. "Do you still miss my dad?"

Tee never called Dave "Daddy." Was that because she'd never known him, despite Corinne's efforts to create a relationship that didn't exist on a physical level? She didn't know. She swiped a wet cloth to the table and answered as honestly as she could. "Every day. But not like it used to be."

Tee scrunched her brow, waiting for a deeper explanation.

"Your dad and I loved each other. And when he died, my heart just about fell apart. It kind of shattered into a gazillion little pieces, like when the ice breaks apart in the spring."

"Crunching and crackling and groaning."

"Exactly. But then you were born, like the best gift God could have possibly given me." Her words inspired Tee's smile. "Callan was two and I was so busy taking care of both of you that I didn't have time to feel sorry for myself. I missed him like crazy, but then it was more like I missed him because of what you both missed. Hearing him laugh. Hearing him sing."

"Was he a good singer?"

"He was a terrible singer, but he was funny, so we all overlooked it. And he loved you guys so much. And me." She wrung the cloth out over the sink. "There was this big, empty hole in our lives because he was missing, but as you guys got older, it wasn't a hole anymore. It was like a space, growing smaller and smaller because we were filling up our lives with our times. Our memories. Our songs."

"I miss having a dad sometimes."

Tee wasn't the type to wax sentimental often, so Corinne set the washcloth down and waited.

"Not like when you'd expect it." Tee wrinkled her face slightly. "You know like the father-daughter breakfast at church and the father-daughter race for the homeless." Tee liked running races for good causes. She was born to run, fearless and free. Organized sports worked well for Callan, but not for Tee, the classic nonconformist.

"I miss it most when we do normal things. Like moving here. Or when there's a school concert. Or even sometimes in church, when it feels like everyone has a father except me." She didn't sigh or whine. She glanced around as if looking for answers and none came. "I'm glad you and Grandma and Grandpa told me all about him. I'm glad we've got his pictures here. But there's still this feeling when I look around, that something's missing. Something important, even though Grandpa always tries to take Dad's place."

"But it isn't the same, is it?" Corinne kept her voice soft.

"No." Ever pragmatic, Tee raised her shoulders. "But it isn't bad, either, Mom. I don't sit around fussing over it."

Tee didn't sit around, ever.

"But I think of it at the weirdest times, and then I wonder what I've missed. At least Callan got to meet him."

Corinne's throat tightened. Her hands tensed, because even though Callan didn't have any real memories of his dad, he was part of Callan's early reality. Not Tee's. Pictures of Dave with Callan had places of honor in several rooms. None of that existed for her precious daughter. "Your dad didn't have to see you born to love you, Tee. He loved you from the moment that pregnancy test said you were on the way."

"I know." Tee edged away, not wanting to be convinced, or maybe not needing to be convinced. Corinne wasn't sure which it was. Not really. "But it's not the same as having him hold you. Is it?" She set the towel down when the phone rang in the next room. "Shana Moyer is going to Skype with me for our project so I can see what she got done today. I'll take it upstairs." She answered the phone and dashed up to her room, leaving Corinne alone.

Tee talked a lot, but she evaded important subjects on purpose. Corinne had learned to wait for Tee to open up most conversations, but now with puberty, would she have that option on a regular basis?

Not always.

She updated her online calendar while things were quiet, and when Tee came back downstairs nearly an hour later, Corinne pointed out their upcoming schedule. "If we want to have time to put up outside decorations, we've got to jump on it quickly. Otherwise the festival takes over our lives and the weather will turn and we'll be making a big job out of a normal one."

"And we still haven't taken the boat out once this fall, and only four times over the summer."

She didn't have to say that Callan's sports schedule took precedence. Corinne already knew the truth in it. "I know."

Tee didn't pout this time, and Corinne was pretty sure that was worse. She was quietly accepting that her mother didn't prioritize her feelings or needs, and when your mother was the only game in town, that had to bite deeply. "I'm sorry, Tee."

Again, no fuss. No whine. Tee gave her an almost no-reaction look, then headed for the stairs. "I'm going to bed, Mom. See you in the morning."

No kiss good-night.

No hug.

And she wasn't being a brat, she was simply guarding herself from disappointment.

Guilt sideswiped Corinne. She was tied up the next

couple of weeks because she'd signed on to run the festival again, but in trying to be a community leader, she was messing up what little time she still had with her daughter.

Callan's baseball team swallowed a huge bunch of family time three seasons a year. Four, if you counted winter workouts.

And all this time Tee had gone along, as if family life centered on Callan. All she'd wanted now that they lived in the lake house was time to enjoy the proximity to the lake. And her mother had been too busy to make that happen.

Lights shone next door as Gabe's car pulled into his driveway, then his garage. She waited, expecting a light to come on inside.

None did.

His house stayed dark.

He was coming home to a shadowed, empty house. Did he know that Drew had asked Kate Gallagher to keep the baby for right now, to give Gabe time? Did he know she was in good hands?

He cared.

She saw that right off, and she saw something more. Much more.

He cared too much, maybe, because when he looked down at that baby, it wasn't just fear that creased worry lines in his face. It was fear mixed with wonder, as if the greatest joy and challenge lay before him.

Lord, help him with whatever this is. Whatever's going on. Help him to come to peace with this, one way or another.

Drew had made an on-the-spot decision to keep the baby out of the system, buying Gabe time. But little

Jessie couldn't be left in limbo forever, which meant Gabe needed to make either peace or a decision before too long.

Gabe woke up from a broken sleep possibly more tired than when he lay down. He needed coffee and maybe a run to clear his brain. A few miles of fresh air and a quick pace might help him figure things out. He stepped out of the house with Tucker by his side. Tee's voice hailed him almost instantly.

"Hey, Coach!"

She waved furiously from the deck as she crossed toward the car. She was dressed for church, and while a part of him wanted to take off, he couldn't do it. He paused as she approached, looking vibrant and full of life and love. "Mom said we've got to get going on our outside Christmas stuff today because the weather's supposed to be nice, only we don't have a ladder high enough for over there." Tee pointed to the roofline facing the water. "Everybody that stays for the winter decorates both sides so that folks can see the ring of lights around the water."

Another thing he'd never considered, how a small-town lakeside community would have its holiday traditions even though he'd noticed the lit houses reflected in December waters.

"It's really beautiful to see," Tee added. "Do you have a taller ladder at your house?"

Christmas lights. Decorations. No place to run, nowhere to hide. That reality broadsided Gabe as he faced his excited young neighbor. "In the garage, hanging on the wall."

"Tee. I told you not to bother Coach." Corinne came

out of the house just then. She had her purse over her shoulder and keys clutched in her hand, clearly in a hurry. "Grandpa has a tall ladder. I'm sure he'll be happy to bring it over." She faced Gabe and he saw it again, the concern he'd read in her eyes the day before. "Each season I discover something else I didn't realize I'd need living down here. The tall ladder is only the latest item. My grandfather didn't hang lights from the roof, but the kids love them."

"My ladder is right here." He pointed backward. "No sense bothering Pete to come over."

"That's actually a good point," Corinne noted before she called out Callan's name. She moved toward the car as Callan appeared on the deck steps. "Pete's doing great since his cancer treatment, but he suffers from vertigo if he's up too high. If he brings the ladder, he'll want to do the upper reaches himself. I'm not after a trip to the ER today."

"And Coach said we can borrow his," Tee reminded her.

"Then thank you, Gabe. We'll grab it after church." She made no mention of yesterday's drama, and drove off with the kids as if it was all normal.

It wasn't normal, and he didn't like people knowing that.

He'd traded the anonymity of being in a small house on a farm-friendly country road for this spot on the water, next door to people who knew him as well as anyone from Grace Haven. He'd kept his life private, purposely, but now...here...doors of silence were being wrenched open.

He took the first mile too fast.

Not for Tucker. The tricolored collie mix took everything in stride, unlike his owner. And by the time they finished mile three, not knowing what had happened with Adrianna's baby was driving him crazy. He texted Drew when he and Tucker got back from the run. How is Jessie? Can I see her?

Drew texted back quickly. Tucked in temporary care. Doing fine. And yes. On my way to church right now. Is later okay?

Gabe typed quickly. Yes.

The house felt emptier when they returned. The unlikelihood of that weighed on him, because the house was the same as it had been when he bought it a few weeks before.

And yet different, somehow, because there'd been a baby here, as if she belonged here. She didn't, of course. And yet…

Tucker nuzzled his snout beneath Gabe's hand, and then he went to the door and cocked one ear, as if asking a question.

Stop thinking about it. If this was a police case, how would you handle it?

Only he couldn't relegate it to impersonal status.

He looked next door.

What did Corinne think of him? Of his behavior? His reaction?

It shouldn't matter what she thought, but something in her expression made him think she might understand.

Well, she can't if you don't talk about it. And you never talk about it.

He hit his mother's number on his cell phone. The call went straight to voice mail.

Agitation spiked his pulse. He didn't like things in flux. He liked to know what was happening, and when, every single day. He didn't consider himself regimented. He was…orderly.

Think. Pray. And maybe giving yourself over to God's plans would be a good start.

He carried the ladder next door so he could lock the house, then gathered his fishing gear. Yesterday's cold blast had mellowed to a soft, fall day. He'd take the boat out, drop a line and think things through. He liked praying in church most times, but nothing beat a man, a lake and a solid-grip fishing pole.

Corinne stretched from the upper rungs, trying to loop as many feet of lights as she could without climbing down and moving the ladder, but when it began to list with her at the top, she was really glad the porch roof kept the whole thing from skidding to the ground.

"Come down from there. Please."

She turned, startled by Gabe's deep voice. "Gabe. You scared me. I didn't see you come back."

"Well, I did just in time to see this ladder almost fall over. Come down, there're plenty of things to do at ground level. I'll do this."

She shook her head instantly. "Don't be silly. I've got this, I—"

He stared up at her. The look on his face managed to erase any form of rational thought. She didn't dare let that become a regular occurrence, but how could she stop it with him living next door? He kept his voice softer now, but not much. "Please? My arms are longer."

They were, and she knew she'd been stretching the limits by leaning so far to the left… "Are you sure?"

"Yes."

Finally she climbed down. He held the ladder firm

until she was on the ground, then he hoisted it. "I should have offered to do this for you earlier. I'm sorry I didn't."

"Gabe, it's fine. We don't expect you to jump in on every crazy family project we do, and this…" Corinne indicated the various lighted projects with a wince. "This is what happens when you combine my grandparents' decorations with ours and Tee wants to use every single one."

"Sounds like Tee."

"Or a *National Lampoon* movie," Corinne muttered. "But they're growing up so fast that I hate to say no over something like this."

"Do you want the lights to wrap the porch posts, too?"

"If you don't mind."

"Got it."

He didn't say anything about yesterday's events. Neither did she. As she helped organize the resin nativity set, a group of lighted reindeer, two inflatable Charlie Brown and Snoopy scenes from her grandfather's favorite Christmas special and cord after cord of twinkle lights, Tee's chatter and Christmas music filled the air with promise of the upcoming holiday season.

Gabe worked, eyes forward, focused and silent.

He didn't sing. He didn't smile. He didn't join in Tee's chatter.

Tucker sat at the base of the ladder, looking up. He wagged his tail whenever Gabe glanced down, and even a firm curmudgeon couldn't ignore the dog's obvious affection. And when Callan called Tucker over for a game of Frisbee catch midday, the dog didn't move. He stayed right by Gabe's side until his master's work was done.

"Such loyalty deserves a reward, my friend." Corinne slipped Tucker a piece of sliced ham, then petted his shaggy head. "You're such a good boy."

"He is." Gabe tipped the ladder down, then balanced it carefully from the middle.

"Coach, I'll help you carry it back." Callan took the front end without being asked. "Mom made sandwiches and the one o'clock game started half an hour ago. Wanna watch it with us?"

"Wish I could, but I've got some things to take care of this afternoon."

"Oh. Yeah. Sure." Callan fumbled the words, as if embarrassed he'd had the audacity to ask. His quieter nature meant he didn't put himself out there like his younger sister, so he wasn't as accustomed to rejection.

"Next week?" Gabe's question smoothed what could have been an awkward moment, and Corinne blessed him for it. "I'll be ready to relax over a game once the festival is over."

Callan's eyes lit up. "That would be great."

"Is that all right with you, Corinne?"

What choice did she have? It wasn't a date. It was a neighbor, coming by for football and nachos. "Sounds good. I'll put a pot of something on and we can just relax for the afternoon." That was what she said, but the thought of relaxing around Gabe Cutler was an impossibility. But that was her problem. Not his.

His phone rang after they'd rehung the ladder. He took the call and paced toward the water, talking quietly. And when he disconnected the call, he stayed where he was, staring at the calm, thin stretch of Canandaigua Lake, unmoving.

"Coach, I can't wait to try the lights tonight! Our

first Christmas on the water and so many decorations! Isn't it the coolest ever?"

Quiet moments of grave introspection were brief when Tee was around. She raced across the yard and seized Gabe's hand. "Won't it be beautiful?"

He looked down, as if he couldn't help himself. Did Tee recognize the pain in his face?

Probably not, but her mother did. Gabe looked at Tee, then the house. He tried to smile, but it was more of a grimace. "Sure will."

"And I'm turning every radio station we have to the Christmas channel," she declared, still wringing the big guy's hand.

"Tee, it's not even Thanksgiving yet," Callan protested as he stowed a box of supplies in the back of their detached garage. "Give us a break, okay?"

"If we weren't supposed to listen, the radio station wouldn't play them all day. But I'll leave yours alone," she added as if being magnanimous. "Mostly because you'll kill me if I mess with your stuff."

Callan laughed. "Glad we see eye-to-eye on that." A car pulled into the driveway to drop off two of Tee's friends. Callan made a pretend face of fear, and headed for the house. "Family room is off-limits to girls during football if they giggle and talk like you do."

"Worse than me, by far," Tee promised him, then laughed. "See ya, Coach! Thanks for helping!"

She ran to greet her friends, and then they disappeared into the house, too, leaving Corinne with Gabe. She crossed the driveway to thank him. "I appreciate the help, Gabe."

His jaw firmed. He glanced from decoration to decoration, almost grim. "It's okay."

Not "happy to help" or "glad to do it," and that was all right, because Corinne was pretty sure he wasn't happy to do it. And yet he had.

"Coffee?"

That perked his interest, but then he surprised her by pointing at his place. Not hers. "Drew's coming by in a few minutes."

If ever a man looked like he bore the weight of the world on his shoulders, it was her new neighbor. "With the baby?"

"Yes." He didn't sound one bit resolved. "I haven't heard back from my mother. I don't know if she's aware of any of this, but I can't leave it like this. Babies don't belong in limbo. They belong somewhere. With someone."

She believed that, too. "Then coffee at your place sounds good to me." She didn't ask if he'd made any decisions. It wasn't her business. But she'd dealt with parents in crisis and grief far too many times over the years, and Gabe Cutler fit the profile.

Whatever he chose—whatever he decided—she prayed it might relieve some of the angst he tried so hard to hide. Angst that seemed to go far deeper than a thirtysomething bachelor, trying to live his life. And how did she know this?

Because she was guilty of the very same thing.

Chapter Six

Drew pulled into Gabe's driveway a quarter hour later. Pete and Kate Gallagher followed him into the drive. Once Pete parked the car, Gabe realized why.

Pete and Kate had Jessie with them.

His heart sped up as Kate lifted the baby carrier from the car seat base. His hands flexed. His palms went damp. He swung the door wide. Pete caught it on his side, then stepped back for Kate to come through. "You kept her overnight?" Gabe wasn't sure what to say. How to react. He was used to being the one taking care of things. Not the one being helped. "Thank you."

"Kept things simple," Pete said. "If we're doing a friend a favor by babysitting, county protocol becomes a non-issue."

"I'm grateful, sir." He was, too, because once legal wheels got rolling, putting the brakes on was next to impossible. "I want to apologize for taking off yesterday."

"None needed," Drew told him. "And Pete and Kate have offered to babysit longer if you need them to step in."

Kind people. Caring people. The Gallaghers reached

out to help others all the time. Only Gabe wasn't used to getting help, or accepting it.

Corinne undid the car seat straps and lifted the baby from the seat as Mack and Susie's car rolled into his driveway. They'd stayed by his side through thick and thin and they understood his mixed emotions better than anyone.

"Hey, precious. How are you?" Corinne nuzzled the baby's soft cheek. "Oh, I could just eat you up, you are that sweet!"

"She's happy for the moment because she downed a full six ounces just before we came over," Kate offered. "She loves to eat, and that's never a bad thing, is it, Shnookums?"

"A good appetite is a wonderful thing in a baby." Corinne blew bubbly kisses against the baby's cheek, laughing, then drew back, totally relaxed, and Gabe had another flash of intuition.

Corinne didn't relax often. Not fully, anyway. Another trait they shared. But here, holding a baby, he glimpsed the tender woman within her.

The baby's face split into a wide smile. She opened her mouth, staring up at Corinne, and tried to smile wider but couldn't. It was…adorable.

"Are you just so happy to be here?" Corinne cooed the words gently, still smiling.

Jessie batted her hands. She kicked her feet, cooing soft sounds that sure sounded like she was happy to be here.

His heart stretched open, watching.

What if Adrianna hadn't made her arrangements ahead of time? What if she'd left this baby with whomever? Then Jessie would be a cog in the system. If she even made it to the system.

"Your cousin went to great lengths to find a safe place for her baby." Drew stated the truth in a matter-of-fact voice as Susie and Mack slipped in through the front door. "She might have been over the edge, but she jumped through a lot of hoops to make sure Jessie would be cared for. The ball's in your court, Gabe. We can have the county step in if that's what you want, but if you need more time, we can do that for you."

Could he actually hand this baby over to Child Protective Services? Turn his back on her?

No.

But did he trust himself enough to care for her?

His pulse increased. A cool sweat broke out on his neck. The room felt cold and hot, all at once.

Serious discussion paused when Tee raced through the back door, skidded to a stop and whistled like a pro. "Who's under arrest? The baby?" she teased as she crossed the room to where Corinne had Jessie snugged in the curve of her arm. "Are you a hardened criminal?" She spoke in a baby-friendly voice. She leaned down into the baby's face, and when Jessie burbled up at her and smiled, Tee burst out laughing. "Uncle Drew, you can't arrest her unless the charge is too cute for her own good. Can I hold her?"

Corinne said yes before Gabe could utter a word. "Of course. Have you washed your hands?"

"Just did. We made PB&J with marshmallow fluff and I was pretty sticky." Tee reached out and lifted the baby from her mother.

Gabe moved forward to explain how she needed to

support the baby's head, and to hang on tight, and not to slip on the floor in her sock-clad feet.

Tee turned, one hand behind the baby's bald head, the other supporting the lower end like a pro. "Oh, she is the sweetest thing, isn't she, Mom? I love being surrounded by babies now! It was like forever since I was born, and no babies in all that time, and now with all the aunts getting married, we seem to have babies and cute little kids everywhere."

Corinne's phone jangled an upbeat song in Tee's pocket. "Oops, Mom, someone's been trying to get you. That's why I ran over here. And to see what all the commotion was about, of course." She grinned in admission. "Here." In total tween nonchalance, she passed Jessie to Gabe before she withdrew the phone and handed it to her mother.

Maybe if he held on tight and didn't look down, it would be all right.

If he just—

Too late.

He looked down.

Wide blue eyes looked back at him. Blue eyes surrounded by fair lashes and a pale head with just a whisper of hair.

Oh, his heart…

She reached up. Touched his chin. The bristle made her face scrunch, as if wondering why he felt rough.

He felt rough because he was rough, inside and out, but when he breathed in the scent of her, a hint of baby powder and baby soap…

He was hooked. Mesmerized.

He reached out a finger.

She grasped it, quick as a wink, folding a tiny hand around his big pointer finger as if holding on forever.

His heart clenched tight, then began to ease as if it had been waiting for this moment a long, long time. It opened just enough for him to say, "We won't be needing a place for her." He took a deep breath, a big, deep breath, then lifted his gaze to Drew's. "It seems she's got a place. Right here."

The room seemed to breathe again.

"Consider it done," Drew said. "We're set for the moment. I'll follow through with the report on our end. We'll have to let Saratoga know what's gone on."

"Let's hold off on telling Adrianna's parents about this," Gabe said. "They're quite rigid, and wanted nothing to do with their daughter or this child. They've kept themselves estranged from most of the family for years. I want to keep it from them just long enough for me to talk with my mother."

Corinne had reentered the room while he was talking. "The letter said they wanted nothing to do with the baby," she reminded them. "I think that's grounds for keeping things quiet for a bit. At least long enough for Gabe to do some checking."

"I'll advise Saratoga, but it will be their call. Still…" Drew shrugged. "They'll probably be glad to let us handle things here because the baby's here."

"Where will she sleep?" asked Corinne.

"We put our extra portable crib in the back of the SUV, just in case," said Kate. "And Emily sent a bag of baby girl clothes over. They need a quick washing because they've been in storage."

A crib. Baby clothes from Kate and Pete's middle daughter. A new reality emerging…

"And I got a box of diapers and an extra can of formula last night, so we have the important bases covered." Drew made the baseball analogy with a knowing grin, and he was right. Food and diapers were two very important things when it came to babies.

Gabe swallowed hard. "That's great. I'll grab some money from my—"

"I don't want your money," Drew cut in. He waved Gabe off. "Keep it to buy her something pretty. Pretend this is a baby shower and that's my gift. Pete and I will get the crib and the clothes for you."

"Where should we set it up?" asked Mack. "Down here or upstairs?"

Gabe hesitated, then pointed to the living room. "Here is good. Closer to bottles. I can sleep on the couch until we've got some kind of schedule worked out."

"Nothing like a baby to set their own schedule." Kate sounded downright cheerful about the whole thing.

"Coaching is done for now, so that's good." Corinne's sensibility helped him see the positive side of this timing. "No extra-long days or weekends away. What about child care while you're working?"

"I'm off on Monday. That will give me time to check things out."

"Sounds good." Drew lifted a hand in farewell. "I'm heading out. I told Kimberly I'd get some outside stuff done while the weather cooperates. We'll talk soon, Gabe." He moved toward the door.

"Drew."

The chief of police paused.

"Thanks."

Drew acknowledged that with a quiet look. "It's all right."

* * *

Gabe snugged Jessie farther into the curve of his arm. She pulled his finger toward her mouth, gave him a toothless grin, then yawned, clutching his rusty heart a little firmer with each baby move. She yawned again, in earnest. "Ready for a nap, little lady? How about a fresh diaper first?"

"Right here." Corinne handed him a diaper from the bag. "Would you like me to change her?"

"I've got it."

He settled her down on the cushioned carpet and undid a puzzle's worth of snaps. When he had the new diaper in place, she scowled and batted tiny hands at his face.

"She says you're slow."

He almost laughed, then winced instead. "She's right. This stuff takes practice."

"Gabe, I've got some unused vacation." Susie moved two steps closer. "I could watch her for a week or two. Give you time to get used to things."

Susie would be great with her. He knew that. But what if she grew too attached?

He glimpsed Mack's frown behind her, as if he worried about the same thing. "Susie, can I put that offer on hold? Let me get my bearings, but there could be times when I need you and I don't want to wear out my welcome this quick."

"Of course." She tried to smile, and remorse hit him square.

Why was such a nice couple denied the chance to be parents and an irresponsible young woman like Adrianna given a perfectly gorgeous child? He had no answers, only more questions. He didn't want this surprise baby to drive a wedge between him and two dear friends. But he didn't feel right accepting Susie's quick offer, either, because he wasn't blind to the longing in her voice. The hope in her eyes. He'd been praying daily for a healthy baby for them because he understood their round of losses far too well.

"Rory has contacts with several local day care facilities," Pete said.

Rory was a regular at Callan's baseball games, enthusiastic, funny and recently married with two adopted children who were quickly becoming ardent baseball fans. "She's got the preschool at the vineyard south of town, right?"

Corinne nodded. "Casa Blanca. I'm sure she can hook you up with someone who's got an opening for a baby."

"Can you have her call me later?" He hated to hurt Susie's feelings, but what if this whole thing got messed up once Adrianna's parents found out he had their granddaughter in Grace Haven? He'd be wrong to pile more anxiety on Susie's already full plate.

"I'll text her right now," said Kate. "She'll be glad to help."

Gabe didn't look up. He couldn't. If he did, he'd recognize the hurt he put on his good friend's face.

Tee had taken Tucker over to meet her friends. In typical Tee fashion, she bounded back into the room. "So fill me in! Whose baby are we watching? And can I help? And how long is she here for?"

Tee's entrance offered a welcome interruption to the awkward exchange. Susie put a hand on his shoulder. "Gabe, I think you've got this under control. We're going to head out. Call if you need anything, okay?"

The tremor in her voice made him nod without making eye contact. "Absolutely. And thank you for running right over, guys."

Mack clapped him on the other shoulder. "That's what friends are for. See you Tuesday at work."

"Will do."

Tee slipped onto the floor. "No toys?" She peeked into the diaper bag and frowned. "This is totally wrong by anyone's standards. Mom, we should bring that bag of toys over that we get out for babies."

"You head back to your friends and I'll get the bag while I check the pot of tomato sauce."

"Great! I'm starved!" She darted out, closed the door snugly and dashed next door.

Corinne touched the baby's cheek. "She's precious, Gabe."

"Yes."

"And Susie told me they've been trying to have a baby for a long time with no success. She said that's why she can't just relax and enjoy her pregnancy like a normal person would, because they've all ended the same way. Sadly."

"I know." His jaw went tight. "And it would be an easy answer one way, wouldn't it?" He looked up and met her gaze. He read sympathy and understanding in her troubled look. "But then what if something weird happens? What if the court denies me custody, or Adrianna's parents contest it and I have to give her to them? I can't imagine putting her and Mack through that."

"I agree totally. But I saw how hard it was on you and I wanted you to know I think you're a very special man to do this."

He wasn't one bit special. Not in his estimation. "I'm

not special, Corinne." He said the words firmly. "I'm barely good by some standards. And just all right by others."

"You're wrong." She laid a cool, soft hand against his cheek, and the gentle touch made him look up. "Whatever it is that makes you feel that way is wrong, too. But at this moment, the pragmatic task of dinner calls me back to my kitchen. And consider this an invite because there's plenty of sauce and meatballs to go around."

He hadn't bothered with food the night before. And he'd never given it consideration this morning, so the thought of a home-cooked meal sounded better than good. It sounded wonderful.

His life had changed instantly, much like the fall weather. He'd been trudging along, minding his own business and then…

Jessie cooed from the floor. She dimpled, writhed, frowned, then burped. And then she dimpled again, smiling at him.

He couldn't do this. He knew that. And yet—he couldn't not do it, either.

Once the house cleared he'd call his mother and discern what she knew, but for now…

He sank onto the floor while Kate started a load of baby laundry and Pete wrestled the crib into a more usable state.

For now, he'd sit and marvel at the tiny blessing cooing on the floor before him.

Chapter Seven

Don't get attached, not to the cop or the baby.

The mental warning repeated itself every time Corinne thought about the abandoned baby in Gabe's living room.

Her job brought her face-to-face with a full spectrum of situations and lots of parents, some good, some bad. She'd witnessed young mothers as they gave their newborns up for adoption, and she'd witnessed grievously sad pregnancies gone wrong.

But much of her workload brought happy endings to scared parents facing medical trauma. She clung to that reality during dark days.

She'd just finished arranging hot garlic bread on a platter when Gabe walked through her lakeside door. "Kate commandeered the baby, and I thought you might need some help."

"Your timing is perfect." He looked pained when she said that, but there wasn't time to delve. Not when freshly cooked pasta and sizzling garlic bread was involved. She laid a sheet of aluminum foil over the bread and tucked the ends as Pete followed Gabe through the door.

"Mom said I should make myself useful, but I think she was just trying to get rid of us so Jessie would fall asleep," he announced. He leaned the door shut. "It's getting colder out there. If it frosts tonight, we'll say goodbye to the last leaves."

"And hello to the holidays and snow and the festival," added Corinne. "Gabe, can you set those plates on the table? The girls were recording their harmonic version of 'Santa Claus Is Coming to Town' upstairs, and I promise you that we're all better off with them up there and Tee's door closed."

He set the plates onto the table, then the bread. He glanced around as if worried. About the house? The girls? The baby? Germs?

She wished she could tell him it would all be all right…to relax, let go and "let God," a favorite saying in the Gallagher house, but she understood the reality too well. He'd just been handed an unexpected and very precious situation to handle on his own. She understood that scenario better than most. It would take a dull-witted person to miss the struggle on his face. In his bearing. The verse she loved came to her, telling and true. "There is a time for every purpose under the heaven."

Brave words from the book of Ecclesiastes.

She tried to live the simplicity of the verse, but it wasn't easy. Her faith had been thrown a challenge when Dave died. She'd felt bereft and alone, watching his metal coffin be lowered into the ground, a toddler clutching one hand while pregnant.

What purpose had Dave's death served? She saw the downsides. No, scratch that, she *lived* them, but if everything had a purpose, what reason was there in a young officer's death?

None that she knew of, and that reality challenged the wise words.

"Have we got everything we need?" Pete asked as she set the large bowl of meatballs and sauce in the center of the island.

"I think so. The kids can serve themselves at the island and that frees up some room at the table."

"Corinne."

"Yes, Gabe?"

He moved toward the door. "I know this will sound like I'm being overprotective, but I'm going to keep Jessie over at the house for now. She's little and with so many kids around..."

A shout from one of Tee's girlfriends punctuated the air, and his voice trailed off.

"That's not being overprotective," she told him. "It's smart. I'm not a big fan of dragging tiny babies who haven't had all their shots out into public all the time. Let's let them build up some resistance. And it will give the two of you time to get to know one another. But give me two minutes to dish you up some supper. From one neighbor to another." She dished up pasta and sauce into a plastic container and handed it to him, calm and cool.

"Here's bread, too." Pete hadn't bothered with anything as civilized as a knife. He'd torn off a man-sized hunk of bread and wrapped it in a piece of foil. "I'll walk over with you. It might take two of us to pry Kate away from that baby."

"I'd appreciate the help, sir." He turned at the door and lifted the container. "Thanks for this."

"We're even," she said lightly, not looking his way, because that's how they needed to leave things. Neighborly. Nothing more. Nothing less. "Thanks for helping with the lights. Hey, guys!" She focused her attention upstairs and not on the handsome man standing in her kitchen. "Dinner's ready."

"Coming!"

"Great!"

Callan came up from the family room while Tee and her two friends dashed down from upstairs, and when Corinne turned around, Pete and Gabe were crossing the deck.

She watched them go.

Gabe touched something inside her. A longing or yearning she couldn't afford to let happen. And when Tee, Callan and the other girls had slipped into the chairs she'd placed around the table, she saw validation for her concerns in her children's faces.

They were too young to know what they'd lost twelve years before. She knew. And it was her job to make sure they never had to go through that again.

Once Tee's friends were picked up by their parents, she popped through the hedge. She wasn't dashing over to help, but to make sure that Gabe knew help was available, if needed. She tapped on his side door. When it swung open, he looked surprised and pleased to see her. "Supper was great. Best meatballs I've ever had."

"Going without food for a day might have shaded your opinion my way, but I'll take the compliment as given. Listen, I'm not interfering..."

"That's what people say when they're about to interfere," Gabe cut in. "It's like saying 'It's not about the money' when of course it's absolutely about the money."

She laughed lightly. "Fair enough. I figured I'd come by and collect my container and remind you that I'm right next door. If you need my help with the baby overnight, I'll have my phone by the bed. Or if you want to do shifts, Gabe." She turned to face him. "I'll be glad to help."

Did she sense the gut-clenching fear inside at the thought of being left alone, responsible for an infant's well-being? She seemed to, and that understanding helped lighten his load.

"You'll be fine. Babies aren't as scary or as fragile as they look."

He knew that wasn't true. He'd known ultimate failure once.

His heart knotted, but what could he do? He'd already refused Susie's offer of help, and that would have been an easily justifiable lifeline, except he couldn't put her in that position. He'd broken enough hearts in his time.

"Call if you need me." She lifted her phone as a reminder. "I'll come running."

"I will."

She slipped out, sent him a quick salute and crossed their connected yards. He watched her disappear inside, then stood there, disjointed, staring at nothing until a peep brought his attention around.

Jessie had rolled over. She had both hands stuffed into her little mouth, peeking up at him with just enough interest that he figured he better mix a couple of bottles ahead of time.

His hands shook.

He breathed deep, through his nose, wanting them to stop.

They didn't, and when he sloshed the first bottle onto

the countertop, he righted it and gripped the counter edge so tightly that his knuckles strained white.

He wouldn't be able to sleep.

How could he?

Responsibility rose like a Saturday matinee monster, all-consuming.

He breathed again, released the counter and got two bottles ready before she set up a fuss. He put one in the fridge and brought the other over to the living room.

He needed noise. Something to make it seem like he wasn't here, alone with his greatest fear, a needy child.

She fussed a little louder, announcing her growing impatience.

He clicked on the Sunday night football game, then crossed the room to the patterned Pack 'n Play. He looked down.

Sky blue eyes stared up at him, round and wide. She looked worried.

Well, that made two of them.

She batted little arms as if wondering what was taking him so long. Then her lower lip trembled slightly, leaving him no choice.

He bent low and picked her up.

So light.

So small.

So precious.

Adrenaline rushed through his system.

He shoved it aside.

Every self-preservation instinct he'd been honing for nine years told him to run next door, hand this baby to Corinne and head for the hills.

Of course he couldn't do that because Adrianna had

trusted him to oversee things. Small matter that her judgment was obviously twisted.

He snugged Jessie into his left arm in a hold he'd never forgotten and adjusted her bottle. She drank eagerly, fists bound tight as if worried that food might not arrive on time. He muted the TV, turned his phone on speaker and called his mother. If anyone knew the background story, it would be Linda Cutler. This time the call went right through.

"Gabe, hey!"

Her voice made the baby lurch, and he fumbled to turn the phone volume down.

"You never call on a Sunday night. What's up?"

"Mom, did you know that Adrianna had a child?"

She sighed and went quiet. For long seconds the only sound was the baby's murmurs of growing contentment as she slurped a bottle in what might be record time. "Yes, I knew. She'd gone to an agency to give the baby up for adoption in her last trimester, and then I heard nothing. I'm sure the baby's in good hands with a family longing for a child. We have to commend her for that."

"Did Aunt Maureen and Uncle Blake know she was pregnant?"

"Yes."

"And they did nothing to help?"

"They'd given up on her, Gabe. They didn't want her or that baby around. They considered the thought of the baby a culmination of sin. They made that quite clear."

Anger rose within him. He was thirteen years older than Adrianna, and they hadn't known each other well, but Gabe was pretty sure her parents had given up on the girl a long time ago. "Who does that, Mom? Who gives up on a kid because they've made mistakes? She'd been clean for nearly two years."

"Maureen and Blake have strict beliefs."

He knew that, but didn't Christ forgive sinners? Didn't he bring the outsiders into his realm purposely?

"I told Adrianna I'd be glad to help her, but she sent me a nice note about the agency, then disappeared. And that's all I knew until..." She sighed again and when she spoke, her voice went thick with regret. "Until she was gone."

The image of his younger cousin, who'd tried to straighten herself out after a two-year stint in women's prison, haunted him.

"How did you find out, Gabe? I've never said anything to anyone, and I can't imagine Maureen and Blake are talking about it."

"I found out because someone dropped off a four-month-old baby girl on my doorstep yesterday afternoon. She came with a handful of diapers and an envelope of custody papers tucked into a diaper bag."

"That can't be." He could almost see his mother standing, pacing. "She was giving the baby up for adoption. She told me her plan and it didn't include robbing places at gunpoint with a baby. Gabe, are you sure?"

He glanced down at the baby girl snugged into the crook of his arm. "Reasonably certain. I'm giving her a bottle right now. Her note said she didn't want strangers to have her baby. So she chose me. You really didn't know that she hadn't given up the baby?"

"No. I'm sure no one knew. Oh, Gabe." She sighed softly. "Wait until her parents hear this. They wanted nothing to do with their own daughter when she was less than perfect, and the thought that they could put those demands on another generation is scary, isn't it? My sister was never cut out to be a mother, I'm afraid."

He frowned, confused by her assumption that his aunt and uncle would want—and be awarded—guardianship of Jessie. "Why would they get custody?" he asked bluntly. "Adrianna clearly signed the baby over to me, complete with witnesses and a notary." Jessie blinked up at him. A tiny dribble of milk ran out of the corner of her mouth, and when he dabbed it away with a soft towel, oh, that smile!

His heart softened, and his resolve firmed up. "Mom, there's no way Aunt Maureen and Uncle Blake are getting their hands on this baby. They don't know she's here. They don't know where she is, and I don't think they care."

"But we'll have to tell them," she said softly. "It's the right thing to do."

Was it?

Gabe wasn't so sure, and the whole thing was too new to figure out right now. "Well, they don't need to know right away. I've got enough on my plate right now."

"I can come help."

He'd like that, actually. His mother had always been a voice of common sense in the middle of her crazy family dynamics. "Can you come next weekend? We've got the Christkindl festival, and I'm working the whole three days. If you could drive up here and take charge of Jessie, that would be wonderful."

"Jessie. That's her name?"

"Jessica Anne, according to the birth certificate, but Adrianna called her Jessie in the letter. She's beautiful, Mom."

"Of course she is." She sighed. "I'll come Friday morning and spend the weekend. But you need to think about telling your aunt and uncle. At some point," she added softly.

He would, but not now. Not yet. "I will. But the thought that they might fight for custody and mess up her life..." He passed a hand over the nape of his neck, then brought the baby up for a burp as naturally as if he'd been doing these things right along. "I can't wrap my head around that, Mom."

"We'll talk next weekend. And we'll pray, Gabe. For you, for this baby—and for guidance."

He could use prayer for all of the above. "Thanks, Mom. I've got to go, she needs a diaper change."

"All right. I'll call tomorrow to see how things are going. Are you okay with this, Gabe?" He sensed the hesitation in her voice. "I mean really okay?"

He wasn't, but worrying his mother didn't cut it. "Fine. Yes."

"Then I'll talk to you tomorrow. I can't say this was the phone call I ever expected to get, but there's a part of me that's proud of what Adrianna did. She took steps to ensure her baby's well-being in the thick of poor choices. For all of her faults, that shows a mother's love."

"It does. Good night, Mom."

"Good night, son."

He stood and paced the room, patting the baby's back.

She belched, then brought her head around to smile at him, thoroughly pleased with herself.

A text came in. He looked at the phone. Call or text if you need me. Walking that baby around the living room might get old around 1 a.m.

He moved toward the window.

Corinne was silhouetted in her living room window, watching him. She waved, and he waved back, suddenly not as alone.

He texted back, Appreciate it. Thanks.

You're welcome, came the reply.

Her window went dark, but knowing she was there, ready to help, meant more than being a good neighbor.

It meant everything.

Chapter Eight

Corinne got home midday Monday.

She hadn't heard from Gabe during the night. Had things gone well? She hoped so.

She needed to check on him.

Needed or wanted?

Both, she decided. She'd grabbed a submarine sandwich at the deli. A man who moves into a new house, then gets a baby dropped on his doorstep, all within twenty-four hours, probably didn't have time to shop for groceries. She tapped lightly. He swung open the door, looking positively haggard. She frowned in understanding and sympathy. "No sleep, huh?"

"An hour. Once. She's got her day and night reversed, as you can see."

She peeked around him and spied the baby curled up, sound asleep in the portable crib. Tucker lay nearby, also sound asleep. She redirected her attention up to Gabe. He looked done in, and she remembered those times too well. She thrust the sandwich into his plans and walked in. "So here's the plan."

"Don't wake her, Corinne." He made a mock-desperate face that was probably more real than fake. He added a pretend growl, as if ready to stand his ground. "For the love of all that's good and holy, don't wake her."

She almost laughed out loud but caught herself just in time because she understood the joy of a sleeping baby. "I'm going to babysit right now so you can sleep. I'll take Jessie to my place, so you can relax."

Yesterday he had refused offers of help. A sleepless night managed to change his tune. "You wouldn't mind?"

Mind? Not in the least, but if she sounded too anxious he'd hear the ticktock of her rusting biological clock. "I'd love it. And you'll feel better after some rest. Why didn't you call me last night?"

"Guilt. I kept thinking of how nice it is to get a good night's sleep, and it felt mean to wake you up. And I knew you had to work today, so I persevered."

"I'm on half days today and tomorrow because of the festival, then I took vacation for the rest of the week. And when someone makes you an offer of help, the right thing to do is take them up on that offer. Which means you should have called. But I do understand, because I was the same way, always insisting I could do everything myself. I was a single-parent dork. I kind of still am." She couldn't believe she was admitting that out loud, but she just did. "I'm not exactly proud of it."

"I don't think you're a dork, Corinne."

That voice. The look, as if he understood more than he possibly could.

"I can own it," she admitted. "Right now I'm going to enjoy an afternoon with this sweet baby while you rest. Got it?" She lifted the sleeping infant and wrapped her in a blanket. "Can you hook me up with a couple of bottles and diapers?"

"Gratefully."

He looked done in. Worn out. But she sensed strength, too. Strength from within.

She wanted to reach up a hand. Touch his tired cheek. Assure him everything would be okay.

But she couldn't do that and maintain her strict boundaries. His living so close had already messed up her strictly from-a-distance policy when it came to Gabe Cutler.

His being next door and needing help with a four-month-old baby turned the tables completely.

A baby changes everything... The words of the country song came back to her, a beautiful ballad of the first Christmas, still true today. A baby *did* change everything, which meant she had to harden her heart and stand firm. As she crossed the yard, she didn't try to pretend it would be easy. Because the stakes had gone up. Way up.

He followed her into the house. She tucked the baby onto the quilt she'd spread on the floor. Jessie wriggled, sighed, then latched onto her pacifier and dozed back off.

"That's what I call an excellent transfer of goods," she said softly as she stood. "Transporting sleeping children without waking them is a highly desired parenting skill. Phase one of Operation Gabe Sleeps is complete."

His hand on her shoulder made her pause, and then turn.

"This means a lot to me, Corinne." His gaze went from her to the baby, and she sensed more than fatigue behind his words. "I'll be able to relax, knowing she's in good hands."

"Good." This time she did reach up and touch his cheek.

He leaned into her touch, then smiled.

Her heart went crazy.

Her pulse fluttered in a way that couldn't possibly be good for either of them, but it didn't just feel *good.*

It felt marvelous. She withdrew her hand from his stubbly cheek. "See you later."

He didn't hurry across the yard like she expected.

He walked, eyes down, but when he got to his yard, he turned, looking tired but focused, too. He spotted her in the window and waved. And then he smiled.

The smile brightened everything. The angst of his cousin's life, the crush of festival prep, the gray November day…

Amazing how one sincere smile helped make everything seem more doable. She loved his smile. That frank grin had attracted her over two years ago, but she couldn't think about that now.

For the moment she'd focus on the baby and the festival and her job and kids. That was plenty.

She put on a pot of soup, then brought her laptop to the couch while Jessie slept. When Tee walked in at 2:55, she spotted the baby and almost squealed.

She fought the urge when she realized Jessie was sleeping. "Mom, how cool! This is like the best surprise. Can I hold her when she's awake?" She whispered the words, a rare occurrence where Tee was concerned.

"Sure. If you get your homework done now, it should work out."

"I had a study hall so there isn't much."

"Bonus!"

Tee grinned. She took her backpack to the table and got to work, but every couple of minutes she glanced over and couldn't hold back a smile.

Some kids liked the idea of babies and little kids but couldn't deal with the reality. Not Tee. Her new little cousins could be pesky, cute, whiny or messy and Tee took it in stride. She had the makings of a good babysitter and was getting plenty of practice with Corinne's new nieces and nephews. But every now and then Corinne caught her watching the uncles with their babies. With their toddlers. A look of longing, or maybe *wonder* was a better word, would soften Tee's face.

Was she imagining what it would be like to have a dad? What her life would be like if Dave had lived?

He'd have made sure she got out on the water.

He'd have taken her fishing every week. He'd have enjoyed her tomboy aspects and cherished her feminine side.

But he wasn't here, and that loss left Corinne to fill the void somehow. She'd make sure things were different next year. But that didn't fix the mistakes she'd already made this year.

Gabe woke at 3:37, befuddled. He stared at the clock, wondering if it was a.m. or p.m., then noted the cloudy but light afternoon.

He jumped up, panicked, and stared at the empty crib.

Jessie.

His heart raced before reality dawned.

Corinne had taken her next door.

He breathed as fear and relief battled within. His pulse pounded. His breath slammed tight against his chest.

His fingers shook. The ends tingled as if on fire.

Shell shock grabbed him in a whole-body press and refused to let go.

He couldn't do this. The thought of something happening to this baby didn't scare him. It drove him positively, absolutely insane. No way could he handle the day-to-day responsibility of a child again. He'd been granted that gift once and lost it of his own accord. He didn't deserve a second chance, despite Adrianna's words to the contrary.

Make some coffee and get hold of yourself.

Then think: life has thrust you into a new situation that pushes old buttons. What would you tell a friend? What advice would you have?

He knew the answer to that.

He'd tell them to get back on the horse that threw them and ride, but they weren't talking theory here. The blessing of a child, a living, breathing human being, should never be taken lightly.

His conscience stayed strangely quiet. Agreeing?

Possibly.

But maybe wishing he would move on, only he couldn't. He shouldn't. And if his head didn't understand that, his heart did.

He made a quick cup of coffee and took a sip before he should have. The pain on the roof of his mouth was nothing compared with the ache in his chest, but he'd dealt with both before. He'd do it again.

He cleaned up in a hurry, then thought twice and shaved. The baby had seemed taken aback by his whiskers, and the last thing he wanted to do was make her cry.

He jogged next door, raised his hand to knock and paused. Then his heart jump-started again, but for a very different reason.

Corinne was curled against the nearest corner of the

couch, feet propped on a pillow, with the baby snuggled against her chest.

Utter contentment.

The beauty of the moment calmed his turmoil but not his pulse.

Corinne had been denied a lot in life. Watching her with the baby made him wish things could have been different for her.

She leaned back slightly, pressed a kiss to Jessie's soft head and glanced up.

Their eyes met.

His heart beat harder. Stronger. The breath he'd just gotten back seemed taken away, but not by fear this time. By something else, an emotion so tender and raw it seemed to swallow him whole.

She waved him in, breaking the moment, and by the time he crossed the floor, he second-guessed himself. It would be foolish to be caught up in the romance of a moment when life held so many turns and twists he wasn't free to take. He crouched down by her side and lifted a brow.

"She likes being cuddled," Corinne whispered, the baby's eyes pinched closed in sleep.

"I see that." He whispered, too. "I think you're both enjoying this."

"Immensely." She had the baseball channel on, with the volume turned down but not off. "Callan, Brandon, Eric and Tee are in the family room getting ready for game seven."

He'd missed game six of the current World Series yesterday, and hadn't even given it a thought.

"Since my Yankees didn't even make the playoffs, I can be indifferent to the outcome."

"No stake in the game, less emotion."

"Exactly. A means to avoid utter disappointment. But a woman must learn to guard her heart, right?"

Her expression indicated she meant more than sports teams. He knew he shouldn't follow that up, but he couldn't help himself, another unusual move. "Except that if we guard against everything, do we block all of our chances at joy?"

"Not with two kids," she whispered, smiling. "They're priority number one, and the years are flying by with them. I kind of hate that."

Her regret painted another picture for him.

Corinne.

A baby.

A child to raise, together.

The thought held an appealing mix of hope for the future.

His palms grew itchy, and he backed off the image instantly. He couldn't trust his brain or his emotional reactions to be normal about kids, and being sleep deprived was obviously not in his best interests.

Until he could—if he ever could—he had no right to tempt fate. "Do you want me to take her?" Part of him wanted her to say no, while another part longed to protect.

"Yes. The soup is all set, but the rolls need to go into the oven."

"Everything smells amazing."

"A cozy fire, homemade soup and a clean baby." She handed him the baby and stood. "A recipe for pure happiness. The simple things in life are the best. And if having Jessie here means you need someone to cover for you at the festival, Gabe, that's fine." She spoke softly as she moved to the kitchen. "Between the troopers and Drew's officers, we'll be covered throughout."

"My mom's coming up for the weekend." He kept his voice quiet, too, as he settled himself into the broad recliner. "I called her last night. She filled me in on some family history and said she'd head this way and watch Jessie. She's nice, Corinne. And she loves babies. She knew Adrianna was expecting, but everyone there thought that Jessie had been given up for adoption. My phone call was a pretty big surprise."

"I expect it was."

He leaned back, almost loving the feel of the baby on his chest, and scared about how easy it would be to fall into a trap he couldn't afford, the trap of love. He'd been there before and had nothing to show for it, but somehow, holding Jessie in Corinne's cozy room made it feel almost possible, and that might be scarier yet.

Gabe's mother was coming to help, and that meant he'd be at the festival next weekend. She hadn't realized how much she counted on that until she made the offer to let him shrug off the commitment. But it didn't matter because he'd already taken care of things. She liked that about him. Not every sports coach dotted *i*'s and crossed *t*'s. A lot of them left the organizational skills to others.

Not Gabe. He accepted help, but he liked being in charge. So did she. Maybe that's why she wasn't as irked when he'd agreed with the new festival changes against her wishes. He wasn't on the committee to promote himself or a local business like some others. He was there because he truly liked to give back to the community. That meant a great to deal to all of the Gallagher clan, but especially to Corinne. She'd grown up in the midst of dysfunction, so she enjoyed doing whatever she could do to make the community a solid place for families. While that was noble enough, she'd stretched herself too thin, and time with Tee had suffered by her choices. But no more.

She puttered about the kitchen, pretending to be busy, avoiding the inviting picture of Gabe snuggling that baby in her living room. Tonight she'd sit down and make a list of why she needed to downplay her attraction, especially with this new turn of events.

She'd been raising kids on her own for a dozen years. She loved the gift of them, and she'd made a pledge to never put Tee and Callan into a heartbreaking situation. She wasn't foolish enough to think romance developed in a vacuum when a whole family was involved. She knew better. And she'd made cops firmly off-limits years ago.

But this...

She peeked into the living room. Jessie was splayed out against the big guy's chest, sound asleep and perfectly content.

Old dreams resurfaced. Thoughts of the happily-ever-after that had been wrenched away came forth. This was exactly how she'd envisioned her life with Dave, and then suddenly he was gone.

"Mom, is supper almost ready?" Callan's question made for a perfect interruption.

"Yes. Twenty minutes. Can you get out the plates and silverware?"

"Can it wait till a commercial?"

She raised an eyebrow. "Missing sixty seconds of the pregame won't kill you."

"I'll do it." Tee came into the dining area separating the living room from the kitchen of her own accord. "You can watch the pregame, Cal."

He stared at her as if she'd just grown two heads for good reason. Tee might like her brother most of the time, but she championed equal distribution of chores. Volunteering to do double duty wasn't exactly her norm, but Callan was smart enough to grab the offer and run. "Thanks."

Tee set the table carefully. She didn't slide the plates somewhat close to a chair and pile the silverware into the middle like she usually did. Rounding the curve of the oval table, every fork and knife and spoon went into its proper place.

She put matching glasses at each place, just above the spoons, and Corinne wasn't sure if she should comment on the pretty table or call for a medical intervention. She leaned in close as Tee put fresh butter—not the half-used stick on the counter—at each end of the table. "This looks great, Tee. Thank you."

Tee folded napkins—real napkins, not half sheets of paper toweling, which was their norm—beneath each fork. "Everyone should know how to set a table, right?"

Sure they should. And Corinne had been showing them the right way for years, but with the exception of Christmas and Easter, this was the first time one of her kids actually did it. "Yes. They should."

The buzzer for the warmed bread sounded as the boys came up the four steps from the lower-level family room. Brandon whistled in appreciation when he saw the food and the perfect table. "Wow. This looks nice, Mrs. Gallagher."

"Tee did it," Corinne replied before she looked up,

but when she raised her gaze, she glimpsed her new reality.

A flush of color brightened Tee's cheeks.

Her normally nonchalant, take-no-prisoners daughter blushed with pleasure over a simple housekeeping task because a boy commented on it. And not just any boy… Callan's friend Brandon.

"Yeah, and I didn't have to do it," Callan added. He slapped Tee lightly on the back like she was one of the guys. "She's all right. Some of the time," he added. "Hey, did you guys see Coach's baby?"

"Coach has a baby?" Brandon asked.

"Shh. She's sleeping," Tee cautioned.

"She was, but I think the smell of good food has lured her awake." Gabe stood up and raised the baby to his broad shoulder as if he'd been doing it for years.

"Is she yours, Coach?" Brandon's brows shot up as if the image of his coach with a baby didn't add up.

"I'm babysitting her for a while." Gabe handled the boys' curiosity as if he fielded awkward questions on a regular basis. As a cop, he probably did. "And from the scrunched-up look on her face, I think she's going to need a bottle."

Corinne had set one in a small pot of hot water earlier. She tested the temperature on her wrist and reached for the baby. "You come eat. I'll feed her."

"No, I've got it." His hand closed over the bottle. "I can eat when she's done."

"So can I," Corinne argued.

"How about this?" Tee swiped the bottle from her mother's hands and took a seat on the recliner. "I took the babysitting course the town offered last spring, and I want people to hire me for babysitting this year, so I can practice on Jessie. Okay?" She tipped her face up with such a sweet, sincere smile that Corinne had to pause.

"You don't mind, Tee?" Gabe asked. Mixed emotions played across his face. He looked hungry, still tired and a little nervous.

"There's only one way to get practice, Coach. And that's by practicing."

"True words." He handed her the baby, watched while she settled her into a proper position for feeding, and then as she touched the bottle to the baby's soft, pink lips.

Jessie rooted instantly, hands clenched, so happy to be fed, a delightfully normal reaction.

"Coach, do you think we can do batting practice sessions at the dome this week?" Eric asked as he buttered a hunk of warm bread. The dome was a huge, rounded, tent-like facility where kids could sharpen their athletic skills indoors during the winter.

Gabe shook his head. "Not until January, guys. I've got to juggle babysitting, work, the festival and help cover a couple of guys who are taking vacation in December. Once January hits, we'll book time there, twice a week. Same as always."

"And the weather's been unusually mild," Corinne noted. "Can't you guys do batting practice right here at Welch Grove Park?"

"It gets dark early now." Callan shrugged. "By the time we get home from school and get to the park it's already dusk."

"The shortened days make a difference," Gabe agreed. He paused as he ladled soup into his bowl, then breathed deep and faced Corinne. "I don't think I've ever smelled anything so good, Corinne." He smiled her way, the ladle paused midair.

Pleasure warmed her cheeks, much the way her daughter's had a few minutes before. "Thank you."

"You're welcome."

Behind them, the baby gasped like they often do when they need to burp after a milky feast.

Gabe shot out of his chair. "I'll take her, Tee."

Tee wasn't exactly the acquiescent type. "Coach, I've got her. She's fine." She stood up and walked the baby around the room, patting her back like an expert. "I had to do this with Davy last year. And Emily's baby, too. Practice, remember?"

Gabe's hands clenched. His face went tight.

"Hey, you're actually pretty good with a kid, Tee." Brandon offered the praise around a bite of bread, total boy. "I wouldn't have a clue what to do with a baby, and I sure wouldn't touch it. I think they're breakable. They've got to be. They're so small."

"Mom says they're tougher than they look," Tee offered over her shoulder.

"I'll take her, Tee. Go grab some food." Gabe's voice didn't leave room for argument. He reached out and took Jessie into his arms, then picked up the bottle to continue feeding her.

An awkward silence descended.

Tee's expression spoke plainly. Gabe was making a big deal out of nothing, but Corinne was grateful when she held her tongue. She came to the table and took the remaining seat, facing Brandon, then proceeded to look anywhere but at him.

Smitten.

The boys talked sports, ranging from current football

to the last baseball game of the year, being played that night. Instead of wolfing her food, Tee ate in tiny bites, eyes down. She didn't join in the conversation and the boys didn't appear to notice, too busy dissecting team moves and managers and unanimously deciding that Mike Trout was the best player in baseball.

And Gabe sat straight and still, not leaning against the recliner's cushioned back, as if he didn't dare allow himself to be comfortable with the baby in his arms but couldn't let her go, either.

Seeing that, Corinne couldn't help but wonder why.

Corinne thought babies were tougher than they looked.

She was wrong, and Gabe understood that better than most. Kids were delicate creatures in so many ways. Gifts from God, deserving of love and attention and protection.

Aware of Corinne's gaze, he kept his eyes trained on Jessie. She squirmed, then did that gasping thing again as she tried to pull back from the bottle.

Gracie had never done that, she'd never made that strangling sound that made him leap out of his chair a few moments before. Jessie appeared to think it was quite normal, but that was because she didn't know how his heart rose up in his chest, strangling him from within. She scrunched up her little face, writhed as if in dire pain, burped and smiled.

And not just any smile.

She pulled back from his chest with her head still a little wobbly, and that precious baby met him eye-to-eye and grinned as if happy to be fed and proud to have burped.

He grinned back.

He didn't want to, but he couldn't help it. The response was automatic, and when she read his smile, hers grew.

She reached out to touch his face like she'd done the previous day, and this time she didn't frown.

"She's glad you shaved," Corinne observed. She moved to his side and rubbed her head against the baby's onesie-covered belly.

Jessie laughed, grabbed for Corinne's hair and missed because Corinne drew back.

"I've got her." Corinne reached for the baby. "Go eat, and don't give me a hard time, Coach. House rules."

"Did you get enough?" He glanced at the table and was amazed by how much food three teenage boys had plowed through. "Never mind. If I don't eat now, I'll miss my chance."

"Growing boys." Corinne settled the baby onto the floor and changed her diaper while he returned to the table. "Cal, since Tee set the table, can you and the guys load the dishwasher?"

"Sure," Eric answered as he stood. "That was great, Mrs. G. Thanks for letting us stay and watch the first half of the game with you guys tonight."

"It's a school night, but when it's the World Series, exceptions must be made," she told him. "And we're happy to have you guys over." She finished changing the baby, then set up a play mat with overhanging arches. "I'm glad I kept this tucked away when Emily's baby got too big for it. Gabe, look." She tucked the baby onto the mat, face up. Jessie began reaching and kicking immediately, batting at the soft-sided toys suspended above. "She loves this."

She did, and that spawned another memory. He and Elise, watching Grace's growth, noting every one of her newly acquired skills in a baby book. Rolling over, first smile, first tooth, first tear…

His heart tripped again.

There was no way he could do this, not when every time he looked at Jessie, all he could see was Grace at the same age. He wasn't sure his head could handle it, and he knew his heart couldn't, but what could he do?

No answers came, and maybe that was because God wanted him to make up his own mind.

He knew what he'd tell someone else. He'd done it often enough. He'd tell them to move forward, grasp the good of today and forge on.

That was easy advice to give away, but wretchedly hard to follow himself.

"Stop fretting over whatever and eat," Corinne scolded from the floor. "Take it day by day, the same kind of thing you'd tell the team, I expect."

She was right. He didn't think he could eat a bite, then proceeded to wolf down a monster-sized bowl of soup and two thick slices of her homemade bread, drizzled with garlic butter. When he finally pushed back from the table, he stared down, dumbfounded. "I can't believe I ate all that."

"You have to remember to take care of yourself in order to take care of her," she reminded him softly. The baby started fussing, and Corinne turned her over on her tummy and rubbed her back. A little burp followed, then a sigh of contentment when she took her pacifier and dozed off. Eat and sleep, with occasional diaper changes.

The normal routine came roaring back to him, the beloved sameness of it all amid the wonder of new life.

"Come sit or stretch out. And if you doze off, I'll watch her for you. I'll stay right here," Corinne promised. She stood and crossed the room to retrieve her laptop, then settled onto the floor alongside the sofa. "That recliner is mighty comfy, and if she stays awake tonight, a little extra rest now isn't a bad idea."

He was 100 percent sure he wouldn't fall asleep, so when he awakened during the fourth inning, he was surprised. The baby was still sleeping, Tee was watching the game and Corinne was stretching tired joints. "Hey. Look who's awake," she teased softly, smiling. "Mr. I'm-Sure-I-Won't-Fall-Asleep has rejoined us."

"I crashed." He pushed the recliner more upright and yawned. "I thought I was tougher than that."

"Food, cozy fire and sleeping baby." Corinne set the laptop aside and stood. "Perfect combination. Coffee?"

"I'll get it. You've been working."

"Well, I'm done working, and I'm having tea, so I'm heading that way." She popped a refillable pod into the coffee dispenser and hit the button just as Jessie began to squeak. "And it looks like we've got company."

He bent low to pick up the baby. She blinked round eyes at him, yawned, stretched and blinked again. "I'll do the diaper if you do coffee."

"Deal." She brought two mugs to the living room almost instantly and Gabe realized how much he loved the new single-cup brewing system when she set the coffee on the table to his left. "I've got her bottle ready whenever she is."

"How are you so good at this when it's been twelve years?" he asked with a nod toward Tee.

She ticked off her fingers. “Kimberly and Drew’s little guy, Davy; Emily’s baby, Katelyn; not to mention the twins, Timmy and Dolly. And I work with expectant parents. Lots of times I dash across the floor to meet their tiny blessings when they come.”

She went above and beyond. He’d noticed that quality in her right off, but he’d noticed something else, too. Corinne kept an intentional cool distance around him. At least she had until he found a bundle of joy on his doorstep. Funny how a baby changed all kinds of boundaries when you least expected it.

He walked Jessie around the room. Tee glanced up, then down.

He’d hurt her feelings.

What an oaf.

He sat on the edge of the window seat and pointed to the homework pile next to her. “Social studies?”

“A geographical map of the New England colonies with at least ten topographical features.”

It looked pretty good from where he was sitting. “If you’re ready for a break, would you like to feed her so I can talk to your mom about the Christkindl festival next week?”

Her eyes lit up, but Tee feared nothing, a fact he liked. “Are you going to get all nervous and overreact if she makes a noise?”

Corinne kept her eyes down across the room, but he was pretty sure she choked back a laugh.

“No, and I’m sorry I did. You were doing fine. Blame it on my inexperience and nerves, okay?”

She met his gaze and drew her forehead tight. “Coach, I’ve never seen you get nervous like that before.

Even in the championships. Not like..." She shrugged, thinking. "Ever."

"Babies are way more important than any game," he answered softly, and when he did, he read acceptance in her gaze.

"My mom would say the same thing." She flipped her notebook closed, set it on top of the poster board and stood. "I'd love to feed Jessie."

"Here you go." He handed her the baby, then brought her the bottle and a cotton towel for burping. "You feed. I'll work."

"Gotcha."

And when Jessie gurgled that weird sound a few minutes later, he steeled himself not to turn, look or jump out of his skin. Tee handled her just fine. Now if he could only learn to do the same.

Chapter Nine

Gabe's living room lights were dimmed but still glowing late that evening. Should she offer to help? Or leave him to his struggles?

Corinne's hand hesitated over the light switch, and then she flicked it off, darkening the first floor. He'd be fine. He seemed to almost have an affinity for baby care, unusual for someone with no experience, but his fear was real and she'd seen that often at the hospital. It would dissipate in a few days, and by then he'd have child care lined up from the list she'd given him, and a few days with his mother around. That week of organization and help should bolster his confidence.

By Thursday night, when vendors had rolled into town and the huge tents had been erected on the Shelby/Gallagher Farm, she was ready to head home when Susie MacIntosh hailed her from the shuttle bus drop-off loop. She crossed her way quickly. "How are you doing? I keep thinking about you and this baby." Corinne kept her voice soft on purpose.

"Good so far," Susie whispered back. "Mack is so excited, and we've never gotten past three months before, so there's reason to be optimistic, right? We're almost halfway there!"

"Yes, absolutely." Corinne gave her a quick hug. "Infertility is a wretched business, Susie, and I'm praying for you guys and this baby. Every single day. Are you helping with the festival?"

Susie shook her head. "No, but Mack is, and I decided to check things out as the vendors put things in place."

"Wasn't Gabe on tonight's schedule?" Corinne asked. Susie's quick expression of regret was enough of an answer. "Did he take the night off because of the baby?"

"He took the whole week off," said Mack as he came up alongside. "He's nervous about day care. And maybe still wondering what to do."

"I assumed he'd found someone and went to work like usual." The past few days had been a whirlwind of work and festival organization. She hadn't noticed that Gabe wasn't leaving the house. "Mack, thank you for jumping in to help. It's greatly appreciated. Are you covering his schedule for tomorrow, too?"

"He's done the same for me many times." He looped an arm around his wife and shared a sad kind of smile with her. "His mom rolls in tonight, so he's fine for the weekend. But he needs to figure this out. If you have any influence, Corinne..."

He said the words as if he thought she did, and the minute he said it, she wished it were true. She moved toward her car and hit the key fob to disengage the locks. "I don't, but I'm bossy. We'll see. Thanks again for stepping in tonight."

They waved goodbye and headed in the opposite direction while she navigated trucks and trailers to get out onto the road.

Gabe hadn't worked all week.

She needed to smack him.

She pulled into her driveway, dead tired from the craziness of festival prep, but headed across the yard first. If she went inside her cozy home, she'd never have the energy to come back out and scold her tall, good-looking, stubborn neighbor. She rapped on his door lightly.

He opened it a few seconds later, looking surprised. "Hey. Come on in, it's getting cold out there."

"The weather's ready to turn, for sure," she answered as he swung the door shut behind her. "Mack ratted you out tonight."

He frowned.

"He said you took this week off and that you're not sure what to do about day care for Jessie, which means you didn't go visit any of the places I gave you."

"I did go, actually." He looked uncomfortable and swiped a hand to the nape of his neck. "I didn't like them, Corinne. They seemed so..." He hesitated, then said, "Sterile. Like it was a schoolhouse setting for infants. And who wants that for a baby?"

She didn't tell him that lots of people preferred the more professional setting, because it was clear that he wasn't a fan. "So you're just going to stay home for the next five years until she's in kindergarten?"

He grimaced. She took pity on him because he seemed truly uncomfortable about leaving the baby in a structured day care facility. "Kate is free right now, and she offered to watch her, but I thought we had this all set. She managed to raise a bunch of Gallaghers, so why don't you think about that. If nothing else, it buys you some time."

"You think she'd do it?" Gabe's expression was like

a drowning man, grabbing for a newly extended lifeline. "Seriously?"

"She said she would, and when Drew needed a place for Jessie to stay overnight, Kate jumped all over the opportunity," she reminded him. "Kimberly has the event center running smoothly, and Kate likes that she can actually be retired unless needed. So yes, she'd love it."

"I would be okay with that," he told her, and the relief on his face agreed. "I've got their number, I just didn't want to impose. I'll call her."

"Good. And even if having Jess is temporary, at least you can both get into some kind of normal routine. I know you've been up late and up early because I see the lights, but one lesson that every new parent learns is that they have to try to work in some sort of normal. Otherwise they drive themselves crazy trying to be all things to all people. Especially babies. Like the one peeking up at me over there."

She crossed the room.

The minute Jess spotted her, she grinned and batted little arms, wanting to be lifted and held. "Oh, you absolutely marvelous, adorable thing." Corinne scooped her up and laughed into her happy baby face. "You are beyond precious, my darling. And have you been keeping my friend up night and day?" When the baby laughed, Corinne nuzzled her cheek, then scolded. "Shame on you, but I do understand the attraction."

Did she just say that out loud?

Heat rose from somewhere in her middle, a reaction she couldn't let him see. Eyes down, she kept her attention firmly on the baby.

"You understand the attraction, Corinne?" He'd moved closer, and the deep note of his voice commanded the tiny hairs along her neck to attention. He sounded…interested. The very thing she'd been trying to guard against.

"We girls are always attracted to anyone who brings us food," she offered lightly, as if his proximity wasn't tempting her forward. "And this happy smile says you're doing something right. She's absolutely content."

"She is. I'm growing attached." Gabe frowned and rubbed his neck again, then geared his attention toward the baby. "I probably shouldn't, right?"

"Oh, Gabe. You'd be wrong not to, but I can't speak to that. I know there are a lot of variables to consider."

Twin headlights flashed in the driveway. A car pulled up, shut off the engine, and then a lithe woman crossed the concrete walk. "Mom's here."

He crossed the room and opened the door.

His mother blew in like a category three hurricane, laughing and hugging him, scolding and then hugging him again before she spotted Corinne. "Oh, well, well, well! Gabe Cutler, who is this lovely woman holding this equally lovely baby? And this baby looks just like Adrianna, doesn't she?"

Gabe sent an incredulous look from her to Jessie and back. "You can't possibly expect me to know this. I was a kid, and I sure wasn't paying attention to babies."

"Good point." His mother crossed the room and extended a hand. "I'm Linda Cutler. It is so nice to meet you. Whoever you are."

Funny, warm and a little cryptic. Corinne liked her on the spot. She hooked her thumb toward the north and said, "Next-door neighbor and festival committee member. And I help with the baseball team during the season."

"And she's great with babies," Gabe added. "And makes the best soup I've had in a long while."

"Hmm?" Linda's eyes lit with interest. "All things that are good to know. May I take her?" She reached for Jessie and Corinne handed her over.

"Of course. I'm heading out, and Gabe, call Kate," she reminded him. "Watching Jess will give her so much pleasure, and she'll show her off all over town."

"A Gallagher trait."

"Yes." She smiled because he was right, and she was okay with that. "The town will fall in love with their new resident, and that's never a bad thing. Mrs. Cutler." She extended her hand toward Gabe's mother. "So nice to meet you. And you." She faced Gabe as she crossed to the side door. "I'll see you at the festival tomorrow, okay?"

"I'll be there. Corinne?"

She'd been heading out but paused and looked back.

"Thanks for checking up on me."

His mother hummed again, a soft sound of approval that they both ignored. "That's what neighbors are for, right?"

"Right."

His smile deepened, but she was pretty sure that was pure relief. His mother had come for the weekend, Kate would jump at the chance to help out with the baby while Gabe sorted things out, and the combination had just lifted stress off his shoulders. Reason enough to smile, right there. She wrote it off as that, when he followed her out the door. "I'll see you home."

"It's a hundred feet, Gabe."

"It's dark and cold and I wanted to thank you in private." He glanced toward his house and the silhouette of his mother, walking the baby inside. "I appreciate it, Corinne. More than you know."

"Gabe." She shivered and made a face at him. "It's getting colder out here and you've already thanked me. Go visit with your mother."

She gazed up at him, letting her smile soften the words, and when he gazed down…when his attention drifted to her lips as if wondering…her heart sped up.

She wondered, too. She'd been wondering for what seemed like a long while, and it was ridiculous because she knew better. She'd set limits purposely, for good reason.

He settled his hands on her shoulders, and his touch was enough to warm her one way and inspire shivers in a very different manner.

He leaned in slightly.

So did she.

Cool fresh air puffed the scent of baby powder and coffee around her.

Then her cell phone signaled a call from her house phone. Tee, wondering what was keeping her so long.

She took a step back.

Tee thought the world of Gabe. Callan did, too. So how weird would it get if the responsible adults began a relationship that didn't work out?

Gabe was Callan's coach, and now their neighbor. A bad move for either of them could have disastrous effects, with way too much fallout. How could they risk roughing up their current dynamics?

They couldn't. Callan's baseball talent could take him places she'd never dreamed of. College scouts had already told the local varsity coach that they were watching three local players develop, and that Callan Gallagher topped their lists.

And Tee thought the world of Gabe.

No, romance gone bad messed things up, and even if he wasn't a state trooper, she had to put kids first.

Or you could admit that you're scared. That burying your husband rocked you to the core and you're afraid to take chances again.

Corinne ignored the mental scolding as she hurried back to the warmth of her living room. There was nothing wrong with being protective. With putting others first. With watching out for her children.

Did that mean she limited her options?

Yes, by choice.

But when she turned off the kitchen light a little later, lamplight spilled across Gabe's side yard.

The Penski house had been dark for a long time, and while the new occupant managed to jumble her nerves, the sight of that slanted glow seemed nice. She'd have to learn to be his neighbor. Just his neighbor. But she couldn't deny liking that she had a big, broad-shouldered cop living right next door.

Gabe had volunteered his time with the Christkindl for the past three years because it was the right thing to do. A fundraiser that helped the families of fallen first responders meant a lot. But he'd always taken road duty before. His presence kept folks safe as they crossed the busy road leading into town, and the sight of his light-flashing cruiser kept speeds down on the main road. His assignment offered enough degrees of separation to keep him focused on the normal, everyday busyness of traffic control and leave the holiday hoopla to others.

Not this year. He'd been home all week and the

commander had put him on festival detail, right at the sprawling tent site on the vintage Gallagher farm.

He exited his car only to be immediately engulfed in all things Christmas.

Twinkle lights surrounded him.

A surround-sound speaker system played upbeat carols.

Decorations lined booth after booth, pretty and poignant.

The man who avoided Christmas found himself immersed. Five minutes in and he wanted to make a mad dash to the road, grab a comrade and change assignments.

Are you going to make the holidays dark and silent for that baby? How is that the right thing to do? his inner voice mocked him softly.

He kept to the outside of the tents as much as he could, but that didn't negate the music and the merry lights, or festooned fresh wreaths in an open-air nursery set up just inside the festival entrance.

"Gabe."

Corinne's voice called to him. He turned quickly because this close to the festival entrance, he might still be able to make a run for it.

He paused in his tracks and couldn't hold back a grin when he spotted her over-the-top holiday outfit.

"I'm rockin' the Ugliest Christmas Sweater, right?" She turned, laughing, and he had to scrub his hand to his jaw to control his response.

"You've entered the festival contest, I take it."

She beamed. "I could win with this, don't you think?"

Oh, he thought all right. He thought she was the cutest, sassiest woman he'd met in a long time. He thought she rocked that sweater, because while the ornamentation on the sweater was boldly Christmas-themed to the point of disbelief, the figure inside was total woman. "They could not have fit another clichéd holiday image on that thing."

She nodded, smug, and looped her arm through his. "Exactly why I grabbed it at the thrift store for three whole dollars." She leaned closer, smelling of some kind of holiday cheer. Cookies and fruit, maybe? He wasn't sure, but he longed to lean closer. "I'm steering you this way before you make a run for it, because you appeared to be looking for an escape hatch when I spotted you."

He couldn't deny it. Not with her, and that surprised him. "I was, actually."

She didn't push. She simply squeezed his arm lightly as she pointed out all the different vendors, and the massive heaters blowing warm air into the house-sized canvas tents. "With the festival site over a mile from town, we always provide a police escort to vendors who do money drops at noon and three. If you or one of the other officers can escort them to their cars, they can go to the Grace Haven banks and make deposits."

"Don't most of them use debit cards?"

She lifted one pretty shoulder, and the sweet scent assailed him again. "A lot of folks do, but there're a few who use cash. Of course, with the shuttle buses to town, sales here might take a downturn." She swept the crowded tent with a pensive look. "We'll see."

"Have you had to take it on the chin from the vendors?" he asked softly. She shook her head, but he read more in her expression. "From some, I take it."

"That's accurate enough," she admitted. "I'm hoping their concerns are overdone and that they go home happy after a successful sale. Which means they'll come back next year."

"And will you chair it again?" He kept the low tone purposely because she didn't need others overhearing her concerns.

She shook her head. "It's time to move on. Not so much because of the changes, but because I've put in my time. In a few years the kids will be off to college." She made a face of regret. "It's gone so fast, and I can't believe that part of my life is close to being over. That was never the plan, but plans change, it seems."

He knew that as well as she did, but she handled it better. So much better. Probably because she was an innocent victim while he carried a yoke of guilt.

"How's your mom doing with Jess?" she asked as they moved toward the food tent. Delicious scents filled the air. Simmering apple, sweet cinnamon and some kind of fried-dough decadence mingled with German strudels baking in an oven adapted for outdoor use.

"She's great," he admitted. "And she filled me in on some things that need consideration. Have you got time to talk later?" He faced her fully. "Like at the end of the day? Or tomorrow?" The shuttles were scheduled to pick up the first festivalgoers at the high school now, which meant the time for conversation would be over once the first bus rolled through the loop. "This whole thing with my aunt and uncle has me confused. I know what I want to do, but I'm not sure it's the right thing."

"Tonight is good because the kids are staying at Kate and Pete's house this weekend. They both had things on their schedules, so it was easier on everyone if they stay in town with Grandma and Grandpa."

"Then how about if we hit the Thruway Café about six o'clock? Is that good?"

A voice called her name. Then another, from the opposite side of the long tented aisle. She fluttered a hand as she moved to the first vendor. "I'll meet you there."

He moved toward a less holiday-themed side of the tent. He passed jams and jellies and candles and jewelry booths, but came to a complete stop when he spotted baby clothes.

He swallowed hard but couldn't resist running his finger along the soft, nubbed bright red fabric hanging at the booth's edge.

"So beautiful, right?" An older woman smiled at him as she entered the booth with a steaming cup of hot chocolate. She set the mug down on the back table, far from the handmade goods, then moved forward. "My daughter does the baby clothes and blankets. And she can embroider names on them, see?" She held up a blanket and he saw the name "Annie" embroidered around the satin binding. "We can customize most anything, but of course, a beautiful dress like this one." She pointed to the one he'd paused to admire. "Needs nothing else. It says Christmas without being ostentatious."

That's what drew him to the red-and-white dress. It was tastefully simple and not overdone with holiday adornment. "How big is it? I mean what size is it?" he corrected himself, flustered. He hadn't bought a little girl outfit in a long, long time.

"This one is six months. How old is your baby?"

His heart scrunched because Jess wasn't his for real. But she was his for now, and so he lifted his shoulders. "Jess is four and a half months old, and she's not real big for her age, according to my mother."

"With Christmas next month, I think this size would work. And being a dress, you don't have to worry about length so much. Not with the pretty little stockings." The vendor had attached a pair of white stockings to the hanger, and the feet of the stockings looked like an old-school pair of black patent leather shoes. Like the ones Grace used to wear. She'd pretend they were tap shoes and dance around the house, tapping her toes with or without music.

He pulled his hand back.

And then the rest of his body followed.

His radio came alive and he eased away from the booth as if he was needed someplace else. He wasn't, it was a general check-in call from the road, but the thought of buying that dress pushed his heart into overdrive.

He went through the morning pretending he had blinders on. He ignored the fuss and fun, he kept his eyes on people, not things, and by midafternoon he was congratulating himself that he'd almost made it when an old-fashioned Kris Kringle strolled through the tent crowds, handing out peppermint sticks to the shoppers.

As Gabe lingered along the back row, keeping a quiet eye on things, a shopper lifted the red dress from the crochet vendor's display.

A part of him hoped she'd buy the tiny dress and take it out of temptation's reach.

Another part wanted to cut across the floor and snatch it out of her hands, and when she flipped the price tag over, scanned it and set the dress down with regret, relief swept him.

He was being ridiculous. Jess needed clothes, he was

her guardian at least for the time being, and the outfit was charming.

But what if his aunt and uncle fought for custody once they discovered he had this baby?

Should he fight to keep her? Was he being too judgmental? Or was it important for someone to finally recognize Adrianna's right as a mother to help form her child's future?

He moved away from the pretty dress and the older woman's understanding gaze and made himself a deal. If the dress was still there near closing time on Saturday, he'd buy it. If not…then it wasn't meant to be.

Chapter Ten

Coffee with Gabe.

Not a date, not a date, not a date...

Corinne muttered the phrase repeatedly as she headed for the café not far from the Thruway exit. The café in town was lovely, and she loved the Grace Haven diner, but both would be mobbed with people they knew. This one was just far enough outside town to draw travelers, not locals. Here they could sit and talk in relative peace without becoming gossip fodder. She parked the car and spotted Gabe, waiting outside.

Chivalrous.

He could have escaped the brisk wind and the growing chill by grabbing a table for them, but he didn't. He'd waited in the cold for her, and that made everything so much nicer. "Hey."

He reached out a hand for hers as naturally as if he did it every day, and that made her wish he did. "They're calling for snow by midweek. And not a few flakes, either. The real thing."

His hand clasped hers in a move so smooth she wasn't

sure where his skin began and hers ended. "Thanks for meeting me."

"Glad to do it," she told him, looking up.

Big mistake.

The minute her gaze met his, all she could think of was that near kiss on the deck, and wonder what she was missing by not kissing Gabe.

She dropped her gaze and spotted an empty corner table as they moved indoors. "How about that one? Quiet enough to be private, open enough to enjoy the carols."

"As if we didn't have enough of those today."

She settled into her side of the booth and frowned. "I love Christmas music. I love the sweet ones, the romantic ones, the funny ones. I love hymns and carols, and I will admit to playing Christmas music throughout the year as the spirit moves me. Does that make me crazy?"

"The fact that you asked the question should be enough of an answer," he teased, but she wasn't immune to the sorrow in his manner.

"The pain of Christmas." She said the words softly and covered his hand with hers. "When things go well, the holidays are such a joy. But in despair or sorrow, they become a sharp-edged sword. I've seen many a grief-stricken family through those first holidays after a loss, and it's heartbreaking, Gabe."

"I bet it is."

His simple words agreed, but she'd read the anguish in his face over the past week. The holidays had a way of magnifying loss. She understood that from a personal and professional perspective. But Gabe's angst had fired up the moment he'd found that baby at his door and hadn't dissipated yet.

"Are you hungry, Corinne?"

She shook her head. "I stopped by the strudel booth twice today. Hannah Guerst's homemade strudels are my guilty pleasure. Her shop is far enough away that I don't get them often, but during festival time I eat as much as I want. My reward for a year of work well done."

"Do you have a favorite?"

"Too many," she admitted, but the question made her smile. "Anything with cinnamon. I love the apple varieties, but I think the brown sugar pecan with maple glaze is my favorite."

"Anything with brown sugar, maple and nuts should be a favorite," he agreed. He stood to place their order with the barista. "Do you want a regular coffee? Or something fancier?"

"Tea," she replied and tapped her slim gold watch. "I've got to be up early and back to the festival grounds, so no coffee tonight. A hot raspberry peach tea sounds marvelous."

He crossed to the barista station and when he came back, he set her tea down first, then sipped his coffee before settling into the booth again. "This is amazingly good coffee. That would be my suggestion to the festival committee for next year. Get someone on-site that can make a decent cup of coffee."

She didn't disagree. "You're right, and that's part of the reason I need to step down. I can't hurt old Milt's feelings by refusing him a spot. He's such a sweet old guy. But his coffee has taken a nosedive, and that's a problem that needs to be solved by someone else. And while I can make small talk as well as anyone, I don't think we came here to talk about coffee, did we?"

"No." He gripped his cup and faced her. "I've filled you in on my cousin and how her parents reacted to her choices and her pregnancy. At this point, they think she gave Jess up for adoption when she was born over four months ago."

Corinne cringed slightly. "Ouch."

"I know." He sipped his coffee with deliberation, then said, "I'm procrastinating purposely, for a mix of reasons, but I'm not sure how to move forward. My fear is that once they know, they'll plead for custody."

"Most grandparents would," she acknowledged. She really couldn't imagine many grandparents who wouldn't.

"That's just it." He leaned forward, hands clasped as he continued in a serious tone. "They're unforgiving people. Their brand of religion doesn't allow for mistakes. They get harsh. And I'm not saying that to excuse what Adrianna's done over the years, but it was almost as if nothing she did would ever please them. So maybe she simply gave up." He studied his mug with grave intent. A muscle in his lower right cheek twitched slightly. "They didn't want damaged goods in a child. They threw Adrianna out. I can't imagine turning Jessie over to them and witnessing the same thing happening again. How unfair would that be to an innocent baby, to knowingly place her into that kind of a situation? And if Adrianna had wanted her parents to have the baby, she'd have arranged it that way. She didn't. That's the stumbling block, because she specifically asked for her parents to be denied custody in her papers."

She lifted her eyebrows, inviting him to continue.

"I'm not perfect, either," he said softly. "I've made mistakes in life, and the thought of raising a baby scares me. But the thought of going against Adrianna's wishes and letting my aunt and uncle take Jess just doesn't sit right. And once they realize where she is, I think they'll fight for her. Or find some way within the family to try to make her life miserable. And I'm not sure I'm strong enough for that."

"For a fight? You?" She sat back, amazed. "Gabe Cutler, I've never met a stronger or fairer man in my life. Of course you're up for it. You rise to any occasion. It's part of who you are. Why is this different? Are you hesitating for the financial reasons of hiring a lawyer? I don't have much, but I'll help if I can."

His smile was part grimace. "Thank you. I love your generous spirit, but, no. It's not money. It's me, Corinne."

"You?" She watched him, puzzled, then sighed. "The past likes to step on the heels of the present, doesn't it? It's so hard to walk fully forward when regret tugs us backward. Do you want to tell me about it? If you do, that's fine. And if not, that's fine, too, Gabe. Either way, I'm giving you the top slot on my prayer list because I don't like to see you hurting. And I expect," she added softly, leaning forward so no one would hear, "that you've been hurting for a while."

He'd been hurting for more than a while. The ache in his heart had been raw for a very long time. Corinne's sympathy helped, maybe because she sympathized without knowing a thing. He took a deep breath and began. "I was married years ago."

Her open look invited him to continue.

"We had a daughter. Grace." He loosed his hands and gripped the coffee cup hard. "She would have been Tee's age. And she was like Tee in so many ways. Funny. Laughing. Always talking, spontaneous, bright. She was a ray of sunshine that just never seemed to draw a cloud. Beautiful and dear and amazing." His eyes grew wet.

He didn't care.

Because talking about Grace was worth risking his tough-guy image.

"We went to a party, a football party at a friend's house. A bunch of kids, moms and dads. A perfect day. My buddy had put a man cave in his barn. Just a spot where he could watch the games and eat pizza and wings and be loud on game days." He lifted his coffee, changed his mind and set it down again. "Somehow I must have left the door to the car open. It was a beautiful day, the first game of the season, and I disappeared while the women and kids hung out in the backyard and the upstairs family room. It was all so perfect…" He breathed deeply. "Until I heard the scream."

Her hand touched his gently. So gently.

"Somehow Grace had gotten into the car and shut the door. I was the last one out of the car, I was the last one to go into the party, and I must not have shut it right. I was carrying a small cooler of food and shoved it shut with my knee. I thought it closed." He sighed, then shook his head. "It didn't. My wife found Grace in the car, in the hot sun. She thought Grace was playing with the other kids. I was inside, oblivious to my beautiful daughter. And just like that, she was gone."

"Oh, Gabe."

Did she know that tears were streaming down her cheeks? Maybe not, because she did nothing to blot them.

She covered his wrists with her hands. "I am so, so sorry. I can't even imagine your loss."

He pulled one hand free and slid a stack of napkins her way. "I didn't mean to upset you, Corinne. I'm sorry."

"Don't say that. Don't ever say that," she scolded as the warm Christmas hymn about a holy night wove poignant notes in the background. "Sharing hopes and fears and sadness is important. But I'm brokenhearted for you, Gabe. What a weight to carry around for so long." Her expression deepened. She kept her hand on his wrist and squeezed lightly. "No wonder Jessie scares you to death."

"She does," he admitted. "But I'm just as worried about letting her go to her grandparents, because then I'm breaking another sacred trust. And I can't do that, Corinne. I've done it once already, so which fear do I face? The fear of making another grave mistake with an innocent child or the fear of letting others hurt her emotionally for the rest of her life?"

"You didn't ask to be her guardian," she reminded him. "But I can understand your cousin's decision. She looked for someone fair, wise and strong to take care of her baby. She wasn't looking back, Gabe. Adrianna was looking forward. And I think that's what you need to do, too."

Forward.

He'd moved forward physically because he had no choice, but emotionally he'd stayed mired in personal tragedy for years. "There's more, Corinne."

She frowned in sympathy.

"My wife died the next year. We weren't able to get over our loss, and she slipped into a cycle of drinking the pain away. She left me on the one-year anniversary of losing Grace and died in a one-car crash three months later while under the influence of alcohol. And nothing's been quite right since."

She stood, came around the table and slipped in beside him.

And then she hugged him.

She wrapped her arms around him and held him close.

He felt treasured.

He felt undone, unwound, as if part of that tight knot coiled within him had worked itself loose. He cherished the embrace, and the woman offering it. Her solace blessed him, and the scent of her hair mingled with brewing coffee and baking gingerbread. Too soon she released him and leaned back. "You should keep Jessie."

"And shrug off her family?"

"You're her family now. You're the one chosen by the distraught mother. There were reasons she sent her daughter to your protection in her hour of need. Her actions show intent and follow-through. She made her decision known and legalized it as best she could. I can see this is a hard step forward for you. You don't trust yourself."

The accuracy of her words made him swallow hard.

"But you *should* trust yourself, because you've got every quality a child would want in a parent."

Except the one that mattered nine years ago. Protection.

"And I cannot pretend to imagine your pain at losing Grace, but I wish one of those grown-ups who were outside had been paying more attention, too. And I expect there were several who feel just as guilty as you do."

Her words took him by surprise.

He'd heard them before, sure, but this was the first

time they'd really registered. Maybe because he hadn't talked about losing Grace and Elise for long, long years. "I can't blame others for my carelessness, Corinne. It would be wrong."

"It would," she whispered back with a gaze so soft and caring that his heart yearned to know hers. To see the world through Corinne's pragmatic optimism for the rest of his life. "It's not about blaming others, Gabe. It never is. It's about forgiving ourselves, and I think Adrianna has given you the best chance to do exactly that. She's offered to let you make decisions for her child during a season of loving and forgiving. The best season of all. Now it's up to you to grab hold and hop on the roller coaster of being a single parent."

She thought he could do this and believed it was in Jessie's best interests.

His phone buzzed a text from his mother. He pulled it out, saw the photo and held it up for Corinne to see.

Baby Jessie, curled up in the soft-sided crib, sound asleep with a hinted smile, and the caption below read Smiling and dreaming of great things to come.

His heart stretched wider, opening the door of possibilities. "I hate that my choice might hurt my aunt and uncle, but my conscience won't let me give Jessie up to them." He took in a deep breath. "I'll let them know I have her, and that I'm her legal guardian. Then we'll take it from there."

"And I'll be right next door, helping all I can," she promised. "We single parents have to stick together."

He turned to smile at her.

She was close.

So close that he could lean just a tiny bit closer and whisper a kiss to that beautiful mouth. And as he contemplated that, he realized he didn't want just a sweet little kiss of friendship.

He wanted to let her know that she wasn't just a neighbor and a friend. She was beyond special and every part of his being wanted her to realize that. He dropped his gaze to her lips again. "Corinne..."

She came closer, so close he felt the warmth of her breath flutter the hairs along his temple.

And then she stopped. She drew back.

Regret shadowed her face. She bit her lip lightly, pensive. "I made a promise to myself, too. When Dave died, and I went through that pain of loss firsthand, I promised myself I would never get involved with another lawman. How could I knowingly put Callan and Tee through that if something were to happen? So as much as I'd love to pursue this—" she indicated his mouth "—I can't, Gabe. I don't think I have it in me to take that risk again."

"But you're tempted? A little?" He raised one brow slightly while he waited, watching her eyes widen in sweet reaction. And then he waited some more.

She was tempted more than a little, and the look on Gabe's face suggested he suspected as much. He'd shared his heart and his pain with her. He'd bared his soul.

More than ever, she longed to care for him. Comfort him.

But her pledge had never been about her. She was tough, faithful and independent enough to trust God's goodness. But to knowingly thrust her children into that situation would be wrong. "Lots of things are tempting, Gabe. But single parents have to weigh a lot more than attraction. I've got three hearts to protect under my roof."

He acknowledged that with a look of acceptance. Then he leaned closer, just a little. "Nothing has to be decided tonight, does it?"

"No," she agreed. But she needed to make herself clear, she needed him to hear her. "But—"

"May I suggest to the committee chairwoman that we table this discussion until our next meeting?" His gentle look warmed her from within, even as he teased her. "That will give all parties time to reevaluate their positions."

"What if I can't change my position, Gabe?" She asked the question straight out. "What if I can't take the risk?"

He smiled right at her, the kind of endearing smile that had drawn her in from the beginning. "That just means I need to try harder, doesn't it?"

Oh, those words.

That look.

That smile.

She couldn't help but smile back. It felt wonderful to be wooed by a strong man who thought she was special. Who thought her children were special. She slid out of the booth and stood. Gabe followed. "Sure you don't want supper, Corinne? You've got to be hungry, and a few pieces of strudel aren't considered a meal. Plus I've got a built-in babysitter for the night. Wow, those are words I never thought I'd hear coming out of my mouth again."

She smiled and shook her head. "I've got to stop by Mom and Dad's and see the kids. But if you offer me supper tomorrow night..." She let the words float back to him as she walked to the door. "I will forgo my urge for strudel and enjoy a good meal. Pete and Kate are taking the kids into the city to see a holiday musical, so I'm on my own."

"I'd like that." He opened her car door for her once they were outside, then leaned down to hold her gaze. "See you in the morning."

She would see him then. And all day. And then for supper.

Suddenly the risk of the attraction seemed outweighed by the strength of the attraction, but was that the smart thing to do?

She didn't know. And until she did know, she should raise her guard, but when she was around Gabe Cutler, keeping her walls up was proving to be more than difficult.

It was next to impossible.

Chapter Eleven

"I can't believe we've lived on the lake all spring, summer and fall and we've only been on the water a few times." Tee flopped onto Kate and Pete's couch, thirty minutes later, grumbling. "That can't be right. Why do we live on the water if there's never time to take the boat out? And now it's supposed to get crazy cold and we'll pack it away until next spring."

"So much for having quality time with the kids," Kate whispered to Corinne. Louder she added, "I hear you, Tee. It can be tough in a big family like ours, especially with weddings and babies and new businesses opening up like we had this past year. It was a little crazy, wasn't it?"

Corinne's sister-in-law Rory and her new husband had adopted his late cousin's two small children when his mother passed away, Emily had purchased a bridal store and had a baby, and the oldest sister, Kimberly, was expecting her second child. For a family where not much had changed in a decade, so much had changed in the last eighteen months. "Next year won't be so wild. I don't think," Kate added. "Although I hadn't predicted this past year's increase in activity, so don't quote me on any of this."

"I'll have more free time next summer," Pete added from his recliner near the cozy fireplace.

"So will I," Corinne told them. "I'm going to step down as festival chairperson, to give me more time, Tee. I realized when we talked about this that I need to pay more attention to my current priorities. It's a good time for others to take over the civic stuff."

"You're sure about this, Corinne?" Kate slid a tray of very unhealthy cake squares her way, and Corinne took one.

"Yes. I want to do more things with Tee, and between Callan's baseball schedule and the festival meetings and follow-ups, Tee's getting left out." She met Tee's frown and blew her a kiss. "I will make this up to you, honey. I promise. I'm just sorry I was shortsighted this year."

"So we really have to put the boat away?"

"We should have taken care of it already. Thanksgiving is coming up, which means another busy week."

"I can do it," Pete offered. "I'm happy to help."

"That would be great," Corinne told him before she waded in with a question she almost hated to ask. "About Thanksgiving..."

Kate looked up with interest.

Pete barely heard her—total male.

"We've got Gabe and the baby next door, and his family is almost four hours away. I don't think he should be alone for Thanksgiving."

Kate did exactly what Corinne was hoping she'd do. "Invite him here. There's plenty of space once we open the enclosed porch and plug in the heater. I expect he'd like that baby to be around other little ones, don't you?"

She did, but she had a more selfish reason for wanting Gabe to be comfortable around Dave's family. She wanted them to like him because she was sliding well past "like" when it came to her neighbor, and the Gallaghers had been her staunch support for years. Their acceptance of him meant a great deal to her. "That's fine with you?"

Kate held her gaze long enough to send a silent message of approval. "It's not only fine, honey. It's wonderful."

Heat stained her cheeks. She'd considered this attraction impossible for a long time, and the thought of new possibilities seemed wrong and right. The fact that she still hesitated added to her confusion.

"I'm going to bed." Tee didn't pause to kiss anyone good-night. She didn't look left or right. Corinne's funny, vibrant daughter trudged up the stairs looking tired and unhappy.

"Romance problems," Kate whispered once Tee was gone.

"She's twelve," Corinne whispered back. "We're not allowing her to think about boys for another four years. Do you think she missed the memo?"

Kate sent a rueful look toward the stairs. "Callan's friend Brandon was here today."

"She's crushing on him." Corinne scrunched her brow, because how did one handle this? She was out of her element, which meant she needed to figure this out. Quickly.

"He's nice as can be and paid her absolutely no attention while he and Callan arranged to go to the batting cages and the opening basketball game at the high school. Without her. We offered to take her, but her feelings were hurt at being left out. She and Callan used to do everything together, so his quest for independence is a touchy subject right now."

"I'll go talk to her." Corinne climbed the stairs. She found Tee in Kimberly's old room, a longtime favorite place to be at Grandma's house. "Hey. I didn't want to leave before saying good night to my best girl."

"G'night." Tee muttered the word, eyes pinched closed, much like she'd done as a baby. Only she wasn't a baby anymore.

"Tee." Corinne eased down on the side of the bed. "I really am sorry about the boat and the water and the stupid boys."

Tee's eyes flashed open. "I don't care about any of it. Not one speck. At all."

Corinne weighed Tee's declaration with a slight frown. "Even if you don't care, I'm still sorry. I won't let time get away from me again. I promise."

"Why are boys so dumb?"

"Are they all dumb?"

Tee sat up partway, eyes flashing. "I believe so."

Corinne had to laugh. "Oh, darling, they can be a frustrating lot, can't they? Why didn't you just go to the basketball game with your friends?"

Tee blew out a breath. "I was too mad. I had it all planned out."

Corinne waited for her to go on.

"Brandon was coming over, I knew they'd want to go to the game, and I kept waiting and waiting for them to invite me. And they didn't."

"You could have invited yourself," Corinne reminded her. "Or just gone along and then you could have gone off with your friends from school."

"It wouldn't have been the same."

"The same as what you dreamed of?"

Tee flushed.

"If I say that Brandon's a clueless lout, that might make you feel better. But sometimes the person we're interested in just doesn't see us the same way, at the same time."

"The whole stupid 'He's So Not Into You' stuff," Tee declared. "So we wait?" Tee's brows shot up at the futility of that. "I hate waiting."

A trait from her father, absolutely. "Then don't wait. Shrug it off until the timing is better, honey. Give yourself some space. I'd hate to see you waste junior high on crushes when there's so much out there beyond boys. The romance thing will come, but I'd be okay if you gave it a little time. I think that would be the best thing to do, but not because I want to keep you a little kid. You only get one chance to be this age at this time. I'd like to see you enjoy it."

"And when Brandon does notice me, I'll ignore him completely and he'll regret his inattention the rest of his days."

"You've been reading *Anne of Green Gables*."

Tee nodded. "Anne and I have a lot in common, it seems."

"Oh, you do, darling." Corinne leaned down and hugged her too-eager-to-grow-up daughter. "And Anne turned out just fine, didn't she?" When Tee said yes, Corinne kissed her cheek. "And so will you. I'll see you Sunday, okay?"

"Yes. And Mom?"

Corinne stood. "Mmm-hmm?"

"Will I always be nervous and weird around boys? Because I hate that."

"No." Corinne shoved her personal reaction to Gabe aside. "No, you will be confident and self-assured. Eventually. I promise."

"Okay." Her beautiful, spunky daughter sank back down into the pillow. "G'night."

"Good night, darling."

Corinne closed the door softly. Regret pinged from within. She'd been foolish to let the nice weather get away from her, and more so to not take time with Tee. She'd do better next year, mostly because she really couldn't do worse.

Corinne.

Gabe shaved quickly the next morning, then called next door. "Hey." He tried to sound casual when Corinne answered her phone, even though he felt anything but casual when thinking about her. "If we're having supper together tonight, it's silly to take two cars to the festival. How about we ride together?"

"What an absolutely sensible idea!"

Her teasing tone made him grin. "Can you be ready to leave in fifteen minutes?"

"I'm kidless so I'm ready now," she told him. "I'll walk over and see your mom and the baby for a few minutes."

"Perfect." He hadn't thought anything would seem perfect again, but opening up to Corinne had dulled his shadowed thoughts. She believed in him. Now if he could just learn to believe in himself. "See you shortly."

"I'm on my way."

He finished getting ready, rued another weekend

gone without putting his boat up for the winter and hurried downstairs.

He paused, midstep.

Corinne was holding Jessie. Her soft blond hair shone beneath the overhead kitchen light, and the baby's pale skin made a contrast against Corinne's forest green turtleneck. The snug sweater and the infant's curve created a living portrait of motherhood.

She'd said she hated for this time in her life to be over. She'd rued that plans had changed without her consent, years before.

The image of mother and child ramped up his heart. Maybe it didn't have to be over, for either of them.

She turned just then, spotted him and smiled. "This baby is intoxicating. I could snuggle her all day."

"She gets under your skin, that's for sure." He finished coming down the stairs and kissed the baby. "I'm pretty sure she flirts with me."

At that very moment, Jess peeked up at him and flashed a coy smile.

Corinne laughed. "She does! Oh, you sweet thing!" She nuzzled the baby's neck, making her laugh out loud, then handed her over to Gabe's mother. "Take her, Linda. Otherwise I'll stay right here where it's warm and cozy, just to get some baby time."

"I've got her." Linda shooed them toward the door. "Go make money for a good cause, and I'll see you after your date tonight."

"It's not a date," Corinne assured her.

Gabe grabbed his leather bomber jacket and gloves. "Thanks, Mom. Call me if you need me. And now that I've heard from the family court lawyer, I'll call Adrianna's parents. Might as well get things out in the open."

"Then I'm staying on hand," Linda declared, "just in case they make the drive over here. When they get their minds set on the right or wrong of anything, they dig their heels in. My sister has never seen a shade of gray she liked," she added to Corinne. "She lives in a world of absolutes, and that can make a hard climate for raising children."

"See you tonight." Gabe kissed his mother, then the baby as Corinne went out the door. He shut the door firmly, made sure it was locked and climbed into the warming SUV.

"You heard back from the lawyer?"

He answered as he backed the car out onto the quiet road. "He sent me an email after examining the paperwork. He says Adrianna did all the right things. There is no father of record, and she acted responsibly in the best interests of her child. The fact that she revoked her parents' rights to custody in writing weighs against them, but I'm hoping they don't have to know she did that. There's been enough damage done already, from both sides. They kicked her out, knowing she was giving the baby up for adoption. I don't want to add more emotional injury to anyone's plate."

"Then why the concern that they might react badly to this? If they turned their backs on her, why would they do a quick turnaround?" Corinne wondered.

"Because it's me," he admitted. "My aunt has always been competitive. If my mother does something well, Aunt Maureen has to do it better. My mother raised me on her own, under a cloud of family backlash. In their minds, I turned out okay while both of Maureen's daughters have had successive problems. She's not going to like that Adrianna picked me because that means my mother did the better job of parenting. Stupid, right?"

"That's a competition with no winners, and too many losers," Corinne answered softly. "My mom was like that. I think that's why I bonded so well with Pete and Kate. They're so normal. They're strong but simple. And they're never in your face about things. I love them, and when I'm faced with a dilemma, I never think, 'What would my mother do?' I think, 'What would Kate do?' So I understand perfectly."

"Is your mother living?" He'd never heard her talk about family except the Gallaghers. There was so much he didn't know about her, but not nearly as much as he longed to know.

"No." She lifted her travel mug to sip her coffee, then didn't. "She died eight years ago. My grandparents raised me off and on. When she was sober, she'd take custody back. When she fell off the wagon, she'd let me live with them. I like that Adrianna has made a very tough decision by making this a clean break. She's put this baby first. My mother could never bring herself to do that, and it made for a wild ride when I was with her."

"I'm sorry, Corinne." He was, too. He'd gone into parenthood thinking it was a breeze when Grace was born. Life and experience had schooled him into a different reality. "But I'm glad you took the negatives and turned them into positives. It takes a lot of strength to do that, and you're amazing with those kids."

"Faith," she said softly. "My faith in God has been my solid ground. I'd have crashed and burned without that, Gabe."

He understood that, too. "It's my rock and my fortress. I hear you. Although sometimes I wonder what

God thinks when my name crosses his desk? Does he see the darkness? Or does he focus on the light?"

"Oh, Gabe." She reached over and touched his cheek as he made the turn into a parking spot in the festival vendors area. "All he sees is the light of a good man who strives to be a better person, every day. He sees the pure light inside you, and I bet he wishes you could see it, too."

And just for a moment, he could. Turning, looking into her eyes, seeing her pretty countenance, the look of trust…

In that instant he saw himself like she did, and it felt wonderful.

Chapter Twelve

She could do this, Corinne realized as they finished a quiet—and yes, *romantic*—dinner that night. With Gabe, she felt able to let her guard down. Maybe even to let go and let God rule the day, and cast her safety-first pledge aside.

The festival was over. The vendors had done well even with the shuttle buses running folks into the village. When she and Gabe had left to go to dinner, most of the vendors were loading excess goods into vans and trucks while wearing smiles of success.

That was good, but sitting here, having dinner with Gabe, laughing about funny incidents through the day…

This was wonderful and normal and she was pretty sure she'd be downright foolish not to grab hold of this man and then keep him, like say…forever?

The waiter brought their desserts in a to-go bag. Corinne shrugged into her coat as Gabe held it out. Then he tugged the sides together for her.

Her heart opened more, and she hadn't thought that possible. She held his gaze and covered one of his hands with her free one. "This was marvelous, Gabe."

He smiled down at her, his hands clutching the twin lapels of her coat. "Yeah?" His gaze dropped to her lips, and his smile grew. "I'm in total agreement." He moved closer.

Then he paused, winked and handed her the take-out bag of tiramisu. "Let's go check out that baby. I must be going soft on her because when I'm not there, I can't get her out of my mind. Even with my mother there."

"You're not going crazy overprotective, are you?"

He began to shake his head, then frowned slightly. "Possibly. But I'm working on it. I promise."

"Good." He reached around her to open the car door for her, then didn't. He paused instead.

Chill air surrounded them. The leaves had long since drifted from the trees, but twinkle lights took their place, marking the change of seasons and a month of holiday festivities.

He lowered his gaze again, and this time he didn't wait. Didn't hesitate. Didn't tease.

This time he gathered her in and took his own sweet time kissing her. A kiss that offered love and support with no words needed. A kiss that spoke to promises and pledges and so much more. And when he drew back, he laid his forehead against hers and whispered, "My lips like getting to know yours. They're so happy right now. Thank you for making them happy, Corinne."

She laughed and ducked her head against the smooth leather of his rugged jacket. It felt good to laugh in this man's arms, to be sheltered in his strong embrace, and when he kissed her again, Corinne was sure of one thing. She'd fallen head over heels for Gabe Cutler, and she wanted nothing more than to spend the rest of her life showing him that. And she was pretty sure he felt exactly the same way. She let herself get lost in the moment, because in Gabe's arms, she knew anything was possible, and Corinne hadn't felt that way in a long time.

A wonderful evening, full of possibilities of a new today and a better tomorrow.

He'd kissed his beautiful neighbor. He'd taken his own sweet time kissing Corinne, and she'd kissed him back. He felt wonderful. Marvelous. Delightfully invigorated with new possibilities opening before him.

Corinne hit a Christmas music station on the radio as he pulled out onto the road. When she began to change it, he reached out a hand to stop her. "It's okay. I don't mind so much."

She slanted a smile his way, and the rusty hinges on his heart crept open wider. Her expression held hope and promise and affection. His courting skills were as rusty as his heart, but Gabe wasn't afraid to brush up on his skills with Corinne for however long it might take.

He'd been in love once, a long time ago.

Now he was falling in love again. He wanted everything right for her, and he was willing to do whatever it took to make that happen.

His tires hit a patch of black ice.

The car skidded sideways, then recovered. He gripped the wheel tightly, watching ahead for more rogue patches. Damp days and quick-chilling nights left drivers susceptible to ice slicks on country roads. Just as he thought that, the car ahead of them spun out of control.

The lights careened in a full circle, slid left, then right, then shot off the road, into a copse of tall, broad evergreens.

"Gabe!" Corinne's hand went to her mouth. She grabbed for her phone instantly and hit 9-1-1. She was offering direction and location before he'd come to a full stop on the icy shoulder of the four-lane road.

"Don't stay in the car," he warned as he jumped out. "Just in case someone else spins out. And have Grant call out salt trucks ASAP."

Emily's husband Grant was the highway superintendent for Grace Haven. "I will." She climbed out of her side of the car as she made the call to her brother-in-law's cell phone.

Gabe rushed to the most accessible door of the damaged car, but the sedan was wedged between the trunks of two trees. Branches blocked his way and his vision. He'd grabbed his flashlight from the backseat, and wished it was the high-intensity model tacked to his service weapon. Still, it was better than nothing. He pulled branches back, but couldn't make progress on the door and hold the wide, draping spruce boughs at bay.

"I've got these." Corinne pulled the branches back, leaving him a clearer view. "I'll hold, you figure out how we can help them."

His light noted two passengers and a car seat.

His heart shoved up, into his throat. He pounded on the glass of the front door.

The air bags had deployed.

He detected movement on the far side. The driver was slumped, and the angle of the door's damage didn't allow Gabe access. He moved to the other side of the car.

Cars streamed by. A couple of them stopped. And in the distance, he heard the welcome sound of sirens. Backup was approaching.

The woman in the passenger's seat reached over and unlocked the door.

He pulled her door open. She struggled toward him, crying and gesturing. "My husband. He's not talking. He's not talking to me. Help him!"

"We will." Gabe guided her out. A man from a stopped car took Corinne's place at the branches, tugging them away from the vehicle.

Corinne circled the car and took the woman's arm. "Let's have a look, okay?"

The woman pushed away. "We have to get my husband out. I smell gas!"

Gabe smelled it, too. He reached in the passenger side, shut the engine down and hoped it was enough to prevent a fiery explosion.

"Can you get him out? Please, you have to help him!" Her tone begged and her face pleaded, and Gabe knew exactly how she felt. He knew it too well.

"Is the baby with you?" Gabe asked.

The woman squinted hard. "I don't think so." She gripped her head. "My head hurts. It hurts so much." Pain contorted her features as she tried to answer his question. "No, she's with my mother. We were having a date night. Oh, no..." she wailed, as if re-realizing her husband's state while Gabe searched the man's neck for a pulse. When he felt the soft beat beneath the pads of two fingers, he sighed in relief.

"He's got a pulse. And help's coming." He called the words across the small grassy incline. Corinne had moved the woman into the clearing and was using the flashlight on her phone to check her over.

Sirens came closer. Flashing lights approached from both directions.

And then a car approaching from the north tried to brake quickly. It spun hard, just like the previous car had done.

The sleek coupe hit Gabe's SUV, did a three-sixty, bounced off Gabe's car again, then hurtled through the air, straight at the original vehicle. And Gabe.

Gabe took the ditch, headfirst.

The car sailed over him and into the stand of trees just in front of the first car.

He held his breath, certain that gravity was going to drop the car back into the ditch and take him out. When it sailed over his head, he made a leap for the embankment behind him and scrambled up the slick hill as if his life depended on it because it did.

The thick branches slowed the car enough to avoid hitting the tree trunks or the initial automobile, but then the car crashed down, into the ditch, onto the same hollow Gabe had sought as refuge.

He couldn't think about what might have been. There was no time for that.

He directed the EMTs and the firefighters with the Jaws of Life to the first car while he helped the driver and a little boy out of the second car.

He ran on adrenaline for nearly an hour.

At some point he noticed that Corinne was guiding the woman into an ambulance.

When the husband was finally extracted, a second ambulance took him to Rochester, where more serious injuries could be effectively treated.

Salt trucks peppered both sides of the road.

On-duty officers took statements.

Tow trucks arrived to clean up the extensive aftermath. The damage from the second accident left Gabe's

SUV undrivable. Drew Slade and Grant McCarthy both showed up during the melee. "Gabe, you're not dressed for this. Go home," Drew told him. He motioned to Grant's SUV parked just up the road. "Corinne's in Grant's car. He'll drive you guys. Do you need to see a doctor? Did you get injured at all when that car went airborne?"

"Nothing," Gabe assured him. "I got out of the way in time."

"Then head home, I'll let you know how it all comes out. Corinne looks shaken up. I think she could use some warmth, peace and quiet right about now."

Of course she could, and he was so busy playing the hero that he'd lost track of her. What kind of man did that?

He strode to Grant's SUV and climbed into the backseat next to Corinne. "Hey. Are you okay? Are you warming up?"

She stayed on her side of the car and nodded. "Yes, Grant left the heater running and I'm thawing out. Any word on the injured?"

He shook his head as Grant swung the driver's door wide. "Drew said he'd let us know."

Grant settled into the driver's seat and eased the SUV onto the road. "Let's get you two home so you can relax. This was a crummy way to end a great festival weekend." He frowned at them through the rearview mirror. "But witnesses are calling both of you heroes. I'm glad you happened along when you did. And Corinne, thanks for the quick call. That might have prevented a lot more problems tonight."

"It was Gabe's idea." Her voice was soft. She looked tired and worn. "Grant, can you drop me at Mom and

Dad's place? I know they're at the musical, but I'd like to spend the night there. Be near the kids. And I texted them to watch out for black ice."

"Sure." He nodded and when they got into the town, he pulled into Kate and Pete's driveway.

Gabe got out to walk her to the door.

She waved him off. "It's fine, Gabe. You've had a rougher night than I did. I can let myself in."

Nerves tightened her tone. Her hands gripped her keys as if frozen to them.

"I'll just see you to the door, then."

"Okay." She walked forward, used the key and pushed the door open. "Good night."

She shut the door.

He stared at it, wishing they could decompress the evening together. As a cop, he understood the need to dissect a trauma, to talk about the good, the bad, the ugly…and then to put it behind you. He'd been able to do that in his professional life, if not his personal one.

He contemplated his options, then realized it might be best to wait until tomorrow. She deserved a good night's sleep.

He didn't like the idea of walking away, but the closed door left few choices. He got back into Grant's vehicle, and when Grant dropped him off at the door, his mother was anxiously waiting for an update.

Jessie lay sound asleep in the crib. The lights were turned low, and the house next door sat black in the darkness. A night that began with such promise and light had turned dark in an instant.

He hugged his mother. "Let's talk in the morning, okay? I'm beat."

"Okay. I'll sleep by Jessie tonight. I don't mind a bit,"

she insisted, “and you’ve got a lot on your plate for to-morrow with Maureen and Blake.”

He didn’t refuse her kind offer. “I appreciate it, Mom. All of it.”

She hugged him again, then reached up to kiss his cold, weathered cheek. “I know.”

Chapter Thirteen

I can't do this. Not now. Not later. Not ever.

Corinne curled up in the corner of Rory's old bed, trying to get warm, trying to calm the gut-clenching fear that grabbed hold nearly three hours before and hadn't let go. No matter what she tried, she couldn't get the images out of her mind.

The coupe spinning out, ricocheting off Gabe's SUV, then sailing off the road, right at him.

Her heart had stopped while her pulse kicked into high. She'd run forward, wanting to save him, knowing she couldn't, and when the car settled and Gabe scrambled up the slope of the ditch, unharmed, she knew.

His death would paralyze her. His death would plunge her into depths of despair. Single mothers couldn't afford despair. They could barely afford to get sentimental over greeting card commercials because being a mom meant being on the job 24/7.

She clenched her hands, wanting to pray, but far too angry to find words.

She'd been so close to a new adventure, a new normal. So very close.

Was this God's way of showing her the dangers involved with loving a lawman? Or was it a test to see if she had what it took to be a trooper's wife?

She didn't.

She recognized that tonight.

Her heart ached. Her hands trembled, more with anger than fear, and her feet refused to warm up.

She'd nearly watched Gabe die, and it about did her in.

She'd overseen life-and-death situations in the crisis pregnancy unit often. She'd laughed and cried, prayed and comforted and was glad to do it.

But this…

She shuddered, replaying the scene in her head as the car sailed off the road. The look on Gabe's face, caught in the glow of airborne headlights. She saw him try to jump out of the way as the car blocked her view, then the long seconds of thinking the worst…

She stood and paced the room.

Sleep wouldn't come.

Her head ached from the intensity of it all.

What if he'd died?

But he didn't, her conscience scolded softly.

Corinne shrugged that off. Gabe was hero-quality. He didn't hesitate to pull that SUV over, and do what needed to be done. A deed that could have spelled his death sentence.

Would you prefer he pass people by? Would you want a man who drives on through, coolly calling 9-1-1 instead of pausing to help? And since when did life come with guarantees? Are we numbered by our timelines or God's?

She scowled.

God's, of course, but there was little use in tempting fate. And yet…

She loved that he waded into the fray instantly, that he took charge in order to save lives. Wasn't that what being a lawman was all about?

Yes.

But that didn't mean she could mentally and emotionally handle the possible outcomes, because tonight's emergency played in her mind like a broken record, spinning out of control. She'd pledged that she'd never live like that again.

Tonight's accident proved her right.

Aunt Maureen and Uncle Blake were on their way to Grace Haven, and they weren't happy. Were they coming to demand their granddaughter, or just complain that Gabe had her? He wasn't sure, but in either case, he wasn't about to subject the baby to a shouting match.

He tucked Jessie's car seat into the SUV and drove to the Gallaghers' house midday Sunday. Kate answered the door. "Gabe! Oh my gosh, come in and bring that little one with you. I think she's grown, Gabe!" She cooed to the baby as Gabe set the seat on the broad kitchen table. "What's up?"

"Is Corinne here?"

"She's not," Kate told him. She looked apologetic and worried all at once. "She took the kids shopping after church for some things they've been needing."

"Oh." Why did that seem odd to him? That she hadn't called or checked in or let him know? Mothers taking kids shopping was absolutely normal, especially on weekends. And yet… Something seemed amiss. "Kate, I know you're going to start watching Jessie tomorrow, but her grandparents are on their way from Saratoga and they're angry that I've got custody. I'm concerned that there might be a scene. Can you look after her this afternoon until the coast is clear?"

Pete came through the doorway leading to the front living room. "Are you expecting trouble?"

Gabe wasn't sure. "I'm preparing for the worst and hoping for the best. I've got Adrianna's paperwork, and the advice of an attorney, but I don't want Jess in the house when they arrive. They're angry and insulted, and my aunt tends to be melodramatic on a regular basis."

"No place for a baby, then." Kate released the seat belt clasps and lifted Jessie up. "Come here, sweetness." She nuzzled the baby's cheek, making her smile. "You go do what you have to do, Gabe. And if there's anything you need, just let us know."

"Do you want police backup?" As the former chief of police, Pete Gallagher never minced words.

Gabe shook his head. "My mother's there and I'm hoping we can sit down and talk things through. But in case it doesn't go like that, I want Jessie in a safe place."

"Sensible," Kate said. "We've got everything we need for a happy baby, and Sunday afternoon football, Gabe."

"Thank you. And can you have Corinne call me when she gets back?"

Kate's expression didn't quite match the cordial tone of her words. "Or you can pop next door later. I'm not sure if she's coming back here or heading straight home."

The feeling of unease crept farther up his back, but that could be anticipation of the upcoming standoff, too. Either way, he needed to get back to his place. "Right."

He kissed Jessie goodbye and headed home, determined to make some kind of right out of too many wrongs.

A text from Mack came through as he pulled into his driveway. Taking Susie to ER. Something's wrong. Pray for us.

Grief flooded Gabe.

He sat in the car, head bowed, praying.

Mack and Susie had been his best friends since high school. They'd loved him throughout his losses, and as they'd tried to start a family of their own, he'd watched helplessly as their attempts came to nothing time and time again.

It made no sense. Why could his cousin conceive and deliver a healthy child while Mack and Susie met chronic failure? He texted back Praying! and he was, but the unfairness of it all angered him.

Don't look at Gabe's house.

Grab your bags and go straight in, eyes front.

Corinne followed her own directive, but when a text came through from Kate, it held a picture of a smiling baby curled up on Pete Gallagher's lap. Someone likes football! tagged the photo, and now Corinne looked toward Gabe's house.

A strange car sat in the driveway, parked crookedly across the asphalt.

Jessie's grandparents?

He'd said he was going to call them, and the baby had been removed from the house. Corinne had watched enough family dramas play out in the hospital to recognize the foresight in Gabe's preemptive strike. As she watched, his front door flew open.

A couple stormed out. The man banged a fist against

a porch pillar, yelled, then strode to the car and slammed the door shut once he climbed in.

The woman stood, facing the door.

Was Gabe in the doorway? Or his mom?

Corinne couldn't see, but she read the anger and pain on the woman's face. Her mouth moved in quick fashion. Begging? Pleading? Yelling?

Corinne moved away from the window.

This wasn't her business. And after last night, she didn't dare make it her business. She'd been raised on family drama and hated it. She didn't want to face the angry woman, or the heroic man who'd narrowly escaped death the night before.

She wanted calm. She wanted structure and order, the peace and quiet she'd carefully orchestrated for years. How could she even consider risking that kind of loss for her kids?

"Mom! Can I run over to Coach's and ask him about the January schedule?" Callan half shouted the question as he loped toward the door. He spotted the woman on Gabe's porch and reconsidered his request. "On second thought, I'll wait. I can ask him on Thanksgiving."

Thanksgiving.

She'd invited Gabe to the Gallagher family meal and he'd accepted happily. Could she rescind the invitation?

Only a heartless creep would do that, but how could she spend a beautiful holiday with him under these circumstances? Especially a holiday based on faith and gratitude?

She couldn't. And yet, she had no choice. If she opted out of the family meal, her kids would think she'd gone crazy. Right about now, she wasn't sure she hadn't.

She put things away methodically, and when Gabe's

footsteps sounded on the deck, her pulse sped up. She was scared to face him and afraid to lose him, two weak responses. How could she consider herself a strong woman if she allowed fear to guide her days? But was it fear? Or common sense because she'd lived through grievous loss once?

She sucked in a breath and crossed to swing open the door before he had a chance to knock. And the minute she saw his shell-shocked face, she grabbed hold of his big, strong hand and pulled him inside. "Come in, have some coffee and tell me what happened."

"I can't stay. I've got to get to Kate and Pete's and pick up Jessie." He frowned, facing her. "Corinne, about last night. We should talk about it. We shouldn't have left it like that and just gone our separate ways afterward. It was a stupid thing to do on my part, and I know better. I'm sorry."

Her heart shook harder than her hands, and both grew chill. "What was there to say, Gabe?"

He tipped his head in question.

"We were both there. We did what we could. And it looks like everyone is going to be okay, and I'm thrilled about that. You should be, too."

"I am." He spoke slowly, watching her make busywork with her hands as she brewed his coffee. "What concerns me is your reaction, Corinne. You've barely looked at me since the accident. You haven't answered my texts—"

"Busy with the kids."

His frown lines deepened. "But I think the twelve-point-six seconds it takes to answer a text isn't the big deal you're making it out to be. Unless..." He took a step closer. "It is a big deal."

She couldn't do this.

She knew cops. She'd married one, her father-in-law had been one for decades and now her brother-in-law ran the police force. They were skilled in brushing off danger, shrugging off risk.

She possessed none of those skills, and she'd seen the risks Gabe was willing to take firsthand. She'd watched that car fly right over Gabe's beautiful, stubborn, thick head and felt the life drain right out of her until he scrambled up the opposite incline.

Her gut recoiled, remembering.

She forced her hands to stop shaking by clutching her mug. "Gabe, we've been friends for a long time. We've worked together on the baseball team and the festival. We like each other."

Her words disappointed him. She read it in his face, and in the set of his shoulders.

"But I have to keep my focus on raising my two kids for the next five years. They have to be my first priority. I'm sure you can understand that better than most."

"You're tired."

She started to argue, but she couldn't. He was correct. She was tired of being alone, of running the show, of missing the sweet things that seemed so near last evening. What if they'd passed through that slicked-up area two minutes before? None of this would have happened, and she'd be in this man's arms right now.

But it *did* happen, and her reaction was an eye-opener and a deal breaker.

"You want to brush me off."

That sounded harsh. She winced.

"All right. I get it." He didn't reach for the coffee. "But what I don't get is why everything changed. What turned everything upside-down. And while I'd love to have time to get to the bottom of it, Jessie's grandparents have just reminded me that my carelessness took the life of one little girl..."

Could his aunt and uncle really have said such a thing? She reached out a hand to his arm. He moved back just enough to avoid the touch, and that tiny action pained her heart.

"They wanted to face me personally to let me know that they're disgusted by their daughter's choices yet again, but also that they have no interest in raising a child born of sin, and they'll make sure everyone in the family knows she's a tainted child. No big news there, right? On that note, I'm going to drive into town, pick up that precious baby and take care of her." He didn't wait for her to reply.

He strode to the door, head down.

She wanted him to hesitate. She longed for him to dissemble her fears, tease her out of her funk and move on through life together.

He did none of those things.

He stepped through the door, pulled it gently shut behind him and crossed the deck.

He didn't look back. Not once.

Her chest ached.

Tears filled her eyes, then rolled down her cheeks.

Tee was studying.

Callan was watching football and pretending to do homework.

And here she was alone, again, by her own doing.

The rights and wrongs didn't matter at the moment. Not when the hollowness in her chest weighed her down.

She reached for her phone to call him, then stopped.

This was what she wanted, wasn't it? She'd pulled back purposely with this result in mind, a measure of firm separation between her and the man she'd come to love so dearly.

She'd forgotten how real the pain of separation could be.

A car cruised by her front windows, driving slowly toward the town. Gabe, going to pick up the baby and bring her home.

"...my carelessness cost the life of one little girl..."

How could they have thrown that up to him?

And how could you not offer comfort and warmth upon hearing it? You stood here, knowing how that must have hurt, and did nothing to assuage his guilt.

She dumped her coffee into the sink.

Her laptop buzzed messages repeatedly, follow-ups to the well-orchestrated festival. She slipped to the floor, drew the computer into her lap and answered each one with false cheer.

Yes, the festival had been a great success. But what seemed important a few months ago dimmed in the glow of real-life issues.

For a little while she'd moved forward, thrilled with the idea of having it all. But now...

She swallowed a sigh, bit her lip and kept right on pretending everything was all right as she answered questions and posts about the Christkindl.

She'd get by, like she'd been doing for so long. Only now it seemed like a shallow shadow of how sweet life could be if only she was brave enough to live it. But in her heart and in her soul Corinne was pretty sure she lacked the courage Gabe needed in a woman. And that wasn't good for either of them.

* * *

Another miscarriage. Staying strong for Susie. Trying anyway. Heartbroken again.

Gabe wanted to throw the phone at the text from Mack.

He wanted to rail at God, at life, at fate, at whatever governed the stupidity of parenting and infertility. His friends had been so close to the dream they'd been chasing for years.

I'm so sorry. So dreadfully sorry. He texted the words back as Jessie slept in her little padded crib.

I know you are. That message came through. Several seconds later another one followed. Us, too.

Gabe's heart broke for them. He got things ready for the morning, and made sure everything was in order for an overnight bottle. Jessie was quite predictable that way. The thought of eight hours of sleep clearly meant nothing to her.

He didn't look out his window.

He tried not to think about Corinne next door, about Callan and Tee, so full of life. She'd shrugged him off, and the standoff with Maureen and Blake had left him unnerved.

How could people be that way? He didn't know, but there was only so much rejection he could handle in one day. He stretched out on the couch, and didn't turn on the late game. He needed sleep because tomorrow was a workday. When he didn't doze off, he shut his eyes and pretended to rest. With his eyes closed, he had no reminders of the beautiful family next door, or those kisses the night before. But even with his eyes deliberately shut, he couldn't get Corinne out of his mind, and sleep was a long time coming.

Chapter Fourteen

Corinne spotted Susie's name on the patient roster the next morning.

No.

Susie was solidly into her second trimester, further than she'd ever gotten before. Two days ago she'd been wide-eyed with hope, and now she was tucked in the crisis pregnancy unit of the third floor.

Corinne set her purse and folders down and hurried to room 3102. She scanned the notes at the nurse's station, then approached the room, heart-heavy. "Hey."

"Corinne." Sorrow filled Susie's red-rimmed eyes. Mack's were no better. "I was so hopeful this time."

"I know." Corinne sank onto the small stool alongside the bed and took Susie's hand. She had no words of comfort for the heartbroken couple. In this line of work, you either won the race or you didn't. There was no second prize. "I'm so sorry."

Mack's chest heaved.

Susie gazed up at him with such a look of love and loss that Corinne's eyes filled, seeing it. "We've been here before, darling. And we've always gotten through. This time's no different."

He clutched her hand, and leaned down. "I am so mad at God right now. I can't even describe it, Susie." He clamped his lips tight, trying to hold back a torrent of emotion.

"God doesn't do this," Susie whispered, holding his gaze. She squeezed his hand lightly. "God wants us happy, Mack, but bodies are imperfect vessels. For some reason, mine doesn't work right when it comes to babies."

"Don't take this on yourself." Mack bent and pressed a kiss to Susie's flushed cheek.

"I'm not," she whispered. "I've done that in the past and it's gotten us nowhere. There's no time to sit around and cast blame, is there? Not when there's so much suffering in the world. We'll get through this, with God's help. And with each other."

He hugged her, swiped a big ol' trooper hand to his streaming eyes, and nodded. "We will, honey. We will."

"Mack, can you get me a cup of tea?" she asked. "That orange tea would be nice. The spiced one."

"Sure."

He left, almost glad for something helpful to do, and when he'd disappeared through the door, Susie broke down.

Corinne slipped onto the side of the bed and held her.

How hard her job was in moments like this.

She celebrated the triumphs of modern medicine and healthy babies under crushing circumstances, but this… the loss of a planned-for infant, the loss of a blessed child…

Oh, her heart ached for them right now.

Susie pulled back and grabbed a stash of tissues. "I don't want Mack to see me like this. We were so excited, Corinne." She smiled through red-rimmed eyes. "Halfway there, and then..."

"I know." Susie's report indicated no fetal heartbeat as of Sunday night. So now they waited for the inevitable.

"I wish this baby had a chance to know us."

Corinne's heart gripped tight. She'd felt the same way with Tee and Dave, two souls, passing in the night, with never a chance to speak.

"I'd have told him what a great dad he had. How amazing Mack is, how brave and strong and true. How I can count on him in every way. Oh, Corinne, I'd have given anything just to have a chance to tell my baby son what an amazing man his father is. Do you think he knew? Someway, somehow, in his little baby haven? Did he know how much we loved him?"

"I'm sure he did." She whispered the words of comfort and held Susie's hand. "I'm sure he knows it now, as well, tucked in the arms of our Savior. And I don't have any pretty words, Susie, and no way to make this better, but I truly believe that your son knows you and you'll know him one day. Pure and perfect, in God's kingdom. And he'll be yours forevermore."

Footsteps sounded in the hallway.

Mack came in, carrying Susie's tea. "One sugar and no lemon."

"Perfect, Mack. Thank you."

Corinne stood. "I've got a meeting coming up, but I'm available the rest of the day. Let me know if you need anything, okay? Anything at all."

They nodded, but Corinne understood the truth better than most. The one thing they needed was a successful pregnancy, and that had been denied again.

She waded through the day, and then the night, and then the day again.

She didn't want to celebrate Thanksgiving this week. She didn't want to pretend she was grateful when she was mostly angry.

She felt like a fake, talking to Kate about pies and cranberry relish. She didn't care about it, about any of it. Not right now.

Susie was discharged late Tuesday, going home with empty arms and womb.

Gabe was doing a good job of avoiding his closest neighbor, and his absence only exacerbated the ache in her soul.

And Tee was trying to figure out what to do with the half day off before Thanksgiving. Callan was spending the afternoon at a friend's, and Tee grudgingly decided to work on her long-term history project while home alone. "Although I don't know why I can't do something fun," she grumbled Tuesday night. "Callan gets to do whatever he wants and I get to come home alone. Again."

"You don't have to come home and work on history," Corinne reminded her. "You could go to Grandma's house and help with the babies. She'll have Jessie there, and Aunt Kimberly is bringing Davy over so she can help Grandma with the squash and sweet potato casserole."

"I hate sweet potato casserole."

That wasn't the point, but Corinne let it slide. "But you love babies."

Tee stared out, into the night, then shrugged. "I

wanted to go to Melody's house, but they've got to drive to Cooperstown to be with family. And Gen's family is going to visit her grandpa in a nursing home for a holiday thing. And you said I couldn't go to Jason's house and hang out with them."

"I don't know Jason and I don't know his parents, Tee."

"I know him. That should be enough," Tee spouted. "If you trusted my judgment."

"It's not about trusting you, it's about being a responsible parent and keeping my daughter safe."

Tee sighed.

"Should we turn on the lights?" Switching on the monstrous array of outdoor Christmas lights wouldn't fix Tee's conundrum, but it might brighten the dark night stretching far beyond their windows. "I know we usually wait until Thanksgiving, but I think we're close enough. Don't you?" She went outside and plugged in the solar-activated displays.

The yard sprang to life around her. Merry lights chased along the dock, and twinkle lights gleamed from the roofline. Ground spotlights illuminated the glowing family of deer and the beautiful Nativity set while Snoopy and Woodstock inflated in the front yard.

When she went inside, Tee had disappeared upstairs. Was she peeking out the window at the fun-filled yard? Or was she moping on her bed? At twelve years old, Tee needed to learn to deal with things a little better. Sure, life wasn't always the way you wanted it to be, but part of growing up was developing a thick skin and moving on. She'd have fun at Kate's house. They both knew that, but Tee was stubborn enough—and mad enough—to obstinately choose to come home on her own, and it wouldn't surprise Corinne if she did exactly that.

* * *

As she drove into work on Wednesday morning, it seemed like the simple joys of Thanksgiving had escaped her and she had no idea how to get them back.

Maybe it's time to ease up on the reins. To take a step back and let life unfurl as it should. You don't have to control everything. Do you?

She never used to, she realized as an unusually warm sun bathed her car. A weak jet stream had been pushed high by a strong warm front out of the Deep South, a front that would be pushed east quickly by an approaching Midwest winter storm system. But for now the day dawned warm and dry for late November, a true surprise. Who expected T-shirt weather in late November? No one in Central New York, and yet the reality surrounded her.

Things had changed on that fateful day that took her husband's life. She'd worked hard to raise normal, grounded children, rich in faith and hope, but she'd stood guard all the while.

Now they were chomping at the bit for more freedom, and that unnerved her a little. Some days, more than a little.

Dear God...

She started the prayer and didn't finish it.

Her faith had been her stronghold through so much, but even that felt threatened recently. Was that her fault?

She pulled into the staff parking area, flashed her badge to security and took the elevator upstairs. Tonight she'd bake a pie and make cranberry relish and pretend everything was all right. It wasn't, but she had years of pretending under her belt. She'd gotten quite good at it, thank you very much.

* * *

"Where are you spending Thanksgiving?" Gabe's mother had called first thing Wednesday morning to see how everything was going. She'd called every day, just to touch base, the kind of thing that mothers do when distance creates concern. "That nice family next door? Or should I come up there and spend Thanksgiving with you? I can cook turkey there as easily as I can cook it here, Gabe."

Gabe sidestepped her hints with an agility refined by years of his mother's matchmaking. "We're having dinner at the Gallaghers' house. The folks who've been watching Jessie for me."

"Good," she said. She knew they were Corinne's family, and that seemed to please her. There was no way in the world he could tell her that Corinne had moved herself out of the picture completely, mostly because he didn't want to believe it himself. "And how are Mack and Susie doing? Are they all right?"

His lungs went tight. He had to pause before answering, long enough to gather his wits and his breath. "Like you'd expect. Heartbroken and disappointed that they got so close to their dream and had it snatched away again."

"Miscarriages are like that," she answered softly. "There's so much silent loss and guilt involved. I'm heartbroken that this happened again, Gabe. It's an awful wound for them."

It was.

He'd visited Susie and Mack in the hospital. He'd watched his best friend cry when they pretended to go for a walk to let Susie rest. And he'd gotten teary-eyed right along with Mack.

They didn't deserve these constant failures, and yet Susie refused to blame God or take out her anger on others.

Kate's phone buzzed into his Bluetooth. "Gabe, I know you were going to pick Jess up early, but she just fell asleep. Why don't you leave her here for a couple of hours and let her get a good nap in?"

"You don't mind?" he asked, but he already knew the answer.

"Not at all! Waking a sleeping baby goes against everything I believe in. I'll call you when she wakes up, and that'll give me time to feed her before you get here."

"Perfect. I'll take this couple of hours to drain the boat's oil and get it put up for the winter."

"Pete was going to do Corinne's, but hasn't gotten over there yet. Maybe I'll send him along to join you," she suggested. "We'll get them both done and he won't be underfoot while we get the squash baked for tomorrow."

He heard Pete's laugh in the background, followed by his voice. "I can take a hint, and you couldn't ask for a nicer day to get this done. Tell Gabe I'll be at the lake in about fifteen minutes."

"I heard him," Gabe told her. "Thanks, Kate."

"No problem."

He hung up the phone, pulled into his drive and changed into old clothes quickly. He had just enough time to grab coffee before Pete pulled in next door. "Hey, Pete. You want coffee before we get started?"

"Don't mind if I do." Pete moved his way and held out a travel mug. "We can make it right in here and I'll drink it while we take care of these boats. The weather's about to change on us, and I'll be mad at myself for not taking care of things I should have done weeks ago. With that storm approaching, we're on borrowed time as it is."

"Our sweet reprieve today is coming to an end," Gabe agreed. "The storm front is moving in fast, according to the radio." He filled Pete's travel mug. Thick gray clouds had started to approach from the west, and when the wind licked the curtains with a distinct chill, he closed the front window and headed toward the door. "Let's get this done."

Gabe stepped outside.

He stopped, stared, then pointed. "Did you move Corinne's boat?"

Pete came through behind him. His gaze followed the direction of Gabe's hand. "No, of course not. I just got here. Do you think someone stole it?"

A wave of wind came through again, a gust that meant the early-day respite of warmth was drawing to a swift end. "Tee."

Pete went pale. "You think she took the boat out?"

"She had this afternoon off, right? And Callan texted me that he and Brandon and Tyler were going to the batting cages to stay in shape."

Pete raced for the shore, peering out across the blue-gray water. "I don't see her, and we've got choppy conditions already."

"Call Corinne. Make sure she didn't hide the boat someplace before we panic."

Pete hit Speed Dial on his cell phone, then scowled. "It's dead."

"I'll call." Gabe hit the number, praying she'd answer. She'd ignored his text messages, but he couldn't afford her fear to mess up this call. This one was too important.

No answer.

He flipped to text, hit her number and put in 9-1-1. Answer ASAP.

And then he called again.

"Gabe, what's wrong? What's happened? Is Jessie all right?"

Her voice was worried for him, worried for that beautiful baby when she should be concerned for her precocious, headstrong daughter. "Corinne, where's your boat?"

"In the yard where I left it." Her voice sounded pragmatic at first, but he could tell when she put one and one together. "Gabe. Tee's home for a half day, working on a project. Is she in the house?"

Her tone had changed completely, because she knew the answer before she asked the question. "Did she take that boat out alone, Gabe? With a storm coming?"

"Pete just checked the house. There are lights on, and her laptop is open on the table, but the boat key isn't on the rack. She's gone and the boat's gone."

"Aaarrrggghhh!" He heard a door close, then another. "I'm on my way, but Gabe, by the time I drive home, the weather will have changed. It's already snowing here, and I'm thirty minutes west of you guys." He heard her call out an emergency goodbye to the charge nurse at the desk. "I can't get there in time to make a difference."

"Pete's here, we'll go after her in my boat. Call it in so I don't wear my battery down or lose a signal. Give them the address, her favorite spots and the boat description. Tell them anything you can tell them to help locate her. She's a strong swimmer and she knows to wear a life vest. The sheriff's department will send their boat patrol. So will Grace Haven. But hurry, Corinne. Hurry."

* * *

She didn't have to be told twice.

She called in the emergency, then called Drew directly. Drew knew Tee. He'd be able to advise where the water rescue patrol should launch to minimize search time.

Tee...

She couldn't let herself cry.

She couldn't let herself come undone.

There would be plenty of time for that later, when Tee was safe and sound and grumbling about boys, school and anything else that messed up an adolescent girl's love of life.

She should have taken the kids out on the water more. She knew that, and the truth came roaring back now. She'd spent her time trying to be everything to everyone and forgot to prioritize her daughter's love of the water. Of boating and tubing and fishing. And how much she loved going out with her grandpa.

For years Tee had been dragged to game after game to support her big brother's love of baseball. How had she been so careless with Tee's hopes and desires? She ran to her car, headed for the interstate and got instantly bogged down in pre–Thanksgiving Day traffic, slowed by the thickening snow.

Kate called just as Corinne realized her predicament. "I'm talking you home so you don't lose it on the way," her mother-in-law announced when Corinne took the call on the car's hands-free phone system. "It's a terrible day to hurry anywhere, Corinne, especially with the weather and holiday traffic."

She'd found that out, and should have stayed off the interstate. Why hadn't she considered that before taking the entrance? Because she was scared. Scared for her daughter and scared for Tee's safety, and she was over twenty miles away, unable to do a thing about it. "I can't believe this, Mom. Tee taking the boat out alone. The traffic. The snow. Any of it."

"I love that Tee is so much like her father," Kate replied softly. "She's Dave, through and through. But in times like this I wish she had a little more of you in her. That hint of caution."

Corinne bit her lip because what used to be caution had become fear somewhere along the way. "Have you heard from them? Anything?"

"Nothing yet. Gabe took his boat out and Dad's at your place in case she makes it back there. They wanted someone to be at home base."

Oh, Tee...

Her heart ached. Her hands trembled. Why hadn't she paid more attention to her daughter? She was so busy being cautious that she forgot to let Tee be Tee. "I can't stand the thought of something happening to her." She whispered the words around the hard swell of her throat. "I can't even imagine my life without her, Mom."

"Then, don't." Kate stayed strong and simple, qualities she exampled every day. "Imagine how we're going to celebrate Thanksgiving with her safe return, and all the stories we'll have to tell. If we don't kill her first once they get her back to shore."

"You think they will? Get to her in time? Get her back safely?" There. She said it.

She'd lived on the water for a lot of years. She understood how quickly a calm lake could become a dangerous thing, and the slanted snow and strong winds surrounding her meant visibility would diminish rapidly. Creeping along the short stretch of interstate, she could barely see two car lengths ahead. How could Gabe and the others possibly find Tee on the lake in these conditions?

"I think Jesus has calmed the waters before. He can do it now." Kate's voice was both firm and gentle. "I'm placing our girl and these rescuers in God's hands, Corinne. And the fact that Tee loves the water and has a knack for handling anything she tackles."

"Like her father."

"Yes."

Awareness broadsided her as she crept along in bumper-to-bumper traffic. "I tried to keep her safe by clipping her wings. Not letting her be herself, not letting her fly free. And I probably put her in more danger because of it."

Kate laughed lightly. "Oh, Corinne. Kids like Tee and her father will always find danger. It's their nature. But their fearlessness is also their strength. They're not timid, or intimidated by much of anything. Although I'm pretty sure that David inspired every gray hair I have. Well, Kimberly gave me her share, too. Rory and Emily were almost a relief by comparison."

Corinne understood completely. Kimberly and Dave were always ready to take the plunge into anything and everything. That aptly described her daughter, too. "Will you pray with me, Mom?"

Kate exhaled a soft breath into the phone, then said, "I'd be happy to."

Chapter Fifteen

Gabe scoured several eastern-shore coves at their end of the long, tapering lake, but didn't see Corinne's boat.

Would Tee have had sense enough to seek the far shore as the storm rolled in? Or would she try to make it back home?

She'd aim for home, he decided. Mostly because she'd get in huge trouble for taking the boat out on her own, but also because she was Tee. If it looked like a challenge, she was the first one on board.

He gunned the engine, heading south, binoculars raised. The wind sliced across the lake, bearing straight east. The drop in temperature was record-setting, even for Central New York. Pete would call him if Tee showed up back home, but as the first snowflakes began to fall, Gabe understood the seriousness of the worsening conditions. He needed to find her soon and get her home, warm, safe and dry.

He headed east, then slowed the engine.

Tee loved boating. More than that she loved fishing. She'd fished with Corinne's grandfather when he was alive, so maybe taking the boat out wasn't so much of a joy ride as it was a way to remember those special times with her great-grandpa.

He turned southwest, aiming for Caldecott Beach. Fish liked to hang out in the warmer, shallower waters a quarter mile out of the rocky cove marking the hotel's sandy beach. Buoys marked the dredged channel, allowing boats to tie up at the Caldecott Hotel docks, but with the rising chop and snow, the buoys wouldn't be visible. That meant Tee had nowhere to go but home, and that was a long ride north in these conditions.

He thought he'd see the rescue boats manning the waters from multiple directions.

He saw nothing as visibility and temperature dropped moment to moment.

He used his navigation system to guide him toward Caldecott. If he drifted too near the shore, he'd hit those rocks himself. If he stayed too far out, he might miss Tee altogether, if she was here. He could only pray that if she wasn't here, that one of the other boats would find her and haul her into safety.

He slowed the motor just enough to churn through the water and called Drew. "I'm at Caldecott. Where are you guys?"

"South of you, Meyering's Cove, heading east."

"Anything?"

"No. And with the decreasing visibility, we're flying blind."

"I'm moving slow. Chop's increasing."

"Watch those rocks."

"Roger." He hung up the phone, scanning as best he could.

He thought he'd hear her motor.

He heard nothing over the slap of waves and the increasing wind. Visibility had gone minimal, but his location system had him coasting into the fishing nook area. He dulled the engine and yelled, "Tee! Can you hear me?"

Nothing.

He crept forward, praying with every passing moment, then again yelled, "Tee! Tee, can you hear me?"

Still nothing.

He started to turn, then paused, feeling stupid.

The horn. He hit the horn three times, quickly. He paused, waiting. Just as he was about to turn outward, he heard something ahead and to the right. Near the rocky outcroppings. Three short beeps. Three long. Three short. They were faint, but they were audible.

S.O.S.

He answered with three short beeps again, and edged her way, praying she'd repeat the signal.

She did, and it was louder this time, which meant he was getting closer.

"Tee!" He yelled her name repeatedly, wanting to see her. To grab hold of her and take care of her and return her to her mother, safe and sound. He hit the horn again, and when she replied with the S.O.S. signal, Corinne's boat appeared before him almost instantly, off to his right. "I've got you, honey. Grab hold of this." He threw her a rope. "Tie it down so I can come alongside."

She was scared, soaked and cold. He watched her try to maneuver the rope to no avail. Time for plan B. "Are you anchored?" He raised his anchor to help her understand the question over the sound of the wind and water slapping waves against her boat.

She frowned, then nodded.

"Okay." He couldn't command two boats back to safety. He knew his vessel better, but he couldn't risk getting Tee on board, even with her life jacket on. If someone needed to switch up boats, it was him, and it was now. He stuffed his cell phone and his waterproof flashlight into the coat pocket of an old extra coat he kept stowed in the boat hatch. He threw the coat to her, then did the same with his jacket. He kicked off his shoes, anchored his boat and jumped into the water.

Weight pulled him down. The cold water made him suck a breath. He pushed back up, spitting and sputtering, spotted Tee's boat and swam her way. The wind and waves doubled his work.

He cut the angle, finally got alongside and reached up. Now he needed to board her boat without tipping them—and the boat—into the water.

She reached out a hand with such a look of determination, he grabbed hold, and with her balance and his effort, he heaved himself up and in.

He stared up at her for a few seconds, then flashed her a grin. "Catch any fish?"

"Oh, Coach." She threw herself at him as he scrambled up. "I'm so dumb! I just wanted to…" Uncontrolled shivering stole her words away, but he got the gist.

"Put that coat on and sit right there. We're going to get back to safety. Grab my torchlight and aim it toward the water in front of the boat, to the right side."

She tugged the coat on. He helped her zip it when her hands refused to work, and then she held the strong, waterproof flashlight as steady as she could with chilled hands while he pulled his jacket back on.

He aimed for the hotel.

He'd fished out here several times over the years,

but not often enough to remember the channel buoys. He turned the boat into the snow but lost his bearings instantly and rethought his choices.

He couldn't chance it. He was more familiar with the northern end. He'd have to make the wild ride back there and pray them to safety. He turned about, increased the motor and pointed north. "We're going home, kid."

She nodded, too cold to talk.

He headed north, praying silently, hoping for just enough of a break in the snow that he could spot houses, lights or a spot to pull up. He watched the speedometer and the gas gauge. It was tipping to the left, getting dangerously low. He tried to reach Drew.

Nothing.

He couldn't text and drive the boat at the same time.

He tried Corinne's number, and she answered immediately. "Gabe? Where are you?"

"I've got her." He had the phone tucked against his shoulder. "We're low on fuel, we're heading your way, alert Drew and all law enforcement, whoever you can contact. I'm snow-blind, but I should be getting close. I think."

"We lit a fire."

"You what?" He couldn't have heard that right.

"On the shore. We lit a fire on the beach to help guide you in. Grandpa taught me that. Watch for it, Gabe. It's pretty big."

She'd no more than said the words when he spotted an orange haze behind them, to his left. He'd gone past their beach, and if his call hadn't gone through, he'd still be searching. "I've got it. Coming about. We're not going to try to dock. I'm running aground."

"I'm praying you in safely."

Those words. The gentleness in her tone.

He couldn't think about that, or let it mean too much. She'd made herself clear, and he had a lot of his own reckoning to manage. Nothing like a near-death experience to reevaluate just about everything there was in life that matters.

"Hunker down, Tee, just in case we bump hard." She followed his shouted direction, peering at the fire ahead.

The wind didn't allow the luxury of coasting in. He'd have to go aground swift and hard, then cut the engine, and that's exactly what he did.

He pitched forward. His head took a nasty shot from the windshield, but Tee stayed tucked between the seats without a scratch from their hard landing.

People streamed forth.

EMTs helped them from the boat. Tee's legs buckled the moment she tried to stand. They called for a stretcher, but she'd been cold too long already.

Gabe rounded the hull, lifted her up and carried her to the waiting ambulance. Corinne raced to them. She gripped Tee's hand. "Come on, sweetness, let's get you warmed up, okay?"

Tee blinked up at her mother. Her eyes mixed sorrow and joy. "I'm s-sorry, M-Mom." Shivers grabbed hold as she tried to speak again.

"We'll save the apologies for later, okay?" Corinne climbed into the ambulance as the medics took over. "Right now let's just get you warmed up."

He backed away, letting mother and daughter have their moment.

Corinne turned and put a hand out. "Gabe."

She wanted to thank him.

He saw it in her face, her gaze.

He didn't need thanks. He'd done exactly what he had to do, answering the pledge he'd made long years before.

He lifted his hand. "I'll see you later. I want to make sure everyone gets in all right. And you." He leaned in far enough so Tee could see him. "Drag me along on your next fishing trip, okay? I guarantee we'll have better luck together than you do on your own."

She tried to smile as silent tears rolled down her chilled white cheeks. "Okay."

He moved back and closed the rescue wagon doors.

Tee needed warmth and time with her mother. A trip to Grace Haven Memorial would give her both.

He scrubbed a hand to his face.

Pete called to him from inside, but he couldn't face questions right now. When Drew called in the "all clear" that all units had made it out of the water, Gabe trudged back to his house.

Pete and Callan had doused the fire with the garden hose and sand while reporters snapped pictures left and right.

Medics wanted to take Gabe in and check him out.

He refused.

He was fine, or would be once he got out of the frigid wet clothes. His long, cold boat ride had given him time to assess a few things. Now he needed enough faith and courage to see those things through.

"Mom, I am so sorry." It was after ten when a very contrite Tee appeared on the stairs facing the kitchen on Thanksgiving morning.

Relief flooded Corinne the moment she spotted her beautiful girl. Tee looked so much better than she had fifteen hours before.

Fear had struck an arrow into Corinne's heart yesterday, a sharp piercing of how quickly life could change, a lesson she'd thought she'd learned a long time ago. But life hadn't changed because Gabe Cutler was brave enough to rush to a kid's rescue when needed.

She hated herself for thinking his raw courage could be a bad thing after the car accident.

If Gabe wasn't strong and brave and true, she might not have a daughter today. She owed Gabe an apology at the very least, and maybe…just maybe…he'd give her the second chance to be the brave woman she'd claimed to be long years ago.

"Is that apple pie I smell?"

"It is." Corinne pointed to the island behind her. "I made a little one, just for you, for breakfast."

"Pie for breakfast?" That thought relieved Tee's features quickly. "With ice cream?"

"If you'd like." She finished grinding the cranberries and nodded to the oranges. "I'm going to have you finish this up for me, okay? And then we'll talk about how I'm going to lock you in your room for four or five years until common sense prevails. But I'll save that lecture until after the cranberry-orange relish is ready."

Tee crossed the room and hugged her tight. "I will never do something that stupid again. I was so mad that we live on the water and almost never take the boat out. I felt like I never get to just sit and fish since Great-Grandpa died. And the weather was so beautiful." She sighed and laid her head against Corinne's shoulder. "I'm so sorry, Mom. You can lock me away. I deserve it."

"How come I get All-County in baseball and you get the newspaper headlines?" Callan pretended to be insulted as he came in with an armload of firewood and the daily paper. "You're all over the news, Tee. Well. You and Coach."

"We're in the paper?" She squealed softly, then shifted gears again, total Tee. "I have to thank Coach. He knew where to come because we talked about it before, and he sacrificed his boat. I've got to pay him back, somehow. I can't believe he did that for me, Mom." She raised her gaze to Corinne's. "He didn't even hesitate, he just jumped into the water, came aboard and brought me home."

"Well, that's how Coach is," Callan offered. He slung his arm around Tee and gave her a sideways hug. "He always puts the other guy first. That's where I learned it from." He shrugged. "Glad you're okay." He tipped his gaze down to Tee. "But try not to do anything stupid again. At least for a while. Okay?"

"Deal. And I'll figure things out with Coach at Grandma's today. Should I save him some of my pie?" She looked back at Corinne, and Corinne shook her head.

"I made another one for dessert. I'll make sure he gets some."

"Okay." She took the pie into the living room and turned on the Thanksgiving Day Parade, and for a few minutes she was the little girl Corinne had worked so hard to raise alone.

But she wasn't that little girl anymore. She was almost a teenager, and Corinne had been so busy trying to be perfect, she'd forgotten how important it was to just "be."

God and Gabe had given her a second chance yesterday evening. One way or another she wanted to make the very best of this new opportunity.

Chapter Sixteen

Gabe knocked at Susie and Mack's door shortly before eleven on Thanksgiving morning. He had a diaper bag slung over one shoulder as Jessie gurgled and batted her hands in the car carrier he clutched in the opposite hand.

Mack opened the door. He looked tired at first glance, but when he saw it was Gabe, he threw the door wide. "Come on in, we'll give you a hero's welcome! I'm so glad you're all right, man!" Mack clapped him on the back as Susie came through from the kitchen area. "Happy Thanksgiving!"

Susie echoed Mack's words, proud of him despite their grievous loss. She came forward, smiled down at the baby, then hugged her old friend. The hug didn't seem forced, even after their recent hardship. It seemed sincere and good, Susie to the max. "Happy Thanksgiving, Gabe. I'm so glad you're all right, and that Tee is okay." She winced in empathy. "That had to be such a scare for Corinne. I'm not sure I could handle that kind of thing. I'd have been turned inside out."

"I think she'd agree with that assessment one hundred percent," Gabe told her. He motioned to the living room. "Can we sit?"

"Yes, of course, you're probably tired." Susie moved forward. Gabe followed, set the baby seat on the couch and undid Jess's straps.

The beautiful, perfect baby gave him a happy, blue-eyed stare, as if pondering their earlier conversation, then grinned.

He grinned back, kissed her cheek and gently touched his forehead to hers, hoping and praying he could do this right. He took one deep, lingering sniff of Jessie's sweetness, then turned and set the nearly five-month-old baby into Susie's arms. "Here you go."

"Oh, Gabe." Susie's eyes went damp as she dropped her gaze, but not before he read the longing in her eyes. "She's growing."

"She is. And she eats a lot. And she still likes to wrestle me awake at night, so prepare yourselves to take the occasional nap."

Mack frowned. "Do you need us to babysit?"

"Here's what I need." Gabe set the car seat onto the floor and sat down. "I need you to take her and be the best parents you can possibly be to her. I'm pretty sure you can do that, right?"

Susie swallowed hard, staring at him with wide eyes, instinctively holding the baby a little closer. A little tighter. "What?"

Mack leaned forward, concerned. "Gabe, you can't be serious. If this is because you think you can't do a good job with a kid, man, you're wrong. So wrong." He got up and paced away, then back. "You'll be a great dad to her." He nodded to Susie. "We both know that. You need to kick the self-doubt to the curb and believe in yourself again. You saved a kid's life yesterday, Gabe. That's got to be worth something, right?"

Gabe had watched Mack run his hand through his hair, pace the floor and then stop in front of him, face-to-face. He held Mack's gaze. "Are you done?"

Surprise furrowed Mack's brow. "Yes."

"Good. Listen." He turned to include Susie in his line of vision. "I love you guys. You've been with me through thick and thin, you stuck by me through the bad years and the worse years, and I know I can always count on you."

Susie reached out and touched a hand to his leg. "That's what friends are for, Gabe. That's kind of like the meaning of the word, isn't it?"

Gabe knew it didn't always work out that way. Their special brand of friendship was a rare jewel. Seldom found and always treasured. "Yeah, but you know that runs amok for lots of folks. Anyway, Jessie needs a home. Her grandparents will do everything they can to undermine her happy existence within our family, and what way is that to start a beautiful new life?"

"There are jerks in every family, Gabe." Mack uttered the words, but Gabe heard the note of hope and wonder in his voice. "You can't be serious."

"I'm quite serious. You'll have to go through the proper channels with the county for adoption, and I'd like to be considered as her godfather when the need arises, but if you'd like to become parents sooner rather than later, I'll be glad to have the lawyer draw up the change of custody papers on Monday and we can get the process going."

"Sooner, meaning…?"

Gabe stood, leaned down and kissed Susie's cheek.

They were tear-stained once more, but this time for a very different reason. "How does now sound?"

"You're serious." Mack stared at him, openmouthed, while Susie rose with a now-fidgety baby.

"Come help me unload the portable crib."

"You packed it?"

"I figured if you said yes, you'd need it, and you can return it to Drew and Kimberly when you're done because I'm willing to bet the kid's going to get a really cute nursery makeover." He grinned at Susie.

"Gabe, are you sure? Really sure?" She gripped his arm, then hugged him, baby and all. "I don't even know how to talk you out of it, because I'd much rather just scream 'yes!' and be done."

"She doesn't like screaming, so just love her, okay? Love her like her young mother wanted her loved, in a way my cousin never knew in all of her twenty-one years. Just love her the way God loves his people."

"We will." Susie gripped his arm tighter as tears streamed down her cheeks. "Oh, we will do that so happily, my friend."

"Good. What are you guys doing for Thanksgiving?"

They exchanged guilty looks that Gabe had anticipated because celebrating Thanksgiving had probably been the last thing on their sorrowed minds.

"I thought as much. I'm going to see if the Gallaghers have room for two more. I expect they do. I promised them we'd have Thanksgiving together, but I think it would be nicer to have all of Jessie's family there. Me. Her Auntie Corinne. And her new mom and dad."

"Dad." Mack ran his hand through his hair again, clapped his hands together, then paused. "I'm a dad."

Susie nodded.

Did she know she was crying? Did she care?

Gabe had no idea as he and his best friend unloaded a car full of baby things into Mack and Susie's living room.

They set up the crib and arranged the necessities, and when things were somewhat organized, Gabe squared his shoulders.

This was the hard part.

He'd done the easy part because he knew it was the right thing to do. He'd known it when the wind and ice and snow pelted his face and arms the day before. And when he'd gone to Kate Gallagher's to pick up the happy baby, he knew it would be his last time doing it, and not because he wasn't capable.

He'd learned his lesson about that.

He knew because this was the right thing to do after seeing his aunt and uncle last weekend. Jessie MacIntosh would start life with a new name and a clean slate, a gift bestowed on her by the mother and cousin who loved her enough to put her needs first.

"Bye, pumpkin."

His eyes grew moist as he bent to kiss her.

She reached up for him, to play with his face. His nose. His eyes.

And then that sweet baby made everything easier by smiling at him, then burrowing her tired little self into Susie's loving arms.

It would all be fine.

He'd been sure of it mentally, and now he was sure of it completely. "I'll see you guys later."

"Three o'clock?"

"That's what Kate said. Just in time to eat before the late-game kickoff."

"Gabe."

He turned.

Mack grabbed hold of Gabe's hand, then hugged him instead. "I love you, man. We both do."

"It's mutual. I'll see you in a few hours, for the best Thanksgiving I've had in a long time. Okay?"

"Okay."

He strode to the empty vehicle, refusing to dwell on what he'd just given up because he'd figured out yesterday that none of this was about him.

It was about others, just as it should be, and just like his mother taught him years ago.

He climbed into the car and didn't look at the suddenly empty space. Instead, he steered the car toward the lake because it was time for him and his neighbor to have a little talk. He wasn't sure what her side of the conversation would be, but he knew what he wanted to say…and then he'd take it from there.

His sound system advised him of an incoming call as he took the turn toward Canandaigua Lake. He recognized the name in the hands-free display and pulled onto the road's shoulder. He hadn't talked to Elise's sister in a long time. That made him fairly certain that whatever she had to say after all this time was better with his full concentration. "Amelia?"

"Gabe." He noted the hesitancy in her voice and waited.

"I saw the news report about you today," she continued. Now anxiety mixed into her tone. "How you rescued that girl, caught in the storm."

It was the kind of story the press ate up on a holiday, so the downstate coverage wasn't a big surprise to him. "I'm just glad it worked out the way it did. How are you,

Amelia?" She'd taken the loss of her niece and sister hard, and she hadn't talked to him since a few months after Elise's funeral. And that discussion hadn't gone well for either of them.

"I'm okay, Gabe. I'm—" She drew a harsh breath then raced on. "I'm calling to apologize. I should have done this a long time ago, and I didn't and that makes me a horrible person, Gabe. And I'm sorry about that." Another short gasp indicated she was fighting tears and losing. "So sorry."

"Amelia, you're not a horrible person." Hadn't God been teaching him that same lesson lately? To unleash the shackles of the past and move on? To embrace the future God laid so lovingly before him?

"I am, Gabe," she went on in a stronger voice. "Because I'm the only one who knew what really happened that day, and I never told anyone because I promised my sister I wouldn't. I said nothing, not to my parents, my husband or my friends. It's been eating me alive for years, and when I saw that picture of you after that rescue yesterday, and that look in your eyes…" She stopped, and he heard her trying to catch her breath. "I realized you hadn't moved on like I hoped. That you still wore that guilt like a weight around your neck, and it wasn't fair. Not one bit fair."

"Amelia." He kept his voice soft but firm. "It's a long time ago. We've both got to go forward."

"But I can't. Not until I tell you the truth, Gabe. You didn't leave that car door open that day. Elise did."

Every hair on the back of his neck stood straight up. What did she say? That Elise had left their car door ajar the day they lost their beloved child?

An adrenaline buzz kicked in. He gazed out the window, seeing the upper curve of the lake in front of him. Yesterday's waves had calmed to a placid blue, lapping the sand along the north-end beach in a gentle give-and-take while his pulse roared like a wild ride in his ears. "What do you mean, Amelia?"

"She confessed to me, Gabe." Her voice went soft. "I told her she should come to you, that you'd understand, but she couldn't face the truth. She knew you'd be disappointed in her, and that you didn't like her drinking when she was with the other moms.

"She made me promise not to tell, and I thought once she was gone, that you'd move on with your life. I imagined you married, with kids, and everything nice and normal. I convinced myself that keeping my sister's secret preserved her memory for our family, but it's been eating at me like crazy lately. When I saw your face in that picture, I realized what losing Gracie did to you, and that I was the only one who could speak the truth and rid you of that horrible guilt. I'm just so sorry it took me this long. Forgive me. Please."

Elise left the door open.

He scrubbed his hands to his face, thinking. It all made sense. Her reaction, the drinking, the guilt and then her untimely death.

"I've felt guilty ever since she told me, because what if I'd come to you, Gabe? What if I'd had the courage to break my promise and tell you what happened? Could we have saved my sister?" Grief deepened her voice. "I'll never know because I said nothing. And I've regretted it ever since."

So much guilt. So many regrets. So much pain.

Forgive us our trespasses, as we forgive those who trespass against us...

Gabe swallowed hard.

A kaleidoscope of images danced through his brain. Elise. Grace. Corinne. Tee. Baby Jessie in Susie's arms…

He drew a deep breath. "Amelia." He pinched the bridge of his nose, then said, "I forgive you. And I'll ask you to do the same for me."

"But, Gabe—"

"Elise liked to drink too much when she got together with the girls. I knew that. She'd promised she wouldn't overdo it that day, and it was only at parties, but I should have been double-checking things myself. I had promised to be the designated driver so she could relax, when I should have made it more important to be the designated parent."

He paused, then sat straighter in his seat. "We've all made mistakes, Amelia. It's Thanksgiving. A day to give thanks for what we have. How about if you and I make a pact that from now on, on every holiday, we look forward, not back? I think it's time for us to do that, don't you?"

"You don't hate me?"

He didn't. He felt sorry for her, and for himself, that they'd both allowed Elise's drinking to be treated casually until it was too late. And then everything had snowballed from that moment. "Not at all. I wish she'd told me. Maybe then we could have gotten through it together." He breathed in. "I'm glad you called, Amelia. I hope you have a blessed holiday."

"You, too."

She disconnected the call.

He sat in his seat, watching the water ebb and flow against the cream-colored sand on the lakeshore.

The snow hadn't lasted on the sand. It rarely did because even oblique sun rays were enough to heat sand quickly, melting the snow.

This tiny view of the lake offered new hope, a fresh start. And Amelia's phone call augmented that new beginning.

And yet it didn't matter now. Not really. Not like it would have. There was plenty of guilt to go around in any tragedy. He'd witnessed that often in his years on the force.

The clean slate along the water's edge called to him. He put the car into gear and edged onto Lakeshore Drive. He knew what kind of new beginning he wanted and needed, and he only hoped the lady in question felt the same way. If not?

He lived next door, and he wasn't afraid to use proximity to his advantage. He wanted a wife, and he wanted a family, and he wanted it all with Corinne.

He didn't want to give up being a cop. It was who he was, and what he did.

But he had every intention of convincing her that loving a cop was worth the risk involved.

Chapter Seventeen

Corinne parked her car along the narrow stone path of the Grace Haven Cemetery like she always did. She and Tee climbed out one side of the car. Callan stepped out of the other. Together they crossed the shallow incline to the patriotic garden and simple monument marking David Gallagher's grave.

Callan moved forward. He set a thick-stemmed pumpkin against the marbled gray stone, then three little gourds alongside it, one for each of them.

Tee tucked a small American flag into a potted chrysanthemum and set it to the right of the pumpkin. Corinne bent low and added a spray of three red roses, their salute of love for a man gone too soon.

She stood back up, quiet. They didn't have to talk or pray out loud when they visited Dave's grave. Words weren't necessary. But then Callan pointed to the thin script along the stone's center. They'd tucked one of Dave's favorite sayings there, just below his name and above the scripture notation. "Today *is* someday."

Dave had lived those words. He always pushed to get things done, not to put tasks off to a random someday.

He was a doer, a take-charge kind of personality with a great sense of humor, much like his adolescent daughter, two peas in a pod, as Kate liked to say.

Callan braced his arms around his middle in a firm stance. "I've made a decision, Mom."

She looked his way and read his intent.

"I'm still aiming for baseball, but only two percent of people who want to play in the majors get to play in the majors."

She nodded. She knew the stats.

"If that doesn't work out, I'm going blue. Like Dad and Grandpa and Uncle Drew."

His pronouncement should have surprised her. Callan was more like her, careful, assessing and cautious, but gazing at the rapidly growing young man, she realized that those qualities would serve him well, no matter what he chose to do in life. She pulled in a deep breath and smiled. "This isn't the shock you think it is."

"No?" He'd looked worried to make the announcement, but a little excited, too.

"It's in your blood, Callan. It's a bond that's never broken, even by death. A brotherhood of officers."

"You won't try to stop me because of what happened to Dad?"

She might have, a few months ago. She might have two days ago, before Gabe swooped in to rescue her daughter.

Now…she shook her head. "Your dad and I would both want you to follow your conscience, Cal. To do what you think God wants you to do. And if that is serving your community as an officer, I will be proud of your service. Every single minute of it."

He looked relieved by her words. He turned and offered a short salute to Dave's grave, but not to the lifeless stone or pretty autumn arrangement.

To his father, gone before the kids really had a chance to know him.

"Are we going back home before we go to Grandma's?" Tee asked.

"No, we've got everything we need in the car. Let's head that way. Aunt Kimberly is bringing a frozen pumpkin ice cream pie from Stan's custard stand, and I'm going to take a little of my own advice today and eat dessert first."

"Whoa." Tee flashed her a teasing grin. "Mom is walking on the wild side!"

"Totally," Callan added in a dry tone. "But if Mom gets to do it, we all get to do it, so what are we waiting for?"

"Race!" Tee was off like a flash. Callan, too. They hit the car at the same time, laughing like the delightful normal kids they were.

She didn't cry as she faced the grave. She read the inscription again, out loud. "Today *is* someday."

A day for new choices and new roads. Dave wouldn't have wanted her to live her life worried. He'd have teased her out of her funk and moved on, and that's what she needed to do now. She'd probably messed up her chance with Gabe Cutler. She'd read the angst on his face the previous day, and she hadn't even gotten a chance to properly thank him for rescuing Tee. He must think her ungrateful and stupidly stubborn.

She'd thank him today.

She'd make sure everyone knew how grateful she was for the rescue and for him. Just him.

She strode to the car, determined to make things right. She climbed in and turned the key.

Nothing.

She frowned, checked to make sure the steering wheel was locked and tried again.

Still nothing.

"It won't start?" Tee leaned up and over the seat.

"For real?" Callan asked. He pulled out his phone before she could say anything and hit a number. "Coach, we're stuck in the cemetery. Mom's car won't start and we're in danger of missing pumpkin ice cream pie. Can you save us? Again?"

Heat climbed Corinne's cheeks. Callan hit the speaker button, and Gabe's voice came through loud and clear. "On my way. Be there in ten minutes."

Drew and Kimberly pulled in ahead of them. They trekked to the grave, adorned it with a holiday wreath. They paused, gazing down, remembering Drew's best friend and Kimberly's big brother...and then they came their way. "Why are you sitting in the car in the cemetery?"

"Car won't start."

"No?" Drew arched his brows. "I'll call Grant."

"Coach is on his way to rescue us," Tee told them, hanging out her window. "I think this is getting to be a thing. We get into trouble—"

"Or cause trouble," Callan deadpanned with a look in Tee's direction.

"—and then Coach rescues us."

"Well, how about if we take you two with us? Because that ice cream pie is waiting at the house, and as much as I love the Gallagher clan, I don't trust them to leave the pie alone until after dinner."

Tee poked Corinne's shoulder. "They're on to us, Mom."

"So it would seem." She turned her gaze back to Drew and Kimberly. "You guys don't mind taking them?"

Drew opened Tee's door. "Of course not, although I feel funny leaving you here alone."

"I'm fine. And Gabe will be here soon."

"We could just call him and tell him we're rescued," Tee suggested. "Save him a trip."

"It's on his way, and there's food at Grandma's," noted Kimberly.

"Reason enough to ride with you guys." Callan fist-pumped the air as he loped to their car. "Tell Coach I'll save him a piece."

Corinne shot Kimberly a quick look of thanks. She wanted a minute or two alone with Gabe, long enough to apologize and thank him. Kimberly and Drew pulled out of the knoll about two minutes before Gabe pulled in.

He parked his SUV, climbed out and came her way.

Her heart sped up. She started to climb out of the car, but he leaned down, blocking the door. "What seems to be the problem, ma'am?"

She gazed into his gorgeous light brown eyes, sparked with humor and something else. Something deliciously indefinable. "My car won't start, Officer."

"That's 'Trooper,' ma'am."

She inclined her head with a slight smile as she corrected herself. "Trooper."

He grinned, held her gaze, then stepped back. "Pop the hood."

She did.

He gave a look underneath as she climbed out of the car. "Do you see anything?"

He shook his head. "No. But then I use Frank at Pieroni's Garage because I know nothing about engines. I called him on my way. He should be here soon."

"But you had me pop the hood." She moved toward him, puzzled.

"For effect." He straightened as she laughed, and then he looked around. He spotted the fresh arrangement of tributes on the incline and jutted his chin. "Your husband's grave?"

"We stop by on holidays or just any old day. I've always wanted to give the kids a sense of who Dave was, because they never got a chance to know him personally. Callan was a toddler when he died, and I was pregnant with Tee."

"That's a tough set of circumstances."

It had been, so she acknowledged it with a lift of her shoulder. "But we did okay."

"You did more than okay. Corinne, listen—" he began, but she had started in at the same time.

"Gabe, I—"

They both paused. Gabe motioned her to go ahead. "Ladies first. Are you cold? Because we can talk in my car. It's got heat and everything. Unlike yours that won't turn on."

"I'm fine. And I've got to say this to you, and it's easier face-to-face."

He waited solemnly, but his eyes still twinkled, as if he had a secret. A happy kind of secret, and she liked seeing him that way.

"I want to thank you for yesterday." He waved that off as no big deal, but Corinne knew better. "Don't brush it off, Gabe Cutler. You risked your life and sacrificed your boat to save my daughter. I can't even begin to tell you how scared I was when that call came in, and then to be stuck in traffic, unable to get here quickly."

"Horrible, I expect."

She nodded, then shrugged. "It was and it wasn't. It was the wake-up call I needed." She drew a deep breath and looked up. "I've been so busy trying to be a great mom and trying to keep them safe and sound, proving I could do it all, that I lost track of some of the important things. I forgot to trust in God, because when I *did* trust him, I lost Dave. I think I never quite forgave God for that, and couldn't hand over the reins because I'd been let down before. And even though I know it was a human decision that put my husband in harm's way..." She hesitated. "He took a chance that day and lost. I still felt like God let me down."

"And now?"

"I realized as I drove home yesterday, completely powerless to help, that I've gotten power hungry," she admitted. "I like being the decision maker. I like being the person in charge. That power is being wrenched out of my hands as the kids grow up, and I realized yesterday that it was never really in my hands. I wanted it to be, but the true power and strength was beyond me. And with Him. He sent you to me. He sent you to coach my son, and He sent you this year to be my next-door neighbor." She put her hands on his arms. "And you saved my little girl's life. I can never thank you enough for that."

Chapter Eighteen

Gazing down into her pretty blue eyes, he could think of several ways, all of them amazing and wonderful, but he didn't have the right to make fear a central part of her life. "I love being a cop, Corinne."

She held his gaze and didn't blink.

"It became my stronghold when I lost my daughter, and then my wife. I couldn't help them, but I could make amends by helping others, and that meant so much to me."

"Did it mean enough to take foolish risks?"

He shook his head firmly. "It meant enough to do what needs to be done. My love for police work isn't about the perils. It's about keeping people safe. Helping others. And sometimes, catching the bad guys, because that's part of the job. But mostly, it's about watching out for danger and avoiding it before it happens. I love what I do, Corinne. I haven't always loved who I am, but I love what I do. And I need you to be okay with that. And to be okay with this." He pulled out his phone, swept open a picture and held it up. "I'm signing custody of Jessie over to Mack and Susie."

Her eyes went wide. She looked at him, the photo, then him again. “You’re giving them the baby?”

“It’s the right thing to do.” He stared at the picture Mack and Susie had sent minutes ago, their first family selfie. And he smiled. “If I keep Jessie, my aunt will make sure my family stays fractured. To her, Jessie was born of sin and can’t escape that, and I would never want Jessie to hear her hateful words of condemnation. This way I can ensure that never happens, and make two of the best people I know very happy.”

“That’s an incredible sacrifice.” She whispered the words because she knew how much he’d bonded with Jessie, and how easy it would have been to keep her. “Gabe, you’re amazing.”

He wasn’t, but it felt good to hear her say it.

“Truly amazing.” She gripped his arms again, and the look she gave him, as if he were something special and wonderful and true…it was the kind of look he’d like to see the rest of his life. “And inspiring,” she whispered, her eyes locked on his.

“Well, I have an ulterior motive. But it hinges on you, and I’m not sure I should bring it up right now.”

“Of course you should,” she argued. “I want to know everything about you, Gabe. If you’re willing to give me a second chance at this whole romance thing, we need to start with a clean slate. Don’t you think?”

Oh, he thought so all right. He locked his hands around her waist and gazed down. “Here’s what I’m thinking.” He dropped his mouth to hers and kissed her, long and slow. “I think we should keep doing things like this forever. I think we should let ourselves be in love and stay in love and take Tee fishing a lot.”

She laughed against his cheek, and it felt good to feel the warmth of her laughter ruffle his cool skin.

"And I'd like to have a family with you, Corinne."

"Gabe—" She sounded surprised, and she had good reason to be, because her kids were almost grown.

"I know you've done this all before." He kissed her cheeks, her ear, her forehead, and then took her mouth again. And when he stopped kissing her, he drew her up against his chest, holding her close. So close. "But I'd love to have another chance to raise kids. With you. If you're willing."

Willing?

Corinne was pretty sure her heart had just been swept away by this rugged lawman. "You're wondering if I'd be willing to have your baby, Gabe? Our baby?"

"That would be the question. And it's not a deal breaker, Corinne." He leaned back to see her face, still holding her. "There's nothing I want in this life more than you, and a chance to be a good friend and dad to Tee and Callan. But if you're willing to increase our family, I'd be the happiest man in town."

She reached up and kissed him. She kissed him until he was convinced of her answer with no words needed, then added the words. Just to be sure. "I would love to have more kids. And I would be honored to be your wife, if you ever get around to asking me, that is."

"Corinne." He snugged her close, then turned her loose and took a knee. "Corinne, I think I've been falling in love with you for a long while, but I was too stubborn to let myself be happy and you were too stubborn to flirt with me. Except you couldn't exactly help it."

She laughed because every word of that was truth.

"And while I make a really good neighbor, I'd like the chance to be an even better husband. Will you marry me?"

"In a heartbeat."

He kissed her again.

Frank's tow truck rumbled into the far lane. He backed the rig up to Corinne's vehicle, hoisted it onto the bed, wished them a happy Thanksgiving and was back on his way in less than five minutes.

Corinne turned toward Gabe. "I'd like a Christmas Eve wedding."

His eyes went wide before he grinned. "Four weeks away. Perfect. We don't want to interrupt the winter baseball practice season with wedding planning."

She laughed and looped her hands around his neck. "Nope. That's not why I want to hurry. This is." She gave him a most convincing kiss. "We've already spent too much time apart. I'm totally unwilling to waste another minute of not being your wife, but with two wedding planners in the family, I'll be killed if I don't give them at least a few weeks to plan things."

Gabe couldn't possibly be happier than he was at this moment.

To spend Christmas with Corinne by his side. With Tee and Callan at church and at the Gallagher family dinner. And here, on the solemn grounds of Grace Haven Memorial Cemetery, commending their father. As it should be. "It sounds perfect. And now we should go because I think we just let Frank drive off with the apple pie and the cranberry relish."

"No!" She stared down the now-empty lane and sighed. "It was a really good pie, too."

"I bet it was, but we've already pulled him out once on the holiday. We could chase him down..." he supposed.

"Or we can call him and tell him to take it into town when he visits his dad in the hospice house."

Gabe thought he couldn't love her more.

He was wrong.

He texted Frank to take the pie and cranberry relish to share with others as Corinne climbed into the car. He climbed in beside her, turned the car on, then turned her way. "You ready for this, my love?"

She feathered a kiss to his cheek, a kiss of faith, hope, love and promise. "I am."

He put the car in gear and drove down the lane, then out onto the road.

A new chance.

A new beginning, for both of them, and for Jessie, too.

As he drove toward town, church bells chimed in unison, marking the hour in joyful abandon. And when they were done tolling, the old stone church carillon rang out the poignant notes of "How Great Thou Art" for the entire town to hear, a Grace Haven Thanksgiving tradition.

And it was good.

Chapter Nineteen

Gabe tucked extra twinkle lights, a fresh evergreens wreath and baby clothes into the back of the car, then spotted a missed call from Corinne. He called her back, delighted by his list of accomplishments.

She answered quickly. Too quickly for a pregnant woman who was supposed to spend the next three weeks resting. "You're supposed to be off your feet. I told you I'd handle everything, didn't I?"

"You did, and I'm beyond blessed, but darling, there's one thing you can't handle, and it's this. I'm in labor."

He couldn't have heard her correctly, because his son and daughter weren't due for nearly three weeks. "You can't be."

"Well, I tried telling the twins that, but they seem to have a mind of their own. Stubborn little things. Oh..." She started breathing in that way women do as a contraction takes hold and won't let go.

"Honey. Honey, I'm on my way, and I've got the twinkle lights!"

She laughed and spoke quickly. "Dad's bringing me

and the kids to the hospital. Meet us there. And I think it would be best to leave the twinkle lights in the car."

He knew that. Could anyone blame a guy for being a tad nervous when his beautiful wife was carrying not one, but two tiny babies?

He stopped shopping for the perfect Christmas decorations she thought she needed to make things just right, climbed into the driver's seat and drove to the hospital in Rochester. Corinne's doctor didn't anticipate problems, but she wanted Corinne in a facility with an NICU in case the babies came early or needed extra help.

By the time he got up to the third floor, Corinne had been admitted and full-blown panic set in.

How could he do this? How could he put her through this? What if something happened to her? Or to the babies?

Pete intercepted him, smacked him on the back and met his look, man-to-man. "It will be fine. I promise."

Pete couldn't promise that. No one could. "You don't know that."

"Maybe not, but if you go into that room—" he pointed to the waiting room behind him where Kate and the kids had gathered "—or that one—" he pointed through the locking double doors separating them from the labor and delivery unit "—looking scared, I'll mop the floor with you."

His tough words helped. Plus, Gabe was pretty sure Pete meant it. He breathed deep, then stopped by the waiting room door. When Tee and Callan spotted him, he jerked a thumb toward the birthing center. "I'm going in, and I'll keep you guys updated, okay?"

"Yes." Callan nodded, calm but concerned.

Tee practically bounced in her seat. "I can't wait!"

A nurse appeared behind him. "Mr. Cutler? We're getting close, and your wife is refusing to deliver either baby until you're with her."

Close? That was impossible. Wasn't it? "She just got here. Are you sure?"

"Reasonably certain." She held the door for him, winked at the family and then showed him where to wash up and grab a gown.

He jumped into the hospital-issued clothing and rushed to Corinne's room.

"Gabe." She looked up at him as a contraction rocked her. He grasped her hand, wishing he could do more, wishing he could—

And then Jacob Gabriel appeared into the world, all six pounds, four ounces of him, and Gabe Cutler fell in love all over again. With his wife, with his life and with this amazing creation who squalled for short seconds, then paused, peeking here and there as if wondering what just happened.

"How is he?" Corinne pushed herself more upright to see, but Gabe brought the tiny fellow down to her level. "Is he fine? He's so quiet."

"He's perfect," the doctor declared. "Absolutely perfect, Corinne. And it's not going to take long to deliver his sister, so be ready. And it might have been a while for you, but remember—" the doctor smiled at her "—a quiet baby isn't necessarily a bad thing."

"Those are true words," she whispered, gazing on the wonder of her baby son. But then the rise of another contraction pulled her attention in another direction. "Hang on to him, Gabe." She laid her hand against baby Jacob's hospital blanket and whispered the words up to him. "I want him to know how much we love him even when I'm busy with his sister."

"I've got him, darling," he promised as the contraction took hold. "I won't let go. I won't let go of any of you."

"And here we go again." The doctor smiled at Corinne over her surgical mask. "You're doing great, Corinne."

Weighing in at nine ounces less than her brother, Isabella Katherine Cutler made her appearance, and let the entire room know she wasn't all that happy about the environmental changes she'd just endured.

Baby Jacob blinked twice, snuggled into Gabe's chest and dozed off, ignoring his sister's newborn theatrics.

"How we doing, Dad?" Corinne reached up a hand to him as the NICU crew checked Isabella.

How was he doing?

There were no words, but he tried. He slipped into the chair next to her bed, leaned in and kissed her sweetly. Gently. And then he laid his forehead to hers. "I have never been happier in my life. That's how I'm doing."

"Me, too."

They brought Isabella to Corinne, wrapped in a traditional hospital blanket. They'd snugged a tiny pink crocheted hat onto her head, and a blue one on Jacob. And then one of the nurses began to take a photo. "First family shot," she announced, happily.

Gabe stood, messing up the shot. He handed her the baby and said, "Hold that thought." He hurried down the hall, through the doors, and had Callan and Tee come back into the room with him. "Big brother and sister have to be in on the act," he explained. "It's not a family shot without them."

"That's right," Corinne agreed.

Eyes wide, the older kids took a spot on opposite sides of the hospital bed, and when the nurse snapped the picture, she held up the camera for all of them to see. "You are now a family of six."

"Perfect." Corinne smiled at the kids, then him, and the two utterly beautiful babies that had just joined the family. "Everything is absolutely perfect."

And it was.

* * * * *

THE DEPUTY'S HOLIDAY FAMILY

Mindy Obenhaus

To my loving husband, Richard. You are my hero.

Acknowledgments

Many thanks to former Ouray County deputy
Betty Wolfe and theater arts teacher Alyssa Preston
for all of your valuable input.
I couldn't have done this without you.

For all have sinned and fall short of the glory of God,
and all are justified freely by His grace
through the redemption that came by Christ Jesus.
—*Romans* 3:23–24

Chapter One

Coming home had never been so bittersweet.

Lacie Collier tapped her brakes at the Ouray city limit sign, observing the snowcapped mountains that closed in around her. Okay, so her trip home in February for her sister's funeral ranked right up there, too. But this was different.

She glimpsed the brown-eyed little girl in her rear-view mirror. The last nine months had been quite an adjustment period for both her and Kenzie. And while her niece seemed to finally be adapting to life without her mother, Lacie was still struggling to balance motherhood and work. Or was anyway, until her employer decided the addition of a child was too distracting and let Lacie go.

Her heart ached as she approached the hot springs pool. She'd wanted so badly to make this the best Christmas ever for Kenzie. Now they didn't even have a home.

Still, God had a plan, of that she was certain. She just wished He'd give her some clue as to what lay ahead.

"Are we there yet?" Poor Kenzie. They'd spent the

last five-plus hours driving across Colorado. A trip Lacie never relished, but throw a four-year-old into the mix and it became an even greater challenge.

"Almost, sweetie. We'll be at Grandma's in just a few more minutes." She knew the kid was eager to break free of the booster seat that held her captive.

Past the park, Main Street greeted them with all of its intimate charm. To the unsuspecting traveler, Ouray was simply a slowdown on their journey along Highway 550, but to those who had taken the time to stop, it was a treasure trove of everything from arts to adventure, four-wheeling to hiking, ice climbing to hot springs.

She slowed the car to almost a crawl, taking in the Victorian-era buildings and the sidewalks bustling with activity. Though it was only the Saturday before Thanksgiving, the town was already decked out for Christmas. Giant lighted snowflakes and evergreen garlands adorned every light post, stores sparkled with holiday-themed window displays, and twinkling lights were everywhere you looked. Everywhere except Barbara Collier's house. Because her mom didn't do Christmas.

She let go a frustrated sigh. How was she ever going to make this Christmas special for Kenzie?

A squeal erupted from the back seat.

Lacie's gaze instantly jerked to her niece and the toy-filled back seat. "What's wrong?"

"My drink," Kenzie whined, her light-up shoes flickering with each and every kick of her suddenly wet legging-clad legs.

"Oh, no." Lacie grabbed the wad of fast-food napkins from the passenger seat. "Did you spill?" With one hand still on the steering wheel, she tried in vain to blot the little girl's legs.

Kenzie merely nodded, her bottom lip pooched out.

Still attempting to console the child, Lacie glanced at the road in front of her, sympathy instantaneously morphing into horror as a pedestrian dodged out of her way.

With a loud gasp, she slammed on the brakes, her seat belt tightening in protest.

Kenzie cried in earnest now as Lacie put the vehicle into Park and fumbled to release her restraint. Her heart thudding, she pushed her door open, the cold air slapping her in the face as she rushed toward the gray-haired woman. "I am so sorry. Are you okay?"

"I'm fine, young lady." Aged green eyes narrowed on her. "But you need to watch where you're going."

"I know. I apologize."

"And you also need to think about moving your car." The woman pointed.

Lacie turned to see a line of vehicles behind her. Not to mention all the people who'd gathered at the corner to see what was happening.

"Yes, ma'am." She hurried back to her SUV, praying nobody recognized her. Then, with Kenzie's whimpers still echoing from the back seat, Lacie double-checked for pedestrians and continued up the street. *Thank You, God, that I didn't hit that woman.*

Half a block later, she heard the whine of a siren. She eyed her mirrors to discover flashing lights bearing down on her. "Perfect."

With not a parking spot to be had on Main Street, she turned at the next corner and eased into the first available space.

"Are we there?" Hope laced Kenzie's voice.

"Sorry, sweetie." She again put the vehicle into Park, gathered her courage, along with her license, registration and proof of insurance, and drew in a shaky breath before rolling down her window. This day couldn't possibly get any worse.

Shielding her eyes from the sun, she watched as the deputy exited his Tahoe and started toward her. Somewhere around six foot and well-built, he wore a black ball cap embroidered with a gold sheriff's badge over his short dark hair, but sunglasses made it impossible to see his eyes. A tactical vest with a plethora of pockets covered his tan shirt and she caught the name on his badge as the sunglasses came off.

Stephens.

One look at his dark gaze and her insides cringed. Obviously, she was wrong, because things had just gotten worse.

Out of the five Stephens brothers, why did it have to be Matt? The one who'd been her good friend through most of high school and the one she'd secretly crushed on…until he started dating her sister.

She sank lower into her seat. Their friendship was never the same after that.

"I thought that was you, Lacie."

She had to force herself to look at him, though when she did, his smile made it impossible to turn away. "Yep, it's me, all right." How could it be that he was even more handsome than she remembered when he hadn't really changed at all, save for the slight creases around his almond-shaped eyes. And those lips with that perfect Cupid's bow—

Whoa! Wrong train of thought for Matt Stephens or any other guy. While Marissa may have thought it fine to have a bunch of men traipsing in and out of her life, Lacie wanted better for Kenzie. She deserved security, a good home and a happy life. Which was why Lacie had to find another job and get back to Denver as soon as possible.

Matt rested a forearm against the roof of her vehicle and glanced toward the back seat. "You doin' okay? Looked like you were having a little problem back there on Main Street."

"Yeah." She brushed a wayward hair away from her face. "I got distracted, that's all."

"That's *all*?" He straightened then, crossing his arms over his chest. "You almost took out Mrs. Wells."

"I know." Her shoulders sagged. "I'm sorry. My niece was having a problem and I—"

"Could have killed somebody."

Was he deliberately trying to make her feel worse?

"Lacie, you know you're supposed to stop for pedestrians in the crosswalk."

"Yes, yes, I do. And it won't happen again. I promise."

"I'm sure it won't." His breath puffed in the cold afternoon air. "But I'm afraid I'm still going to have to give you ticket."

Indignation had her sitting taller. "A ticket? Why? Nobody got hurt."

"I'm sorry, Lacie, but you broke the law."

"It wasn't like I did it on purpose."

"Nobody ever plans to have an accident." He pulled a pad from his vest. "I'll need to see your license, registration and proof of—"

"Yeah, yeah." She shoved the documents toward him.

"You know, you could cut me a little slack. I'm just doing my job."

She forced herself to smile. "Or you could cut me some and let me off with a warning."

Chuckling, he patted her on the arm. "I'll be right back."

She could hardly wait.

"Aunt Lacie?"

"What is it, sweetie?" Turning, she noticed that not only was Kenzie no longer crying, but her deep brown eyes were as wide as she'd ever seen them.

"Are we going to go to jail?"

She couldn't help smiling. "No, we are not going to jail. As soon as we're done here, we're going straight to Grandma's to get you cleaned up and into some dry clothes. Okay?"

The little girl grinned. "Okay."

"All right. Here you go, Lacie."

She twisted back toward the door to accept her documents from Matt.

"And if I could just get you to sign here." Pointing with his pen, he handed her his ticket pad. "You two in for Thanksgiving?"

And then some, but he didn't need to know that.

"We are, yeah." She scrawled her name. Why did he make her so nervous? After all, it wasn't like they were in high school anymore. She was thirty-four years old, for crying out loud.

Must be the uniform.

She handed him his pad.

Or the fact that he's every bit as good-looking as you remembered.

He tore off her copy then bent to hand it to her, his seemingly curious gaze drifting from her to Kenzie. "Be safe and I hope you guys have a happy Thanksgiving." With a wink, he walked away.

She looked at the ticket in her hand. So much for old friends.

No telling how much it was going to cost her for almost killing someone. Yet as she continued to study the paper, she suddenly found herself smiling.

It wasn't a ticket at all. He *had* given her a warning.

Matt couldn't seem to get Lacie out of his mind. And, for the life of him, he couldn't figure out why. Nonetheless, he'd spent the last twenty-four hours thinking of little else.

Was it the frazzled state she seemed to be in? Or the way she'd glared at him with those pretty gray-blue eyes?

Perhaps it was the little girl in the back seat. Though he may have been much older, he knew the pain of losing a mother. And with no father in the picture, Marissa's death had likely rocked the kid's world.

Memories of the child's mother played across his mind. The last time he'd seen Marissa was six years ago, when he was stationed in Hawaii with the navy. Her visit had been a pleasant surprise. And for a brief time, he'd even thought their failed relationship might have a second chance. Instead, he'd gotten burned, and discovered the kind of person Marissa had really been. Evidently the old adage was true. Beauty is only skin-deep.

He scrubbed a hand over his face. The Collier women were the last thing he should be dwelling on. Not when he had plenty of other things to worry about. Like work, his father and the town's annual Christmas play. He could only imagine what Dad would think of him taking on the role of director.

Something Matt wasn't 100 percent sure of himself.

He was just a deputy sheriff who barely knew stage right from stage left. Yet when he heard rumors that they were thinking about canceling the play, he'd felt compelled to do something. He couldn't let the event his mother had begun over a decade ago die. That would be like losing Mama all over again.

So here he sat in the cab of his Jeep, staring at the two-story cream-and-blue brick building that was the Wright Opera House, praying he wouldn't let her down.

Drawing in a deep breath, he grabbed the stack of scripts from the passenger seat and stepped out into the chilly late-afternoon air. The cast would be arriving soon, so he'd better get inside and at least pretend he knew what he was doing. He refused to let other people see him as the screwup his father believed him to be. Because regardless of the what the old man thought, Matt was not responsible for his mother's death.

He flipped on the lights inside the circa 1888 building that smelled of lemon oil and popcorn. Moving past the box office with its intricately carved moldings, he continued up the curved staircase to the second floor. The view at the top never ceased to stop him in his tracks.

Beyond the expanse of arched windows, the gray volcanic peaks of the Amphitheater enveloped the town's eastern edge. Cloaked in white and skirted with conifers, they were a sight to behold. God's majesty on full display.

A few steps closer and his gaze fell to a nearly empty Main Street. He could only imagine how things must have looked back when Ouray was a thriving mining town. Carriages lining Main Street as people turned out in their finest for some cultural enrichment.

With an about-face, he moved into the theater opposite the windows and brought up the house lights. Unexpected emotion clogged his throat as he took in the large space with its brick walls, wooden floor and the original stage curtain that now served as a mural. Mama used to think of the Wright as her second home. He could still see her, taking the stage in an array of roles—everything from a soldier to a nun. She may have been a country girl, but she loved the theater. And this play was her legacy. Meaning as long as Matt lived and breathed, the show would go on.

"Oh, good. I'm not the first one here."

The voice had him whirling to find Lacie standing behind him. Her caramel-colored hair, which had been pulled back into a ponytail yesterday, now spilled over her shoulders and down her back. Much longer than the no-nonsense, chin-length style she'd worn throughout high school. And with her pale pink peacoat cinched around her waist, she was quite the contrast to the tomboy who had once run circles around him and just about every other guy on the basketball court at Ouray High. She'd always steered clear of anything remotely feminine. That is, until she took the stage their senior year. Watching her transform from the Cockney Eliza Doolittle into a refined lady in their school play had had everyone's jaw dropping.

Her smile wavered as he approached, her expression suddenly curious. "What are you doing here?"

He cleared his throat. "I'm directing the Christmas play. Why are you here?"

"I'm *in* the play." Hands stuffed inside the pockets of her coat, she shifted from one stylishly booted foot to the other. "I thought Mrs. Nichols was directing.

That's what she said when she called and invited me to be a part of it."

"You're only in town for Thanksgiving. Why would she ask you to be in the play?"

Lacie hesitated a moment before jutting her chin out. "Actually… I'm here throughout WinterFest."

But that ran from Thanksgiving all the way to the ice festival in January, so— "Why would you do that?"

A hint of annoyance pinched her brow. "Not that it's any of your business, but my mom needed some holiday help at the boutique." Removing her hands from her pockets, she brushed something from her coat sleeve. "And since I no longer have a job…"

She'd lost her job? Now he was really glad he'd given her only a warning. After all, she had a child to care for. "I'm sorry to hear that."

"It's only temporary." She looked everywhere but at him, seemingly studying everything from ceiling to floor. "So where's Mrs. Nichols?"

"Rehab."

Eyes wide, she finally met his gaze.

"She broke her hip."

"Ooh, that's rough. She's such a sweet woman."

"Yes, she is."

Lacie meandered toward the windows. "Great theater teacher, too. I hope she recovers soon."

"We all do."

After a silent moment, she faced him. "So you're directing the play in her stead?"

"Yes, I am."

"I…didn't realize you were into theater."

"I'm not. But my mother was. The Christmas play

was her baby." He lifted a shoulder. "And since there was no one else willing to direct..."

A hint of a smile played across her pink lips. "That's actually very sweet. I know how close you were to your mother."

Sentiment prevented him from responding with anything but a nod.

"That reminds me, though," she continued. "I wanted to thank you."

"For what?"

"For giving me a warning instead of a ticket." Hands back in her pockets, she shrugged. "In case you couldn't tell, I was kind of freaked out about what had happened. That warning made my day a little bit better."

Something about that last statement warmed him. "Glad I could help."

"So where is everyone else?" She looked to the street as an echo of voices drifted from downstairs.

"Sounds like they just arrived."

A short time later, after moving a few rows of chairs out of the way, he gathered in front of the stage with the dozen or so cast members comprised of townsfolk ranging in age from eighteen to seventy.

"I want to thank you all for coming and for being a part of this play." He filled them in on Mrs. Nichols's condition. "Now, I know many of you have been involved in this event for many years. However, I'm new to this directing thing, so if any of you would like to bow out, this would be your chance."

"Don't be silly, Matt." Valerie Dawson waved off his comment. She'd been a good friend of his mother's and a part of this event since its inception. "We're just happy you were willing to step in on such short notice. Besides, it'll be nice to have a Stephens leading us again."

A round of nods and "that's rights" followed, bolstering his confidence. Maybe this wouldn't be so hard, after all.

"All right, then. Since this is supposed to be a read-through, I guess I'll just pass out these scripts—" he picked up the stack from the edge of the stage "—and we'll get started."

"Excuse me." Lacie held up her hand. "Are we not going to go over show expectations?"

Show expectations? What were those?

"Do you have our call times?" asked someone else.

Call times? Okay, that was rehearsals. At least he thought that's what they were.

"Oh, and what about costumes?" asked another. "When will we be fitted?"

Matt wasn't used to having his authority questioned. Then again, he wasn't wearing a uniform, either. He was completely out of his element.

He scanned the expectant faces before him, not wanting to let them down. Yet there was one glaring factor he couldn't ignore.

He was in *way* over his head. Having Lacie here only amplified his incompetence. And he got the feeling she didn't like him much, either. Two things he was determined to change.

Chapter Two

He was crashing and burning. And Lacie couldn't bear to watch. Not after hearing why he'd chosen to become their director. She had to help him out.

Suddenly nervous, though, she hesitated, glancing at the faces around her. While she knew most of the people, one she even used to babysit, she'd been gone from Ouray for a long time. She didn't want to come across as a know-it-all, no matter how much community theater she'd done. A cast was a team, no one person better than another. She supposed she should have remembered that when she brought up the show expectations.

Still, she had to do something.

With lights glaring overhead, she raised her hand again and mustered her most charming smile. "You know what? I think we're all eager to do the read-through, so let's not worry about the technicalities right now."

"You are absolutely right, Lacie," said Valerie. "Let's get on with the read-through."

"No, no." Matt set the scripts back down on the edge of the stage. "If the show expectations come first, then we will cover them now."

What? It was obvious he didn't have a clue what show expectations were. And yet when she'd given him an out, he ignored it.

Let him fail then.

No, that wasn't right or Christian of her. Though it was apparent he didn't want anyone to interfere.

Hands slung low on his denim-clad hips, he continued, "I want to do this right. So let's go ahead and discuss our expectations." He scanned the group before him. "Rehearsal times are firm. In case you aren't aware, I'm former military, which means I'm a stickler for promptness."

The cast was silent, giving him their full attention. The military reference must have scared them.

The corners of his mouth lifted a notch. "However, I'm also a realist. As a law enforcement officer, I know how life can interfere. Before you leave tonight, I will give each of you my cell number. If you're going to be late, please let me know."

She had to give him credit for trying.

"Now that we've got that out of the way—" he reached for the scripts "—let's continue with the read-through."

One by one he passed out the scripts, though she was beginning to wish she hadn't signed on for this. No matter how much she loved acting, she'd agreed to work with Mrs. Nichols, not Matt Stephens, the man who didn't have a clue he'd broken her heart.

"*The Bishop's Wife*." His baritone voice carried throughout the space. "Mr. Garcia, would you get us started, please?"

For the next hour and a half, Lacie focused on the script as well as the rest of the cast instead of the man leading them. And once they were finished, she was eager to leave. After chatting with Clare Droste, the girl she'd once babysat, Lacie donned her coat and started across the wooden floor. Maybe she'd even make it back to her mother's in time for dinner.

"Lacie?"

Her steps slowed. Matt's voice set her nerves on edge.

Hands in her pockets, she turned on her heel. "Yes?"

He took a step closer. "Would you mind staying? I'd like to talk with you."

Talk with or talk to? She had questioned him, after all.

Reluctantly, she made her way through the cluster of exiting cast members, toward the stage and the man she'd seen more of in the past two days than she had in the past sixteen years.

"Was there something you needed?"

"Yes." Hands clasped, he leaned against the edge of the stage. "How much acting have you done?"

She crossed her arms over her chest. "Until Kenzie came to live with me, quite a bit."

"I suspected as much."

"Is that a problem?"

"No. It's just that—" he pushed away from the stage "—well, I have no idea what I'm doing here. I was wondering if you'd be willing to teach me?"

Her arms fell to her sides. "Teach you?"

"Yes."

"Teach you what? Acting?"

"What I'm supposed to be doing as a director."

"Oh. You mean you really don't know?"

He shook his head. "All I ever did was help with the

set crew. And even that was only for a couple of years before Mama got sick."

Why did he have to keep bringing up his mother? Just thinking about Mona made it much more difficult to say no. And she wanted to say no. Just the thought of being with Matt made her edgy. "If you could just walk me through some of the terminology and what I need to do at each step in the process."

"I really should be getting home to Kenzie." She poked a thumb toward the exit.

"It doesn't have to be tonight. The group doesn't meet again until next Sunday."

"Yes, and there's Thanksgiving and—"

"Please?" His velvet brown eyes pleaded with her. "I don't want to mess this up, Lacie."

She did not want to be around Matt Stephens any more than necessary. Unfortunately, a successful play fell into the "necessary" category. The entire town looked forward to this event.

"Okay, I'll help." Letting go a sigh, she pulled her phone from her pocket. "What's your email address?"

"Email?"

"Yes, so I can send you a list of things you need to do."

"Okay. But can we meet at least once to go over it?"

She'd rather have a root canal. They gave you painkillers for that. "Fine. But I hope you don't mind kids, because Kenzie will likely be accompanying me."

"Not a problem. We can even meet at your mother's, if you like."

She typed in the email address he gave her. "I'll send you something later tonight or tomorrow morning. Then we can schedule a meeting." Tucking her phone back into her pocket, she continued. "Right now, I need to get home to my niece."

Outside, she tightened the belt on her peacoat and shivered. Seemed the temperatures had gone down along with the sun. It was downright freezing.

She hurried across the darkened street to her SUV, wishing she'd brought her gloves. She'd forgotten how much colder it could be here than in Denver. Of course, Ouray was also more than two thousand feet higher in altitude.

Under the glow of a street lamp, she threw herself into the driver's seat, shoved the key into the ignition and gave it a twist. Except instead of the engine roaring to life, it simply clicked. Weird. She turned the key again. *Weeneeneeneenee... Weeneenee, weeneenee...*

She groaned, recalling the words of the mechanic who'd done her last oil change.

"You're probably going to want to think about changing out that battery soon."

And she'd just driven all the way across the state.

Stupid! How could she have let that slip?

As the windows started to fog, she willed herself to calm down. All she needed was someone to give her a jump.

She opened her door and stepped out onto Ouray's only paved street, looking around for anyone who might be able to help her. But with the other cast members long gone, things were pretty deserted.

A gust of wind sent her back inside her vehicle. "Lord, please help me to get this started."

Once again, she twisted the key and was met with the same result.

Tap, tap, tap.

She jumped, jerking her head toward the window.

"Need a little help?" Matt stood on the other side, wearing a smile that would melt most women's hearts. But she wasn't most women.

She pushed the door open. "My battery could use a jump."

"Sure. Just let me swing my Jeep over here."

"I've got jumper cables," she called after him. No point in having him think she was incapable of taking care of herself.

In no time, his vehicle was nose-to-nose with hers, cables extending between them, and she was back behind the wheel, praying her car would start.

"All right, Lacie," he hollered from outside. "Give it a try."

With a nod, she turned the key.

Weenee...

"No, please don't do this to me."

"One more time." He sent her a thumbs-up.

Please, please, please... She tried again.

Nothing. Not one sound.

Matt opened her door then. "I'm afraid your battery is dead."

She wanted to cry. Though not in front of him.

So she grabbed her purse and keys and stepped outside. "I guess I'll just have to walk home."

"No, I'll give you a ride."

She dared to look at him now. "It's not that far. I'll be perfectly—"

"You're just as stubborn as ever, aren't you, Lace?"

She froze. Lace? He was the only one who'd ever called her that. Something just between them, an endearment that made her feel…special.

"Well, so am I," he continued. "And I am not about to let you walk. So get in the Jeep while I take care of these cables."

She simply stared at him, though she wasn't sure what bugged her most. The fact that he called her stubborn or that he thought he could tell her what to do. However, since her teeth were chattering and her fingers and toes were numb, she climbed into the passenger seat and waited.

He tossed the cables into the back before getting in the driver's seat. "All right, let's get you home."

Couldn't come soon enough for her. Being around Matt was so…nerve-racking.

He put the vehicle into gear and turned at the corner. "So are you hoping to find a job closer to Ouray?"

"Oh, no." Looking out the window, she watched the houses go by. "Denver is our home. Kenzie has her daycare, our friends are there, our church… I don't want to uproot her. I'm just biding my time until I have something else lined up." Unfortunately, none of the home builders in the Denver area were looking to hire anyone, including interior designers/stagers until after the holidays.

"That's very commendable." He turned onto her mother's street. "A shame, too."

"Why?"

"I'm sure your mother would enjoy having both you and your niece near."

"Oh." She tamped down the unwanted disappointment. "Well, I just want what's best for Kenzie." Not to mention herself. And that meant keeping her heart closed to Matt Stephens.

She reached for the door handle as he eased to a stop in front of Mom's house. "Thanks for the ride."

* * *

Gray clouds and freezing temperatures were the order of the day as Matt climbed the front steps at the Collier house shortly before nine the next morning. When he'd dropped Lacie off last night, he'd barely brought his Jeep to a stop before she hopped out. Leaving him to wonder why she was being so standoffish.

Sure they hadn't seen each other in years, but time couldn't erase the fact that they'd once been really good friends. From seventh to eleventh grade, they'd had no problem confiding in one another. Then he'd started dating Marissa and Lacie no longer wanted anything to do with him. Just like last night.

Later Marissa told him Lacie had had a crush on him. Making him feel like the biggest jerk ever for not recognizing it.

But that was sixteen years ago. That couldn't be the problem now, could it?

Regardless, his friend had a dead battery to contend with and her mother had a business to run. Even if Lacie were to use Barbara's car, she'd still have to remove the battery and find a replacement all with a child in tow. He couldn't let her do that. Not in this weather.

He knocked on the door of the slate-colored, sixties-era, single-story rambler, thinking of all the times he'd been there before. Back when two teenage girls lived there and the house was an ugly pea green. Much had changed in the last sixteen years. And not all for the better.

The door swung open then and Barbara Collier smiled at him, just as she had all those years ago. These days, her short, dark blond hair sported a little more gray and her blue eyes had lost some of their spark, but given what she'd been through, having lost her husband and a daughter, he supposed it was understandable.

She pushed open the storm door. "Matt, what a pleasant surprise." Her gaze skimmed his uniform. "At least, I hope so." She looked him in the eye again. "You're not here on official business, are you?"

He couldn't help chuckling. "No, ma'am. You're in the clear."

"Well, in that case, come on in."

He wiped his booted feet on the mat before following her inside the comfortable living room with its pale yellow walls and overstuffed beige furniture.

"Can I get you some coffee?" She gestured to the adjoining kitchen.

"No, thank you. I don't suppose Lacie's up, is sh—"

"I'm gonna get you, you little stinker." Lacie's voice trailed down the hallway to the right, as a small child came running into the room wearing bright pink pajamas.

"No..." The little girl laughed and bounded onto the couch.

"I've got you now." Lacie closed in on her, stopping short when she spotted Matt. "I didn't know we had company."

"Don't let me interrupt your fun," he said with a smile.

She grabbed the small shirt and pants that were draped over her shoulder. "Somebody's giving me a hard time about getting dressed this morning."

The child grew quiet and clung to her aunt's leg once she realized there was a stranger in the house. She was a cute little thing. Dark brown curls, dark eyes... Not at all like Marissa. Yet there was something about her.

Obviously sensing the girl's hesitation, Barbara said, "Kenzie, this is our friend Officer Matt."

Did she remember him from the other day, when he'd pulled Lacie over?

Moving closer, he felt almost mesmerized as he crouched to her level. She was little, all right. How old was she anyway? Three? Maybe four?

"It's nice to meet you, Kenzie."

Her smile returned, albeit a shy one as she tightened her hold on Lacie. Still, the pleasure it brought him was inexplicable. Never had a stranger's eyes looked so familiar.

"What brings you by?" Lacie's tone carried that same stubborn edge he'd heard yesterday.

"You."

Her eyes widened as he stood. "Me?"

"Yes. You have a dead battery that needs to be replaced. I'm here to help."

"Oh, that won't be—"

"That is so sweet of you, Matt." Barbara made her way toward them. "Lacie's been stressing all morning, wondering if she was going to need to have her car towed or not."

One glance at a chagrined Lacie had him biting back a smile. "Nope, no towing needed. We'll simply take out the old battery, pick up a new one and put it in right there on Main Street."

"We?" Lacie's glare bounced between him and her mother.

"Okay, you'll just be there to supervise and pay for the battery. I'll do the rest."

She looked over his uniform. "But you're working.

I'm sure you have plenty of deputy things to keep you busy."

"Helping the community *is* part of my work."

She paused. "Well, what about Kenzie? I can't let her ride in the back seat of a sheriff's vehicle."

Man, she really did not want his help. Or was simply too obstinate to accept it.

"That's all right, dear," said Barbara. "Kenzie can come to the shop with me." She smiled at her granddaughter. "You want to come to work with Grandma?"

"Uh-huh."

"Okay, we'll have to get you dressed first." Barbara snagged the clothes from Lacie, then held out her other hand to Kenzie, who promptly took hold and accompanied her grandmother down the hall.

He managed to contain the laughter bubbling inside him. "Looks like we're free to go whenever you're ready."

Lacie continued to stare down the hall. While he'd appreciated her mother's intervention, it was obvious Lacie didn't share his opinion. "I'll get my coat."

"Might want to grab some gloves, too. It's kind of cold out there." After last night, he figured a friendly reminder wouldn't hurt.

Though, based on the look she sent him, she found his suggestion more irritating than friendly.

A short time later, he pulled behind her SUV on a slowly awakening Main Street.

"You can wait here, if you like. I just need to remove the old battery and—"

Lacie unhooked her seat belt. "I want you to show me how to do it."

He glanced across the center console to her lined

jacket. Definitely more work appropriate than that pink coat she'd worn yesterday. "That's admirable. Most women leave this sort of stuff to someone else."

"Yeah, well, maybe I'm not most women. Should I ever find myself in this situation again—"

"Hopefully you won't, but I understand. Why don't you go pop the hood while I grab a couple of tools?"

He watched the set of her shoulders and the determination in her stride as she walked toward her vehicle. He had no doubt that Lacie could do anything she set her mind to, whether it was acting, becoming an instant mother or auto repair.

"First thing we need to do is remove the cables from the battery." A semi rumbled past as he hovered over the frozen engine. "A wrench is better, but you could also use pliers."

"Okay." The expectant look on her face was beyond endearing.

He continued, explaining each step until the battery was freed. "All we have to do now is lift it out, go get a new one and we're golden."

"Golden," she said with a rapt smile on her face. "Where do we find a new one?"

"At the service station north of town. That is, assuming they have one in stock."

"And if they don't?" Worry creased her pretty brow.

"You pick it up tomorrow. No big deal."

Fortunately, they had one in stock. And when they returned to her SUV, Lacie insisted on carrying it. No small feat, since it weighed almost forty pounds. About the size of a small child. Though he doubted Kenzie weighed that much.

He shook his head. He couldn't seem to stop thinking about the kid. Her dark eyes had grabbed hold of him and refused to let go.

"All right, Lace, this is your chance."

"Chance for what?"

Strange. Until now, he never realized how much he'd missed that smile. The one that hinted at the tender heart behind the tough facade. The one that never failed to draw him in. "You get to install the battery."

Still hunched over with the weight of her load, she said, "Seriously?"

"I'm only here for assistance."

Her eyes sparkled. "Cool!"

Her attempts to lift the battery to the proper height failed immediately, though. She flared her nostrils. "Grrr..."

"Easy." He moved to the back seat and grabbed Kenzie's car seat. Setting it on the asphalt, he said, "Try standing on this."

She did, and it was just the boost she needed to set the battery into place.

"All right, Lace, what's next?"

"I don't know." A moment of panic flitted across her face. "The negative cable?"

"That's right." He handed her the wrench.

She cinched it into place, then connected the positive. "Screwdriver," she said, moving the bracket into position.

Finished, she handed him his tools, her gaze expectant.

"Go fire it up and let's see what we've got."

She hurried behind the wheel and a moment later the engine roared to life. "I did it!" She hopped out onto the pavement, thrusting a fist into the air. "Yes!"

This time he did laugh. He'd never seen someone get so excited over a battery.

Suddenly more subdued, she moved toward him, her expression softening. "Thank you for teaching me." The pink tinge of her cheeks grew deeper, heightening his awareness of just how pretty she was. Why hadn't he noticed that before? "I really appreciate it."

"And I appreciate your willingness to help me understand my job as director. It's important to me."

Peering up at him through long lashes, she said, "I know it is." Her gray-blue eyes held his for a moment, allowing him the slightest glimpse of the Lacie he'd once shared his secrets with. Then she stepped away to close the hood. "That reminds me, I still need to send you that list."

"That's okay. You had other things to worry about."

She nodded. "Well, I…guess I'd better go get Kenzie. We need to run to Montrose to pick up a birthday cake."

"Looks like we got this taken care of just in time then. Whose birthday?"

"Kenzie's." Her smile was like any proud mother's. "I can't believe she's five already."

"Five?" He took a step back. "But she's so small. I would have thought she was younger."

"Nope." She glanced up and down the street, as though unable to look at him. "So I should go."

"Yeah, of course." He gathered up his tools and placed them in the back of his vehicle as she drove away. What was wrong with him? This nagging sensation that twisted through him hadn't been there before. Was it Lacie's appreciation getting to him? Or something more?

Chapter Three

Lacie pulled into a parking spot in front of her mother's shop, mentally chastising herself. In all her gratitude, she'd almost let her guard down with Matt. Something she couldn't afford to do with any man. She owed it to her niece to be that one constant in her life, instead of allowing herself to be distracted the way Marissa so often had.

Like the night her boyfriend crashed his car, robbing Kenzie of her mother and forever changing her life.

Still, Lacie appreciated Matt's willingness to guide her through the process of installing her new battery. Not dismissing her or trying to take over the way Brandon would have. In the two years they'd dated, Brandon had insisted on doing everything for her. At first, she thought he was just being chivalrous, but later realized Mr. Know-It-All had a deep-seated need to feel superior to anyone and everyone. Including her.

Shaking off the unwanted thoughts, she exited her vehicle into the cold late-morning air. Judging by the gray clouds obscuring the tops of the mountains along the town's western edge, they'd soon be in for some snow. Kenzie would love that. Good thing Lacie had scooped up a couple of coats and some snow pants on clearance for her back in the spring when she still had a job. She didn't want to have to tap into her savings any more than necessary.

Turning, she glimpsed the beginnings of her mother's window display at The Paisley Elk, a little clothing boutique that catered mostly to women. So far, it consisted of batting "snow" and white lights, but then the contest for best Christmas display didn't start in earnest until next week, so there was likely plenty more to come.

Inside was another story, though. Lacie had to hand it to her mother. The boutique was definitely festive. Standing under a ceiling adorned with hundreds of twinkling LED lights, she realized just how adept her mother had become at feigning Christmas. Not a Christmas tree in sight. No nativity of any kind. Not even a hint of the traditional red and green, save for the occasional evergreen bough. No, this was commercialism at its best. And if there wasn't a prize involved—even if it wasn't anything more than bragging rights—she doubted Mom would do any decorations at all.

Still, The Paisley Elk had an undeniable appeal that would draw people in. Like the glistening purple and silver balls that appeared to float in midair just below the lights, adding a touch of color to the overhead charm. And, of course, everything was perfectly merchandised for maximum effect, with pops of glitz and glam everywhere you looked.

Now if Lacie could just convince her mother to decorate the house…

December 23 would mark twelve years since Lacie's father's death. She'd never forget coming home from the hospital and watching her mother take down every decoration in the house. They hadn't even opened their presents. Mom said she'd never celebrate Christmas again. And, so far, she'd held true to her word.

However, this was Kenzie's first Christmas without Marissa. They owed it to her to make it the best Christmas the kid could possibly have. That meant having a tree, presents and everything else Lacie and Marissa had enjoyed as kids.

"There you are." Mom draped a glittering silver pashmina scarf around the neck of a dress form sporting a pine-bough skirt adorned with silver ribbon, purple and silver balls, and peacock feathers. "How's the car?"

"Up and running again, I'm happy to say." She spotted Kenzie off to one side playing with— "Mom, is that Marissa's and my old dollhouse?"

"Sure is. I thought, since Kenzie will be here with us a lot and that old thing was just collecting dust in the basement, she might enjoy playing with it." Moving beside Lacie, she lowered her voice. "And I was right. She's been playing with it this entire time."

Lacie's heart grew hopeful. Perhaps Mom hadn't lost all sentiment.

She crossed to the small table where Kenzie was carefully moving the tiny furniture pieces, her smile widening with each step. The kid must have been having fun because she hadn't even noticed that Lacie was there.

Kneeling beside her niece, she said, "What are you doing?"

"Playing house." Tongue peeking out the corner of her mouth, Kenzie placed the miniature baby into the tiny crib.

"Are you having fun?"

Kenzie nodded, her expression somewhere between determined and delighted.

"I know just how you feel, Kenzikins." Lacie's father had built the dollhouse when she and Marissa were little. Like Kenzie, Lacie would spend hours rearranging furniture and contemplating different wall colors. No wonder she'd gone into interior design.

"Would you mind helping me assemble these, dear?" At the counter beside the cash register, Mom shoved glitter-covered branches into one of five tall galvanized buckets.

"Sure." She shrugged out of her coat, setting it beside the dollhouse before joining her mother.

Reaching for a trio of sparkling white branches, she mustered the courage to broach the topic of the holidays. "I noticed there wasn't a turkey in the fridge or freezer. Would you like me to pick one up?" One at a time, she plunged the stems into the Epsom salt snow.

"That won't be necessary." After admiring her handiwork, Mom picked up a spool of wide purple ribbon and stretched a length around the first bucket. "I thought we'd just go to Bon Ton or The Outlaw. No point in spending our day off in the kitchen when for all intents and purposes, Thanksgiving is just another day."

Had Mom's heart really grown that hard?

"No, it's not." She stared at the woman in disbelief. "Thanksgiving is when family and friends come together to give thanks for their blessings." *Like we used to do when Daddy was alive.*

Her mother smiled, seemingly unaffected by Lacie's comments. "Okay, you pick where we should eat then."

Passing the first bucket off to Mom for ribbon, Lacie reached for another cluster of branches. "Actually, I was kind of looking forward to some of your homemade dressing."

No response. Barbara Collier had always been good at avoiding conflict.

But Lacie wasn't willing to let it drop. "What if *I* cooked Thanksgiving dinner? Nothing fancy. Just some turkey, dressing—I'll need your recipe—and maybe a pumpkin pie. You wouldn't have to lift a finger."

"I don't know." Mom tied another swath of ribbon. "I hate for you to go to so much trouble."

"It's no trouble. I like to cook." Especially when she had people to cook for. "Throw in those traditional recipes and I'm a goner."

Mom was silent for a long moment. Finally, "Oh, all right. If you insist."

She wasn't aware she was insisting, but as long as they were on a roll… "And then, after dinner, maybe we could put up the Christmas tree." Biting her lip, she held her breath and stabbed another twig in the bucket.

But her mother remained focused on the task at hand. Without so much as flinching, she said, "Lacie, you know I don't celebrate Christmas anymore. If you want to take Kenzie to some of the festivities around town, that's fine. But there is no Christmas at the house."

She glared at her mother. "There used to be."

How she used to love coming down the hallway Christmas morning to the glow of twinkling lights and the soft sound of Christmas carols playing in the background. So many memories. Memories she desperately wanted to recreate for Kenzie. *God, please soften Mom's heart.*

"That was a long time ago." Her mother moved her reading glasses to the top of her head and looked at Lacie. "People change."

"And you won't change for your granddaughter?"

Scooping up the two completed buckets, she whisked past Lacie to disperse them throughout the store. "We all have our beliefs and convictions. I have chosen not to celebrate Christmas."

The bell over the door jangled then, ushering in a customer and effectively ending their conversation. Even though Lacie had so much more to say.

She glimpsed the little girl across the room. No, that wasn't a discussion to be had while Kenzie was within earshot.

So she finished the other three buckets while Mom assisted her customer, then went to check on Kenzie. "Are you about ready to go pick out your birthday cake?"

The child beamed. "I want chocolate."

Turning her gaze to the window, Lacie couldn't help smiling. "Chocolate it is then."

Maybe she'd even get the kid to take a nap this afternoon, allowing Lacie to work on that list for Matt.

Thoughts of the deputy had her wondering what he was doing for Thanksgiving. Perhaps they should invite him to join them. As a thank-you for helping her today.

She rubbed her arms, quickly dismissing the ridiculous notion. He had his own family. A rather large one, at that.

Besides, she had better things to do than worry about Matt Stephens's Thanksgiving plans. Like figuring out how on earth she was going to have a Christmas for Kenzie when her mom was dead set against it.

An hour after Lacie pulled away, Matt sat at the counter at Granny's Kitchen, a local diner, staring at his untouched burger. Seemed no matter how hard he tried to erase the memory, his mind kept rewinding to one February night nearly six years ago. Marissa's last in Hawaii. A night that never should have happened.

His insides churned. The math added up. But still…

Marissa may have done him wrong, but she would have told him he had a child, wouldn't she? Then again, she hadn't told him she was dating someone else, either.

So why isn't Kenzie's dad raising her?

He picked up a fry and forced himself to take a bite. He didn't want to believe it. But he couldn't ignore it, either. Could Kenzie be his daughter?

"What's up with the sad face?" A hand clamped on to Matt's shoulder.

He looked up as his brother Andrew helped himself to one of his fries. "What are you doing here?"

Andrew plopped down in the seat beside him. "Carly's putting up the Christmas decorations at Granger House, so I'm on my own for lunch." For the past nineteen years, Andrew had lived in Denver, where he ran a multimillion-dollar commercial construction company. Until last spring when he sold it, came back to Ouray and married his high school sweetheart. Now they were stuck with him.

"Christmas decorations? It's not even Thanksgiving yet."

Andrew snagged another fry. "True, but we've got guests booked for this weekend, so the bed-and-breakfast portion of the house needs to be ready before then." His gaze drifted to Matt's plate. "Something wrong with your burger? You haven't touched it."

"Guess I'm not very hungry."

His cell buzzed in his pocket. He pulled it out to

see Gladys Bricker's name on the screen. His favorite teacher must be baking again, because that was the only reason she ever called. A fiercely independent gal, Gladys had never married, but considered many of her former students her children. Himself included.

"Hello, Gladys."

"Oh, Matt, I hate to bother you."

Something in the eighty-one-year-old woman's voice wasn't quite right. "Gladys, you are never a bother. What can I do for you?"

"I'm afraid I need some wood brought in. It's already cut, but I just can't seem to make it outside to get it." His unease rose. That was definitely not like Gladys.

He stood. "Not to worry. I'm on my way." He ended the call. "Looks like your timing is perfect, bro." He slid his plate toward Andrew. "Duty calls."

His older brother reached for the burger. "I'll get the tab."

"You do that," said Matt as he made his way out the door into the brisk midday air. Honestly, he was grateful for Gladys's call. He wasn't exactly in the mood for a lengthy conversation with Andrew today. However, he was worried about the older woman.

He slid behind the wheel of his Tahoe and headed north, continuing outside of town. Gladys had always been faithful in keeping in touch with him over the years. He still had all the letters she'd sent him while he was in the navy.

A few minutes later, he pulled into her drive, gravel crunching beneath his tires. Exiting the vehicle, he spotted the large pile of wood near the barn at the back of the property. He made his way there first and filled his arms before heading to the small, white, single-story house with green trim.

He tugged open the screen door and knocked. "Gladys? It's Matt."

His anxiety heightened as the seconds dragged on. Reaching for the knob, he gave it a twist and inched the door open. "Gladys?"

"In—" coughing echoed from the living room that sat at the opposite end of the kitchen "—in here."

He continued into the house, moving through the compact yet tidy kitchen and into the chilly living room. There, on the other side of the room, in front of the big picture window, the elderly woman lay in her recliner, buried under a stack of blankets, her short gray hair sticking up every which way. She looked frailer than he'd ever imagined.

Crossing to the wood-burning stove in the corner of the room, he dropped the wood before touching a hand to the side of the stove. "This thing is stone-cold." He opened the door to see only ashes in the bottom.

He twisted around. "What's going on, Gladys? Why don't you have a fire going?"

Her face was pale, but she sent him weak smile. "I ran out of wood."

This wasn't good. "You're sick, aren't you?"

"Just a little cold." One wrinkled hand clasped the blankets to her chest while the other held tightly to a handkerchief she used to cover her mouth when she coughed.

A few quick strides put him at her side. He touched her forehead. "You're burning up."

"Am I?" Clouded blue eyes met his. "Feels pretty chilly to me."

He knelt beside her. "Have you been to see the doctor?"

"No."

He knew what he had to do, but Gladys wasn't going to like it. The best thing he could do was to make her a little more comfortable before bringing up the ambulance. A few more minutes wouldn't make that much difference.

"Okay, let me get this fire started." Back at the stove, he removed the ashes before adding a starter stick from the box he spotted on the shelf and a couple of thin logs.

After closing the doors, he went into the kitchen and set the four-cup coffeepot to brew. Probably not the best thing, but she needed something warm. A few minutes later, he filled an old green coffee cup halfway and took it to her. "Careful, it's hot."

"Thank you, Matt. You're a good boy."

No, a good boy would have checked on her more often.

After adding another log to the firebox, he pulled up a chair and sat beside her. "I wish you had called me earlier."

"I know. But I—"

"Hate to bother me, I know." Resting his forearms on his thighs, he leaned closer. "Gladys, I need to call an ambulance."

Her eyes widened slightly as she passed him her cup.

"I'm afraid you have more than just a cold and I want the EMTs to come and check you out."

"Can't I just go to the doctor?" She coughed.

"And how are you going to get there? You're in no condition to drive yourself." Any other time he'd take her himself, but since he was the only deputy on duty… Besides, she'd likely be going to the hospital in Montrose anyway.

Her thin lips pursed as she turned her gaze to the conifer-dotted landscape outside the window. "If you think that would be best."

He laid a hand atop hers. "I do. I want you to get better."

He made the call, then monitored the fire and paced the beige carpet as he waited for the EMTs to arrive.

"When did you do this?" He pointed to two photos, one color, the other black-and-white, encased in a single frame on the wall near the opening to the kitchen.

"About a month ago. That's my first graduating class—" more coughing "—and my last graduating class." Forty years of teaching. Definitely impressive.

"Hey, there's me." He pointed to the newer photo.

"Bring it over here, please."

He lifted the frame and took it to her.

She smiled as she touched the glass. "You and your brothers all had your father's dark eyes."

"Except Daniel," he said. The baby of the family was the polar opposite with his blond hair and blue eyes.

"Oh, yes. He took after your mother. But the rest of you… Anyone could tell you were a Stephens."

His gut clenched, images of Kenzie flashing through his mind. Her dark eyes. That sense of familiarity washed over him again. Could it be true?

Thirty minutes after the EMTs arrived, he watched as they loaded Gladys into the back of the ambulance. While bronchitis was a good bet, given her age, the doctors wanted to observe her to be certain there was nothing else going on.

He returned to the house to make sure everything was in order and the fire in the wood stove was put out. He'd have to touch base with the church and others in town so Gladys would have plenty of folks to check on her and bring her food once she returned home.

Before leaving, he picked up the framed photo and hung it back on the wall. *Anyone could tell you were a Stephens.*

His eyes closed. *God, forgive me. I know I made a mistake all those years ago. How do I know if Kenzie is my child?*

By the time his shift ended, he could hardly wait to get home. He didn't want to get his hopes up, but if what played across his brain was truly from God, he might have the answer he'd prayed for.

He pulled his Tahoe into the drive, ditched his gear at the back door and headed straight for the bookshelves surrounding the fireplace in the living room. Quickly locating the scrapbook his mother had compiled for him and his sister-in-law Carly had assembled, he flipped past the baby pictures and those of him as a toddler, his heart pounding when he came to a photo of him at age four and a half. Except the face staring back at him was Kenzie's. The nose, the eyes— He touched a finger to his forehead—even that little widow's peak had Stephens written all over it.

He dropped onto the couch, feeling as though the air had been sucked from his lungs.

Kenzie was his daughter.

Chapter Four

Standing at the island in her mother's kitchen, Lacie transferred the remnants of Kenzie's birthday cake to a large plastic container then licked a smudge of the super sweet frosting from her finger. Thanks to no nap earlier in the day, save for fifteen short minutes in the car on the way back from Montrose, the little girl had crashed early. Still, it had been a good birthday. Mom had gone above and beyond on the gifts. Clothes, toys, books… Yet she refused to do Christmas. Unless the abundance was to make up for *not* celebrating Christmas.

Whatever the case, they'd all had a pleasant evening.

She stowed the cake in the fridge, rinsed and dried her hands, then grabbed her laptop and settled on the couch in the living room. Since she'd sent off Matt's list this afternoon, she was now free to see if any new job listings had been posted. Because if she could find something that started before Christmas, her problems would be solved.

"I see you got a turkey." Sitting in an adjacent chair near the window, Mom looked up from her book and moved her reading glasses to the top of her head.

Lacie lifted a brow. Was that merely an observation or were they about to enter round two of holiday discussions? If so, she'd better prepare to stand her ground.

"Just a small one." She snagged the deep purple plush throw from the back of the sofa and tossed it over her legs while she waited for the website to load. "Oh, and don't forget to give me your dressing recipe."

"It's in the recipe file in the cupboard." Mom reached for her herbal tea on the side table. "It's fairly basic, no special ingredients, so you shouldn't have any trouble finding what you need at Duckett's."

Contemplating an inevitable trip to Ouray's one and only grocer, Lacie was pleased to see that her mother had embraced the idea of having Thanksgiving here at the house. Now if she would just come around to Lacie's way of thinking regarding Christmas…

A knock sounded at the door.

She and her mother exchanged quizzical looks.

"I wonder who that could be." Mom set her cup down, stood and started for the door. Fingering the sheer curtain aside, she peered through the sidelight window and smiled. "I have a feeling it's for you."

"Me?" Lacie set her computer on the coffee table, tossed the throw aside and stood in her socked feet. Who would be here to see her? The only person she'd had contact with since she'd been back was—

Her gut tightened. Oh, please don't let it be—

"Matt, this makes twice in one day." Mom held the door, allowing him and a blast of cold air to enter. "To what do we owe this pleasure?"

Pleasure? Lacie tugged at the sleeves of her bulky sweater. That was debatable.

"Hey, Barbara." He wore a heavy coat, a pair of well-worn jeans, gloves and a black beanie. And if the hefty dose of pink coloring in his cheeks and nose was any indication, he'd walked. "I'm sorry to stop by so late."

"Nonsense." Mom closed the door behind him. "It's only eight thirty."

Yeah, never mind the fact that they were settling in for a cozy evening.

When Matt's dark gaze moved to Lacie, she noticed something different, though. His shoulders seemed to slump, as though he were carrying a heavy burden, and there was something sad in his expression. Something that made her heart go out to him, though she quickly snatched it back.

Had something happened with the play? Mrs. Nichols?

"Is Kenzie in bed?" He watched her intently.

Uncertain how she felt about this side of Matt, she crossed her arms over her chest. "Yes. Why?"

"Could we take a walk?"

A walk? Now? But it was late. Moreover, it was cold.

"We won't be long," he added.

She looked to her mother.

"I'll keep an ear out for Kenzie." Obviously the woman had read her mind.

Lacie glanced down at her computer. So much for job hunting. "Give me a sec to get ready."

She donned her coat, scarf, hat and boots, all the while trying to figure out why Matt would suddenly feel like taking a walk. With her of all people. Unless something *had* happened. Or he simply wanted to discuss his duties as director? But couldn't they do that here or someplace else that was warm?

Tugging on her gloves, she let go a sigh. She'd find out soon enough.

Outside, the air was still as they started up the darkened street. The clouds that had plagued them all day had finally dissipated, leaving a plethora of stars in their wake. It also meant they were likely in for a very cold night. Perhaps a hot bath would be in order when she got back.

"How'd the party go?" Matt's breath hung in the freezing night air.

"Not too bad, considering there were only three of us." She stuffed her hands into her pockets. "Kenzie made out like a bandit."

"I'm guessing she'd consider it a success then." Though she didn't look at him, she could hear a hint of a smile in his voice.

"Probably."

They walked in silence for a few moments, seemingly heading nowhere in particular, which had her wondering what this walk was all about.

Approaching a dim streetlight at the corner, she said, "Did you want to discuss the email I sent you?"

He glanced her way, his expression somber. "You sent me an email?"

"I told you I would."

Again looking straight ahead, he said, "I haven't checked. Had other stuff on my mind."

Okay, then what—

Hands in his pockets, he kept walking. "I'm curious—why isn't Kenzie's father raising her?"

"What?" How dare he ask something so personal?

"I mean, typically when one parent passes, the other assumes custody."

"Unless there's a will that stipulates otherwise. Kenzie's father wanted nothing to do with her. My sister wanted me to raise Kenzie. Not that it's any business of yours."

"Were you planning to keep it a secret like Marissa did?"

"I have no idea what you're talking about. What secret?"

"That I'm Kenzie's father."

Dumbfounded, she stopped and simply stared at him. "If you're trying to be funny, you missed the mark by a long shot."

He stared back at her. "No, I'm quite serious."

Not to mention crazy. She shook her head. "Did you not pay attention in ninth grade biology? It only takes nine months to have a baby. It's been sixteen years since you and Marissa were a couple, so even if you had—"

"Marissa came to Hawaii." The intensity of his gaze heightened and bore straight into her. "The February before Kenzie was born. But then you probably knew that."

Her mind raced to keep up. Of course, she remembered her sister's trip. Marissa and Grant had just broken up for the umpteenth time.

"I was there with the navy," Matt continued. "I spent the week showing her around Oahu. And then …" He turned away as though embarrassed.

She burrowed her hands deeper into her coat. Her sister never said anything about seeing Matt. And as she recalled, Marissa and Grant got back together shortly after she returned from her trip.

February? She ticked off the months on her frozen fingers. March, April, May, June, July, August, September, October, Novem…

A sickening flurry of emotions began to churn in

her belly, spaghetti and chocolate cake morphing into a lead weight. She swallowed hard as the potential reality of Matt's confession sank in.

It couldn't be true, though. Grant was Kenzie's father. He and Marissa had dated off and on for years. Until shortly before Kenzie was born, when he walked away for good.

She dared a glance at Matt, squaring her shoulders. Marissa would have told her if he was Kenzie's father. "Matt, I don't know how you came up with such a crazy notion, but I can assure you that you are not Kenzie's father."

He twisted toward her. "Really? Then how do you explain this?" He held out a five-by-seven photo. A little boy with dark eyes alight with amusement and dark brown hair that had been combed back to reveal a slight widow's peak… Just like Kenzie. "That's me at four years old. When your mother introduced me to Kenzie earlier today, I felt as though I'd met her before. I didn't get it at first. Until you told me how old she was." His voice cracked. "I'm not imagining this, Lace. I truly believe that Kenzie is my daughter."

She stared at the photo, feeling as though she might be sick. Grant was as fair-haired as Marissa had been, with eyes just as blue. Why hadn't her sister told her she saw Matt? That there was a possibility he could be Kenzie's father?

She looked away. It couldn't be true. It wasn't true. Jutting her chin into the frigid air, she glared right at Matt. "It's not true." Then, before he could say another word, she turned and ran back home.

Thanks to Lacie's abrupt departure last night, sleep had evaded Matt. Now as midafternoon approached, he was starting to feel the effects. Unfortunately, his shift wasn't over for another three hours.

Under what he would normally consider a beautiful blue sky, he maneuvered his Tahoe through the neighboring town of Ridgway, eyeing the jagged, snow-covered peaks of the Cimarrons to the east. He wanted to kick himself for accusing Lacie of hiding Kenzie's paternity, when it was obvious she was as shocked by the revelation as he was. What he couldn't figure out, though, was why she refused to believe him.

Because maybe you're not Kenzie's father.

Yet he'd gone off half-cocked with no concrete proof to back up his supposition.

Anyone could tell you were a Stephens.

The image of Kenzie's face haunted him. Wouldn't a father know his own child? After all, it wasn't like he was looking to be a dad. And while the evidence he had was circumstantial, it all added up and was impossible to ignore. At least until he had proof to the contrary.

So where did he go from here? And how was he going to convince Lacie that he wasn't crazy?

His radio went off. Possible poachers. He waited for the address, cringing when it came. He did not need this today. Or any other day, for that matter. With the mood he was in, the last person he wanted to see was his father.

Why'd he have to call while Matt was the only deputy on duty? Couldn't he have waited a few more hours for the next shift? Sure, it would be dark, but at least he'd have been off the hook.

Bound by duty, he reluctantly responded to dispatch and headed south on Highway 550. *God, I'm going to need Your help.*

Ten minutes later, his vehicle bumped across the cattle guard beneath the arched metal sign that read Abundant Blessings Ranch. He crept up the long gravel drive, praying that perhaps it had been his oldest brother, Noah, who'd made the call. Yet as he passed the recently expanded stable, his hopes were dashed when he glimpsed Noah tending the horses. He thought about stopping to check, but knew he'd simply be postponing the inevitable.

Approaching the ranch house, memories of that day nearly three years ago filled his mind. All he'd wanted to do was make Mama happy. And he had. For a short time, she'd forgotten the pain and weakness that had plagued her for months.

But Dad didn't see it that way. *Are you trying to kill her?*

Ten days later, she was gone. The cancer had finally gotten the better of her.

Just then he spotted his father exiting the new barn his brother Andrew had built over the summer.

You're nothing but a screwup, Matt. Always have been, always will be.

Clint Stephens's words didn't sting quite as much today as they had when he'd first spat them at Matt. And while Matt tried to pretend his father's opinion didn't matter, it seemed he'd been trying to disprove his father ever since. Yet for all of his trying, he'd only succeeded in proving him correct.

While Dad looked on, he parked beside the old man's dually, in front of the long wooden deck that spanned the length of the single-story cedar ranch house. Thanks to Andrew and a good power washing, the place looked almost new. The ugly black buildup from years of neglect had been whisked away. If only the damage to his heart could be so easily erased.

His father was waiting as Matt exited his truck, felt cowboy hat perched upon his graying head, hands buried in the pockets of his Carhartt coveralls. "Wondered if you'd be working today."

"I am. So whatcha got?" Because the sooner he could get away from here, the better off he'd be.

"A decapitated mule deer." The old man poked a thumb over his shoulder toward the pasture. "Near Smugglers Bend."

Matt knew the area well as he used to hunt there all the time. There wasn't an inch on the ranch that he and his brothers hadn't explored at some point in their young lives. "I'll drive over there and walk in from the road."

His father's gaze narrowed. "He's tucked in amongst the brush. Might have a hard time findin' him, so I'd best take you."

The dread Matt had felt earlier amplified. Did Dad think he was incapable of finding it? Or that he needed a chaperone to make sure he got things right?

Whatever the case, the old man remained quiet during the ride out there on one of the utility vehicles they used to get around the ranch. Despite an abundance of sunshine, the bitter cold air stung Matt's face as they thudded over the now-dormant rangeland, carving a path around cattle and the occasional tree.

A short time later, his father brought the vehicle to a halt beside a small wooded area. Scruffy conifers and barren deciduous trees blanketed with underbrush. A hiding place for wildlife. "He was a big fella." Dad stepped off the vehicle and led Matt several feet into the thicket.

Matt eyed the once-majestic buck. "Yes, sir. But then, poachers don't make a habit of going after the little guys." He surveyed the overgrowth around the animal. "How'd you find him?"

"Neighbor called and said I had cows on the road. When I went to get 'em, I discovered somebody had cut the fence." Dad glanced some hundred yards in the distance. "Wasn't long after that I saw the blood trail." He looked down at the dead animal. "Looks like a clean shot, though." He pointed to the entry wound behind the animal's left shoulder. "Fella never knew what hit him."

"I'm guessing they shot from the road." Matt dared a look at his dad. "Then walked in to claim their trophy."

Dad shook his head. "Them poachers are the ones that ought to be shot."

Matt took some photos and jotted down a few notes before following the trail to the road and doing more of the same. "Unfortunately, this isn't the first incident we've seen," he told his father when he returned. "I'll hand this information over to investigators, though with little to go on, catching anyone isn't likely."

They again climbed on the UTV and started back to the ranch house in silence. Matt took the opportunity to survey the land he loved so much. He gazed at the river as they passed, wishing he could spend more time there. How he used to enjoy walking the property, communing with nature, hunting, fishing… Except now he felt like an outsider. Unwelcome in his own home.

"Well, I suppose you need to get on, don't you?" His father stopped the vehicle in front of the house. "Probably have reports and such to take care of, huh?"

If Matt were anyone else, Dad would have offered him a cup of coffee. But he wasn't anyone else. No matter what he did, he was a disappointment to his father. The son who was arrested for underage drinking, then let his parents down by joining the navy without ever consulting them.

"Yes, sir."

The old man followed him to his Tahoe. "I've been hearing rumors that you're directing your mama's play."

Matt's entire body tensed. "Yes."

Hands shoved in his pockets, the old man rocked back on the heels of his worn work boots. "I gotta say, I'm kinda curious as to why you decided to do that."

Turning, he looked at his father. "They were talking about canceling the play and I couldn't let Mama's legacy die."

"I can appreciate that." Dad nodded, his lips drawn into a thin line. "But don't you think it would have been better to leave it in the hands of someone who knew what they were doing?"

Matt's blood boiled. The old man would never cut him any slack. "Why? Because you think I'll screw that up, too?"

When his father didn't respond, Matt turned on his own booted heel. "I'm out of here." He threw himself into his vehicle, fired up the engine and exited the ranch at a much faster pace than he'd arrived.

As far as Clint Stephens was concerned, his middle son had no redeeming qualities. Just wait until he found out about Kenzie. The fact that Matt had fathered a child out of wedlock would only amplify the old man's belief that Matt was nothing but a failure, unworthy of his father's love. And as much as it killed Matt to admit it, even to himself, that's the one thing he desperately wanted.

Chapter Five

Matt could not be Kenzie's father. That's all there was to it.

Darkness had already settled over Ouray as Lacie stood at the stove in her mother's kitchen, stirring noodles into the beef Stroganoff, its savory aroma filling the air. While she welcomed the opportunity to cook for more than just herself and Kenzie, the task did little to distract her from the annoying thoughts that had plagued her brain all day. How could one brief meeting have Matt believing he was Kenzie's father? Talk about nerve.

"I'm hungry." Kenzie approached from the living room, where an educational cartoon had held her attention for the past twenty minutes.

"I know, sweetie." Lacie put the lid on the skillet, annoyed that she'd wasted most of her day, mentally rehashing last night's conversation with Matt instead of interacting with Kenzie. "How about a piece of string cheese to tide you over until Grandma gets home?"

"Okay." Her niece beamed at the prospect. "Can I play with my ponies?"

Lacie opened the refrigerator and grabbed a cheese stick. "You like those, huh?"

"Uh-huh." Kenzie nodded, accepting her snack.

She had to hand it to her mother, she'd done a good job anticipating what toys Kenzie would and would not like. "Then yes, you may. I'll let you know when dinner is ready."

"Okay." She grinned up at Lacie with a smile that reached her big brown eyes. Eyes not at all like Marissa's or even Grant's. Instead, they reminded Lacie of—

No. She shut the refrigerator door with a little too much force, rattling its contents. She wasn't going to go there because it wasn't true. Grant was Kenzie's father, even if he was a deadbeat dad.

While Kenzie played and they waited for Mom to get home from the shop, Lacie seized the opportunity to focus on something besides Matt. She crossed to the table and opened her laptop to check those job listings she'd planned to research last night before she'd been so rudely interrupted. Yet even as she stared at the computer screen, her thoughts kept returning to Matt. To the pain and conviction in his dark eyes.

She let go a groan and returned to the stove to give the Stroganoff another stir. This was ridiculous. If Matt had been Kenzie's father, Marissa would have told her. There were no secrets between them. They—

She froze. Kenzie's birth certificate. She had Kenzie's birth certificate in her files in the bedroom. Strange that she thought to keep it close by in case she needed it, yet had never taken the time to look over the document.

Quickly replacing the lid, she set the wooden spoon on its rest and started down the hall. Grant would be listed as Kenzie's father on the birth certificate, putting this nonsense to rest once and for all.

Inside her old bedroom, she opened the closet door and grabbed the plastic file box that contained all of her and Kenzie's important documents and set it on the bed. She lifted the plastic lid and fingered past shot records, guardianship papers and tax records until she located the folder labeled Birth Certificates.

She removed it from the box, opened it and read. Mackenzie Elizabeth Collier. Date of birth. Place of birth. Father…

Unknown?

Lifting her head, she stared at the glowing numbers on the bedside clock. Why would Marissa have listed the father as unknown? Did she not want Grant to be a part of Kenzie's life or—

A sick feeling in the pit of her stomach had her easing onto the same bed she'd slept in as a teenager. Grant wasn't Kenzie's father.

Her mind's eye recalled the picture Matt had shown her last night. Sure there were similarities, but that didn't mean he was Kenzie's father. A lot of people had dark hair and eyes.

And the widow's peak?

Her confusion persisted into dinner and throughout the evening. She barely touched her food. Even as she tucked Kenzie into bed, the fact that her sister had listed the girl's father as unknown not only perplexed but annoyed her. Who did that to a child?

Returning to the living room, she absently flopped onto the sofa, drawing her legs under her as she stared at nothing in particular.

"Can I get you a cup of tea?" Mom approached from the kitchen.

"No, thanks." Lacie reached for a throw pillow and hugged it against her chest.

"Care to talk about it?" Mom eased into her chair.

"Talk about what?"

"Whatever it is that's bothering you." Her mother set her cup on the side table. "You've been in a funk ever since you came back from your walk with Matt last night."

If there was anyone she should talk to about this situation, she supposed it would be her mother. After all, she and Lacie were the only family Kenzie had left. And despite Mom's refusal to celebrate Christmas, she still cared about her granddaughter and had her best interests at heart.

"Matt has this crazy notion that he is Kenzie's father." She fixed her gaze on her sister's graduation photo hanging on the far wall. "Seems he and Marissa spent some time together while she was in Hawaii. So when he learned when Kenzie's birthday was, he automatically decided she was his daughter." She puffed out a disbelieving laugh. "He even showed me a picture of himself at the same age. As if *that* was supposed to convince me." No matter how alike they might have looked.

"Did it?"

"No." Toying with the pillow's silky fringe, she continued. "So I pulled out Kenzie's birth certificate to prove him wrong."

"And?"

She looked at her mother. "Marissa listed Kenzie's father as Unknown."

Mom drew in a long breath. "I was afraid that might be the case." Standing, she came to sit beside Lacie.

"What?" She twisted to face her mother. "That she'd not name a father?"

"No. That Matt is Kenzie's father."

Lacie recoiled at the statement. "Why on earth would you think that?"

"Marissa told me she'd seen Matt while she was in Hawaii." Her mother rested a hand on Lacie's knee. "I know she was seeing Grant around that same time, but I also know your sister. Throw in the fact that Kenzie looks just like Matt and even I can do the math."

Lacie didn't get it. "Why didn't you say anything?"

"It wasn't my place."

"Not even after Marissa died?"

"I had no proof." Mom shrugged. "Just mother's intuition." After a silent moment, she went on. "I am curious, though." Her mother watched her intently. "Why is it so difficult for you to believe that Matt could be Kenzie's father?"

Because it means Marissa got a part of him I'll never have.

Shocked by the juvenile notion, she tossed the pillow aside and stood. What was she, back in high school? She had no interest in Matt, let alone bearing his children.

"Just blindsided, I guess." She let go a sigh before turning back to her mother. "I mean, what am I supposed to do now?"

"You could always ask for a DNA test."

She lifted a shoulder. "I hate to put Kenzie through that."

"It's only a cheek swab." Mom stood and went to retrieve her tea. "That's hardly traumatic." Cup cradled in her hands, she eyed Lacie again. "Don't you want to know the truth?"

Lacie rubbed her arms. Only if it meant Matt *wasn't* Kenzie's father.

"Sweetheart—" her mother moved closer "—I know how much you love Kenzie. But do you think it would be fair to keep her from having a relationship with her father? Especially now that her mother's gone?"

While Lacie knew the correct answer to her mother's question, she didn't necessarily like it.

"No. But how do you even begin to explain something like that to a four—I mean, five-year-old?"

"Slowly." Mom was beside her now, cup in hand. "And probably not fully until she's older. Right now the best thing would be to let them forge a relationship. After all, she just met him."

Again, she knew her mother was right. But if Matt was Kenzie's father, where did that leave her?

She paced to the window and peered through the blinds. "What if he wants her? What if he tries to take her away from me?"

"Lacie, Matt is a good man. Don't try to paint him as vengeful."

Turning, she said, "He thinks I knew. That I was keeping the truth from him right along with Marissa."

Mom's expression softened. "Just like you, once he has a chance to process things, I'm sure he'll realize you're telling the truth."

"But what if he doesn't?" What if he decided to fight for custody of Kenzie? What would that do to Kenzie? And what would that do to her?

By Wednesday, Matt had pulled himself together enough to know that he had to talk to Lacie again. At least to apologize for accusing her of lying. But with the majority of his shift still stretched out in front of him, he wasn't at liberty to have a lengthy conversation. That didn't mean he couldn't be proactive, though.

So shortly after ten thirty, when he knew Barbara would be at the shop, he stopped by the Collier house. He knocked on the door, praying Lacie would answer. After the way she left him the other night, there were no guarantees. One glimpse of his sheriff's Tahoe and she might pretend no one was home. Even if her SUV was still in the drive.

Just when he was thinking about knocking a second time, the door slowly opened.

Dressed in jeans and a bulky gray cable-knit sweater, Lacie clutched the knob, looking far more vulnerable than the stubborn woman he was used to butting heads with. Her caramel-colored hair was pulled back into a messy ponytail and lines he'd never noticed before creased her forehead, as though she were just as distressed about Monday night's conversation as he was. Making it even more imperative that they talk.

After a long moment, she cracked open the storm door. "What's up?"

"I was wondering if you and Kenzie would meet me at Mouse's later today. After my shift."

"I don't know, Matt. I'm pretty busy getting things ready for Thanksgiving tomorrow. Lots of cooking and such."

"It won't take long. I promise. Just give me thirty minutes."

She studied him, her gaze narrowing before she glanced back into the house, and he couldn't help wondering if she was looking at Kenzie. When she looked at him again, she let go a sigh. "I suppose I can afford thirty minutes to meet and talk about your director duties…and let you see Kenzie."

Let him see Kenzie? Did that mean she believed he was Kenzie's father?

"I get off at five. How about five thirty?"

She nodded. "That should be fine."

His hopes soared. "Okay. I'll see you then."

Excitement coursed through his body as he dashed back down the walk and climbed into his vehicle. He could hardly wait until tonight. Though he was also a little on the nervous side about spending time with Kenzie. It was one thing when he believed her just any other little girl, but now that he knew she was his own flesh and blood, his daughter, well, he wasn't quite sure what to do.

Driving away from Lacie's, he remembered Kenzie's birthday. He needed to get her a gift.

With that in mind, he headed straight for the toy store. Yet once he was inside, he found himself overwhelmed by the multitude of books, dolls, stuffed animals, games, you name it. There were things for babies and toddlers. Little kids and big kids. Outdoor toys, indoor toys.

Then it hit him. He knew absolutely nothing about Kenzie. Her likes and dislikes. What kind of toys she preferred, her favorite food, even her favorite color.

Sadness mingled with anger, twisting his gut. Thanks to Marissa, he'd missed out on everything. Every birthday, every first. So many years that could never be recaptured.

His body sagged under the weight of grief. Maybe he shouldn't get Kenzie anything. At least not until he knew her better.

He started toward the door.

"Can I help you find something?"

He turned to see Hank Marshall approaching. Hank was close to his father's age and the owner of Ouray's lone toy store. The man always claimed he loved what he did because he was nothing but a big kid himself.

"No, that won't be—"

Hank continued toward him, undeterred. "Since I usually don't see you in here, Matt, I'm guessing you're looking for a gift."

"I was, yes. But—"

"Boy or a girl?"

"Girl."

"That would explain the distressed look on your face." The older man who'd always reminded him of Mr. Rogers smiled. "How old is she?"

"Five. It's a—a birthday present." Matt swiped a hand over the sweat suddenly beading his brow.

"Well, we'll just have to find her something special."

Matt glimpsed a stack of oversize stuffed animals. "How about that stuffed dog? Do you think she'd like that?"

"For about ten minutes."

"Oh." Matt felt his shoulders droop.

"Follow me." Hank walked deeper into the store. "Kids that age want to be entertained, but they also want to be challenged. After all, they'll soon be starting school."

School? But she was so small.

Ten minutes later, Matt was feeling much better about the whole gift thing. With Hank's help, he finally decided on a set of wooden puzzle boards with pictures and letters, though, just for good measure, Matt also threw in a small stuffed kitten.

Armed with a gift bag brimming with colorful tissue paper, he exited the store, even more eager for his meeting tonight. Unfortunately, that made the rest of the day stretch on forever. Until a call came in late afternoon about an accident north of town.

He barreled down Highway 550, sirens blaring. Approaching the scene, he saw vehicles lining the road. He methodically maneuvered past them, taking in his surroundings. The sun was shining and the road was dry, so weather couldn't have been an issue. Nonetheless, traffic was at a standstill and that usually spelled bad news.

Moments later, he spotted a late-model sedan to his right, nose-first in the ditch. In the middle of the road, an older-model pickup truck sat at an angle, straddling both north and southbound lanes. The driver's-side bumper was crumpled and the headlight crushed.

He parked and exited his Tahoe as the two occupants of the car emerged with the assistance of passersby. Glancing toward the truck, he saw only one person standing guard, but making no attempt to help the person or persons inside.

By the time EMS arrived, he understood why. The elderly gentleman in the truck was deceased, though seemingly from natural causes, not as a result of the accident. According to the occupants of the sedan, the truck drifted into their lane and while they tried to swerve out of the way, the pickup struck the back end of their vehicle, sending them off the road.

In the end, the highway was temporarily shut down, the middle-aged man and woman in the sedan were treated at the scene and released and, thanks to paperwork and reports, Matt missed his meeting with Lacie and Kenzie by a long shot.

With no way to get in touch with Lacie, he went straight to the Collier house from the sheriff's office, hoping and praying that Kenzie was still awake. And that Lacie would understand.

With Kenzie's gift in his hand and his heart in his throat, he knocked on the door.

A moment later, the porch light came on, the door jerked open and a very unhappy-looking Lacie promptly joined him on the porch.

"Uh-uh. No." She wagged a finger. "You are not going to do this."

"Do what?"

"Kenzie and I waited for you at Mouse's for nearly an hour. And now you think you can just show up here and everything will be hunky-dory?" Her words rose into the chilly night air. She crossed her arms over her chest. "I will *not* let you do that to her. Not now, not ever."

"I'm sorry, Lacie. I promise you, I had no intention of missing our meeting. I've been looking forward to it all day. But there was a fatality accident this afternoon, so I got held over until just a few minutes ago."

"And you couldn't have called?" Her glare only intensified his unease.

"I don't have your number. And it wasn't like I had the time to search for your mother's."

After a silent moment, she took a step closer. "Look, even if a DNA test proves that you're Kenzie's father, you're going to have to earn the right to be a daddy. So don't think you can just step into our life and take over. Because we've done fine without you."

Staring down at her, he shifted the bag from one hand to the next, understanding her desire to protect Kenzie. But then, it wasn't as if he'd ever had a say in the matter.

Her irritated gaze lowered. "What's in the bag?"

"A birthday present for Kenzie. I picked it up this afternoon, before the call came in." And he'd been praying ever since that it was something Kenzie would enjoy. That is, if Lacie allowed him to give it to her.

"Sorry, but it'll have to wait for some other time."

He wanted to argue with her, to tell her he wasn't that kind of guy, but knew it would do no good. She'd made up her mind.

Turning, he stepped off the porch, determination coursing through his veins. No matter what he had to do or how long it took, he would earn Lacie's trust and be the dad that Kenzie deserved.

Chapter Six

Lacie pushed the door closed, leaned against it and let go a sigh. She was proud of herself for standing her ground and giving voice to those things that had been festering inside her all evening. She would not let Matt force his way into their lives and do whatever he pleased. So what if he had a valid excuse for not meeting them earlier? She was the one who'd been stuck at Mouse's with a five-year-old ogling all that chocolate.

"Who was at the door?" Mom eyed her from the kitchen.

"Matt." Turning, she peered through the sidelight. Why was he still out there?

"What did he want?" Mom tossed over her shoulder.

"He had a *g-i-f-t* for someone." Lacie had to spell out the word, otherwise Kenzie would be asking all kinds of questions. "But I told him he'd have to wait." She nudged the sheer curtain ever so slightly with her finger. Just enough to get a better view.

He hadn't even gotten into his Tahoe. He just stood beside it, staring at the ground with that stupid gift hanging from his hand.

"Why would you do that?" asked Mom.

Yeah. Would it have killed you to let him give her the present?

Straightening, she let the curtain fall back into place. She was not the bad guy here. She was simply trying to protect her niece.

You could give the guy a chance.

Huffing out a breath, she reached for the knob. "Fine." She pushed the storm door open and poked her head outside. "Matt."

When he looked her way, she motioned for him to come in.

"Thank you." His smile was one of relief as he stepped onto the porch and followed her into the house.

"Look who's here." With Matt now at her side, she closed the door and continued through the living room to the adjoining kitchen.

Kenzie popped her head up from her coloring book at the kitchen table, while Mom poured herself another cup of tea at the island.

"Always a pleasure, Matt." Mom smiled.

"Trust me, the pleasure is mine." Stopping behind the sofa, he breathed deep. "Something sure smells good. You must be cooking up a storm in there, Barbara."

"Not me." Her mother picked up her mug, bobbing the teabag up and down. "Lacie's the one who's been baking all day. Pumpkin bread, pumpkin pie..."

His attention shifted to Lacie. "I didn't realize you were so domestic."

The sincerity in his dark gaze had her looking away. "There are probably a lot of things about me you don't know." And she'd just as soon keep it that way.

She moved into the kitchen.

Matt did, too, setting his gift bag atop the island before continuing on to the table. "Hi, Kenzie."

The awe in his voice took Lacie by surprise.

The little girl paused, yellow crayon still in hand, and peered up at him. "Want to color with me?"

Seemingly nervous, he darted a glance to Lacie.

She reluctantly nodded her approval.

"It's been a long time but, sure, I'd love to color with you." He pulled out the next chair and sat down beside Kenzie. "What are we coloring?"

"I'm doing the kitty book," Kenzie explained, "but you can color in my pony book." She dropped the crayon and pulled another book from the small stack beside her.

"I like ponies," he said.

"Me, too." Kenzie opened the book and thumbed through it before setting it in front of Matt. "You can color this horsie. He's a boy."

"Oh, I see. What color do you think he should be?"

She dug through her crayon box, coming up with two blue crayons she promptly handed to Matt. "Boy horsies are only blue."

"Really?" Practically beaming, he looked from Kenzie to Lacie and back. "I don't think I knew that."

Arms crossed over her chest, Lacie leaned against the island, watching as Matt set to work with the dark blue crayon.

She still didn't want him here. Appearances could be deceiving. What if he wasn't the good guy he seemed to be?

She felt a nudge against her elbow.

"Still skeptical?" her mother whispered.

Again focusing on the duo at the table, Lacie found it impossible to ignore the resemblance. Seeing Matt and Kenzie side by side…the hair, the eyes, the shape of their faces. Even the silly way each had their tongues peeking out of the corner of their mouths as they colored.

She hugged herself tighter. “Until proven otherwise, yes.” Yet as she watched the two of them, an ache filled her heart that was as unexpected as it was unwanted. Why had Marissa never said anything? All these years she let everyone believe Grant was Kenzie’s father and that he’d run out on them, robbing Kenzie of the father she deserved and Matt or whoever of the right to know his daughter.

How could her sister do such a thing? And now that the truth had been revealed, where did that leave Lacie?

Yeah, she needed to get him out of here as soon as possible. “Matt, wasn’t there something you wanted to give Kenzie?”

“Oh, man, sorry. I got distracted.” He pushed away from the table to retrieve the brightly colored bag. “Happy birthday, Kenzie.” He handed her his gift.

Her niece’s brown eyes went wide as she took hold. “For me?”

“That was pretty nice of Matt, wasn’t it, Kenzie?” Mom watched from the other side of the island.

“Uh-huh.” Standing on her chair, the little girl tossed the pink and orange tissue paper aside and peered into the bag. “A kitty!” She reached inside and pulled out a small gray kitten with a pale pink bow and brilliant blue eyes. “I love her!”

Hugging the toy to her chest, Kenzie looked at Matt. “What’s her name?”

“She doesn’t have one yet,” said Matt. “What do you think her name should be?”

Kenzie scrunched her face up as she studied her gift. "Starlight."

"Starlight?" Matt and Lacie said simultaneously.

"Uh-huh." Kenzie tucked the kitten under her arm. "Her name is Starlight."

Mom shrugged, eyeing Lacie over the rim of her mug. "Reminds me of someone who insisted on naming our toy poodle Killer."

"Hey, the way he used to growl and bare his teeth..."

"There's something else in there, too." Matt pointed to the gift bag.

Setting the kitten on the table, Kenzie again reached inside the sack. "What are these?"

Lacie moved beside her for a closer look. "They're puzzles, Kenz." She glanced at Matt. "You like puzzles. And these have words and letters that will help you get ready for school next year." The perfect combination of education and fun. He'd really put some thought into his gift.

"Yeah." The little girl again picked up the kitten, tucking it under her arm.

Lacie touched her shoulder. "What do you say to Matt?"

"Thank you."

"You're welcome." The guy couldn't seem to stop smiling.

Tilting her head, Kenzie continued, "Can I play with them now?"

"Sure." Matt quickly jerked his head toward Lacie. "That is, if your aunt Lacie says it's all right."

How could she say no? Though it had nothing to do with Matt and everything to do with Kenzie. "Go ahead."

Watching Matt with Kenzie, Lacie couldn't help noticing the wonder in his eyes. But how would he feel a month or a year from now when the novelty of having a child wore off? Or when Kenzie was sick or throwing a temper tantrum? Lacie had altered her entire life for Kenzie. And couldn't imagine being without her.

"Matt—" Mom eyed him across the kitchen "—would you care to join us for Thanksgiving dinner tomorrow?"

Lacie glared at her mother. A few days ago the woman didn't even want to celebrate Thanksgiving, and now she's inviting Matt as though he's part of the family? She could have at least run the idea past Lacie first.

"Thank you, Barbara, but I have to work tomorrow."

Phew!

"Perhaps you can stop by in the evening then," Mom continued. "I'm sure we'll have plenty of leftovers."

Looked like Lacie was going to have to sit down with her mother and set some boundaries. Because the last thing she wanted to do was spend all her time with Matt Stephens. Not when being near him reminded her of the feelings she'd once had for him—and the ache of rejection when he'd chosen her sister.

While Mom gave Kenzie her bath a short time later, Lacie walked Matt to his vehicle.

"The gift was a nice gesture. Thank you."

"No, thank *you* for understanding and for letting me see her." He paused at the curb and looked down at her. "This was, without a doubt, the best night I've ever had. Kenzie is amazing."

Despite wearing her coat, she shivered in the night air. "Yes, she is."

His expression took on a more serious note. "I owe you an apology, though."

"For?" Had he lied to her about the accident? Not that she couldn't easily find out. This was Ouray, after all. Population one thousand.

"For accusing you of hiding Kenzie's paternity from me. I know that you were just as clueless as I was. And if you want me to do some DNA testing or something..."

"Yes, I plan to do that right away." Especially after seeing him and Kenzie side by side. "And just so you'll know, I'm not proud of what my sister did."

Hands shoved in the pockets of his uniform pants, he shrugged. "What's done is done. However, now that the truth is out, I have every intention of building a relationship with Kenzie. I want to be a part of her life."

"You...do know that we'll be going back to Denver after the first of the year, right?" Sooner, if she could find a job.

Looking out over the neighborhood, he nodded. "I'll do whatever I have to."

Lacie's heart nearly stopped beating. Her stomach sank to her knees.

That could only mean one thing. He was going to try to take Kenzie.

Watching Kenzie as she enjoyed a slice of pumpkin pie with him the next night at the Colliers' kitchen table only amplified Matt's knowledge that his life had been forever changed. However, he still had a play to direct. And with only three days until their first real rehearsal, he was growing more nervous by the minute.

Sure, he'd gone over the notes Lacie had sent him

regarding the duties of a director, but that didn't mean he understood them. At least not completely. What he needed was to sit down with her and thoroughly discuss his role. Something he hoped to do tonight. That is, if he could get her to stick around long enough. Seemed she'd been all over this house since he arrived an hour ago, needing to take care of one thing or another. Anything except remaining in the same room with him. As though she were avoiding him.

"Are you finished with your pie, Kenzie?" Barbara brushed a hand across her granddaughter's back.

"Uh-huh."

"How about you, Matt?" The woman turned her attention to him. "Care for some more?"

"No, thank you, Barbara. I'm good." He patted his overstuffed belly, still amazed at how much turkey and dressing he'd eaten. "Matter of fact, I'm more than good."

She chuckled and took his plate along with Kenzie's and started toward the sink.

"I thought Lacie was going to be helping you at The Paisley Elk," he called after her.

"She is. I wanted to give her a few days to settle in. She'll start Saturday."

"Ah, Small Business Saturday."

"That's right." She rinsed the dishes before putting them into the dishwasher. "One of my biggest days of the year."

"What are you going to do with Kenzie?" He glanced at the child as she climbed out of her chair. "Where are you going?"

"I'm going to get my puzzles," she said before scurrying into the adjacent living room.

Her grandmother watched after her, smiling. "She'll come to the shop with us. I've got some toys and a little table there for her. I think she'll do just fine."

"It's time for somebody to get ready for bed." Lacie appeared from the hallway.

"Aww…" Kenzie frowned. "But Matt and I were going to play puzzles."

Lacie paused beside the island, perching a hand on her hip. "Sorry, Kenzikins, you've had a long day with no nap."

"But I'm not tired." The kid's words were quickly followed by a yawn.

"Yeah… I can see that," Lacie said flatly.

"I've got an idea." Barbara closed the dishwasher and moved toward her granddaughter. "How about I give you your bath again—"

Kenzie's eyes widened. "With bubbles?"

Barbara grinned. "With lots of bubbles. And what do you say we let your new mermaid doll take a bath with you."

The little girl immediately returned the puzzles she was holding to the shelf and took off down the hall. "Come on, Grandma."

Matt couldn't help laughing. "I don't think I've ever seen anyone shift gears so fast."

Shaking her head, Lacie chuckled. "You haven't seen anything yet."

"No—" he stood from the table, pushed in his chair "—but I'm looking forward to it."

Lacie's smile evaporated then. "I should probably go check on them." So she was avoiding him.

"Why?" He crossed to where she stood. "It's not like your mother hasn't bathed Kenzie before." After a silent moment, he continued, “Besides, I have something I’d like to talk to you about.”

“I…really should get this food put away.” She side-stepped into the kitchen.

“That’s okay. We can talk while you work.”

If Lacie appeared nervous before, she looked down-right petrified as she picked up the plastic container of leftover turkey.

“Is something wrong?”

Her gaze jerked to his. “No. I’m just concerned about Kenzie, that’s all.”

“Well, I have no doubt that she’s in good hands. Be-sides, they’re right down the hall.”

Lacie nodded, opening the refrigerator. “So what is it you wanted to talk about?”

“The play.”

She set the turkey inside, her shoulders suddenly less rigid. “The play?” Why did she look surprised?

“Yes.” Rounding the island, he picked up the casse-role dish with the dressing and handed it to her. “Re-hearsals start Sunday and I’m scared witless.”

“Didn’t you get my notes?” She tucked it away.

“I’ve been going over them all day. But no matter how hard I try I can’t seem to wrap my brain around this whole directing thing.” Pressing the foil around the edges of the pie plate, he looked her way. “You want this in there?”

“Sure.” She took hold. “Then you’re obviously over-thinking it. Hand me the gravy, please.” She pointed. “This is a small production. All you really need to do is make sure people know their blocks—”

Handing her the bowl, he lifted a brow. “Which are…?”

"Where the actors are to be onstage at any given point. You'll guide them during rehearsals, so by the time opening night arrives, everyone will have things down." She closed the fridge and, for the first time tonight, seemed to relax. "Actually, Mrs. Nichols did the lion's share of a director's job before you ever stepped into the role." Lacie grabbed a rag from the sink. "She casted the play, planned the rehearsals, established a stage manager… Now you just need to bring the play to life."

"Um—" he scratched his head "—I thought that's what the actors did."

"They do." She wiped down the island. "They bring *your* vision to life."

"My vision." He wasn't sure he had one.

Pausing, she set a hand to her hip. "Have you seen *The Bishop's Wife*?"

"Are you kidding? I've been watching the movie at least once a day since I agreed to direct."

"Good. That should give you a basic understanding then." Returning to the sink, she rinsed the rag and turned off the water. "About those actors, though." She faced him now. "I think it might be best if I step down. I only have a minor role, so someone else could easily cover it."

What little hope had begun to take root vanished. "What? Why would you do that?"

She shrugged, grabbed a pot holder from beside the stove and tossed it into a drawer. "With all that's happened this week, things that have come to light, I just feel like it might be awkward."

"Not for me, it wouldn't." Panic morphed into a plea. He took hold of her arms. "I'd be lost without you, Lace.

I can't risk messing this up." The intensity of his words had him quickly letting go. How had he come to depend on her so quickly? As though she were his compass, pointing him in the right direction. Just as she'd been back in school, before he'd lost his way.

"You keep saying that." She looked at him curiously. "I understand that you don't want to fail your mother, but…why are you so afraid?"

Was it that obvious?

Scratching his head, he turned away. After the conversation with his father the other day, his fear of failure was probably greater than ever. But did he dare share that with Lacie? Reveal the chinks in his already loosely held-together armor?

At this point, he supposed he had nothing to lose. Not if he hoped to talk her into continuing on with the play.

He drew in a deep breath before facing her again. "My dad and I aren't on the greatest of terms. Matter of fact, we barely speak at all."

"But I thought the two of you were close. I mean, you worked alongside him at the ranch."

"That was a long time ago." He met her gaze. "Nowadays, he thinks I'm nothing but a screwup."

"Aw, Matt, we all have issues with our parents, but I'm sure—"

"He blames me for my mother's death."

Her mouth formed an O before she pressed her lips together.

Taking a couple of steps, he glanced down the empty hallway before saying any more. "She had cancer and we knew she was nearing the end." His attention shifted back to Lacie. "Dad was out working cattle and Mama was all alone when I came into the house. We visited for a while and she mentioned that she wanted to see Chessie, her horse. It was a nice day. Warm, no wind, so I carried her out to the barn. Even set up a chair for her so she could spend some time without getting worn out."

Arms crossed, Lacie leaned her backside against the counter. "I do remember how much she loved the horses."

He couldn't help smiling. "Yes, she did. And it made her happy to be near them again. But when Dad walked into the barn and saw Mama, well, he wasn't happy, but he kept his cool. At least until Mama fell asleep later. Then he asked me to meet him in the barn. When I did, he went off on me."

Her brow puckered. "What did he say?"

Spotting the forgotten container of cranberry sauce, he picked it up and passed it to Lacie. "He was furious that I'd brought her outside. Accused me of trying to kill her, when all I wanted to do was make her happy."

"Of course you did." She watched him over her shoulder as she again opened the fridge.

"She died the following week. Dad told me that I was nothing but a screwup, pointing out all the things I'd done wrong in my life. Everything from the underage drinking incident after graduation, even though the charges were dropped, to leaving the ranch behind and joining the navy without even consulting him, then getting kicked out—"

"You were kicked out of the navy?" Closing the door, she looked at him.

Why had he said that? "I punched a guy who'd had too much to drink and was getting aggressive with a woman. Problem was, he was one of my superior officers. So I ended up having to choose between a reduction in rank or a general discharge. I took the discharge."

"How long ago was that?"

"Almost five years. Shortly after my mother got sick."

"All because you were trying to help someone?"

"Yeah, well, that's not how my father saw it."

"What did he say?"

"Nothing. He simply shook his head and walked away." Matt raked a hand through his hair. "I can only imagine what he'll have to say when he learns I fathered a child out of wedlock."

She was back against the counter. "When are you going to tell him?"

"The question isn't when, it's if." Suddenly weary, he started toward the door. "Tell Kenzie I said good-night."

"What do you mean *if*?" Lacie followed him. "Suppose you are Kenzie's father. Is that something you're ashamed of?"

He lifted his coat from the rack, feeling as though he couldn't get anything right. "No." Looking down, he saw the fire in Lacie's eyes. "I could never be ashamed of Kenzie. Just my actions, that's all."

She continued to glare at him before finally looking away.

He couldn't blame her for not trusting him. Though he really wished she would.

Arms crossed, she studied the carpet. "Well, you don't have to worry about the play."

Hope ignited. "Are you saying you'll stay?"

She met his gaze. "Not only am I going to stay, I'm going to see to it you put on the best play this town has ever seen."

Chapter Seven

Lacie entered the Wright Opera House Sunday afternoon, wishing she had kept her big mouth shut.

I'm going to see to it you put on the best play this town has ever seen.

What had she been thinking? One week ago, she rued the sight of Matt Stephens. Now she'd barely gone a day without seeing him. And even after he'd said he would do whatever he had to in order to be with Kenzie.

Lacie knew good and well what that meant. Yet she'd thrown away her only opportunity to bow out of the play. All because he was a wounded soul who wanted to make his mother—and father—proud. Sure, he and his father were estranged, but behind that angry facade, Matt wanted nothing more than to earn his father's approval. And like a fool, she said she'd help him.

Continuing past the box office, she took hold of the theater's original walnut railing and stormed up the stairs, thankful for the burgundy-and-gold carpet that muted the thudding of her boots. She needed to have her head examined.

Or better yet, she needed to find a new job and fast.

One that would get her away from Ouray well before December 25. Otherwise, she'd never be able to give Kenzie the Christmas she deserved.

What about Matt?

She'd worry about that *if* and *when* they confirmed he was Kenzie's father.

On the second floor, she peered out the expanse of windows that overlooked Main Street. The sights and sounds of Christmas were all over town, while she and Kenzie were trapped at Scrooge Collier's house, where even the mention of the holiday was sure to bring a swift admonishment.

No kid should have to live like that.

She huffed out a breath. For today, though, she had to make it through the first play rehearsal. Not to mention four subsequent rehearsals in as many nights, culminating with performances Saturday and Sunday. Then she could finally be rid of Matt Stephens. Or, at least, no longer forced to be around him. When it came to Kenzie, though, she had a choice.

Inside the lovely old theater, she took off her coat and draped it over the back of a chair before adjusting the sparkling red scarf looped around her neck. Her mother might not celebrate Christmas, but she definitely did.

Pretending to dig for something in her purse, she discreetly surveyed the space to see who all was there. She recognized Larry Garcia, Valerie and several of the other cast members. The stage manager and, of course, Matt.

"Hi, Lacie." Clare waved as she approached from the back of the room, her long golden brown hair swaying from side to side with each movement. "How was your Thanksgiving?"

"It was good." Lacie set her purse on the chair. "How about you?"

"Crazy." Clare rolled her eyes. "All my nieces and nephews running around. My dad and brothers arguing over a football game."

Lacie tried not to laugh. While Clare might not have appreciated all that family time, Lacie would love nothing more than to be surrounded by such chaos. The way it used to be when she was young.

"Are you ladies ready to get this show on the road?"

She and Clare turned to see Valerie coming toward them. Close to Lacie's mother's age, the spunky brunette was always quick with a smile and never had a bad word to say about anyone.

"I can hardly wait." Clare, who was playing the lead role of Julia, slipped off her coat, practically bubbling with excitement.

Lacie knew how she felt. She always loved the start of a new project. Her gaze inadvertently drifted to the stage where Matt was talking with the guy in charge of the lighting. Of course, back in Denver she didn't have to work with a director who posed a threat to her on more levels than she cared to admit.

Fortunately, he seemed more interested in a successful play than zeroing in on her, so as rehearsal got under way she relaxed and began to enjoy herself. Acting was definitely a therapy for her. Escaping reality and pretending to be someone else. The fact that they were doing one of her favorite plays didn't hurt, either.

The community theater she was a part of back in Denver had put on *The Bishop's Wife* last December and Lacie had been fortunate enough to be cast in the lead role. It was the biggest role she'd ever had and was quite the undertaking, but one she would never regret. Especially with the turn her life had taken since then. This would mark the first time she'd acted since Kenzie came to live with her.

Two hours later, with a successful rehearsal behind her, Lacie met with the stage manager to discuss her costume fitting before gathering her things.

"So how'd I do?" Matt took her coat from her hand and held it up for her.

After a hesitant moment, she shoved in one arm then the other. "You did great." She shrugged the coat over her shoulders and pulled her hair from beneath the collar. "All that time you spent watching the movie and poring over the script came through in your attention to detail."

He winced. "I hope I wasn't too overbearing."

"Not at all."

"Good." He visibly relaxed. "How was your first day at the shop?"

"Surprisingly enjoyable." She buttoned her coat. "We were quite busy."

"Kenzie do okay?"

"Yeah, she had a great time." Something Lacie was more than grateful for. "You wouldn't believe what she did, though." She rested a hand on her hip. "Mom and I were both busy assisting customers, so when another lady came in, Kenzie decided to help. She marched right up to the woman and—"

What was she doing? Rattling on as though she and Matt were doing this parenting thing together. As though he were a part of their lives. So what if he was Kenzie's father? She was the guardian who'd given up everything for a child she loved more than she'd ever thought possible.

Not that that would count for much in a court of law. If Matt sued for custody of Kenzie, how could Lacie ever win?

"Go on." Matt's smile was full of anticipation. "What did she do?"

Lacie's gaze fell to the wooden planks beneath her feet as she pressed a hand against her stomach to quell the rising nausea. "I'm sorry. I'm suddenly not feeling so well."

He took a step closer, the concern in his dark eyes unnerving. "Are you okay? Would you like me to drive you home?"

"No." She picked up her purse. "I'm sure I'll be all right. I just need to lie down for a minute." *And get away from you.*

"In that case, you definitely don't need to be driving. Why don't you give me your keys? I'll drive you, then come back for my Jeep."

"No, really. That's not necessary. Kenzie isn't even home. Mom took her with her to Montrose."

"This isn't about Kenzie, it's about you."

She eyed him suspiciously, recalling the caring boy she once knew. The one who put others before himself and always looked out for his friends. Unlike her sister's, which was purely superficial, Matt's heart was what made Lacie fall in love with him all those years ago.

"I'm not taking no for an answer, Lace." Placing a hand on her shoulder, he turned her around and propelled her toward the exit. "Now let's get you home."

Matt was growing weary of Lacie's stubbornness. Particularly when her face was so pale and it was obvious she needed help.

So despite her objections, he not only took her home and escorted her inside the house, but he was determined to stay until her mother and Kenzie got home. He wanted to see for himself that she was, indeed, going to be okay.

"This is so unnecessary. You don't have to stay." She argued from the couch. "A little herbal tea and I'll be fine."

Arms crossed over his chest, he stared down at her. "Well, you're wrong. I do have to stay. However, if you'll point me in the direction of the tea, I'll be happy to fix it for you."

She huffed out a breath and looked the other way. "Never mind."

"Sorry, no can do." Whisking past her, he made his way into the kitchen and put the kettle on to boil. "Now let's see, if I were an herbal tea bag, where would I be?" He opened the cupboard next to the stove. Nope.

"You're not funny," she said.

"I wasn't trying to be." He moved on to the cupboard near the coffee maker. Score! "Man, who knew there were so many different kinds of tea?" He riffled through the plethora of boxes, locating two that said Herbal. "Which one do you want? Chamomile or ginger peach?"

"Surprise me."

A few minutes later, he returned to the sofa and handed her a steaming mug. "I decided on the ginger since it's supposed to be good for stomach problems."

She looked at him suspiciously. "How do you know that?"

"I just do." Curiosity had him wandering toward a grouping of photos on the white bookshelves against the far wall. "Oh, and be careful, it's hot." He studied a picture of Lacie and Marissa as little girls and another of them with their father when they were teenagers.

Lacie had always been more reserved than her sister. So he'd been pleasantly surprised the day she barreled up the drive of the ranch in her father's Jeep. Even if it was for nothing more than to rub in the fact that she'd gotten her driver's license before he did. Still, he liked that she'd wanted to share that momentous occasion with him.

That kind of stuff stopped after he and Marissa started dating. And though he'd never acknowledged it at the time, he missed Lacie and the camaraderie they'd once shared. She got him in a way no one else ever had.

On the next shelf, he spotted a photo of Marissa in a hospital bed, smiling and holding a newborn.

His heart twisted as he picked it up and touched a finger to Kenzie's face. *I wish I could have been there.*

Clearing the emotion that suddenly clogged his throat, he returned the picture to the shelf and went to check on Lacie.

"How is it?" He picked up the purple throw draped across the back of the sofa and laid it over her stretched-out legs before sitting down on the ottoman opposite her.

"It's fine."

Resting his forearms on his thighs, he clasped his hands together. "There's something I'd like to ask you. I'm just not quite sure how to do it."

She stared into her cup. "Just say it and get it over with." Her words held an air of defensiveness.

"I've heard the stories of how Marissa died, that she was in a car with some guy when it crashed, but...where was Kenzie?"

Finally, she looked at him, her expression softening as it so often did whenever her niece was the topic of conversation. "She was spending the night with me. Something I have thanked God for many, many times."

The corners of his mouth twitched. "Did that happen often? Kenzie staying with you." He wasn't trying to interrogate her, he simply wanted to know about Kenzie's life.

"Sometimes more often than others." She set her cup on the side table. "I never minded, though. I've loved her as though she were my own from the moment she was born." She adjusted her blanket. "I had the privilege of being Marissa's birthing coach."

"So Kenzie has known you all her life?" Something he wished he could say.

"Yeah." She met his gaze with an intensity that hadn't been there before. "There's not much I wouldn't do for that little girl."

"I know." He stretched his legs out in front of him, crossing them at the ankles. "She's blessed to have you, Lacie. Not everyone would be willing to take on the role that you have."

She lifted a shoulder. "I don't know. I think I'm the one who's blessed. There's not a day that goes by that I don't thank God for her."

"Me, either." The words seemed to fall out so naturally. Probably because they were true. "At least not since I found out about her."

Silence fell between them for so long he was afraid he'd offended her. Then again, in her eyes, he was the guy who posed a threat to something she held very dear.

"About that DNA test." She must have read his mind.

And while he knew in his heart that Kenzie was his, he understood Lacie's need for proof.

"I ordered a test kit."

He lifted a brow. "Ordered?"

"Thought that would be the most discreet way to handle this. I'll need a cheek swab from both you and Kenzie to send to the lab. We should have the results by the end of the week."

"Is it reliable?"

"One hundred percent accurate, according to the website."

Restless, he pushed to his feet and started to pace. "I want you to know that I'm not a love-'em-and-leave-'em kind of guy." He probably shouldn't have said that, but for some strange reason, it mattered what Lacie thought of him.

She lifted a shoulder. "We all make mistakes."

"I tried to stay in touch with Marissa, but she never answered my calls." He again dropped onto the ottoman. "When she finally did, she told me that she and her boyfriend were back together, so I shouldn't call anymore." Head in his hands, he stared at the carpet. "I didn't even know she had a boyfriend."

"That must have hurt."

"It did. Made me feel—"

"Like you'd been used."

For a moment he thought she was chastising him. But lifting his head, he saw only understanding in her eyes. "Something like that, yeah."

Sitting straighter, she reached for her tea. "Marissa rarely thought about anyone but Marissa." She took a sip, then cradled the cup in her hands. "I'm not saying she was a bad mother. She loved Kenzie and doted on her. But…there were times when I worried about my niece's safety."

His whole body tensed. His hands fisted. "Did she hurt her?"

"No, Marissa would never do that. But with so many men moving in and out of her life, I…had some concerns."

He knew exactly what she was talking about. "I would, too." An unexpected anger filled his words. "Sorry, that wasn't directed at you. Just the situation."

"I understand. There were times I was pretty upset myself." She set her feet to the floor. "Kenzie should have been Marissa's top priority, not Marissa."

Looking at Lacie now, he couldn't help wondering how two sisters could be so different. One self-serving, the other self-sacrificing. And while most people thought Marissa the prettier of the two Collier girls, he was beginning to see that Lacie's beauty far outshined her sister's. Hers wasn't superficial. Instead, it emanated from inside her, touching those around her.

Including him.

Chapter Eight

Lacie really needed Matt to leave.

This conversation was getting way too intense. Not only had he managed to get her to open up, sharing things she'd never shared with anyone else, she'd also seen the pain that flickered in his dark eyes when he talked about Marissa and the way she'd just cast him aside. Something Lacie had witnessed firsthand on more than one occasion. Why was it always the good guys her sister hurt?

Yes, despite being sucked in by her sister, Matt was one of the good guys. To Lacie's chagrin. Because for as much as she wanted to dislike him, she couldn't bring herself to do so. Not when he was still the same caring guy she'd once lost her heart to.

However, she did not need or want a man in her life. Especially one who held the power to take away the one thing she cherished most in this world.

So she practically jumped for joy when she heard the garage door open. "Sounds like Mom and Kenzie are back."

Thank You, Lord.

Matt stood as the door leading from the kitchen to the garage burst open a few moments later.

"Matt!" Kenzie cheered when she spotted him. She charged across the room, her light-up shoes flickering, and stopped right in front of him.

"Hey, there, small fry," he said, looking down at her.

She giggled. "Want to play puzzles with me now?"

His smile reached from ear to ear. "I live to play puzzles with you."

The kid giggled again. Did he have her wrapped around his finger or what? Or maybe it was the other way around.

Unfortunately for Lacie, though, it meant he wouldn't be leaving right away.

She tossed the throw off her legs and stood as her mother entered, carrying several plastic bags and a massive pizza from the supercenter deli.

"Let me help you, Mom." Grateful for the distraction, she hurried into the kitchen and took hold of the bags.

"Thank you, dear." Her mother set the unbaked pizza on the counter. "Matt, I didn't know you were here. I'm glad I decided to get the larger pizza."

He strode toward them. "Lacie wasn't feeling well after rehearsal, so I wanted to make sure she was okay."

Mom's gaze shifted to Lacie. "Are you all right, dear?"

Not that she was ever really sick. At least, not in the way Matt thought.

"Yes, I'm feeling much better now thanks to Matt and some ginger tea."

"Good," said Mom, turning on the oven. "Ginger is always helpful for an upset stomach."

Matt nudged Lacie with his elbow. "See."

"Come on, Matt." Kenzie tugged on his other hand. "Let's play."

Mom looked at the two of them. "It would appear that you're in high demand around here, Matt."

"I wouldn't have it any other way." He winked at Lacie before heading around the island to join Kenzie at the table.

Unexpected heat crept into her cheeks.

Perhaps *she* should consider leaving.

She didn't, though, and even after Matt had gone home and she helped Kenzie into bed later, thoughts of her time alone with him continued to play through her mind like a sappy movie. The way he'd insisted on taking care of her, even when all she'd really been was heartsick, had her feeling a bit guilty. No one had paid her that much attention in a long time. And while she didn't want to like it, she did.

With Marissa's old Strawberry Shortcake lamp glowing on the night stand, Lacie sat on the edge of the bed as Kenzie pulled her princess comforter up to her neck.

"We seed Santa Clause at the store."

"You did?" Lacie brushed an unruly strand of dark hair away from the child's face.

"Grandma wouldn't let me say hi to him, though."

"Well, maybe we can say hi to him later."

Kenzie pouted then, her brow puckering as she crossed her arms over her chest. "She wouldn't let me look at the Christmas trees, either."

Lacie's heart squeezed. How she wanted this Christmas to be extra special for Kenzie. Unless her mother had a change of heart, though… "Grandma was probably in a hurry to get home."

"But we need a Christmas tree so it can be Christmas."

Lacie swallowed the lump that lodged in her throat. "Kenzie, Christmas is in our hearts. Not in a tree or the decorations. Sometimes we forget that Christmas is Jesus's birthday."

"He was a little, bitty baby." Kenzie sounded like a baby as she held her hands close together.

"That's right."

"But then He growed up to be big." She thrust her arms wide. "Like Matt."

Lacie couldn't help chuckling. "He did."

Kenzie again snuggled under her covers and yawned. "I like Matt."

Lacie thought about all she'd discovered about him today. "Want to know a secret?"

Kenzie nodded, her eyes wide.

"I like him, too." Making it even more imperative that she keep her distance. Although, considering they had rehearsals the rest of the week, that was going to be a challenge.

Smiling, Kenzie held her arms up for a hug.

"Good night, sweetie." Lacie hugged her tight. "I love you."

"Night, night."

Out in the hallway, Lacie closed the door and drew in a deep breath.

Oh, God, I know Christmas isn't about trees, decorations or gifts, but I so want Kenzie to be able to experience all of the joy this special season has to offer. Please, soften Mom's heart and allow her to see things through her granddaughter's eyes.

With Kenzie's words still ringing in her ears, she continued down the hallway and into the living room.

Mom sat in her chair near the window, reading as

usual. She glanced at Lacie as she entered. "Everything okay?"

"Yeah." Pausing behind the sofa, she dug her fingers into the plush throw. "Can I get you some more tea or anything?"

"No. I just poured a fresh cup, so I'm fine."

While her mother went back to reading, Lacie rounded the end of the couch, mustering all of the courage she could find, and sat down. "Mom, I'd like you to reconsider having a Christmas tree for Kenzie. She's just a little girl. Next year, you can go back to—"

"We already had this discussion, Lacie." The woman never even looked up. "I have deliberately chosen *not* to celebrate Christmas."

Lacie willed herself to remain calm, though everything inside her was screaming. "No, you've deliberately chosen to be mad at God for taking Daddy. Do you really think you're going to get back at Him by refusing to celebrate His Son's birthday?"

Without even flinching, her mother finally met her gaze. "I really don't care what God thinks." Then she went back to reading her book. Or at least pretending to.

Lacie's ire did spark now. She shot to her feet, hands fisted at her sides. "I'm sorry you feel that way, Mom. However, I am going to do everything in my power to make this the most special, most amazing Christmas that Kenzie has ever seen."

Mom lowered her book and took off her readers. "There will be no Christmas tree in this house." Her voice was firm, yet even. "No decorations, *no* celebrations."

Lacie thought of her father, her bottom lip trembling. He was the godliest man she'd ever known. One who reveled in the holidays, sharing the good news of Jesus with everyone he came in contact with. "Daddy would be so disappointed in you."

Turning on her heel, she walked to her room and dropped onto the bed, a flurry of emotions darting through her. *God, what am I going to do?*

Matt stood in front of the Collier house Friday evening, filled with gratitude. Not only were rehearsals finally over, Lacie had received the results of the DNA test today, proving beyond a shadow of a doubt that he was, indeed, Kenzie's father. A sense of pride wove through him. He had a daughter. Now if he could just survive this weekend's performances.

Unfortunately, all of the rehearsals this week hadn't allowed him much time with Kenzie. Just a few minutes here and there. So tonight he was looking forward to taking her and Lacie to the town's Christmas tree lighting. The annual event was one of his favorites of WinterFest. Carols, hot cocoa and, of course, the lighting of the tree. He couldn't think of a better way to start the holiday season.

With a spring in his step, he headed up the walk. But before he even made it to the porch, the door flew open and Kenzie bolted toward him in her coat, snow pants and winter boots.

"Matt!" She threw her arms around his legs and squeezed with all her might.

The gesture nearly knocked him over, both physically and emotionally. The way she'd so readily accepted him. He couldn't remember the last time he'd felt so much love or had someone so genuinely happy to see him. He could definitely get used to this.

He lifted her into his arms. "That was some greeting."

"I misseded you." She patted his cheeks, the look in her eyes as sincere as it was innocent.

"I missed you, too, small fry."

She giggled then, a sound he would never tire of hearing, and hugged him around the neck.

"Where's your aunt Lacie?" His breath hung in the chilly night air.

"Right here."

He and Kenzie both turned to see her coming toward them, wearing a light gray puffer jacket over a pair of jeans, a white scarf and a white knit cap.

"You look great." Then again, she always looked good.

"Thank you." Pink tinged her cheeks. "Just trying to keep warm. Which reminds me—" she pulled a small pair of gloves from her pocket "—we need to put your mittens on, Kenzie."

The child held out her hands, allowing Lacie to assist her.

"Are we ready now?" He set Kenzie to the ground.

"Yes!" she cheered.

Lacie tugged on her own gloves. "I believe so."

Through the cold night air, the three of them proceeded the few blocks to the center of town, Matt on one side of Kenzie, Lacie on the other, each holding her hand. Almost as though they were a family. They walked along the sidewalk, past homes with inflatable snowmen and Santas in their yards, others with light displays and most with Christmas trees in their front windows.

"Are you guys getting ready for Christmas yet?" He hadn't thought much about it, but was excited that he'd get to spend this one with his daughter.

"No." Lacie kept her gaze fixed straight ahead, her expression flat. "We've been busy at the shop this week."

"Well, we're barely into December." He shrugged. "You still have plenty of time."

"Hey, Matt," he heard as they rounded the corner onto Main Street.

Turning, he saw his brother Andrew, his wife, Carly, and their ten-year-old daughter, Megan, coming up behind them.

"I thought that was you." His brother looked surprised. Probably because he was used to seeing Matt alone.

"I wondered if you'd be here." Matt's gaze moved from Andrew to Carly. "You remember—"

"Lacie…" A smiling Carly moved in for a hug, her blond curls peeking out from beneath her knit hat. "I haven't seen you in forever." She released her. "When did you get into town?"

He'd forgotten the two women knew each other. Carly had been a couple of grades ahead of them, but everyone knew everyone at Ouray's only school.

"Last week. Kenzie—" Lacie nodded toward her niece "—and I are helping Mom at the store for a while."

"Oh, you two will have to drop by some time then, so we can catch up." Carly touched her daughter's shoulder. "Megan, this is my old friend Lacie."

Bundled up in a purple puffer and purple hat, her strawberry blond hair splayed around her shoulders, his niece smiled.

"Hi, Megan," said Lacie. "This is Kenzie."

While the females continued to chat, Megan and

Kenzie becoming fast friends, Matt took a step back with his brother.

"That's Marissa's daughter, right?" Andrew studied the little girl and Matt couldn't help wondering if his brother could sense that same familiarity he'd had when he first met Kenzie.

"Yes." He leaned closer. "And mine, too."

Andrew stared at him, confused, before looking to Kenzie and back again. "She's your daughter?" he whispered.

"I'll fill you in later." He kept his voice low. "Suffice to say, I only recently found out. Yes, Lacie knows, but Kenzie does not, so mum's the word."

"You got it, bro." A still-looking-stunned Andrew patted him on the back. "Congratulations."

His heart swelling with pride, Matt rejoined the women. "Hey, we'd better get on down to the tree lighting before we miss it."

They continued along the street, Lacie and Carly chatting all the way, as were Megan and Kenzie, until they reached the corner of Main and 7th Avenue. The still-darkened Christmas tree was surrounded by revelers singing "We Wish You a Merry Christmas."

Each of the adults and Megan were handed a piece of paper with the words to the songs they'd be singing. Megan shared hers with Kenzie, even though Kenzie didn't know how to read. Still, he appreciated the gesture.

After a couple more carols and some hot chocolate to chase away the chill, the mayor thanked everyone for coming then started the countdown to the lighting.

"Ten, nine..."

"This is it." Matt lifted Kenzie into his arms so she

could have a better view. He could tell by the way she kept looking around that she wasn't quite sure what was going on.

Lacie must have noticed it, too. Taking hold of Kenzie's hand, she pointed to the tree. "Look, sweetie. They're going to turn the lights on."

"Three, two, one—"

Cheers erupted from the crowd, but Matt kept his gaze fixed on Kenzie.

Her gasp and wide eyes when they flipped the switch were priceless. "I want a Christmas tree like that." She pointed.

"Pretty cool, huh?" He joined his fellow townsfolk in a round of "Oh, Christmas Tree" until he felt Lacie beside him.

"Watch Kenzie for me." The distressed look on her face tore at his heart. And as she turned to walk away, he was pretty sure he saw tears in her eyes.

What could have happened? Had he done something wrong?

Whatever it was, he had to find out.

He caught Andrew's and Carly's attention. "Would you two mind keeping an eye on Kenzie for a few minutes? I need to check on Lacie."

"Is everything okay?" asked Carly.

"That's what I intend to find out." He set Kenzie to the ground. "I need you to stay with Megan and her parents for a few minutes. I promise, I'll be right back."

"Can I have more hot chocolate?" She held out her empty cup.

Carly took hold of it. "Of course you can." She eyed her daughter. "Come on, Megan. Let's get some more cocoa."

Matt scanned the area, looking to see where Lacie had gone. Finally spotting her across the street, he made his way to her.

Her back was to him, so he moved in front of her to discover she was crying.

"What's wrong?" He instinctively put an arm around her.

"I'm sorry." While people continued to sing behind them, she dabbed at her face with a tissue. "It's just that Kenzie was so happy."

"And that's a bad thing?"

"No." She sniffed. "But I wanted to make this Christmas special for her and I can't."

Because she'd lost her job. "Lace, if this has to do with money, I'm more than happy to—"

"No, it's not the money." She drew in a breath. "It's my mother." She looked up at him. "She hasn't celebrated Christmas since my dad died and she's not willing to make any exceptions."

He continued to watch her. "Not even for Kenzie?"

Lacie shook her head. "She refuses to let us have a tree or anything that even remotely resembles Christmas."

"That's crazy."

Her tears were gone now. "No, that's a bitter woman who's mad at God."

No wonder Lacie was so upset. Kenzie was just a kid. And this would be her first Christmas since her mother died. Of course her aunt wanted to make it special.

For that matter, *he* wanted to make it special. He couldn't let his little girl not have a Christmas. Especially when it was the first one he'd get to spend with her.

He laid his gloved hands atop Lacie's delicate shoulders. "All right then, we'll just have to do Christmas at my house."

"Your house?" Her pretty gaze searched his.

"Yes." And the more he thought about it, the more he liked the idea. "We'll have to wait until the play is over, but maybe Monday we can all go to Montrose. We'll pick up a tree and some decorations and we'll give Kenzie the best Christmas a kid could ever have."

He felt her body relax.

And the smile she sent him reached deep inside, warming every part of him.

"Kenzie is one fortunate little girl."

"Yes, she is." He touched a finger to Lacie's cheek. "Because she's got the best aunt ever."

Chapter Nine

Opening night had arrived. Matt wasn't quite as nervous as he'd thought he would be. Still, he prayed things would go well. He did not want to shame his mother's legacy.

Backstage, he fingered the burgundy velvet curtain just far enough apart to watch as people arrived. There sure were a lot of them. Young and old, families…and he knew almost every one of them.

He continued to observe, his chest tightening when he saw his father enter with Hillary Ward-Thompson, an old schoolmate of Dad's that he'd recently become reacquainted with. Now Matt was nervous. The only thing worse than failing would be failing in front of Dad.

"I need you, Matt." Corey Winslow, the play's stage manager, scurried across the wooden floor, looking even more rattled than Matt felt.

He let the curtain fall closed and turned to face her. "What's wrong?"

"It's Clare." He never knew Corey was such a nervous Nellie.

His gaze narrowed. "What about her?"

The petite brunette sucked in a breath. “She’s sick.” The woman cringed. “She can’t go on.”

Can’t go on? How could they perform *The Bishop’s Wife* without the bishop’s wife?

So much for not being nervous. Between this and his father, Matt’s anxiety level just went through the roof.

He shoved both hands through his hair as he started to pace. “This is not good.” What was he going to do?

“No, it’s not,” said Corey. “But at least we have a backup.”

He whirled to face her. “We do?” Why didn’t he know that?

“Yes. Lacie did this same show last year and played the role of Julia.”

He stared at his stage manager. “Well, why are you standing here then? Why aren’t you telling her all of this?”

Corey smiled and nodded. “Because that’s your job.”

“Oh.” Lacie must have left off that portion of a director’s job description. “Where is she?”

Corey shook her head. “She’s here somewhere.”

He took off, nearly running into Lacie as she exited costuming in her maid outfit. “Lace—” he gripped both of her arms “—I need you.”

“What?” She quirked a brow.

“I mean, get back in there. You need to change.”

She glanced down at her costume before again looking at him. “Okay, why don’t you take a deep breath and tell me what’s got you so stirred up?”

Behind him he could hear the audience growing larger, while backstage people were running around like chickens with their heads cut off.

He let go a sigh. "Clare is sick and can't go on. Would you *please* take over as Julia?"

"Oh, no. I hope Clare is all right." She pressed a hand to her chest. "But yes, of course, I'll take over."

He nearly collapsed with relief. Instead, he hugged her like he'd never hugged anyone before. "Thank you, Lace. Thank you."

"Don't you think I'd best go get changed?" Her words were muffled against his shoulder.

He quickly released her. "Yes, definitely. Go change." Turning, he lifted his gaze to the century-old hand-hewn rafters. "Thank You, Lord."

A short time later, he watched from backstage as the house lights went down, feeling a bit like the captain of the *Titanic*. "Here we go."

He wasn't sure he breathed again until the closing lines were uttered. But the cast had done it. They'd pulled off a flawless performance.

The audience applause was overwhelming. Everyone was on their feet as the cast was introduced, though the loudest applause was for Lacie. And rightfully so. Without her, they wouldn't have had a play at all.

Then he was called onstage. Still standing in the wings, he looked all around. Nobody had informed him he'd have to do that. He was a behind-the-scenes kind of guy.

Next thing he knew, Lacie and Valerie Dawson were at his side. They each took hold of an arm and escorted him center stage as the crowd continued to applaud.

Blinking, his gaze again drifted upward. *I hope you approve, Mama.*

Once the introductions were complete, the cast and crew descended the stage to greet those in attendance.

Matt shook hands with everyone who passed, overwhelmed by the number of people congratulating him on a job well done.

"That was wonderful, Matt." Dressed in a stylish pantsuit, her short blond hair perfectly styled, Hillary clasped both of his hands. "I'd forgotten how much I loved that movie, but you brought it all back. Thank you."

"You're welcome. I'm glad you enjoyed it."

"See you at the diner?" She tucked her short blond hair behind one ear.

"Wild horses couldn't keep me away."

She winked and continued down the line.

Then his father stepped in front of him. "The troop did a fine job. Your mama would be proud."

Matt hated the disappointment that wove through him. The ache he felt in his heart. He knew what Mama would have thought. Even if the play had flopped, she would have been proud, because she was always proud of her boys no matter what they did.

But Dad? No, he wasn't proud. If he was, would it have killed him to say so?

Unfortunately, all the praise Matt had received did little to overshadow his father's remarks. Even as he finished putting the props away ninety minutes later, the pain lingered.

"One down, two more to go." Lacie was kind enough to stay and help him.

"If I survive." He shoved the bishop's desk into a corner.

"What are you talking about?" She perched a hand on her now-denim-covered hip. "The play went off without a hitch."

"Thanks to you." He came alongside her. Taking hold of the maid's broom she had yet to put away, he stared into her beautiful blue eyes.

With one hand still on the stick, she studied him a moment. "What's wrong?"

"Nothing."

"Then why are you so bummed?"

He took the broom from her and laid it atop the desk as she gathered up her things. "I don't mean to sound ungrateful. I know that the play was a hit."

Still watching him, she put on her coat. "But…?"

He shrugged into his own jacket as they started for the door. "I'd really hoped I could make my father proud. But he wasn't impressed."

After pausing to turn off the house lights, they started down the stairs.

Lacie remained beside him. "Did he say that?"

"Not in so many words." On the main level, he held the door for her then locked up before joining her on the sidewalk. "He just said that Mama would be proud."

"Matt, that doesn't mean he's not proud." She continued beside him as they moved toward their vehicles. "Maybe he just doesn't know how to express it."

"I wish that were true." His steps slowed.

"It appears we both have issues with our parents," she said.

"Sure looks that way. Let's just hope we never do that to Kenzie." Thoughts of his daughter lifted his spirits.

Lacie stopped and stared at him, though her expression was unreadable. "You're forgetting… I'm not Kenzie's parent."

How could she even think such a thing? After all he'd

learned about her, what he'd witnessed. She was more of a parent than a lot of folks in this world.

"Yes, you are." Standing there in the cold, their breaths swirling together, he touched her cheek. "You're the best mother my little girl could ask for." And a pretty good match for him, too, he was starting to discover.

His gaze fell to her lips. Beautiful lips. Lips that spoke truth and love.

She took a step back then. "I need to go."

Lacie hung up her costume in the prop room after their final performance Sunday afternoon. She'd have to do a better job of steeling her heart against Matt. Though it wasn't easy when he looked at her with those velvet-brown eyes that beckoned her to let him in. Like he'd done last night.

Still, for Kenzie's sake, she couldn't let down her guard. She'd vowed she'd have no men in their lives and that's how she intended to keep it.

Matt isn't any guy. He's Kenzie's father.

But what if she opened herself up to him and things didn't work out? What if he was just using her to get to Kenzie?

No, she wouldn't put herself or Kenzie through that. And with this year's play now in the record books, she couldn't wait to get home and have a quiet evening with her niece.

Returning to the storage-closet-turned-dressing-room to gather up her things, she ran into Valerie.

"Lacie, it sure would be nice if you could stay in Ouray." Valerie picked up her coat. "You've been a great addition to our team."

The compliment warmed her heart. "Thank you, Valerie. Unfortunately, there's not much of a market for interior designers in Ouray."

"No, but there's always Telluride." The woman's green eyes glimmered. "Have you checked with any of the builders over there?"

Telluride. She hadn't even considered it. But it was less than an hour's drive from Ouray. "No, I haven't."

"Something to keep in mind."

Out of the corner of her eye, Lacie saw Matt approaching.

"Great job, everyone."

"Thanks, Matt." Lacie, Valerie and a couple other cast members responded in unison.

He motioned Lacie toward the stage.

Reluctantly, she joined him.

"Hey, what do you say I take you and Kenzie out for a celebration dinner?"

She glanced at the wooden floor. "Actually, I was thinking a quiet evening sounded kind of nice, after all the busyness here." Maybe he'd get the hint.

"Yeah, I guess you're right." He paused, hands on his hips. "So what if I pick up pizza instead and we hang out at your mom's? Maybe watch a Christmas movie— No, I guess that won't be happening. Unless you want to grab Kenzie and come on over to my place."

This time of year, Lacie loved nothing more than curling up with a good Christmas movie. Just not with him.

"So what do you say?" Under the bright lights, he shifted from one foot to the other. "I mean, we need to do something to celebrate me surviving the play. Not to mention your incredible performance." And then he had the nerve to look shy. “Besides, I’d really like to see Kenzie for a little bit.”

“We’ll all be together most of tomorrow, you know? That is, unless you forgot about the decorations.”

“I didn’t forget. I just miss her when I don’t get to see her for a while.” He shrugged. “Oh, and if you two come to my house, maybe you can get a better feel for what we might need in the way of decorations.”

Why was it so hard to tell him no? Then again, he was letting them have Christmas at his house. And while it may not be ideal, it was all she had and, for that, she was grateful.

She adjusted the coat draped over her arm. “Kenzie likes cheese pizza.”

He grinned. “I remember that from last Sunday at your mother’s. But what about you? What’s your favorite?”

“I’m a supreme kind of girl.”

“A woman after my own heart.”

If only things were that simple.

After getting his address, she went by her mother’s to pick up Kenzie, who was beyond excited about going to Matt’s house. Realizing that her niece might get bored, Lacie paused to gather up some coloring books and crayons, reading books, as well as the puzzles Matt had given her for her birthday, and then they were on their way.

Though it was dark outside when she eased to a stop in front of the 1905 two-story craftsman-style home, the lights illuminating the expansive front porch revealed the charm of a bygone era. Matt had said the house was a fixer-upper but, as a designer, she saw a lot of potential. Even if she had yet to see the interior.

"Can I ring the doorbell?" Standing on the porch, Kenzie looked up at her.

"Yes, you may. But only once." As opposed to over and over, which she was fond of doing. "We don't want to give Matt a headache."

"Come on in," he said a few moments later.

They entered into a spacious living room with beautiful dark wood floors and a coffered ceiling. Against the far wall, the original fireplace was flanked by gorgeous glass-front wooden bookcases topped with simple leaded-glass windows.

"Matt, this is incredible." Christmas music played softly in the background as she moved farther into the room, wanting to take it all in. Despite the heavy use of dark woods, the space still felt cozy and inviting thanks to the light-colored furniture and walls.

"Thanks." He moved beside her, holding Kenzie's hand. "Stripping off all of that old paint was a labor of love."

Lacie jerked her head in his direction. "You mean all this wood was painted?"

"Multiple times." He frowned.

"So you stripped and refinished all of this?" Talk about time-consuming.

"It took forever, but yes."

She looked him in the eye. "I must say, I'm very impressed."

"Well, before you get too excited, I should tell you that this and the dining room are the only ones I've finished. The rest is a work in progress."

"Don't sell yourself short, Matt. Anything worthwhile takes time."

He watched her for a moment. "I'll have to remember that." Then with a smile, he said, "Now who's ready for pizza?"

"Me!" Kenzie bounced up and down, her shoes flickering.

Five minutes later, Lacie stood in the opening between the kitchen and living room, holding her plate with two slices of supreme and Kenzie's plate with one slice of cheese, all the while eyeing Matt's light taupe furniture. And even though there was a coffee table...

"You're sure you want us to eat in the living room?"

"Why not?" Standing behind her holding his plate, he continued. "I do it all the time."

Lacie tossed a glance over her shoulder. "Yeah, but you're not five."

"Oh. Good point." His gaze shifted to the other opening that led into the dining room. "But if we're at the table we can't watch the movie. So...how about I grab a blanket for Kenzie and she can have a picnic on the floor in front of the TV?"

"That should work." She looked down at Kenzie. "But we need to keep our drinks in the kitchen, okay?"

"Okay." The kid nodded.

After Kenzie was settled, Matt picked up the television remote. "So let's see what's on."

Within seconds, *Rudolph the Red-Nosed Reindeer* appeared on the screen.

Sitting cross-legged atop the old comforter Matt had spread on the floor, her little mouth full of pizza, Kenzie straightened. "I want to watch this."

Still standing, Matt sent Lacie a questioning look.

She shrugged. "I watch it at least once a year anyway."

"Yeah, me, too." He set the remote on the coffee

table and picked up his plate. "So where do you think we should put the tree?" He took a bite.

"I don't know." Making her way past Kenzie, she stopped beside him. "Where did you put it last year?"

"I didn't have a tree last year." He peered down at her. "Which is why we need to go buy one."

"I see." She set her plate down and moved about the space to get a better feel for things. "How about over there—" she pointed toward the corner "—against the wall, beside the bookcase? That way you can see it wherever you're sitting, but it won't be too close to the fireplace."

"Hey, who am I to argue with a designer?" He took another bite.

"And the mantel would look beautiful with some lighted greenery." Remembering this wasn't her home, she added, "Unless you think it's too much."

"No, I like that look."

His approval had her biting her lip. When did things get so easy between them? Like they'd been back in high school. Like this was the way they were meant to be.

She quickly shook off the crazy notion. She and Matt were not meant to be.

Before the show was over, but after she'd finished her pizza, Kenzie pulled a book from the tote Lacie had brought and handed it to Matt. "Will you read this to me?"

He looked at the cover. "*Goodnight Moon*. I remember this book. Sure, I'll read it." He took a seat on the couch. "Hop on up here."

From across the room, Lacie watched as Kenzie climbed into his lap and snuggled against his broad chest. Definitely one of the sweetest sights she'd seen in a long time.

As Matt started to read, she gathered their plates and took them into the kitchen, then rinsed their glasses. When she returned to the living room to fold the blanket, Kenzie was asleep.

Lacie moved toward the pair. "Would you like me to take her?"

"No." He never took his eyes off his daughter. "I just want to look at her." And he did, for what seemed like forever, as though trying to take in every little nuance.

"She really is a great kid," he finally said.

"You'll get no argument from me there."

It was obvious that Kenzie was growing attached to Matt, making Lacie feel bad about taking her back east. Every little girl needed a daddy. And Matt had already missed so much time.

There's always Telluride. Valerie's words echoed in Lacie's mind.

A job in Telluride would mean she and Kenzie could stay in Ouray. Though it would also mean spending a lot of time with Matt, fighting to keep her feelings in check.

Or you could let them go and see where things lead.

Except that was a risk Lacie wasn't sure she was willing to take.

Chapter Ten

Matt knew that he loved Kenzie. But holding her last night, watching her as she slept, her little body relaxed against his in complete trust… He'd never been more enamored.

So if Lacie wanted Kenzie to have the perfect Christmas, then Matt intended to do everything in his power to make that happen. Even if it meant spending half the day with a bunch of crazed holiday shoppers. At least they'd come on a Monday instead of the weekend.

Christmas music echoed overhead as he pushed the supercenter shopping cart past a small forest of artificial trees. Green trees, white trees, some with fake snow. Some had white lights while others had multicolored ones and still others had no lights at all. Fat trees, skinny trees…

"I like the pink one," said Kenzie.

A pink Christmas tree? He shook his head. Definitely not like the real ones he and his family used to have at the ranch.

His mother would spend months wandering the land, scoping out the perfect tree. Then, shortly after Thanksgiving, they'd hitch a trailer to the tractor and the whole family would go out, cut it down and bring it home. He could still remember how the house would be filled with the scent of fresh pine.

"That is cute." Holding Kenzie's hand, Lacie knelt beside her and admired the pint-size tinsel tree. "But it's pretty small." She grinned up at him. "Matt might trip over it."

Kenzie looked from the tree to Matt as though considering Lacie's advice. After a moment, she said, "We need a *big* tree." She held her arms wide.

"That's right, small fry." He ruffled her soft curls. "The bigger the better."

"Okay, then." Laughing, Lacie pushed to her feet, looking pretty cute herself in her glittering snowman sweater.

"I can't believe I let you talk me into coming out here with everybody and his brother."

Matt's smile faded. He knew that voice.

"Oh, don't be such a stick-in-the-mud, Clint. Where's your Christmas spirit?"

And that one.

He turned, doing a double take when he spotted his father and Hillary standing a few feet away, also looking at Christmas trees.

He inched the cart forward. Perhaps he could pretend he hadn't seen them.

But Lacie nudged him with her elbow. "Are you going to say something or should I?"

Just then, Hillary looked their way, her smile instantaneous. "Well, hello, you two." While Dad scowled at him from behind a flocked faux fir, Hillary continued toward them, wearing a stylish sweater and jeans that had definitely come from a much pricier store than this one.

"Lacie, right?" Hillary shook her hand. "We met after the play."

"Yes, I remember. It's good to see you again, Hillary."

The woman's gaze fell to Kenzie. "And who do we have here?"

Lacie placed her hands on the girl's shoulders. "This is Kenzie."

Hillary introduced herself. "Are you getting a Christmas tree?"

Kenzie leaned into Lacie and nodded.

"Hey, Clint," said Lacie as he approached. "How are you?"

The old man tilted his dirty beige felt Stetson farther back on his head and glared at Hillary. "I'd be a lot better if someone hadn't dragged me all the way to Montrose to pick out a tree."

Matt's gaze shot from Hillary to his dad. "You're getting a tree? But you always cut a fresh one at the ranch."

"Wasn't planning to do one at all, but Ms. Fancy Pants over here says I have to." Dressed in his usual Wranglers, denim work shirt and Carhartt jacket, the old man poked a thumb toward the trees. "At least one of these prelit things ought to be a lot easier."

Easier, yes, but not how Mama would have done it. How could Dad even think about an artificial tree? What about tradition?

So why are you thinking of getting one?

Matt glanced at a superskinny tree. Good question. Of course, until a couple of days ago, he hadn't been planning on having a tree at all. Still, why had his first thought been to go out and buy something fake instead of cutting down the real deal? Especially when this was his first Christmas with Kenzie and both he and Lacie wanted it to be extra special.

"I pointed the ranch out to Kenzie on our way here," said Lacie.

Her shyness abating, Kenzie took a step forward. "I want to see the horsies."

The old man smiled and crouched to her level. "You do?"

Matt's insides tensed. He and three of his brothers looked like his father. And Kenzie was definitely a Stephens. Would his father see the resemblance? Would he figure out that Kenzie was Matt's daughter? His granddaughter?

Kenzie nodded, her brown eyes sparkling, completely unaware that the man she was speaking to was her grandfather.

"Then you need to tell Matt here to bring you on by."

Kenzie's face rivaled the lights on the Christmas trees beside her. "Can we go now?"

"Sure." Dad stood. "We just need to grab us a tree then we're headed right back." Shoving his hands into the pockets of his jeans, he looked from Matt to Lacie. "What do you two have going on?"

"We need to pick out a tree and some decorations," said Lacie.

"But that shouldn't take us too long," Matt was quick to add. Not when he had something in mind that would be far more fun than spending the afternoon at a superstore. Because if they were going to give Kenzie the best Christmas ever, he was going to make sure they did it right.

"Tell you what, let's forget about these phony things." Matt gestured toward the colorful array of plastic and tinsel. "Why don't we all head back to the ranch, let Kenzie see the horses and then I'll cut down a *real* tree for both of us?"

Lacie's smile grew wider by the nanosecond. "I *love* that idea."

"Oh, it does sound like fun, doesn't it?" Hillary clasped her hands together. "Maybe the three of you could even stay for lunch. Clint's got a pot of chili waiting for us at the ranch house. And with the way he cooks, I'm sure there's enough for a small army."

He looked at his father now. "So what do you say, Dad?"

The old man's gaze narrowed. "Shouldn't you be workin' today?"

"Nope. I've got the day off."

His father grunted. "What about them poachers? You got any leads yet?"

Matt tried not to let his father get to him. "No, but the investigators are working hard to find them, and I'm sure they'll be in touch with you soon."

"Come on, Clint." Hillary elbowed him. "It's not like Matt was volunteering you to cut down any trees."

Matt bit back a chuckle. He was growing to like Hillary more all the time.

"Don't know how we'd get it back." Dad scraped a worn cowboy boot across the concrete floor. "Trailer's got a flat."

"I can fix it." Matt wasn't sure if the old man was being ornery in general or because it was Matt who had made the offer. Either way, this wasn't about him. It was about his daughter's Christmas.

His father shifted from one foot to the next. “Them real trees, though, they can get kinda messy. You gotta keep adding water and such.”

Surely the old man could come up with a better excuse than that. “Dad, since when have you ever had anything but a real tree?”

No response.

“Okay, fine.” Matt took hold of the cart. “I’ll just cut one for us then.”

That seemed to get his father’s attention. “Now, you don’t need to go gettin’ all cranky.”

He was being cranky?

“Clint—” Lacie took a step toward him “—if you don’t want us to cut down a tree from the ranch, it’s okay. I understand.”

His father’s expression softened. “I never said I didn’t want you to.” His gaze briefly shifted to Kenzie. “’Course, we can’t let the little one down. She wants to come see the horses.”

The kid grinned. Obviously she’d won Dad over.

He looked at Matt, his countenance more resigned than argumentative. “Guess we’ll see you back at the ranch.”

Excitement bubbled inside Lacie over the unexpected turn of events. She was so glad they had run into Clint and Hillary. Otherwise, they would be back at Matt’s now, decorating an ordinary tree. Instead, they were bumping across the rangeland of Abundant Blessings Ranch in a utility vehicle towing a flatbed trailer, in search of the perfect Christmas tree. And giving Kenzie an experience she was sure to remember.

She looked down at her niece, who was tucked between her and Matt on the lone bench seat, and tightened her seat belt. "What did you think about those horses, Kenzie?" In the open-air vehicle that reminded her of a cross between a dune buggy and a small truck, she had to raise her voice to be heard over the engine.

"They were big." Not nearly as big as her smile, though.

Lacie appreciated the way Matt had lifted Kenzie into his arms, making the massive animals less intimidating for her as he patiently introduced each one.

"Yeah, like the tree we're gonna get, right, Kenzie?" Holding tight to the steering wheel, a grinning Matt nudged the girl with his elbow.

She nodded, adjusting her pink knit cap with her mitten-covered hands.

Lacie eyed the cottonwoods lining the riverbank in the distance. Backdropped by conifer-covered, snow-capped mountains, the scene reminded her of a rustic Christmas card. All it needed was a light-adorned evergreen somewhere and it would be perfect.

"I'm so glad you suggested this, Matt. Hunting for a real tree is beyond anything I could have dreamed of for this Christmas."

"Good." He grinned, his camo ball cap shading his face from the afternoon sun. "I kind of like the idea of making your dreams come true."

Despite the chilly temperature, her cheeks warmed. Seemed he was doing just that, first by offering to give Kenzie the perfect Christmas at his place, then again today. His actions were enough to have gratitude and excitement twisting and tangling into one overwhelming emotion. An emotion she had no business feeling when it came to any man. Except he wasn't just any man. He was Kenzie's father.

Talk about complicated.

Over her shoulder, she glimpsed Clint and Hillary following behind them on another UTV. "So what's the story with your dad and Hillary?"

"I'm not sure." Matt veered northward, his expression taking on a more serious air. "I know they were friends in high school. She left Ouray, but recently moved back to be near her daughter and grandkids." He glanced her way. "Do you remember Mrs. Ward and the Miner's Café?"

"Yes."

"That was Hillary's mother. Hillary's daughter Celeste now owns Granny's Kitchen. She married Gage Purcell." Gage was an old schoolmate of theirs.

She shoved her gloved hands between her knees for the added warmth. "Talk about full circle."

"I've got to admit, it was pretty weird seeing Dad and Hillary together at the store like that."

"Why?"

He shrugged. "She's not Mama."

"I see." If there was one thing she knew for certain, it was how much each of the Stephens boys adored their mother. "Well, is Hillary a bad person?"

"No." The corners of his mouth tipped upward again. "Actually, from what little I've been around her, she's pretty good at putting the old man in his place. As you witnessed today." He made a sharp turn.

Laughing, Lacie grabbed hold of the roll bar to keep her from sliding into Kenzie. "I suspect Mona would approve, then."

"I'm still surprised Dad wanted to come with us."

Matt eyed the rearview mirror as though checking on the vehicle behind them. "After the way he tried to deter me earlier. As if cutting down a tree was the stupidest thing he'd ever heard."

"Don't take it personally."

"How can you say that? Even Hillary came to my defense."

"Yes, but I don't think his avoidance had anything to do with you. I think it's because it reminds him of your mother."

She knew she'd struck a chord when he didn't respond. He simply blinked, continuing to stare straight ahead.

"Bringing in the Christmas tree was something you always did as a family, right?"

He nodded. "Mom picked it out and Dad would cut it down."

"So without Mona at his side, it's not the same. I mean, think about it, Matt. They were married for how long?"

"Forty years." He brought the vehicle to a stop near a wooded area. "You might be right, Lace." He turned off the ignition and reached an arm across the back of the seat to squeeze her shoulder. "Thanks."

Between the warmth of his touch and the intensity of his gaze, her heart pounded.

Finally, his focus shifted to Kenzie. "Now let's go find us a tree."

"Yay!" Kenzie couldn't unbuckle her seat belt fast enough, so Matt helped her as Clint and Hillary pulled alongside them.

Clint killed the engine. "You sure this is where you want to look?"

Matt grabbed the chain saw he'd put in the bed before they left the house. "Mama always seemed to find some good ones in here." He eyed the wooded area. "Since it hasn't been touched in a few years, thought there might be something worthwhile."

"Let's give it a go, then." Clint climbed out of his vehicle.

The five of them moved into the woods where barren deciduous trees mingled with junipers, firs and pines.

"Look, Kenzie." She saw the wonder in her niece's eyes. "This is way better than the store, isn't it?"

The little girl nodded.

"But unlike the trees at the store," Matt said, "no two are going to be the same. They could be tall and skinny, short and fat, full, skimpy…you just never know."

Hands buried in her pockets, Lacie continued beside him. "I'm not sure what I'm looking for exactly, but I'll know it when I see it." Something full, perhaps, but not too wide, with a straight trunk.

"That's how it usually goes, Lacie." Clint's voice echoed from behind them. "You know it when you see it."

Kenzie gasped then. "Look at this." She picked up a pinecone as though she'd found the greatest treasure ever.

"Pretty cool," said Lacie.

Squinting against the sun, the child peered up at her. "Can I keep it?"

"If it's okay with Mr. Clint."

"Sure you can," he said.

Leaves crackled beneath their feet and snow remnants crunched as they moved deeper into the thicket. Overhead, a couple of magpies chattered back and forth.

"That's a nice one there, Clint." Hillary approached a squatty blue spruce. "You said you didn't want a big one."

Matt's father moved closer and circled the tree that didn't quite reach his six feet. "Don't see any big holes." He stepped back, continuing to scrutinize the conifer in question. "I believe it'll do."

"Oh, good." Hillary appeared especially pleased.

"Well, that was easy." Matt approached with the chain saw.

"Everyone get back," hollered Clint as the saw roared to life.

Within seconds the tree crashed to the ground. The women watched as Matt and his father loaded it onto the trailer.

"Looks like it's our turn, Lace." Matt rejoined her and Kenzie.

Along with Clint and Hillary, they resumed their search and in no time Lacie was eyeing a substantial Douglas fir. Not too fat at the bottom, perfectly tapered…

"This one looks good," she and Matt said in unison.

How about that? They actually were in agreement.

Except when she turned, she saw that Matt was looking at an entirely different tree. And while it was still a Douglas fir, it was way too wide with branches so close together it would be hard to place the ornaments.

"I think this one over here would fit in your living room better." She pointed to her tree.

"Are you kidding? That's way too skinny."

"No, it's not. Sure, it's not fat like that tree—" she aimed a finger at his selection "—but at least there's plenty of room for ornaments."

"What are you talking about? Do you see all those branches?" He took hold of his tree. "You can get a ton of ornaments on there."

"But your tree is flat on top," she continued. "How are we going to put the star on?"

"Trust me. The star will fit just fine." He looked at his father and Hillary. "What do you two think?"

Arms crossed, Hillary lifted a shoulder. "I'd have to go with Lacie's tree."

"What?" Clint frowned. "Look how full Matt's tree is."

Matt swiped a hand through the air. "Forget it. There's only one person whose opinion really matters. Kenzie, what do you think?" He turned to the spot where she had been.

Lacie's heart dropped. "Where's Kenzie?" She jerked her head right and left, scanning high and low.

"She was just here." Matt looked every bit as stricken as she felt. He set the chain saw to the ground. "Kenzie?"

"Oh, no." Lacie gripped his arm. "The river."

Eyes wide, he looked at his dad and Hillary. "Stay here in case she comes back. Come on, Lace."

Turning, they ran in the direction of the river.

Blood roared in Lacie's ears. Tears stung the backs of her eyes. Why had they not seen Kenzie wander away?

Conviction pricked her heart. *Because you were so consumed with finding the perfect tree that you weren't paying attention.*

A sob caught in her throat. *God, help us find her. Please, let her be okay.*

Her foot caught on a branch and she fell flat. Air whooshed from her lungs.

Matt helped her up, his expression more panicked than she'd ever seen. "You okay?"

"I'm fine. But we have got to find—" Over Matt's shoulder she spotted Kenzie. "There she is."

He turned. "Oh, thank God."

They rushed to her side.

"Kenzie, sweetie." Lacie dropped to her knees, trying to catch her breath. "We didn't know where you were. You're not supposed to run off like that."

"Are you all right?" Matt asked.

"Uh-huh." She smiled as though she didn't have a care in the world. "I finded the perfect Christmas tree." Her little finger pointed.

Both Matt and Lacie turned to find a tree unlike either of the ones they had chosen. The blue spruce was spindly and misshapen with more bare spots than branches. And while it wasn't quite a Charlie Brown Christmas tree, it was far from perfect.

Matt glanced from the tree to Lacie to Kenzie, then back to the tree. "That's the tree you want?"

"Uh-huh," said Kenzie.

He looked at Lacie.

She shrugged, knowing that she would have done just about anything for Kenzie right now. "If it's the one she wants…"

"I hear ya." His smile echoed Lacie's relief. "I'll go get the chain saw."

Chapter Eleven

After a lunch of chili and corn bread at the ranch, Matt, Lacie and Kenzie returned to his house to decorate their tree. Lacie helped him carry it into the house, set it up and now, as he finished stringing the multicolored LED lights they'd bought in Montrose, she pulled a pan of break-and-bake cookies from his oven. After all, what was a tree-trimming party without cookies and cocoa? Even if they were both instant. She just hoped the decorations would perk up that sad little tree.

Not that she or Matt really cared anymore. Today was all about Kenzie.

"Cookies are done," she hollered from the kitchen.

"So are the lights," Matt responded.

Perfect timing.

She quickly transferred the cookies to a plate then joined Matt and Kenzie in the living room.

He knelt beside the tree, in the corner, near the bookcase as they'd discussed last night. "Are you ladies ready?"

"Yes!" they responded in unison.

Hand perched on her hip, Kenzie looked rather impatient. "Hurry up, Matt."

He laughed. "Okay, here we go."

A split second later the humble tree glowed with brilliant shades of red, green, blue, yellow and orange.

Kenzie gasped, tilting her head all the way back so she could see the top of the tree that almost reached the nine-foot ceiling. "Pretty."

"And we're not even done yet, small fry." Matt joined them at the coffee table. "Your aunt Lacie is going to add some of that ribbon we bought, then we get to put on the ornaments."

She stared up at him very matter-of-factly. "Don't forget the star."

"That's right." He lifted Kenzie into his arms and started back toward the tree. "And since you're going to put it up—" he hoisted her over his head "—we'd better make sure you can reach."

Laughing, she stretched out an arm as he moved her closer. "I toucheded it."

"Good." He lowered her into his arms again. "Then you got the job, kid. Now, what do you say you and I chow down on some of those snowman cookies while Lacie puts the ribbon on the tree."

"Okay." She wriggled free.

Armed with a large spool of burlap ribbon and scissors, Lacie moved toward the tree. "You guys had better leave me some."

"Aww, do we have to?" Matt handed a cookie to Kenzie.

"Yes, you have to."

"Man. You hear that, Kenz? The boss says we can't eat all the cookies."

Her niece scrunched up her nose. "You're so silly, Matt."

Watching the two of them, one would think they'd known each other forever. Kenzie seemed as comfortable with him as she was with Lacie. And Matt…?

The look of horror and desperation on his face when he realized Kenzie was missing was unlike anything Lacie had ever witnessed. And it said a lot about the depth of love he felt for his daughter.

But not only had he been there for Kenzie, he'd been there for Lacie, too. She couldn't imagine what she would have done without his help. Then again, if it weren't for him, she and Kenzie wouldn't have been there in the first place.

She glanced up at the tree. Nor would they be here, getting ready to decorate and celebrate this most wonderful time of the year. And considering the fact that Kenzie was completely unaware anything bad had happened, things still looked pretty special in her eyes. Meaning their goal had been achieved.

When she'd finished adding the ribbon to the tree, she stepped back to inspect.

"Hey, it's looking better already." Matt came alongside her and she inhaled the aroma of fresh air and chocolate.

Talk about a powerful combination.

"Thanks." Setting the remaining ribbon and scissors on the table, she eyed Kenzie enjoying the last of her hot chocolate—in the living room, no less. Definitely a special occasion. "Looks like we're ready for the ornaments."

Kenzie carefully set her cup down on the coffee table then grabbed the massive container of shatterproof ornaments they'd bought at the store. Shiny balls, glittering balls, red ones, silver ones, some with candy cane stripes… And light enough for a five-year-old to carry.

Matt turned on some Christmas music and suddenly Lacie felt as though she'd been transported back in time. The tree trimming, the cookies and cocoa, the music… Just like when she was little and her family would gather.

Now Kenzie would have those same memories. Thanks to Matt.

When all of the ornaments had been placed on the tree, Lacie removed the glittering silver star from its packaging. "This is all that's left."

"That's your cue, small fry." Matt lifted Kenzie into his arms as Lacie handed her the topper. "You're going to stick it on top of this branch right here." He pointed.

"Okay."

Lacie readied the camera on her phone as Matt lifted Kenzie into the air.

Click. Click.

"I did it," said an excited Kenzie as Matt returned her to the floor.

"You sure did." Lacie knelt beside her. "And it's perfect."

Matt took a step back. "Actually, it really is." He motioned for Lacie join him.

"Well, I'll be." If she hadn't seen it, Lacie never would have believed that between the ribbon and the ornaments, this once-pathetic-looking tree was more perfect than anything she'd ever seen.

She held up her phone and snapped another picture. "You two get over there now."

They did and she took a couple more shots.

"Hey, do you have a timer on that thing?" Matt asked.

She glanced at her phone. "I think so. Why?"

"So we can get one of all three of us."

She located the timer, he set the phone on the TV stand and lined up the shot, then they all hurried to get into place in front of the tree. Matt and Lacie on their knees with Kenzie standing in between.

The flash went off.

"Let's see what we got." She hurried to retrieve her phone with Matt at her side. A couple of taps and there on the screen was a perfect picture of all of them and their perfect tree.

"I like it," said Matt.

So did she. Perhaps more than she was willing to admit, even to herself. They looked like a real family. A notion that sounded better every time they were together. Matt's attentiveness to Kenzie was undeniably attractive. Especially when he turned that same attention toward Lacie.

Just then, her phone rang and her friend Jill's name appeared on the screen.

"Sorry." She glanced at Matt.

"You go right ahead," he said. "Come on, Kenzie, let's pick out a Christmas movie."

"Hey, Jill." Phone pressed to her ear, Lacie moved into the kitchen.

"Lacie. Oh, how I've missed you." Jill had also been one of her coworkers.

"Aww, thank you, Jill."

"I'm serious." She could envision her friend pouting. "Work isn't near as fun without you."

She eyed the darkening sky outside the window over the sink. "It's not like it was my idea to leave."

"I know. But I heard some news I wanted to pass along to you."

Lacie straightened. "What is it?"

"I was talking to another designer who told me about a builder down in Colorado Springs who's looking for someone."

"Really?" She leaned against the counter. "The housing market is booming there."

"Which is why they're in need of someone with experience."

"Well, I definitely have that." Almost a decade's worth. And while she'd hoped to find something in the Denver area so she could keep Kenzie in the same daycare with her friends, perhaps this was God's way of nudging her in a different direction. Considering she'd already given up her apartment… "This could be just what I'm looking for."

She took down the info. "Thanks, Jill. I'll give them a call tomorrow."

She ended the call with a renewed sense of optimism. Yet when she returned to the living room and saw Matt and Kenzie cuddled up on the couch, staring at the TV, something twisted inside her.

Perhaps what she was really looking for was right here in Ouray, after all.

Matt came in from work the next day, smiling when he caught sight of the Christmas tree. Aside from that brief scare with Kenzie, it had been one of the best days he'd had in a long time. Even Dad hadn't been able to dampen his spirits. Then Lacie told him about that job in Colorado Springs.

He strolled across the room and plugged in the lights.

Even if he lived to be a hundred, he'd never forget decorating this first tree with Kenzie.

Taking the phone from his pocket, he pulled up the images Lacie had sent him last night. Kenzie and him in front of the tree. Him, Lacie and Kenzie. He stared at the photo. How could Lacie even consider a job on the other side of the state? Sure he understood that she needed a salary and that her given career field was better served back east, but that would mean separating him from Kenzie when he'd already missed out on so much. Didn't that count for something?

He zoomed in on Lacie's image. Truth was, he didn't want either of them to go.

A knock sounded at his door, stirring him from his thoughts. He wasn't expecting anyone, but maybe Lacie and Kenzie had decided to surprise him. Or simply wanted to see their tree. He crossed the living room and swung open the door only to find his father standing on the other side.

Matt's smile evaporated. His entire body tensed. Dad had never come to see him before. Had never even set foot in Matt's house. So what was he doing here now?

After a long moment, his father said, "Mind if I come in?"

Still at a loss for words, Matt stepped back, allowing the man entry.

Continuing into the living room, Dad removed his cowboy hat, revealing his thick salt-and-pepper hair. "Tree looks nice."

Matt closed the door and followed him, still suspicious. "Thanks."

"Your brothers tell me you've done a lot of work on this place." He scanned the space. "Don't know what it looked like before, but I'd say you've done a pretty good job."

"Yeah, well, there's still plenty left to do." He peeled off his tactical vest and set it on the floor. "What can I do for you?"

The old man turned to look at him with those dark eyes Matt had come to appreciate as much as fear. "There are a few things that have been bothering me."

Great. What had he done now?

Matt crossed his arms over his chest. "Such as?"

The muscle in his father's jaw twitched. "Tell me more about little Kenzie."

If Matt thought he was nervous before… "What would you like me to tell you?"

Dad thumped his hat against his denim-clad thigh. "For starters, are you her father?"

For a moment, Matt couldn't breathe. His lungs constricted, tighter and tighter. Digging deep, he willed his pulse to a normal rate. "How did you figure it out?"

"'Cause she looks like a Stephens." The old man glanced away then. "Actually, I couldn't shake the feeling that I'd seen her before. Then, when I mentioned it to Hillary, she's the one who asked if you could be Kenzie's father." He glared at Matt now. "I'm guessing she was right."

Lowering his arms, he took a step closer as though daring his father to do something. "Yes, Dad, she was. Congratulations, your screwup son fathered a child out of wedlock."

The old man never flinched. Didn't bat an eye. "No. My son has a daughter."

Matt couldn't have felt more off balance if his father

had hit him with a left hook. He narrowed his gaze. "What did you say?"

"I owe you an apology, Matt. One that's long overdue."

He blinked as years of pent-up emotions rose to the surface.

"You're no screwup, son. I am."

Matt swallowed the lump that lodged in his throat.

"I was mad that I was losing your mama and needed to lash out." Dad's dark eyes shimmered. "Unfortunately, I took it out on you. Seeing those horses made your mother smile. Yet I let you believe that I held you responsible for her death. And I can't tell you how sorry I am."

Still blinking, Matt stared at the coffered ceiling to keep his tears from falling. He felt as though he were ten years old again. "I know I let you down when I joined the navy and said I didn't want to be a rancher."

"No, you did not." Dad laid a calloused hand on his shoulder and Matt feared he might fall apart completely. "God gave you a different calling, just like your brothers. I understand that." His father let go then and shuffled toward the fireplace, his worn hat still clutched in his hand. "It was me. I let myself down. Not to mention your mama."

Matt couldn't believe what he was hearing. Dad had never talked like this before. "How can you say that? As far as Mama was concerned, you hung the moon."

The old man sniffed. "If I'd have just taken better care of her..." His voice cracked. "Insisted she go to the doctor sooner..."

He moved alongside his father. "Dad, we all know

she wouldn't have listened. She was too busy taking care of all of us."

Dad looked at him, his smile tremulous as a tear trailed down his cheek. "That's because she did it so well."

Matt couldn't help himself. He put an arm around his father's shoulders. "Yes, she did. And we were blessed to have her."

The old man turned into his embrace and hugged him. "I love you, son."

"I love you, too, Dad."

There in front of the Christmas tree, they held on to each other as years of misunderstandings melted away. Something Matt never would have dreamed possible. Yet, by the grace of God, here they stood.

He was curious, though.

Releasing his father, he said, "What prompted you to come here today to tell me all of this?"

Dad wiped his eyes. "Hillary."

"Did she force you?"

"Son, you know me better than that."

True. No one was going to make Clint Stephens do anything he didn't want to do.

"She's a good listener. She suggested I swallow my pride and make amends with you before it was too late."

"Suggested, huh?"

Dad looked a little sheepish. "I do love you, Matt. Always have, always will."

"Same here, Dad."

The old man scratched a hand through his thick hair. "What do you say we go grab some dinner over at Granny's Kitchen?"

The corners of Matt's mouth twitched. "So you can have an excuse to see Hillary?"

"What do you take me for, some teenager? If I want a good meal, Granny's Kitchen is the place to go."

Matt quirked a brow. "And the fact that Hillary will probably be there has nothing to do with it?"

"So I happen to like her. Shoot me."

He laughed. "It's all right, Dad. You're allowed to have a life." He shrugged. "Besides, I like Hillary, too. She knows how to keep you in line."

His father grinned. "Nah, she's just bossy."

Sounded like the pot calling the kettle black. "Give me a minute to change and we'll go."

Twenty minutes later, in a booth at Granny's Kitchen, over a cup of coffee, Matt told his father about Marissa, Kenzie and the phone call Lacie received last night. "I don't know what I'm going to do if she takes that job."

"I know this is pointing out the obvious, but you are Kenzie's father. You could always sue for custody."

And make Lacie hate him? "I couldn't do that. Kenzie barely knows me."

"I understand." Dad wrapped both hands around his own white cup. "Well, a housing boom usually means a greater need for law enforcement. You could always follow them."

He eyed his father across the high-gloss wooden tabletop. "I thought about that."

"But?"

"It wouldn't be the same." He shrugged. "Here I'm able to drop by and see them even when I'm on duty. And Barbara's more than happy to help out with Kenzie, giving Lacie and me time together." He started to take a sip, then stopped. "You know, if we need to discuss something."

Now his father was the one with the curious lift to his brow. “Sounds like this isn't just about Kenzie.”

He thought about Lacie's smile and amazing eyes. “Lacie is unlike any woman I've ever known. Sure, she's pretty, but there's so much more.” He stared into the steaming black liquid. “I mean, she sacrificed everything to be a mother to Kenzie when Marissa died.”

“That takes a special person, all right.”

Turning toward the window, he took in all of the twinkling lights up and down Main Street. “She's definitely special.”

“Sounds to me like you're falling in love.”

His gaze jerked to his father's. “Love?” He scratched his head, hoping to dismiss what he knew in his heart to be true. “I don't know about that. Didn't you see the way we butted heads over a simple Christmas tree yesterday?”

“I saw the way you two worked together when you thought Kenzie was missing.”

Dad lifted his cup. “Either way, I recommend you figure it out before it's too late.”

Chapter Twelve

At The Paisley Elk Thursday afternoon, Lacie parked her laptop on the sales counter beside the cash register. Since Thursdays were usually slow, her mother had stayed home with Kenzie, allowing Lacie to hold down the fort here at the shop. And while Lacie wasn't sure just how much of a break her mother was getting, it enabled her to get in some much-needed online shopping without a five-year-old looking over her shoulder.

Aside from searching for gifts, she really wanted to find a Christmas outfit for Kenzie. Maybe a cute tunic with a ruffled skirt and colorful leggings or even a classic white fur and red velvet dress like Lacie and Marissa used to wear when they were kids.

She typed in the web address for a company that specialized in children's clothing. Concentrating on Christmas would also keep her from dwelling on that job in Colorado Springs. Despite calling them Tuesday and sending her resume and portfolio as they'd requested, she had yet to hear anything regarding an interview. To say she was getting impatient would be an understatement. Even if she wasn't sure how she felt about moving

Kenzie to someplace entirely new. They'd basically be starting over and Kenzie had already faced more than her fair share of changes this past year.

Still, it would be nice to have their own place again. And they'd still be together. That is, unless Matt decided he wanted to keep Kenzie here and took measures to ensure that.

She shrugged off the unsavory thought. With all the fun they'd been having together lately, it was difficult to imagine him doing such a thing. Then again, the more Matt was with Kenzie the more inclined he might be to want permanent custody.

Grabbing her tote bag from the floor, she retrieved her phone and brought up the picture of the three of them in front of their Christmas tree. At times, it felt as though they were a family.

Silly. She clicked off the phone and put it away. The only thing between her and Matt was Kenzie and that's the way it would stay. Or so she kept telling herself. Yet the more time they spent together…

The bell over the door jangled and she looked up to see Valerie coming into the store.

"Hey, Valerie." She hurried around to the other side of the counter, past the ornate chalkboard artfully adorned with the words Happy Holidays and a rack of sweaters to give her fellow thespian a hug. "It's so nice to see you again." After getting to know her during the week of the play, Lacie had grown quite fond of her new friend.

"I just can't seem to stop thinking about you." The woman let go of her with a pat and admired the festive decorations. "Your mother sure knows how to decorate. This place is amazing."

"Yes, Mom is very good at doing festive." So long as it's not Christmas. "Can I help you find something?"

"Not today." Valerie smiled at her. "I just popped in to see if you were here. I have something I want to talk to you about."

"I'm all ears."

"I was having lunch with a friend in Ridgway yesterday and I overheard two gentlemen talking at the next table."

Lacie lifted a brow. "I think that's called eavesdropping, Valerie."

"Not when they're talking loud, it's not." She winked. "Turns out, they were builders. You know, for those really expensive homes over there in Telluride. Anyway—" she waved a hand "—they are in the market for an interior designer. Someone who can work with their clients to help them choose all those decorative things that go into a home."

Though she was definitely intrigued about the job opportunity, she curiously eyed her friend. "You *overheard* all of this?"

"I may have asked them a few questions." Adjusting the purse strap over her shoulder, Valerie blushed. "And when I told them that I knew someone who'd been working in Denver, but was looking for something out here on the Western Slope, they gave me their card—" she pulled it from her pocket and held it out "—and said they'd love to hear from you."

Lacie took hold of the card, feeling rather stupefied. "You did all of that for me?"

"I told you we'd love to keep you here."

Her heart melted into a puddle right there. "Valerie, that is the sweetest thing anyone has ever done for me."

She again hugged the woman, wondering what God might be up to. First the news about Colorado Springs, now this. "Thank you."

The always chipper brunette set Lacie away from her and gave her one of those motherly looks. "Does that mean you're going to call them?"

Lacie met her gaze. "Yes, ma'am, I will definitely call them."

"Oh, good, because I plan to keep on praying they'll hire you."

The door jangled again, ushering in a blast of chilly air as both women turned.

This time, Matt walked in, dressed in his uniform, removing his aviator sunglasses, just as he had that first day Lacie arrived in Ouray. "Afternoon, ladies."

"Hi, Matt." Valerie turned back to Lacie. "You let me know what they say, okay?"

"I will."

Valerie smiled. "Gotta run." She waved. "See you later."

Matt paused beside the chalkboard as the door closed. "What was that all about?"

Lacie chuckled, returning to her computer. "Valerie was telling me about a design job she heard about in Telluride."

Matt followed her. "I like the sound of that." His dark gaze fixed on Lacie, he leaned his elbows against the opposite side of the counter.

For a moment, the hope she saw in his eyes took hold of her. Then she reminded herself it was only about keeping Kenzie close by.

"If you're looking for Kenzie, she's at home with Mom."

"I know. I stopped by there first. I'm here to see you."

Her traitorous heart leaped.

"You know how I told you that Dad and I made amends?"

"How could I forget?" He'd come straight to her house after having dinner with the man, bubbling over with joy as he told her all that had transpired. The news had brought happy tears to her eyes.

"Well, he called me this morning and asked if we would come out to the ranch on Sunday so everyone could meet Kenzie."

So he did only want to see her about Kenzie. "But we haven't told Kenzie that you're her father."

"I know. And I don't intend to tell her any time soon. They're aware of that." He fingered a bar of specialty chocolate displayed on the counter. "But it's never too early to start building relationships with family."

Family. Something she seemed to be losing more of all the time. And if Matt decided to take Kenzie—

She shook her head, disgusted by her self-pity. She couldn't keep Kenzie from knowing Matt or his family. That little girl deserved all the love she could get.

Stiffening her spine, she said, "What time would you like to pick her up?"

Matt straightened, looking confused. "Pick her up? Lacie, I said *we*. That means you, me and Kenzie."

"Oh. I just thought—"

He reached across the counter and took hold of her hand. "I wouldn't exclude you. We're a team."

A team. As in one for all and all for one. Kenzie being that one. Except the gleam in Matt's eye spoke of other things. Things that had her believing that staying in Ouray might not bc so bad after all.

* * *

"Now, this is the Gladys we're all used to seeing." Her blue eyes were bright, her color was good, her spirits were up as Matt would have expected. And even though she was perfectly capable of doing it herself, he added another couple of logs to the wood-burning stove Friday morning.

This was the first time he'd visited his former schoolteacher since she came home from the hospital two weeks ago, but then, with so many others checking on her and bringing her food, he didn't want to wear her out.

"I do have a confession, Matt." Gladys set the cup of coffee he'd made for her on the table beside her recliner. "I was none too pleased with you when they loaded me into that ambulance."

After closing the doors on the stove, he crossed the beige carpet to kneel beside her. "I know. I wasn't too pleased about it, either, but I had to exercise some tough love. You needed the extra care."

Smiling, she patted his hand with her wrinkled one. "And you knew just what you were doing. If I'd have stayed here, I probably would have been dead in days."

While he may have known it to be true, he wasn't ready to acknowledge it. "So what can I do for you today?"

She wrinkled her nose. "Nothing. I'm doing just fine, thanks to you."

"Aw, come on, Gladys." He gently nudged her arm. "There's got to be something you're craving. Help me out and tell me what that is."

She stared out the window for a moment, watching the snow fall to the ground. "Well, I don't expect you to do it now, but I've found myself with a hankering for some of those cinnamon rolls from the Miner's Café. Maybe you could pick me up a few the next time you're in there."

He smiled, knowing he wouldn't wait. "That would be Granny's Kitchen. Remember, Mrs. Ward's granddaughter, Celeste, now owns it."

She wagged a finger. "That's right."

"But she uses her grandmother's recipe."

The older woman perched her clasped hands over her smaller-than-usual belly. "Yes, those are some mighty fine cinnamon rolls."

"They are, indeed." He stood. "Matter of fact, I'm kind of craving one myself. What do you say I go pick us up a pan?"

Gladys looked like she'd just stolen the last cookie from the cookie jar. "Can you do that?"

"Young lady, I have sworn to serve and protect. And I am here to serve you."

The woman snickered into her hand.

"I'll be back in a jiffy." Amid the falling snow, he hurried outside to his Tahoe. Oh, how he loved that woman. And was glad to see her back to her old self.

He pulled out of her drive and, a few minutes later, eased into a parking space near Granny's Kitchen with a smile on his face and a song in his heart. Something that seemed to happen a lot more often lately. Between learning that he had a daughter and a restored relationship with his father, life was sweeter than it had been in a long time. Now if only Lacie would decide to stay in Ouray.

He didn't know what he'd do if she took that job in Colorado Springs. Probably follow them. Because the thought of living without her and Kenzie was more than he could bear.

Thanks to Valerie, though, Colorado Springs might not even be a blip on Lacie's radar anymore. He could only pray that job in Telluride would come through.

Opening the door of his vehicle, he stepped out into the crisp late-morning air and continued onto the sidewalk.

"Morning, Matt." Kaleb Palmer, a wounded warrior and Ouray's most decorated hero who was now owner of Mountain View Jeep Tours, looked a little weary.

"Hey, Kaleb." He shook his old schoolmate's hand. "You doin' all right? You don't look so good."

Kaleb rubbed the back of his neck. "Ah, the twins are teething, so Grace and I had kind of a rough night."

"Yeah, from what I hear teething is tough enough with one, but you've got double trouble."

The corners of Kaleb's mouth lifted. "We wouldn't trade it for the world, though. Will and Whitney have brought so much joy into our lives."

"I hear ya." Just the thought of Kenzie could brighten his spirits. "Hang in there and tell Grace I said merry Christmas." He clapped his friend on the shoulder before he walked away.

"Will do, buddy."

At the corner, Matt reached for the restaurant's door handle.

"Matt!"

Kenzie?

Turning in the direction of Main Street, he saw her happily running across the street all by herself as though she didn't have a care in the world—and a truck moving rapidly toward her.

His gaze jerked from her to the driver. She'd bolted so fast and was so small he knew the driver couldn't see her.

"Kenzie!" Lacie stood frozen on the opposite corner, watching the horror unfold.

His heart jackhammered against his tactical vest. He had to get to his little girl before that truck got to her.

Though adrenaline pushed him forward, his legs felt like lead as he rushed into the wet street.

All around him, everything seemed to be moving in slow motion. Him, Kenzie… Everything except for that truck.

He waved his arms wildly, desperately trying to get the driver's attention.

People on the sidewalks yelled for the man to stop. But he didn't.

All the while, a grinning Kenzie kept moving toward Matt, oblivious to the danger headed straight for her.

God, I need Your help! Please don't let my daughter die!

A guttural sound he didn't even recognize escaped his throat as he made a final lunge toward Kenzie.

His arm made contact.

He scooped her up and dove out of the way as the truck skidded to a halt.

Clutching his daughter to his chest, he sat in the middle of the street, trying to catch his breath. *Thank You, God. Thank You.*

The panicked driver exited the vehicle. "I'm so sorry! I didn't see her."

Matt sucked in a large amount of bone-chilling air and held up a reassuring hand. "I know. You're fine. Just move on." He was too spent to worry about anything besides his little girl.

Those who had been looking on began to clap as Matt stood and continued across the street with Kenzie still in his arms. He didn't care about their applause, though. The simple fact that she was safe was all that mattered.

Pressing his face into her jacket, he willed his emotions to remain at bay. Not only did Kenzie need him, Lacie did, too. And just as God was there for him, he would be there for them.

The flow of traffic had resumed by the time he reached the corner. A frantic Lacie took Kenzie from him and hugged her tight.

"Thank God, you're all right." Her watery eyes found his. "I don't know what happened. I was holding her hand. She took off so fast..." After a final squeeze, she set Kenzie to the ground.

The child who had been unaware of what was going on only a few seconds ago now pooched out her bottom lip as she slowly looked up at him, tears welling in her big brown eyes. "But I wanted to see you."

His heart nearly broke.

He knelt beside her and took hold of her tiny hand. "I want to see you, too, Kenzie. But you're too small to be crossing the street by yourself." The mere thought of what could have happened clogged his throat.

He swallowed hard. "Promise me that next time you will tell your aunt Lacie and wait for her to cross the street with you."

"I promise."

When he glanced up at Lacie, he noticed that all of the color had drained from her face.

Uh-oh.

He shot to his feet. "Lace, you okay?"

She started to sway. Her eyes rolled.

Lifting her into his arms, he said, “Kenzie, you stay right with me.” He moved to a nearby bench and watched as she climbed onto it before he sat down, still holding on to Lacie. “Lace, can you hear me?”

Her head bobbed, sending her caramel waves spilling over her shoulders. “Yeah. I guess I just lost my breath for minute.”

He eased Lacie between him and Kenzie. “I think we both did.”

She wrapped her arms around the child and held her close, tears streaming down her cheeks, which were slowly regaining their color. “Thank you, Matt.” She straightened to look at him. “If you hadn’t been there—”

He touched her cheek and brushed her tears away. “But I was. No thanks necessary.” He pushed the hair away from her face. “I’ve got your back, Lace.”

She turned away then, but not before he realized just how much he meant what he’d said. He wanted to be there for her. To have her in his life. Her and Kenzie.

His dad was right. He was in love with Lacie.

Chapter Thirteen

Lacie had never been more frightened in her entire life. Yet Matt had been there to not only save the day, but to help guide her through the aftermath. Just like he'd been there for her countless other times since she came back to Ouray.

So when he suggested they attend church together on Sunday, she found it difficult to say no. Because, after what had happened in the middle of Main Street Friday, they shared a mutual understanding of just how much they had to be grateful for.

Sitting with Matt's father and three of his brothers, however, gave her pause. Wasn't it enough that they were going to be with them at the ranch later this afternoon? It wasn't that she didn't like them, it was just so...familial. And she wasn't quite prepared for that.

Nonetheless, she supposed she'd better get used to it. After all, that was the whole reason they were going to the ranch. Kenzie was a Stephens, meaning Lacie would likely be seeing all of them a lot.

When the service ended, she and Matt picked up

Kenzie from her class and made their way to his Jeep through a fresh layer of snow.

"I love singing those old Christmas carols." Lacie opened the passenger-side door. "There's something about them that's very comforting."

"I couldn't agree more." Matt carried Kenzie, who insisted on wearing her red patent leather Mary Janes despite the decent amount of snow that had fallen overnight and continued coming down. "It's that sense of tradition, not to mention the true meaning of Christmas within their words, that makes them special."

He hooked Kenzie into her booster seat, which they'd transferred from Lacie's SUV, before sliding into the driver's seat. "Shall we grab some lunch?" Then, since they had yet to say anything to Kenzie, he mouthed the words, *before we head to the ranch.*

"I suppose that would be all right." Lacie adjusted her scarf. "I could go for a hot bowl of stew." Even though it meant they'd be together the entire day. Something that seemed to be happening a lot more often.

"No!" Kenzie pouted in the back seat. "I want to go home."

Lacie twisted to face her. "You don't want to get some chicken nuggets?"

"No." Arms crossed over her chest, Kenzie adamantly shook her head. "I want to see Grandma." Strange, since she usually loved to go out.

Lacie glanced at Matt. "I'm not sure what's gotten into her."

He put the vehicle into gear. "No point in making her go."

She shrugged and faced forward again, debating her next move. But since they'd already agreed to lunch…

"I can make up some soup and sandwiches at home. If you're interested."

He eyed her across the center console. "I'm a bachelor, Lace. I'm always interested in food. Especially the home-cooked variety."

When they arrived at her mother's, Lacie unhooked Kenzie. "You want me to carry you so your feet won't get wet?"

Without responding, the determined child scooted past her and ran right through the snow to the house.

A grinning Matt came alongside her as they followed. "I guess you have your answer."

Lacie shook her head. "She sure is acting weird." Yet she couldn't imagine why.

"I wouldn't worry about it." He leaned closer. "She's going to have a great time once we get to the ranch."

She bent in his direction. "True, but we'd still better keep that to ourselves until after lunch. Otherwise, we'll never get her to eat."

Kenzie let herself in and by the time Matt and Lacie made it inside, she was already in the kitchen.

"How was church?" Mom stood at the island, tossing a salad.

"We learneded about baby Jesus." Still wearing her coat with the mittens dangling from the sleeves, Kenzie crawled up onto one of the stools that lined one side of the island.

Lacie closed the door, but waited in the living room, curious as to what her niece was up to.

"You did?" Mom tried to act engaged.

"Uh-huh," Kenzie continued, more animated than usual. "'Cept He didn't stay a baby. He growed up."

"He did?" Mom looked a little wary, her curious

gaze shifting from Kenzie to Lacie and Matt as they approached the sofa.

"And guess what?" Kenzie's brown eyes were wide, as was her grin. She was in rare form today.

"What?" Mom tried to mimic her granddaughter's excitement, but failed.

"He loves us *this* much." Kenzie stretched her arms as wide as they would go, her mittens swaying to and fro.

Mom didn't respond, though. She simply focused on her salad. The thing should be good and tossed by now.

Seemingly annoyed, Kenzie climbed onto the counter. She was not about to be ignored. Evidently, she had something to say and she was going to say it.

"Young lady—" Mom looked horrified "—you know better than to—"

Undeterred, Kenzie plopped down on her knees in front of her grandmother, laid a hand on either side of the woman's face and forced her to look at her.

Lacie had to put a hand over her mouth to keep from laughing. Glancing over at Matt, she noticed that he was every bit as humored about what was going on as she was.

Nose inches away from her grandmother, Kenzie said, "And He loves you, too, Grandma."

Lacie's mouth fell open now. If she hadn't been here to witness this… But, boy, was she glad she was. She laid a hand to her chest as tears pricked the backs of her eyes. *And a child shall lead them.*

Turning, she started for the hallway before she cried in earnest.

Matt followed her.

She pulled a tissue from her pocket and dabbed her

eyes. "I don't think I've ever been prouder of that little girl. Who knew she could preach like that?"

"No kidding." He smiled. "Though I'm pretty proud of you, too," he whispered.

She peered up at him. "Why?"

"All these years, you were the one who saw to it Kenzie was in church. You helped instill those convictions in her and I, for one, really appreciate that."

Lacie gave a tremulous smile, her heart feeling as though it had been set beside an enormous bonfire. "And if Kenzie's words happen to impact Mom, then even better."

After changing into clothes more appropriate for the ranch, Lacie returned to the kitchen to start on lunch. Now that Kenzie had accomplished what she'd set out to do when they left church, she was more interested in playing with Matt. So Lacie decided to wait until *after* they told her they were going to the ranch to talk her niece into changing. A little motivation never hurt to keep things running smoothly.

She grabbed a can of tomato soup from the cupboard and cheese and butter from the fridge. All the while she could feel her mother watching her from the table as she slowly chewed her salad.

Really? Who had a salad on a cold day like this?

She dared a glance across the island.

Her mother, that was who.

Oh, well. To each her own. Lacie had too many other things to think about besides what her mother thought of Kenzie's little sermon. Like the two job prospects she had looming out there.

After putting the soup on to heat, she readied a skillet and opened the loaf of bread. She'd contacted the gentleman in Telluride, who'd seemed very interested, and sent him her resume. He'd promised to get back in touch with her tomorrow.

In addition, she'd finally heard back from the company in Colorado Springs and had a phone interview scheduled with them for tomorrow afternoon. This was shaping up to be a busy week.

Yet, as she buttered the first slice of bread, she couldn't decide which job she'd prefer more. While staying in Ouray would be nice, there were so many more opportunities in the eastern part of the state. Then again, back there it'd be just her and Kenzie. Here, they'd have all kinds of friends and family. People who could help out, should the need arise.

Lord, show me what You would have me do. Lead me on Your path.

Mom brought her empty bowl to the sink as Lacie laid the first sandwich in the pan. The butter sizzled when it made contact with the heat, much like the feel of her mother's gaze boring into her. It was only a matter of time before—

"So did you put Kenzie up to that?"

Spatula in hand, she faced her mother. "You know, Mom, I wish I could say I did." She couldn't help smiling. "But, like it or not, that was all Kenzie."

To her surprise, Mom didn't respond. She merely lowered her gaze and walked away.

Matt couldn't remember the last time he'd actually looked forward to going to the ranch. Sure there'd been a few times since his mother died that his presence had been requested and he'd forced himself to go, but his visits were always overshadowed by an enormous sense of dread at the thought of seeing his father.

All these years, he'd never imagined his father had been hurting, too. That he'd wanted to reconcile, but had been just as afraid as Matt to make a move. And while Matt had feared the news about Kenzie would have deepened the chasm between them, it had instead brought healing and allowed them to start anew.

Thank You, God, for redeeming something I thought unsalvageable.

Now, as they headed toward the ranch, he could hardly wait to introduce his daughter to everything it had to offer. Fishing, exploring, climbing trees, riding horses and so much more. Not that they'd be able to do many of those things today, but now that the snow had stopped, they might get in something fun.

"Are we there yet?" Kenzie wiggled in her booster seat.

"Almost." In the passenger seat of his Jeep, Lacie rolled her pretty eyes. "Imagine hearing that question over and over for five hours."

He shuddered. That alone should be incentive enough for her *not* to take the job back east, should they offer it to her. That and the fact that he didn't want her to go. Because the more time he spent with her, the more he realized just how special she was.

"Horsies!" Kenzie said as they approached the ranch.

He peered at her via the rearview mirror. "Hey, how would you like to ride one of those horses, Kenzie?"

Her arms shot straight into the air. "Yay!"

"Wh—" Lacie's head jerked in his direction. "You're not serious about that, are you?"

"Sure, why not?" He sent her a curious glance as they

turned into the drive and continued under the arched sign. "I was a lot younger than her the first time I sat on a horse."

"Yeah, but you were around them your entire life. Until Monday, Kenzie had never even seen one up close." Why was she getting so worked up?

"Lacie, it's all right. You know I wouldn't do anything to put her in danger."

Her expression was incredulous. "Oh, you mean like you did Marissa."

"What?"

"You know, the time you took her horseback riding and the horse bolted into the woods." She shook her head. "Her neck was scraped and scratched from one side to the other from being dragged through the trees."

Oops. He'd forgotten about that. "I blame Noah for that. He promised that horse was perfect for a novice."

She cast a wary glance at the stable as they passed. "And that's supposed to make me feel better?"

"I'll be choosing the horse this time." Not to mention that he and his brother were both a lot wiser now.

"It's not you I'm worried about. It's an unpredictable animal."

They bumped the rest of the way up the long drive in silence. He couldn't help wondering if what had happened on Friday was playing a part in Lacie's sudden overprotectiveness. Because when they'd taken Kenzie to see the horses last Monday, Lacie had been fine.

"Pretty lights," said Kenzie when they pulled up to the ranch house. Obviously the heated exchange between him and Lacie hadn't affected her.

He eyed the colorful strands of lights that now adorned the railing of the deck and smiled. Evidently the grouchy old coot they'd run into at the supercenter last week had found his Christmas spirit. And perhaps it had something to do with the little girl in the back seat.

Emerging from his vehicle, he noticed Andrew's truck parked on the other side of their father's dually.

"Looks like Andrew and Carly are already here." Considering Noah, Jude and Daniel lived at the ranch, it looked like he, Lacie and Kenzie were the last to arrive.

He helped Kenzie from the back seat and held her hand as the three of them made their way onto the long deck. Fresh snow crunched under their boots, yet despite the gray clouds overhead, he couldn't help feeling that this was going to be a good day.

When they entered the ranch house, the first thing Matt smelled was pine, reminding him of Christmases from long ago. His heart warmed. Deciding to cut down a real tree had been the right thing to do. In this house, nothing else would do.

After removing their boots in the mudroom, they continued into the family room with its wood-burning stove and overstuffed yet oh-so-comfortable furniture. And there in front of the picture window was the tree. Smaller than he was used to seeing, but magnificent nonetheless.

"There they are." A grinning Dad set his coffee cup on the off-white counter and started toward them from the adjoining kitchen. Stopping, he looked straight at Matt. "Glad you could make it, son."

A lump formed in Matt's throat. It had been a long time since he'd felt welcomed in this house.

He did his best to shake off the emotion. "I wouldn't have missed it, Dad."

"Lacie, good to see you again." The old man patted her on the arm.

"Thank you for inviting us," she said.

Lowering his gaze, Dad smiled at his granddaughter. "And how are you today, Miss Kenzie?"

"Good." She leaned into Lacie. Something Matt had come to expect whenever his daughter was feeling shy or insecure.

Hillary approached then. "Hello, everyone."

Carly followed and hugged Lacie. "I'm so glad you're here." His sister-in-law then knelt in front of Kenzie. "Megan's been looking forward to seeing you again."

His daughter straightened and smiled, obviously feeling more confident. "Where is she?"

Carly stood. "She and Andrew are at the stables." She looked at him now. "Noah is giving her a riding lesson."

Kenzie gasped, her face beaming. "I want to ride the horsies, too."

"I'm sure we can arrange that." Hands resting on his denim-clad hips, Dad continued to watch the little girl.

Recalling their conversation in the Jeep, Matt glanced at Lacie.

Her eyes were wide as she looked at Carly. "Lessons, huh?"

"Oh, yes. Megan loves horses, so the more knowledge she has about them, the safer she'll be."

He'd have to remember to thank his sister-in-law later.

"You think we have a helmet small enough for Kenzie?" He eyed his father, hoping that the mention of safety equipment would help put Lacie at ease.

"Sure. We got all sizes."

He figured as much, considering Abundant Blessings

Ranch not only offered lessons but trail rides during the summer months. Something Noah had been working toward expanding into a full-blown rodeo school.

"Can we go now?" While Lacie might be nervous, Kenzie was more than ready.

Dad looked from his granddaughter to Matt then Lacie. "I don't know why not."

"But she's only five." Lacie fiddled with the zipper on her coat. She still wasn't sold.

"Ah, she'll do just fine," said Dad. "You can even go down there with her."

"C'mon, Aunt Lacie." Kenzie tugged on her arm. "Let's go."

Still looking none too certain, Lacie reluctantly followed Kenzie across the wood laminate flooring toward the mudroom.

Matt fell in beside her, determined to put her at ease. "Don't worry, Lace. I'll be with her the whole time."

However, the glare she sent him said he hadn't reassured her at all.

Chapter Fourteen

Lacie had a bad feeling about this.

Following Matt and a helmeted Kenzie down a long aisle lined with stalls, she drew in a shaky breath, the smell of hay and horse filling her nostrils.

"My brother Noah helped me choose the perfect horse for you." Matt smiled down at Kenzie.

"What's its name?" She tilted her little face to look at him.

"His name is Toby."

"He's a boy?"

Matt chuckled. "That's usually how it works."

He was putting her on a male horse?

Passing another stall, Lacie eyed the big fellow Matt had introduced them to last week. The one he said was Noah's horse. The dark brown creature was huge.

Gentle or not, why would Matt risk putting a little girl on something so massive?

She double stepped to catch up with them. "I'm sorry, Matt. I just don't think this is a good—"

"Here we go, Kenzie." As though ignoring Lacie, Matt stopped in front of one of the stalls and slid the wood-

and-metal door to one side. "Meet Toby." His gaze shifting to Lacie, he motioned for her to have a look.

"Oh…" Hands clasped against her chest, Kenzie eyed the animal with wonder.

Taking a step closer, Lacie peered inside to see a small black-and-white horse. "A pony?" Young and barely trained. She sent Matt a questioning gaze.

He continued into the stall. "A Shetland pony." He rubbed a hand over the animal. "He's eight years old." He sent Lacie a pointed stare. "We keep him especially for kids."

Suddenly embarrassed, she backed off while he bridled and saddled the horse. She shouldn't have doubted him. She'd seen how he responded when Kenzie flew into the street two days ago. He'd put his own life on the line to save her. So why did she think he wouldn't have Kenzie's best interests at heart now?

Still, animals were unpredictable. What if something spooked the horse or it didn't want to be ridden? She closed her eyes. After what happened Friday, she was more afraid than ever.

Matt led Toby into the aisle. "We're ready to go."

Lacie fell in beside Kenzie. "You listen to everything Matt tells you and do exactly what he says."

"Okay."

While Matt continued into the small indoor arena with Kenzie and Toby, Lacie joined Clint, Noah, Andrew and Megan at the railing.

"She'll be just fine." Clint winked.

Matt lifted Kenzie into the saddle and got her situated.

"Aunt Lacie, look at me."

Lacie couldn't help but smile. She pulled out her phone and opened the camera.

"Smile." She snapped a couple of shots.

Matt led the animal and Kenzie around the large circle.

Kenzie's smile had never been bigger, though she also seemed to understand the importance of paying attention to what she was doing.

"That a girl," said Clint.

Kenzie waved as they passed and Lacie caught another picture.

While Noah, Andrew and Megan discussed her lesson, Lacie turned to Clint.

"Thank you for being so good to Kenzie, welcoming her like this."

He perched a boot on one of the fence rungs. "You and Kenzie are welcome here anytime."

She nodded uncomfortably, knowing what she still needed to say. "I also want to apologize for my sister's actions. Keeping Kenzie away from all of you, not letting Matt know..."

The older man's smile was one of understanding. "It doesn't matter how she got here—she's here now. And we couldn't be more pleased."

She again searched out Kenzie. Something wasn't right, though. "Is it my imagination or is she leaning?" And with every step the horse took, the saddle and Kenzie inched farther down Toby's side.

"Saddle isn't cinched," said Clint.

Matt looked at Kenzie then, but it was too late.

Kenzie toppled off the horse.

"No!" Lacie climbed the rungs, thrust herself over the railing and rushed toward Kenzie. What if the horse stepped on her? He may be small, but he still weighed a lot more than a little girl.

She reached them as Matt lifted Kenzie to her feet. "You okay, small fry?"

How could he take this so lightly? It wasn't as though she'd simply stumbled.

Then she heard it. Kenzie was—laughing?

Looking up at Matt, she dusted herself off. "That was fun."

Fun? She was practically having a heart attack and Kenzie thought it was fun?

Matt barely glanced at Lacie before turning his attention back to his daughter. "Let's get this saddle tightened up so you can ride some more."

Feeling like a fool for overreacting, she made her way across the arena.

Clint opened the gate for her. "Looks like we might need to get you on a horse, too."

She faced him as he closed it, only to see a mischievous grin. "I'm sorry. I don't usually overreact like that."

He set a calloused hand on her shoulder. "I guess you're still pretty rattled about what happened Friday."

"That obvious, huh?"

"Just a little." He held up a finger and thumb. "If there's one thing I've learned raising five boys, it's that no matter how good of a parent you are, they're still going to get hurt, they're going to get sick, they're gonna cry and they're going to do some of the *stupidest* things you can imagine."

She laughed then.

His weathered expression turned more serious. "The only thing we can do is love them." His dark eyes so reminiscent of Matt's drifted toward the arena. "And sometimes we don't even get that right." He cleared his throat. "What I'm trying to say is that you're a fine mama to that little girl and, even though he's new to it, I think Matt's going to be a great dad."

Looking over her shoulder, she watched Matt put Kenzie back into the saddle. "I think he already is."

When the ride was over, Kenzie went on back to the house with Clint, Noah, Andrew and Megan while Lacie helped Matt put things away at the stables. He was unusually quiet, though, and she had a pretty good idea why.

"I'm sorry I overreacted." Standing in the doorway of the tack room, hands shoved in the pockets of her puffer, she watched as he put things away.

"Nah, I get it." He hung up the bridle, never even looking her way. "You're still freaked out from the other day."

"That's true, I am. But I don't want you to think that I don't trust you. I mean, after all, you were the one who saved her. I just stood there like a bump on a log." If he hadn't been there, Kenzie could have been killed while she watched.

He stopped what he was doing and finally faced her. "Is that what this is all about?" He moved toward her then. "Are you blaming yourself for what happened?"

All of the emotions she'd been holding in rose to the surface. Her throat thickened. Her bottom lip began to quiver.

She quickly turned away. "I couldn't stop her." Looking toward the rafters, she blinked several times. "One second I had a hold of her hand and the next—" A sob caught in her throat. Her body began to shake.

"Look at me, Lace."

She didn't want to, but he stepped in front of her and made her do it anyway.

"Aw, Lace." He took her into his arms and that was

it. Everything she'd been fighting so hard to keep inside let loose. All of the pent-up angst, disappointment and failure flooded to the surface.

"It's all my fault," she cried. "I should have stopped her, but I didn't."

He tightened his hold. "It's all right. We never know how we're going to react when we're put in situations like that."

"No, it's not all right." Her anger spilled out. Breaking free, she moved into the tack room. "Nothing is all right. I lost my job. I'm the reason we don't have a home. The reason Kenzie isn't going to be able to wake up Christmas morning and walk down the hall in her own house to a tree filled with presents and Christmas music playing in the background. It's all because of me." Exhausted, she dropped onto a bale of hay, covered her face with her hands and, for the first time since she became Kenzie's guardian, she let her tears fall freely.

When she finally stopped, she lifted her head to see Matt kneeling in front of her with a roll of paper towels.

"Not as soft as tissues," he said, "but at least they're absorbent."

Smiling, she pulled off a few sheets and blotted her face. "I'm sorry you had to see that." He probably thought her a lunatic.

"I'm not. Now I know you're human."

She peered up at him. "As opposed to…?"

"Well, we won't go there." Grinning, he tugged her to her feet, but didn't let go of her hands. "You know, a dam can only hold so much before it breaks. Sounds like you've been holding in an awful lot."

She nodded, her cheeks growing warm.

"You're not alone, Lacie. I know you think you need

to do and take care of everything yourself, but there are plenty of us who want to help you. Me, your mom…me."

"I know." Seemed he'd proved that over and over, clear back to that day he helped her with her battery.

He glanced toward the window. "I hate to bring this up, but we should probably head on up to the house for dinner."

She groaned, covering her face. "I must look a mess."

"Not at all." Pulling her hand away, he touched her cheek. "You look beautiful."

"Yeah, right."

"I mean it, Lace. You're the most beautiful woman I've ever known." He looked so serious.

Her insides tangled. But she knew better than to allow herself to be sucked in.

She turned for the door. "They're waiting on us."

Matt finished clearing off the worn-out wooden dining room table that had been left behind by the previous owners when he bought his house. The scarred and scratched surface may not be pretty, but it was flat, making it the perfect spot for wrapping presents.

He retrieved the few gifts he'd already bought for Kenzie, along with scissors and tape. Now he just needed Lacie to get here with the wrapping paper and her presents. Since Barbara had agreed to keep Kenzie, they'd decided this would be a good time to compare each of their gift selections so they could see what else they might need, as well as wrap without fear of Kenzie walking in on them.

Returning to the living room, he turned on some Christmas music and cleared the crumbs littering the coffee table, his gaze drifting from the tree glowing in the corner to the empty fireplace. Something was missing, though he had yet to figure out what that something was. Perhaps it was just the lack of a fire. He'd have to make a point to swing by the ranch to pick up some wood.

A knock sounded at the door.

He opened it to find Lacie holding a large box that obscured her face and plastic bags dangling from both arms, one with two rolls of wrapping paper sticking out.

"A little help, please." She grunted.

He tossed the crumbs out the door and grabbed hold of the box. "I got it." He waited for her to enter then closed the door. "You can put the stuff in the dining room."

She made her way into the space adjacent the living room and dropped the bags into one of four peeling chairs. "Phew! That wasn't quite as easy as I thought it was going to be."

He set the box on the table. "You could have asked for help, you know. Or have you forgotten our conversation yesterday?"

Making a face, she tossed her head back. "Don't remind me. I still can't believe I did that to you."

"Uh, just what was it you did to me?"

"As if you don't remember." Casting an annoyed eye his way, she shrugged out of her puffer. "Having a meltdown is one thing. Doing it in front of someone else is just wrong."

"Not if that someone else doesn't mind." Actually, he kind of liked that she felt comfortable enough with him to let her feelings out. Made him feel as though she finally trusted him.

Now, however, he'd better change the subject. "Can I get you anything? Water, coffee, hot chocolate—it's instant."

"Yeah, I think some hot chocolate would be nice."

At least he got her to smile. "Marshmallows?"

"Of course."

Since he already had the water hot on the stove, suspecting that's what she'd go for, he quickly scooped the powder into a couple of mugs, then added the water and a spoon before grabbing the bag of marshmallows and rejoining her.

He set the items on the table. "I forgot to ask you. How did the interview go?" Today was her phone interview with the company in Colorado Springs. And while he didn't want her to fail, he wouldn't be disappointed if they chose someone else, either.

"It went well." She opened the bag, tossed a handful of marshmallows into one of the cups and stirred. "They said they liked my designs, that my style would work well with their projects..." She shrugged. "I guess I'll find out in a few days." Lifting the cup, she blew on the steaming mixture. "Oh, and I heard from the company in Telluride."

Cradling his mug, he did his best to keep his excitement under wraps. "And?"

"I have an interview with them tomorrow morning." She started to take a sip, then stopped. "In person, of course."

"That always helps. You get a better feel for people when you can see their body language and such."

"Yeah. But I have to admit, I'm a little nervous."

"You shouldn't be. With your experience and sparkling personality, they're sure to love you."

She puffed out a laugh. "I don't know about that, but I appreciate the vote of confidence." She sipped her drink. "Mmm... I like the Christmas music, too. All

Mom plays at the shop is some nonholiday instrumental stuff and then nothing at home." She let go a sigh. "It's kind of depressing. So I'm glad I'm here."

"Me, too." Though he doubted she knew just how much. "You want to show me what you got for Kenzie?"

"Yes." She returned her cup to the table and opened the flaps on the box. "I really haven't gotten her any toys yet, because I wanted to wait until I knew what you were getting her." Reaching inside, she pulled out what looked like a shoe box. "I got her a pair of riding-style boots." She lifted the lid to show him.

"Nice." Though he might be in trouble.

After depositing the boots on the table, she reached inside the larger box again. "And you'll probably love this." Smiling, she pulled out a pink cowboy hat.

"Okay." He smiled back, though he was cringing inside.

"And then I got her a stuffed animal." She showed him a fluffy black-and-white horse that kind of reminded him of Toby. "Seeing as how she's now totally in love with horses."

He drew in a deep breath, set his cup down and picked up the bag of things he'd gotten Kenzie. "Lace, you know how they say 'great minds think alike'?"

"Yeah…"

He dumped the items onto the table. "Boots, cowboy hat and a stuffed horse."

Looking at his gifts, she started to laugh. "Oh, that is too funny." She picked up his pink cowgirl boots and her pink cowboy hat. "These will go perfectly together." After setting those aside, she grabbed the identical stuffed horses. "I'll return mine." She set it in the box as he reached for the black cowboy hat he'd bought.

"And I'll return my hat. Because she's going to be so in love with the pink hat and boots that we may never get her to wear anything else."

"Oh, you're right about that." Hand on her hip, she eyed the three items they were going to give Kenzie. "You know what this means, don't you?"

"Yeah. We have a lot more shopping to do."

"And very little to wrap."

They looked at each other and laughed.

"What's in the other bags?" He pointed to the chair.

"I almost forgot." Taking hold of the first one, she reached inside. "I realized that we didn't have any stockings, so I bought us some, along with these cute stocking holders."

"Stocking holders?" He'd never heard of such a thing. At the ranch, they just hung theirs on a nail.

"I didn't want to mess up that pretty mantel of yours, so…" She held up a silver rectangle with a hook on one side. "They're weighted, so they sit on the mantel like this." She held it so the hook was on the bottom and there was a letter *J* on the top. "And then—" she grabbed one of three furry red-and-white stockings "—you simply hang your stocking on it."

"Clever." He studied it a moment. "Except, why the *J*?"

"Oh. There's also an *O* and a *Y*, so they spell *joy*. I thought about doing our initials, but with a *K*, *L* and *M*, I was afraid it would look like we'd simply carved out the middle of the alphabet."

"Good thinking."

Suddenly looking sheepish, she said, "I hope you don't mind, but I got one more thing to kind of round out the whole look."

"Lacie, you can do whatever you want."

From the final bag, she brought out some evergreen garland. "It's prelit, so I thought it would cast a nice light while illuminating the *J-O-Y*."

"Didn't you mention this that night before we got the tree?"

She tilted her head. "Yeah, you're right. And then we forgot all about it."

"Yeah, well, we took a little detour when we decided to cut down a tree." He picked up the stockings. "Shall we go put them up?" He nodded toward the living room.

In no time, she'd artfully arranged everything. He plugged in the lights before joining her near the couch. And when he turned to look at what she'd done, he could hardly believe his eyes.

"You're not going to believe this, Lace, but all week long I've been looking at the fireplace, knowing that something was missing. I thought it was simply a fire, but you hit the nail on the head."

"What do you mean?"

He turned to face her. "I've lived in this house for over a year now, worked to make it mine, and yet it's never really felt like home. Until now." Unable to stop himself, he caressed her cheek. "The decorations, all of the little touches you've added… Lacie, you've made it feel like a home."

Lowering his head, he kissed her. Something he'd wanted to do for a long time, but the moment had never felt right until tonight. With or without Kenzie, Lacie was the missing piece in his life.

He pulled her closer as her arms wound around his neck. She smelled like the wildflowers that covered the mountains in late July.

And he knew that this was definitely right.

Chapter Fifteen

By Tuesday afternoon, Lacie was sorely in need of a distraction. Something that would take her mind off Matt and that amazing kiss. She'd never been kissed like that before. In Matt's warm embrace, she'd felt safe, wanted…loved.

So she was more than grateful when Carly called, inviting her and Kenzie to come over to Granger House for some cookie decorating.

"Look, Aunt Lacie." Sitting at the table in Carly's kitchen, Kenzie held up her cookie creation. "I maded a Santa Claus."

Armed with a cup of chai tea, Lacie made her way across beautiful dark hardwood floor to where Kenzie and Megan sat surrounded by bowls of frosting and containers of sprinkles and colored sugars.

She eyed Kenzie's sparkling red confection. "Ooh, he looks good enough to eat."

"No." Suddenly perturbed, her niece quickly withdrew her masterpiece. "We hafta save him for Christmas."

"Oh, okay." Considering that Christmas was just

under two weeks away, she doubted the treat would last that long.

"Don't worry, Kenzie." Beside her, ten-year-old Megan carefully frosted a snowman. "We have lots of cookies so you can take home a whole bunch."

"I can?" The little girl's brown eyes went wide as though she'd never imagined she'd get to decorate more than one cookie.

"Yep." Megan took a bite of the snowman, crumbs clinging to the corners of her mouth. "We even get samples."

Kenzie looked from Megan to the Santa cookie she still held in her hand. After a moment of contemplation, she bit into his red beard and grinned. "He tasteses good."

Chuckling, Lacie returned to the large marble-topped island, where her friend was transferring another batch of freshly baked sugar cookies to a cooling rack. "Thanks for inviting us, Carly. Kenzie is having a ball." And it gave her niece the opportunity to participate in some of those things Lacie used to do as a kid but her mother no longer allowed.

"Good." Carly set the now-empty baking sheets atop the large commercial-style range. "The kids get jazzed on sugar and you and I get time to catch up. Sounds like a win-win to me." She picked up two warm Christmas tree–shaped treats and handed one to Lacie. "Cheers."

"Cheers." She took a bite, savoring the unexpected hint of nutmeg as she admired the baking-themed ornaments dangling from an evergreen swag over the window. "You have quite a knack for decorating." From the historic Victorian home's stunning front porch all the way through to the family room at the back, the house was a feast for the eyes with nods to the season everywhere you looked. Wreaths, seasonal vignettes, poinsettias…

Kenzie had been blown away by the fact that they had two Christmas trees. A lovely Victorian-themed one in the parlor of the bed-and-breakfast and a more casual one for Carly, Andrew and Megan in the family room.

"This place is absolutely gorgeous."

Laughing, Carly dusted the crumbs from her hands. "I know I go a little overboard, but I just can't help myself. I love Christmas."

"I know what you mean." Lacie's father used to say the same thing. Even Mom. They could hardly wait to get the Thanksgiving turkey put away so they could start on Christmas. Then Daddy died and Christmas at their house hadn't been the same since.

But that didn't mean she couldn't resurrect those old traditions so Kenzie could experience them. And thanks to Matt and Carly, she was getting to do just that.

Carly poured herself another cup of tea. "How's the job search going? Did you ever hear from the place in Telluride?"

"Actually, I interviewed with them this morning." She eased onto one of the high-backed stools along the island.

"Yay!" Her friend joined her in the next seat. "That would mean you could stay in Ouray."

"Yes, it would." Something she found even more appealing after spending time with Matt last night. She still couldn't believe they'd picked out the same gifts. Or how pleased he'd been with her simple changes to the fireplace.

You've made it feel like home. Her heart thundered just thinking about the look in his eyes right before he kissed her.

She cleared her throat. "Mind if I get some more tea?"

"No, help yourself."

Lacie scurried around to the other side of the island and poured a cup. It would be silly for her to stay in Ouray just because of Matt, no matter how kind he'd been or how spine-tingling his kisses were. After all, there were no guarantees. And she refused to hang her hat on a man the way her sister had.

So why did those crazy notions of her, Matt and Kenzie as a family keep popping up?

"When will you know something?"

Returning to her seat, she said, "Hopefully by next week."

Carly shivered with excitement. "I'll be praying extra hard then."

Lacie cradled the warm cup in her hands. "You know that I also interviewed with a company in Colorado Springs."

Her friend waved her off. "I don't care about them. I want you to stay here." She sipped her tea, her expression taking on a more impish air. "And I'm sure Matt would like that, too."

If only. "I know he doesn't want Kenzie to go away, but—"

"I wasn't referring to Kenzie." Carly set her mug atop the marble surface. "I was talking about you."

"What do you mean? Matt and I are just friends." At least she assumed they were still friends.

Carly's brow arched. "Mmm-hmm. You just keep telling yourself that."

"I'm not sure what you're getting at." She eyed the two giggling girls across the room. Kenzie appeared to have more frosting on her face than the cookies.

"I used to say the same thing about Andrew and me. And look where we are now." She held up her left hand and wiggled her ring finger.

Panic swirled in Lacie's gut. Were her feelings for Matt that obvious? And if Carly had been able to figure it out, did Matt know, too? More important, did he feel that way about her?

No, she refused to get her hopes up.

Then why did you kiss him?

Eager to change the subject, she said, "Matt said you two got married in September. I thought Andrew lived in Denver."

"He did. But after selling his business, he came back here last spring to work on his grandmother's house—" she pointed to the home next door "—not knowing that she'd left half of it to me. Next thing you know—"

Lacie's phone rang. She pulled it from her back pocket to see Matt's name on the screen. Her cheeks heated. Did he know they'd been talking about him?

She glanced at Carly. "I need to take this." Twisting out of the chair, she pressed the button and put the phone to her ear. "Hello."

"Hey, it's me."

"Yeah, hi." Her stomach did that fluttering thing.

"You aren't going to believe this, but I stopped by your mom's shop earlier and she asked me if I would like her to watch Kenzie tomorrow night so that you and I could go shopping."

Lacie felt her eyes widen. "You're kidding." Turning her back to the girls and Carly, she took a few more steps so Kenzie wouldn't hear her. "I mean, yeah, I mentioned about the gifts, but still, we would be *Christmas* shopping and since she doesn't do Christmas..."

"I found it kind of strange myself. However, since she offered… Are you free tomorrow night?"

"Yes, of course." She turned back around. "The sooner we get this out of the way, the better I'll feel."

"Great. I'll pick you up about six then?"

"Sounds good."

"And Lace?"

Seemed her heart did a little quickstep every time he called her that. "Yeah?"

"I'll see you and Kenzie later tonight?"

She couldn't help smiling. "See you then."

Cup in hand, a grinning Carly leaned back in her chair as Lacie ended the call. "And you think you're just friends, huh?"

Matt enjoyed his time with Kenzie Tuesday night, though he couldn't seem to take his eyes off Lacie. Since that kiss, their relationship had drifted into uncharted waters. And all Matt knew was that he couldn't stop thinking about her.

Which made his shift on Wednesday seem excruciatingly long. Yet as the day progressed, there was one thing he began to understand: his life was finally coming together.

For too many years, he'd felt as though he was simply existing. Now he had a purpose. He was a father. And, after Monday night, had begun to entertain the notion of becoming a husband and having a family to call his own.

No doubt about it, he was in love with Lacie.

Now he just needed to find a way to share those thoughts with her.

However, the toy aisle of the supercenter in Montrose was not the right place.

"What about this art easel?" Lacie looked at him over her shoulder as they continued their search for Christmas gifts Wednesday night. "Or is that a disaster waiting to happen?"

Images of Kenzie armed with a paintbrush filled his head. "Hmm, good question. Perhaps we should keep looking."

While "Jingle Bell Rock" played overhead, they strolled from one aisle to the next, dodging other shoppers who were also searching for that perfect present.

"Are you okay?" He watched Lacie, noting how her turquoise scarf deepened the blue of her eyes. "You seem kind of quiet tonight."

"Yeah, I'm fine." She pushed the cart, scanning each and every shelf. "Just worried about finding something that Kenzie will really enjoy. Not just play with Christmas morning and then be done with it."

He froze, a leaden weight suddenly bearing down on him. "Boy, you can tell this is my first Christmas as a dad. I never even thought of that. That would stink." He wanted his little girl to have something momentous.

Smiling, she patted him on the back. "Sorry, I didn't mean to stress you out. Just keep in mind that there are two of us, so I'm sure we can come up with something."

Out of the corner of his eye, he glimpsed the board games. "Hey, does she have a Candyland game? I used to love playing that." Then he spotted the bicycles. "Or what about a bike? One with training wheels and pink streamers hanging off the handlebars. She'd love that."

"Probably so." Resting her elbow on the cart, Lacie looked up at him. "But what if it's snowing Christmas day? She wouldn't be able to try it out."

"Good point. Better wait till spring for that." Another

idea blazed across his brain. "However, we could get her a sled. Or maybe a toboggan. Then we could take her to Vinegar Hill. We'd have a great time sledding with all of the other kids." He took hold of her arm. "I can see us now, zooming down the hill, noses pink from the cold, snow flying..."

She nodded. "That's not a bad idea. I do have one question, though."

"What's that?"

The corners of her pretty mouth tilted upward. "Is this sled for Kenzie or for you?"

He grinned. "Well, she is kind of little to be going all by herself."

"Okay—" she continued down the aisle "—so a sled for Dad and Kenzie."

He followed behind her, his chest puffed out ever so slightly. "I like the way you said that."

She slowed. "Said what?"

"The way you referred to me as Dad." He shrugged. "I'm looking forward to hearing Kenzie say it someday."

She stopped, her expression turning sad. "Matt—"

"No, no." He held up a hand. "It's okay, Lace." He knew what she was thinking. That he was pushing her to tell Kenzie he was her father when they'd agreed to wait until she was old enough to understand. "I was simply making a statement. Now, let's get back to shopping."

An hour and a half later they left the store armed with a couple of board games, some Legos, a princess doll, Christmas pajamas and a promise that he would find them the perfect sled. This Christmas was going to be the best ever.

Now, as they headed south on Highway 550 in his Jeep with Christmas music playing softly on the radio, he could hardly wait to get back to his house so they could wrap the presents and place them under the tree. Kenzie would be so excited when she saw them.

If only he could decide what to get Lacie. Something heartfelt. Jewelry? Clothes, maybe?

He'd worry about those things another day. Tonight, he and Lacie were alone. And even more than wrapping the gifts, he wanted to talk about his and Lacie's future. Not about jobs or moving, but their feelings for each other and where those feelings could ultimately lead.

"I think we did pretty good, don't you?" He watched the darkened road ahead.

"I do. I'm glad we were able to get it out of the way."

He eyed his rearview mirror. "I can't wait to see Kenzie's face on Christmas morning."

The hum of the tires filled the space between them as Lacie stared out the passenger window.

Reaching across the center console, he gave her shoulder a squeeze. "You tired?"

"No, not too bad." She twisted in her seat to face him, but didn't say anything.

He glanced her way, slowing his speed as they came into the town of Ridgway. "Something wrong?"

Appearing somewhat nervous, she drew in a breath. "I heard from the company in Colorado Springs today."

His grip tightened around the steering wheel and he suddenly found it hard to breathe. "What'd they say?" His voice was tight.

"They offered me the job." The smile he saw via the dashboard lights felt like a knife between his shoulder blades.

This couldn't be happening. Not now. Not when they were growing so close. "Are you going to take it?" Regretting the anger that tinged his words, he added, "I mean, what about the job in Telluride? You haven't heard from them, have you?"

"No, not yet." She faced forward again as they passed under the stoplight. "And I'm still not a hundred percent sure about this one. However, it pays very well and there's room for advancement."

"But what about…?" *Us*, he almost said.

She looked at him. "What?"

"Nothing." He shook his head, accelerating again as they continued out of town.

Looking down at her clasped hands, she said, "How would you feel about it? If I decided to take this job?"

How would he feel? Did she even have to ask? Of course he didn't want her to leave. He couldn't believe she was even considering it.

And what about his daughter? Was Lacie planning to keep Kenzie away from him the way Marissa had?

"Lacie, I—" He stopped himself, his nostrils flaring. Arguing would do no good. She'd made up her mind. "You do what you want to do."

Nothing more was spoken. Just the fact that she was still considering taking Kenzie and heading back east said it all. Obviously what happened between them the other night meant nothing to her. So there was no point in going back to his place.

When they hit the Ouray city limits, he took her straight to her mother's.

Bringing the Jeep to a stop, he said, "Let me know what you decide."

Chapter Sixteen

Lacie stood in the cold night air and watched Matt drive away. She knew better than to get her hopes up. Yet she'd done it anyway. Matt wasn't interested in her. Only Kenzie.

Hands buried in her coat pockets, she forced one foot in front of the other, battling back tears as she continued up the front walk at her mother's. She needed to get away from Ouray. And the sooner the better.

Yes, she was in love with Matt, something she could kick herself for, but she'd obviously misread his feelings for her. Otherwise he would have told her not to take the job in Colorado Springs. Instead, he would have asked her to stay.

But he didn't. Leaving her free to do whatever she wanted. So why was she so torn?

She glanced toward the house. The blinds were closed, yet she could see the glow of light beyond them. It was almost nine o'clock, so Kenzie would likely be in bed. Just as well. Lacie wasn't sure she had the strength to pretend that all was well in her world. Facing her mother was going to be tough enough.

Pausing on the porch, she slumped against the wall. *God, my heart is hurting and I don't know what to do. Should I go ahead and accept this job that will take me and Kenzie away from Ouray and Matt? Or should I wait to see what Telluride has to say?*

A chilling breeze sifted through the trees.

Staying here would mean seeing Matt on an almost daily basis. Was she prepared to deal with that?

She squeezed her eyes shut. *My heart is telling me to go, but I want to be in Your will, Lord. Show me what I should do.*

Wiping a tear from her cheek, she took a deep breath, pushed the door open and stepped inside.

"Surprise!" An overly excited Kenzie rushed toward her and took hold of her hand. "Look what we did, Aunt Lacie." She swept her little arm through the air, as if to say *tah-dah.*

Turning, a lump caught in Lacie's throat. There in front of the window was a Christmas tree, its white lights twinkling among the silver bead garland and a multitude of ornaments. And beside it was her mother, smiling as she added another ornament.

Lacie's broken heart now felt as though it might explode.

"What…?" Tears welled in her eyes as they had only moments before. Except these were happy tears. She brought a hand to her mouth as if trying to keep everything inside. For the first time since Daddy died, there was a Christmas tree in the living room.

Mom came toward her then. "You were right, Lacie. I have been trying to get back at God. All these years, I've been angry." She slipped an arm around Kenzie's shoulder. "It made it hard to listen when my granddaughter so joyfully reminded me just how much Jesus loves me. Then I found this." She turned then and picked up a small box.

"What is it?" Lacie's bottom lip trembled as she watched her mother lift out a shimmering ornament that read Jesus Is the Reason for the Season.

"It was your father's last gift to me." Her mother's voice broke, her blue eyes shimmering with unshed tears. "I found it in the closet the other day, still wrapped, with a note that said Never Forget." She sniffed. "Kenzie was right. Jesus does love me. Enough to hear me out when I finally told Him how upset I was about losing your father."

Unable to hold her emotions in any longer, Lacie embraced her mother. "Oh, Mom. I know how much you miss Daddy." She sobbed.

"I do, sweetheart. More than you will ever know." She set Lacie away from her. "But I can't tell you what a burden has been lifted from me these last few days. My bitterness is gone. All because I finally said my piece."

"I'm so happy for you." She hugged her again. "I love you, Mom."

"I love you, too, sweetheart."

"Aunt Lacie." Kenzie tugged on her hand. "You need to come see this."

Swiping a finger across each cheek, Lacie allowed Kenzie to lead her to the tree, where she picked up a glittering Popsicle-stick snowflake ornament.

"My mommy maded this." Her dark eyes that were so like Matt's were alight with what could only be described as pure joy.

"She sure did." Lacie smiled at the memory. "And

I got mad at her for using up all of the purple glitter." She laughed.

Kenzie giggled while Lacie continued to study the tree, which was filled with so many memories. The colorful palm tree ornament they'd gotten that year they vacationed in Florida. It had been her first time at the beach. The salt dough imprints of her and Marissa's hands when they were toddlers. And the Mod Podge photo of Lacie and her dad that she'd made in kindergarten.

She looked at the ceiling, blinking rapidly. So much joy. So much sorrow. *Thank You, Lord.*

Lowering her gaze, she noticed the stockings hanging from the bookshelf.

"My stocking." After grabbing a tissue from the table next to Mom's chair, she moved to the far end of the room to admire the handcrafted labor of love her grandma Collier had made for her before her first Christmas. Running a finger over the felt-and-sequin snowman, she smiled. How proud she'd been of her stocking, always eager to show her friends when they came over. Because no one had a stocking like hers. Except Marissa.

Just as it always had, her sister's teddy bear Santa stocking hung to the right of hers, the white felt cuff forever marked with a few chocolate smudges courtesy of an eight-year-old Marissa.

"I thought maybe Kenzie could use Marissa's stocking," said Mom. "For this year, anyway."

Recalling the three stockings hanging over Matt's fireplace, she sniffed. "I think that's a great idea."

Arms wrapped around her middle, she continued around the room, taking in all of the items that had lived in her memory, but hadn't seen the light of day in twelve years.

"Oh, Grandma Preston's nativity." Kneeling beside the side table, she felt as though she'd been transported back in time. How she used to love playing with the ceramic Mary, Joseph and baby Jesus. And while most adults would have objected, Grandma never took issue. Sometimes, she even joined in.

Standing, she saw her mother across the room, watching Kenzie, looking happier, more carefree, than she'd seen her in a long time. This was truly an answer to prayer. "I'm proud of you, Mom."

The woman hugged herself as she surveyed the space. "I'm kind of proud of me, too."

"Now we need some presents." Kenzie dropped to her knees in front of the tree, her small fingers moving from one ornament to the next.

Mom looked to Lacie. "That reminds me, how was your evening? Were you successful?"

Lacie's heart broke anew. While she and Matt had been successful in picking out gifts, the rest of the night had been a miserable flop. She didn't know what she was going to do. The Christmas they'd planned at Matt's, the one that had seemed so promising, probably wasn't even going to happen now. At least Mom had had a change of heart. Now Kenzie could wake up Christmas morning to a tree filled with presents and carols playing in the background, the same way Lacie had always done.

But what about Matt? What about the gifts they'd picked out? Would he still get Kenzie the sled?

"It was fine. Though we still have some decisions to

make." The biggest one being whether she would stay in Ouray or head back east and away from Matt.

Matt came home from work the next day and dropped his gear at the door, only to spy the Christmas tree at one end of his living room and the bag of unwrapped gifts at the other. The sickening feeling that had plagued him all day intensified. He didn't know what to do now.

Shoving a hand through his hair, he collapsed onto the couch. He was a mess. These last few weeks his life had been fuller than he ever imagined and he didn't want that to change. Not now, not ever. Unfortunately, that's exactly what was about to happen.

All day long he'd tried and tried to make sense of it. He and Lacie had such a good time at the store. Everything had seemed fine. Yet she'd known. The entire time they were there, she'd known about the job offer and didn't say a thing. Why couldn't she have said something before they went to Montrose?

Because they still would have ended up in the same foul mood and that would have made it nearly impossible to think about shopping.

Glimpsing the stockings spread along the mantle, his heart ached. *J-O-Y.* That's exactly what Lacie and Kenzie had brought into his life. Without them he was miserable.

He dropped his head into his hands. *What do I do, God? What do I do?* Staring at the floor, he saw a sliver of white sticking out from beneath the couch. He picked it up, immediately recognizing the card with columbines on the front. It was a note his mother had written to him when she was dying. Something she'd done for each of her five sons. It must have fallen out of his scrapbook that day all those weeks ago when he'd first suspected he was Kenzie's father.

Opening the card, he again read his mother's words:

> My precious Matt,
> As the middle child, I know you often felt as though you didn't stand out, but you were always a shining light to me. A man of great character, with a stubborn edge, you're kind and eager to help others. Traits some people might take advantage of, so guard your heart.

Tears blurred his vision and he looked away. "I wish you were here now, Mama."

He blinked a few times before allowing his gaze to drift back to her handwritten words.

> Traits some people might take advantage of, so guard your heart. However, not so closely that you allow that something or someone special to slip away.

Lowering the card, he thought about Lacie. She was someone special all right.

And you're letting her slip away, doofus.

He shot to his feet. What was he thinking? He couldn't lose them. He had to find a way to convince Lacie to stay. And there was only one thing he could think of.

After a quick change of clothes, he hopped into his Jeep and drove the few blocks to the Collier house. Darkness had already fallen over the town when he pulled up, and while he'd often been to Lacie's at night, this time he found himself doing a double take to make sure he was at the right house.

There was a Christmas tree in the front window.

Deciding he was, indeed, at the correct house, he climbed out and started up the walk, past a dwindling pile of snow. He wasn't sure he'd ever been so nervous. *God, please let this work. I don't want them to go.*

He knocked on the door. A moment later, Lacie stood before him, looking as beautiful as ever in jeans and a sweater, her hair around her shoulders. Her expression unreadable, she simply stared at him through the storm door for the longest time, until he finally said, "Can I come in?"

She stepped back, allowing him entry.

"Matt!" Kenzie barreled toward him in her favorite bright pink outfit, arms outstretched. At least somebody was happy to see him.

He lifted her into his arms, savoring her sweet childlike aroma. "How's it going, small fry?"

"Come see." She was already trying to wiggle free.

He set her to the ground, only to have her hand take hold of his much larger one.

She tugged him into the living room. "We made Christmas!"

Turning, he took in the entire space. It was Christmas, all right. Everywhere he looked. There was even Christmas music playing in the background.

His gaze captured Lacie's before darting back to Kenzie. "Did you and Aunt Lacie do this?"

Kenzie stared up at him, her smile wide. "No. Grandma and me surpriseded her when she got home last night."

Grandma? Wait a minute. Barbara? But she—

He looked at Lacie. "Your mom? Really?"

Arms crossed over her chest, she nodded. "I was pretty surprised myself."

He glanced around. "Is she still at the shop?"

"Yeah."

Just as well. He didn't need an audience.

"Look, Matt." Kenzie held up a small ceramic manger. "It's baby Jesus."

"I see that." He couldn't help wondering what had happened to change Barbara's mind.

Then he recalled Kenzie's determination to get home from church last Sunday and the way she adamantly shared the good news of Jesus with her grandmother. Could that have been what turned her around?

"Want to color with me?" His daughter was beside him again, peering up at him with those big brown eyes. "I gotted a Christmas coloring book." She held it up. "'Cept there aren't any horsies. Only reindeer."

Could the kid possibly get any cuter? No one could say no to that.

"Sure. Let's sit down at the table." Besides, coloring was supposed to be relaxing. He could use a little of that as he gathered his courage.

While Lacie worked on dinner, Matt sat beside Kenzie, though it was difficult to stay focused with all the things he wanted to say to Lacie swimming through his head.

Nonetheless, he colored a reindeer on one page while Kenzie tended to the Christmas tree on the opposite page. Not near as easy as when they each had their own book to color. But since she had only one that was Christmas themed…

Elbow on the table, chin perched on her hand, his

daughter let out a sigh. "I think I want to color by my-self now."

"Are you sure?"

She nodded.

Standing, he ruffled her soft hair. "Okay, small fry. Let me know if you need my help." He sent her a wink before turning his attention to the kitchen.

Lacie was at the stove, stirring a pot of something that smelled really good. Any other time his stomach would have growled, but it was too tied in knots to do so now.

He took a deep breath. *Okay, Stephens, it's now or never.*

Pressing forward, he moved beyond the island to lean against the counter beside the stove. "Smells good." Great, now she probably thought he was looking for a dinner invitation.

"Vegetable soup." She shrugged. "Not exactly a manly meal."

Time to cut to the chase, before he lost his nerve. "Lacie, I don't want you to go to Colorado Springs."

For a split second, he thought he saw a glimmer of hope in her pretty gray-blue eyes. "I know you think the best thing is for you to devote yourself to Kenzie, but she needs more." He lowered his voice. "She deserves two parents who love her. And, honestly, I can't go back to the way things used to be." Looking her straight in the eye, he took a deep breath and went on. "Marry me?"

Her expression went flat. "Very funny." She whisked past him and turned on the water at the sink.

"I'm serious, Lace." He followed her, not that he had that far to go. Smiling, he took hold of her now-wet hands. “I want us to be a family. Lacie Collier, will you marry me?”

Her gaze searched his for a moment and his hopes soared. Then her brow furrowed as she slowly shook her head.

She let go of his hands, wiping them against her jeans as she stepped away. “I—I’m sorry, but I can’t do that.”

He blinked, his heart feeling as though it had been ripped in two. He’d blown it. She wasn’t interested in him.

What was he supposed to do now?

The only thing he could do.

He retreated. Moved to the table and placed a kiss atop his daughter’s head, the first time he’d dared to show her that kind of affection. “See you later, small fry.”

Turning to leave, he couldn’t help noticing the beautifully decorated Christmas tree in the living room. The one at his house was every bit as nice, thanks to Lacie. But the tree at her mother’s made one thing perfectly clear.

Lacie didn’t need him anymore.

Chapter Seventeen

Matt sat behind the wheel of his sheriff's vehicle the next morning, feeling like a fool for leaving Lacie's with his tail between his legs instead of sticking around to ask her some questions he really needed answers to. Such as when was she leaving? What about Kenzie? When would he get to see her? And what about Christmas? Though it was obvious they'd now be celebrating at her mother's. But what about the gifts they'd bought for Kenzie? She was his daughter, after all, and he intended to spend Christmas with her.

Continuing along one of the county's back roads, he eyed the sleet/snow mixture that had been falling since shortly after sunup and racked his brain, trying to decide how to approach Lacie again. Not that his reasons weren't valid. It was just the situation was so… awkward.

His gaze shifted from the conifers lining the road to his right to the snow-covered mountains beyond the dormant rangeland on his left. He needed some advice and soon, otherwise he'd drive himself crazy. But from who? It wasn't like any of his brothers had ever been in a situation like this, or his father. Still, Dad seemed to be the logical choice. Especially since he knew more about Matt and Lacie's relationship than anyone.

By the time he bumped up the ranch's drive around lunchtime, the wintry mixture had turned to all snow. He parked between Noah's pickup and his father's dually, exited his Tahoe and hurried onto the deck. Good thing his father always had a pot of coffee on. Between the cold and lack of sleep, Matt could really use a cup.

He paused at the door, though. It had been a long time since he'd dropped by the ranch unannounced. Or even wanted to. Should he have called first?

No. Dad had shown him nothing but love and acceptance since that day he came to him. So Matt was going to let bygones be bygones.

Opening the door to the mudroom, two things captured his attention: the aroma of pine and the smell of coffee.

"Dad?"

"In the kitchen," the old man responded.

Matt kicked out of his work boots, thinking about that day he, Lacie and Kenzie had come out here to cut down the trees. The day Kenzie got lost. Or so they thought. That was the day he began to think of the three of them as a unit. A family.

Boy, had he been wrong.

Inside the kitchen, Dad sat at the long wooden table, eating his lunch. "There's some roast beef." He pointed toward the counter. "Help yourself if you're hungry."

"No, thanks." He started toward the cupboard. "I'll just take some coffee." He poured a cup, then joined his father.

Dad's dark eyes narrowed. "What's the problem?"

Matt sent him a curious look. He hadn't even said anything yet. "Who said there was a problem?"

"You did. Those lines in your forehead don't show up unless something's got you bothered. So what is it?"

He wrapped his cold fingers around the hot mug. "Lacie's been offered a job in Colorado Springs."

The old man frowned. "Surely she's not going to take it."

"Unfortunately—" he leaned back in his chair "—I'm afraid she is." If she hadn't already. "But there's more to it than that."

His father picked up a potato chip and waited.

"I'm in love with her, Dad."

Shaking his head, the old man popped the chip into his mouth. "I hate to say I told you so—"

"Then don't. Please." He straightened. "I feel bad enough as it is."

"I'm sorry, son."

Matt stared at the black liquid. "It's just… I thought our relationship had moved beyond friendship."

Sliding his plate out of the way, Dad crossed his arms on the table and leaned closer. "I assume you told her you loved her?"

"I was going to, then she told me about the job offer. Even had the nerve to ask me how I'd feel about her taking it." He puffed out a disbelieving laugh. "I mean, you'd think she would have known."

"So what did you say?"

He let go a sigh. "I told her to do what she wanted to do."

Dad's face contorted. "Son, why would you—"

Matt shot to his feet. "I was angry, all right?" Gripping the counter, he stared out the window. "But I knew

I'd made a mistake, so I went to see her last night." Over his shoulder, he looked at his father. "And I asked her to marry me."

Dad's brows lifted. "Well now..." He picked up his plate and moved beside Matt to set it in the sink.

"Yeah, it was kind of spur-of-the-moment, but I was contemplating it even before she said she was leaving."

Inches apart, Dad narrowed his dark gaze. "What did she say?"

"She said no."

"What on—" The old man threw his hands in the air. "Did you tell her you wanted her to stay?"

"Yes."

"Did you tell her you loved her? That it wasn't just about Kenzie? That you wanted to spend your life with her?"

Matt scrubbed a hand over his face. "No, I did not." How could he have been so stupid?

Suddenly still, Dad looked appalled. "You didn't?"

"Apparently, I overlooked some very important points in my speech, okay?"

Hands on his hips, his father glared at him. "Matt, you're my son and I love you. But from one stubborn man to another, you're about to blow this. You need to get yourself over there right now and tell Lacie how you feel about *her*."

He pondered the old man's advice. "You're right, that is what I need to do." Pushing away from the counter, he grabbed his mug and set it near the sink before heading for the door. "I just hope she'll listen to me."

Dad followed him into the mudroom. "Matt, if Lacie is worth having, then she's worth fighting for. You just need to make sure she understands that your feelings for her have nothing to do with Kenzie. You got it."

He shoved into his boots. "Got it." Straightening, he held out his hand. "Thanks, Dad."

The old man took hold and reeled him in for a hug. "I'll be praying for you, son."

"Thanks." He was almost out the door when his radio went off. He listened close.

Shoplifting suspect. Older-model Ford Explorer, dark green. Last seen heading north on 550 out of Ouray.

Right where he was.

"Gotta go, Dad." He radioed dispatch as he closed the door, threw himself into his Tahoe and took off down the drive. Unfortunately, his talk with Lacie was going to have to wait.

The snow had picked up, making it difficult to see. Yet as he reached the end of the drive, a dark green Explorer whizzed past.

"I love it when things are easy." He turned on his siren and lights and took chase. His windshield wipers thumped back and forth across the glass as he bore down on the vehicle in question a half a mile later. But the driver wasn't having any of it. He accelerated, weaving around the vehicle in front of him.

What few cars there were moved out of the way, allowing Matt to follow. The suspect pressed on. Swerved, but regained control.

"Come on, buddy." Matt picked up speed. "Pull over."

They continued through the neighboring town of Ridgway, past the reservoir.

Finally, Matt closed in again.

The fellow veered left.

What was he—

Ice.

The Tahoe went into a spin. Matt took his foot off the gas pedal and tried to regain control. Everything was a blur. Then he saw it. Another truck coming toward him.

Matt did the only thing he could do. He braced for impact.

While the snow continued to fall outside, Lacie hung a shirt on one of the circular racks at The Paisley Elk with a little too much force, causing a portion of the display atop the rack to topple. How blind could she have been? Matt was interested only in Kenzie, not her. Why else would he have proposed a loveless marriage?

Well, loveless for him anyway. Still, she couldn't live that way, hoping, wondering, if someday he might fall in love with her.

But who could blame him? Kenzie was not only his daughter, but adorable in every way. Just look at the way she'd shared her five-year-old faith with her grandmother. And Mom had responded in a way even Lacie couldn't have imagined.

Listening to the Christmas music that her mother was now playing at the store, she righted the black velvet jewelry forms and repositioned their beaded necklaces. As soon as Christmas was over, she needed to leave Ouray. Even though the company in Colorado Springs had given her a week to make her decision, she may as well go ahead and accept their offer. Sure, it would mean being away from Mom again, and there'd be a challenging few months while she and Kenzie adjusted to a new town, new school and new job, but they'd be okay.

At least, she hoped so.

Yet as she returned to the storage room at the back of the store, the sadness and unease lingered. *Help me, God.*

She was about to grab a couple more dresses when her phone vibrated in her back pocket. Pulling it out, she immediately recognized the number on the screen. Her heart raced with anticipation.

A glance over her shoulder revealed an empty shop, so she decided to take the call.

"Lacie, this is Jim Duncan with Bridal Veil Builders in Telluride."

"Yes, sir." Nervously tucking her hair behind her ear, she paced back into the main area of the shop. Why was she so anxious all of a sudden?

"My partner and I have talked things over and we'd like to offer you the job," said Jim. "We were quite impressed with your designs and think that you would be a great addition to our team."

Yes! She mentally thrust a fist into the air.

Of the two positions she'd interviewed for, this was the one that interested her the most. Not only because of the location, but because it was a custom builder, not a big corporate builder, giving her a chance to spread her wings as a designer and try some new things.

But within seconds, her excitement fell flat. Hadn't she just decided it would be best to take the job back east? To get away from Ouray and Matt? "Um, that's great. Really. Thank you."

"You sound hesitant."

She perched on the arm of the black leather love seat near the dressing room, indecision gnawing at her gut. "I've received another offer. And while I haven't accepted it yet…" Though if it wasn't for Matt…not to mention her heart…

"I understand." Jim's voice remained even. Undeterred. "Why don't you take the weekend to think things over, then?" His generosity made her smile.

"Thank you so much." Relief flooded through her, though she was sure it was only temporary. "I promise, I'll be in touch with you first thing Monday morning."

"Looking forward to it. Have a good weekend, Lacie."

Standing, she ended the call, wanting to cry and do a happy dance at the same time.

A job in Telluride was the best of both worlds. Aside from a great position, she could stay in Ouray, where she'd have friends and family to help her with Kenzie. But now that she knew how Matt really felt, she wasn't sure she wanted to. Her heart would break every time she saw him.

But a move to Colorado Springs would mean Kenzie would almost never see Matt. And she didn't want to do that to either of them.

So what was she supposed to do?

She rubbed her forehead. This was going to be a very long weekend.

The door jangled and she looked up to see her mother rushing toward her with Kenzie in tow. And while Kenzie appeared fine, Mom looked distressed.

Lacie approached the front of the shop, watching as her mother settled Kenzie at the table with the dollhouse. "What is it?"

Mom patted her granddaughter on the back. "You stay here, sweetie, while I talk to Aunt Lacie." The woman was practically winded by the time she reached her. She took hold of Lacie's arm, tugging her toward the scarf display at the back of the store.

She couldn't imagine what had her mother so riled up. She sent her a curious look. "Are you okay?"

"Clint called." Mom sucked in a breath, her blue eyes boring into Lacie. "There was a car accident. I don't have many details, just that Matt was unconscious when the ambulance took him to the hospital."

Her throat tightened. She blinked. Several times. *God, please let him be okay. Please!*

Mom put an arm around her shoulders and aimed her toward the door. "I'll stay here while you go on to Montrose—"

Lacie stopped in her tracks. "What for?"

Her mother shot her a disbelieving look. "To the hospital so you can be with Matt."

Lacie felt as though her heart was shattering into a million pieces. If anything happened to Matt… What about Kenzie? She didn't even know he was her father.

She turned away, wrapping her arms around herself, not wanting her mother to see the pain that threatened to swallow her. "It's not my place."

"Not your place?" Taking hold of Lacie's elbows, an incredulous Mom stepped in front of her.

Through tears and the occasional sob, she told her mother everything that had transpired between her and Matt in the last few days. "I love him. But I can't marry someone who doesn't love me."

"Oh, sweetie." Mom hugged her tight. "You are so misguided."

"What do you mean?" She took a step back and stared at her mother.

"Young lady, you told me the truth when I needed to

hear it, so now I'm going to give you some of the same. Matt loves you."

"He loves Kenzie." She sniffed. "And that's okay. I get it."

"Lacie, do you not see the way that man looks at you? The way he lights up whenever you walk into the room?"

"Then why didn't he tell me?" She swiped a finger over each cheek. "I mean, who asks someone to marry them without telling them you love them?"

"Matt Stephens." Mom's head bobbed with each word.

Lacie frowned, too afraid to buy into her mother's observations for fear she'd only be let down again.

"He's a man, Lacie. Sometimes they assume things." Mom crossed her arms. "Your father didn't tell me he loved me very often, but I still knew."

"Yeah, but I bet he told you when he proposed."

Seemingly frustrated, her mother continued to watch her, pinched expression and all. "Okay, Miss Know-It-All, does Matt know how you feel about him?"

Though she'd never said anything, he must have had some clue. Why else would he have thought she'd agree to marry him? "I—I guess so. I mean, it's not like I came out and told him."

"Oh, my dear, sweet daughter." Mom wrapped her arms around Lacie's shoulders. "If Matt doesn't survive this accident, you might never get the chance."

Chapter Eighteen

Matt didn't have to open his eyes to know that his entire family was in the room.

"Why is he asleep?" said Andrew. "I thought people with concussions were supposed to stay awake."

"Sleeping actually helps the brain heal." Noah had been on the rodeo circuit long enough to know. "It's a loss of consciousness they're more concerned about."

"All I know is that he got T-boned pretty good," said Jude. "When I came up on that scene, I wasn't sure he'd even be alive."

"God is good." Dad sounded kind of choked up. "Guess He knows Matt and I have some lost time to make up for."

"I'm just waiting for him to open his eyes and tell all of you to shut up." Did his baby brother, Daniel, know him or what? Because that's exactly what he was about to do.

Except his head was killing him. Not to mention the entire left side of his body. And that incessant beeping noise wasn't helping. *Somebody shut that thing off.*

"Would one of you boys tell someone to get in here

and change his IV bag?" The old man was getting annoyed. "That noise is about to drive me up a wall."

"I got it," said Jude.

Things grew quiet then. Except for that stupid beeping.

"Let me get this taken care of for you." A woman's voice. A nurse maybe?

Whatever the case, the beeping had stopped. *Thank You, Lord.*

"Look who I found out in the hall," said Jude.

Who was it? Matt tried to open his eyes, but the lights were so bright.

"I was hoping you'd come," said Dad.

Who? Who was he hoping would come?

"How is he doing?" Lacie?

"Much better than they first thought." Dad cleared his throat.

"Good." *It was Lacie!* He could tell by the fragrance of her perfume. Like wildflowers in July.

Now if he could only… He struggled to open his eyes, but those lights…

"Would you like us to leave you alone?" asked Dad.

"Oh, that won't be—"

He might not be able to open his eyes, but he could still talk. "*Yes*… Please…"

"Matt?" He felt his father's calloused hand cover his.

"Would somebody kill the lights?" His request, or rather, demand, was followed by the shuffling of boots against linoleum. He could envision his brothers hurrying to do his beckoning. Of course, that would be a first.

"Daniel, close them blinds." A moment later, his father continued. "Okay, Matt. It's as dark as we can possibly get it."

For the first time since they'd moved him to a private

room, he opened his eyes ever so slightly. Enough light from the hallway shone in for him to recognize the standard features—bed rails, TV hanging just below the ceiling, big, round wall clock, uncomfortable-looking chair.

With the head of his bed already elevated, he searched the concerned faces gathered around him until he found Lacie. Man, she was beautiful.

He blinked a couple of times, becoming more alert. "Would you guys mind if I talked to Lacie alone for a few?"

Dad held up a hand. "Whatever you want, Matt." Turning, he nodded toward the door. "Come on, boys. You heard him."

He watched them leave then shifted his attention to a seemingly nervous Lacie. "Where's Kenzie?"

"With my mom."

He figured as much. "Come here." He held out his right hand. To his surprise, she took hold. Despite the throbbing in his head, he tried to smile. "Boy, are you a sight for sore eyes."

Her pretty gray-blue eyes studied him, the corners of her mouth tipping upward. Did she have any idea how much he loved her?

No, she didn't, because he'd never told her.

He caressed her hand with his thumb. "Why are you here?"

Lifting a shoulder, she said, "They said you were hurt."

"Not as badly as they first thought." His gaze briefly traversed the sterile room before returning to her. "Concussion, broken arm, a few bumps and bruises…nothing life threatening."

"I didn't know that, though. And I couldn't…" Pressing her lips tightly together, she looked away.

"Could I get you to put this railing down—" he bumped it with his elbow "—so you can sit beside me?"

Nodding, she did just that, carefully adjusting the IV tubes that extended from his arm before easing onto the side of the bed.

He again took hold of her hand, urging her closer.

Finally, she looked at him, her eyes shimmering. "I couldn't let you die without telling you how I felt."

His heart dared to hope. He moved his hand to her cheek. "Well, I'm not dying, but I'd still like to hear it."

She drew in a deep breath, a tear slipping onto her pretty face, but he brushed it away with his thumb. "I love you."

"Funny, that's—" He cocked his head, the movement making him wince.

"Are you okay?" Her eyes were wide now.

"Yeah." Lowering his hand, he closed his eyes until the pain subsided. "Remind me not to make any sudden movements."

"I'm sorry." She caressed his arm.

Finally, he opened his eyes. "As I was about to say—" his gaze found hers "—that's exactly what I wanted to tell you, before I had to chase that shoplifter."

She laughed ever so softly.

"I messed up, Lace. I mean, sure I'd like Kenzie to stay here in Ouray, but there are plenty of law enforcement jobs near Colorado Springs. If you choose to go, I'll simply have to follow you."

He threaded his fingers into her hair. "But I really wish you'd choose to stay here with me. Not because of Kenzie, but because you're the best thing that's ever happened to me. I love *you*, Lacie Collier, and I want to spend the rest of my life showing you just how much."

Her tears fell in earnest now as he tugged her close and kissed her with everything he had. Which may not be much right now, but if she'd agree to be his, he'd do everything he could to correct that.

When they finally parted, he rested his forehead against hers. "So what do you say, Lace? Will you marry me?"

A teasing smile played across her pretty lips as she placed a hand on his chest and leaned back. "On one condition."

He was in a hospital bed and she wanted conditions?

He lifted a brow. "And that is…?"

"We can be married by Christmas. Assuming you're well enough, that is."

Now, that was a provision he could live with. He'd marry her right now if he could, but— "You know Christmas is only eight days away. I thought weddings usually took months to plan."

"That's for big weddings." She shrugged, adjusting his white blanket. "I prefer something smaller. More intimate. Say, with just family."

Things were looking up. "I think we can make that happen."

"Good." She smiled, but didn't say anything else. Did she know how to make him crazy or what?

He tugged her toward him again. "I'm still waiting for an answer, Lace."

"Looks like I'll be taking that job in Telluride, after all."

"You got it?"

She nodded. "They called this afternoon." Her expression turned serious then, her hand softly touching his chin. "I would love nothing more than to be your wife and grow old with you, Matt. So yes, I will most definitely marry you." She touched her lips to his. "I love you, Matt."

"I love you, too, Lace. Now and always." He brushed a hand over her hair. "Now, why don't you go get my family? Because we've got a wedding to plan."

Lacie made her way through the darkened house in her bare feet Christmas morning, pausing to plug in the lights on the tree and quietly turn on some Christmas tunes before continuing into the kitchen to get the coffee going. This Christmas hadn't turned out at all like she'd expected. Only a month ago, she'd feared she and Kenzie would have no Christmas at all. And now—

One strong arm found its way around her waist. "Merry Christmas, Mrs. Stephens." Matt's whispered words were a caress on her ear.

She turned into his embrace, though his other arm was still in a cast and would be for several more weeks. "Merry Christmas to you, Mr. Stephens." Placing her hands on his broad shoulders, she pushed up on her toes and kissed her husband with no hesitation, and no doubt of his love for her.

They'd married last night, in a quiet ceremony at Granger House, with Mom, Kenzie and all of Matt's family in attendance. There in front of Carly's Victorian Christmas tree, with the snow falling outside and only tiny white lights and candles illuminating the parlor, she and Matt had pledged their love to one another forever. Things couldn't have been more perfect. Then they all celebrated with more food than eleven people could possibly eat. Her new sister-in-law had pulled out all the stops for them.

"I take it Kenzie's not up?" Matt kept his voice low.

"Not yet." Lacie and her mother had taken a couple of

days to overhaul one of the bedrooms at Matt's for Kenzie. They'd painted, hung curtains and bought new bedding, giving the little girl the pony room of her dreams.

Of course, they should have known better than to show it to her earlier in the week, because she'd been a little miffed that she'd had to wait until last night to sleep in it.

Lacie grabbed two mugs from the cupboard as the machine finished brewing. Once Matt was well, they'd need to make a run to Denver to get all of her things out of storage.

"Hey, Lace."

"Yeah." She eyed her husband, who was now standing by the back door.

"Come look at this."

Still holding the cups, she moved beside him, gasping when she looked outside. "It must have snowed all night." The two blue spruces in the backyard bowed under the weight.

"And it's still coming down," he said.

"In that case—" she returned to the coffeepot "—shall we snuggle on the couch while we wait?"

"Mmm, I like the way you think." He gave her another kiss.

"How are you feeling this morning?" Cup in hand, she carefully nestled beside him a few minutes later and took a sip of the hot liquid.

"Well, I just married the woman of my dreams, I'm about to spend my very first Christmas with my daughter and I now have someone to make my coffee for me every morning. I'd say things are pretty good."

She playfully swatted his good arm. "Ha! You just *think* I'm going to make coffee every morning." Setting her cup next to his on the appropriately named coffee table, she twisted to face him. "Seriously, how's the arm? The hip? The leg?" While his head seemed to be fine, he still walked with a slight limp.

"A little better every day."

"Good, but I don't want you overdoing it today." At least they had only one house to go to instead of three. Carly had graciously offered to host everyone at their place so Matt wouldn't have to do so much traveling. And probably so they could help eat all those leftovers. Though if she knew Carly, she'd have a new round of food going today.

"But what about Kenzie's sled?" He motioned a hand toward the window. "I mean, with all this fresh snow..."

Her mouth fell open. "Don't you dare even think—"

He silenced her with another kiss.

Wrapping her arms around his neck, she deepened the kiss, weaving her fingers into his short hair.

"It's Christmas!"

She jumped at Kenzie's excited announcement and pulled herself off the sofa with Matt in tow.

"Merry Christmas, sweetie." She smoothed a hand over her robe. Being a newlywed as well as a parent was going to take some getting used to. She peered up at a blushing Matt. But they'd find some way to balance it all out.

"Hey, small fry." Matt kissed Kenzie's cheek as he scooped her up into his good arm. "Merry Christmas."

"Merry Christmas." Kenzie sleepily brushed the hair away from her face, all the while eyeing the tree surrounded with presents. She'd been so great this week, wanting to help take care of Matt and taking extra care not to bump or hurt him in any way. Of course, her favorite thing had been writing her name on his cast.

"You don't suppose there's anything under that tree for you, do you, small fry?"

Kenzie nodded, her smile no longer sleepy.

"What do you say we check it out, then?" Matt set her to the floor and the three of them inched closer.

"Oh, those stockings look much fatter than they did last night." Lacie retrieved Kenzie's, pausing just long enough to admire the diamond wedding band that now adorned her left hand. She passed the stocking to Kenzie before grabbing hers and Matt's. "Let's see what's in it."

Kenzie sat cross-legged on the floor and shoved her hand inside. "I gotted some new crayons." She reached in again and pulled out a small board book. She studied the cover. "A baby Jesus book."

Matt leaned toward Lacie. "That is one smart kid. She figured that out just by looking at the cover."

She winked at him. "We'll chalk it up to good genes."

"What is that?" Kenzie crawled to her feet, her dark eyes wide as she looked at the tree.

"Whatcha see there, Kenz?" Matt stood beside her.

"This!" She ran to the tree and pointed to the sled that was leaning against the wall.

"Do you know what that is?" asked Lacie.

"Uh-huh." She bobbed her head. "It's for the snow."

"It sure is." Matt's grin had him looking like a kid himself. "What do you say we take it up to the sledding hill later today and you and Lacie can try it out?"

"But don't you want to ride it, too, Matt?"

"I do, but I can't until I'm healed."

"Oh, yeah." She frowned.

"But we've still got a lot more winter ahead of us. So as soon as I'm better, we'll make a day of it, okay?"

"Okay."

It wasn't long before all of the presents had been opened and the living room was littered with the wrapping. So while Matt rested on the couch, Lacie went to the kitchen to heat up the sausage-and-egg breakfast muffins Carly had sent home with them last night. When she returned to the living room, Kenzie was beside him and he was reading her the baby Jesus book that had been in her stocking. He finished the story right about the time Lacie set the platter of muffins and some napkins on the coffee table.

"Matt, are you my daddy now?"

Lacie froze. To have Kenzie call him Daddy would be a dream come true for Matt, even if Kenzie didn't know the truth yet.

"'Cause I never had a daddy before," Kenzie continued.

Matt looked at Lacie, his eyes wide with anticipation. "Well, I guess now that Lacie and I are married and we'll all be living in the same house..." He was trying hard not to insinuate himself.

Lacie sat down beside her niece. "Kenzie, do you want Matt to be your daddy?"

"Uh-huh."

She glanced at her husband, who was blinking heartily. "Why don't you ask him, then?"

Still leaning against Matt's right side, Kenzie peered up at him with eyes just like his. "Matt, will you be my daddy?"

He seemed to have a hard time finding his voice. "Small fry, I would love nothing more than to be your daddy."

Kenzie grinned. "Aunt Lacie, Matt said he'd be my daddy."

"I heard." And she couldn't be happier for both of them.

Kenzie jerked her head back to Matt. "Thank you, Daddy." She giggled, then hugged him before hopping down to play with her new toys.

Lacie watched the man she loved with all of her heart. She'd never seem him so dumbfounded. But then she knew how he'd longed to hear Kenzie call him Daddy.

She took hold of his hand and curled beside him. "I'd say this was a pretty good Christmas, huh?"

"Are you kidding? I've gotten everything I ever could have wanted and more." He wrapped his arm around her. "God has brought me two of the greatest blessings ever. You and Kenzie." He kissed her forehead. "It's a dream come true."

Sitting there in the warmth of his embrace, watching the snow fall outside, with Christmas music playing in the background while Kenzie danced in front of the tree, she realized that her dream had come true, too. She'd wanted Kenzie's Christmas to be extra special, like the kind Lacie'd had when she was a kid. They'd gotten exactly that, plus a husband and a daddy, too.

Kenzie moved in front of them, wearing her new pink cowboy boots and hat with her pajamas. "This is the bestest Christmas ever!"

With more joy in her heart than she'd ever imagined possible, Lacie hugged her niece. "I'd have to agree with you, Kenzie." The three of them were a family. And that was the best gift ever.

* * * * *